IGNITE

BOLT SAGA: VOLUME TWO
PARTS 4 - 5 - 6

ANGEL PAYNE

IGNITE

BOLT SAGA: VOLUME TWO
PARTS 4 - 5 - 6

ANGEL PAYNE

WATERHOUSE PRESS

TABLE OF CONTENTS

Now more than ever, for Thomas:

*The one who taught me to dream big,
then gave me the wings to try.*

*And for Jess, who shows me that weird
is the coolest corner in the universe.*

IGNITE

PART 4

CHAPTER ONE

EMMA

Funny how life changes when the world knows you're sleeping with a superhero.

Funnier still how the differences are most glaring in the tiniest details. Like finally finding one's way to the ladies' room after a five-hour flight and a twenty-minute gate taxi only to have one's three-by-six-foot sanctum pierced by an urgent whisper from the next stall over.

"Hey."

At first, I clear my throat and ignore her. The chick's probably just on the phone with someone and isn't aware of my presence next door.

"Hey. *You*. Emma Crist."

"Uhhhh..." I repeat the throat clearance with a little more emphasis. Believe me, I'm painfully used to being recognized in public these days, but it's usually not when I'm pausing for a second of relief in the airport bathroom. "Yes? Can I help you?" In any case, professional mode is best. She's probably just asking for toilet paper or a tampon.

"So tell me what he's like."

I watch my eyes bug in the reflection from the stainless-steel door. "He...who?"

"Come *on*. You *know* who."

"I...uh..."

"Reece Richards." She adds a conspiratorial giggle. "You know. *Bolt.* What's he like, girlfriend?"

"I beg your pardon?" My confusion is authentic on several levels. I'm really in the weeds about what to do. I'm done with my business but afraid to budge. If I make a move, will she flush just as fast and corner me against the sinks? If I don't, how long will she hold me hostage on the pot in order to win her answer?

"I bet he can fuck like a machine. Right?"

"Pardon *me*?"

"Probably doesn't even need a recharge—even if that cover story you're floating is true, about the thunder and lightning being a big ol' magic trick and all."

"Well." Forget professional. Maybe I just need to show my whole hand now. A full house of irked, peeved, and get-lost-lady. "Reece has already made his official statements on the matter."

Statements that were meant to buy us some time. Badly needed time. A moment's breath to figure out our new reality, which feels no more real now than it did back in July. The night he'd taken off his mask in that room, in front of my family and a hundred other Newport Beach socialites, and changed my life forever. A change I thought I was ready for—but quickly learned I wasn't. Since then, despite the changes and compromises we've both made, life still feels like a gigantic roller coaster, with no return back to the loading platform in sight.

Which means I need to learn to hold on tighter or seriously invest in some barf bags.

"Come on. Just tell me." Annnnd, Stall One is still damned and determined to girl-talk her way into a confession from me.

"He's better than the little battery bunny, isn't he? But does he come with a...*drum*?"

The threads of suspicion in my gut form into a bigger ball. This chica's pushing the metaphors hard. Just like a good gossip reporter would...

"I..."

The trill of my cell can't be better timed. With a whoosh of relief, I grab for the thing. "Sorry. Have to get this."

"Oh, God. Is it *him*?"

Of course it's him. Not that I'm going to tell *her* that.

Using the nickname we openly borrowed from the world's most notable superhero creator provides a perfect way to do that.

"Mr. Lee." Like the real Mr. Lee, my man has a tendency of showing up in the most unexpected places at the oddest times, earning him instant street cred for the designation.

Reece Andrew Richards has a different view on the matter and makes that clear with a dark, dangerous, arousing-as-hell growl.

"How can I be of service to you this afternoon?"

Reece repeats the sound but with more sensual undertones. "That all depends."

"Yes. Go ahead. Of course I'm here." Attempting to keep up the calm, cool, and professional thing is *not* easy when the man has the power to flip my stomach like a pancake simply with the force of his voice.

"On whether you plan on fully apologizing for using that little zinger."

I clear my throat again, using the sound to cover what it takes to clean stuff up and get back to my feet. "We fully understand your frustration with the situation, Mr. Lee.

Richards Resorts wants to make things right. I'm still at the airport, but I'll be back at my desk in about an hour and will be happy to—"

"No."

One word, full of carnal command, turns the pancake to mush—along with my knees. I fight to stay upright with a fortifying breath through my nose. "So sorry. Could you repeat, please? I didn't quite get that."

Reece's grunting laugh fills the line. "Oh, you'll get it, my little velvet bunny. Just not back at the office." He adds a subtle hum because he knows, no matter where I am or what I'm doing, how hot the sound makes me—and exactly where. "It's Friday. You're taking the rest of the day off."

I unlatch the stall door and march to the mirrors and sinks—where my flushed cheeks and aroused eyes are waiting to gloat at me in full. *Damn him. How I've missed him.* "I'll have to double-check that request with upper management."

"*Upper management* is waiting for you at the curb, woman." His tone drops into the rugged valley between seduction and fornication. "Which means get rid of whoever's gawking at you and get your sweet ass out to the VIP pick-up curb."

"Well, I have checked bags—"

"Which Z is already handling," he supplies. "So you have no more excuses. Get out here. Into my arms. *Now.*"

"Wait. What? Into your—" I'm cut off from the rest of my gasp as my new bestie from stall one strides out in all her glossy-lipped, sprayed-on-jeans glory. I can read every thought in her head just by glancing at her knowing smirk. She's on to me. More accurately, she's on to "Mr. Lee's" true identity. "I'm certain that can be arranged, sir. Your satisfaction is always our first priority."

Stall Girl yips out a laugh that echoes in the oddly uncrowded bathroom. The moment couldn't be better timed. Reece's verbal foreplay is causing blood to collect in parts of my body where it shouldn't, and a full-on sprint out to Mr. Snarly and Seductive has started beckoning like the swoony romance-movie cliché it is. Maintaining my cool for the strange woman is really a blessing in disguise, especially because everyone wants—and expects—the whole passionate reunion thing between Reece and me now, with "EmRee's" magic three-month mark just hurdled.

EmRee.

Seriously. That's what they call us in all the papers and tabloids that seem to matter to people like Stall One Girl, who follows me out of the restroom and down the concourse.

EmRee.

It's so stupid, it's cute.

And still a little surreal. And definitely a lot of crazy.

But maybe that last part *does* fit. Because damn, am I crazy about this man—a truth never blazed so boldly into me than the moment I step out of the terminal and into the heat of an LA Indian summer day, only to be riveted by the one sight hotter than the heatwaves rising from the asphalt. Yet oddly, even in the charcoal suit precision-fit to the millimeter for his powerful torso, Reece stands as if he doesn't know the meaning of the word sweat. He's polished and tall and suave and perfect, long legs braced like a Viking atop an iceberg, with the wind blowing his mocha hair back with equal drama. I'm unable to see his eyes due to the photo-gray film on his glasses, but the subtle shift in the right side of his jaw already betrays how intense his silver gaze must be.

Holy. Freaking. God.

I stop for a second, visually pinned by him—until the ache of missing him is suddenly replaced by the need to be with him. Against him. All over him. The craving is so urgent, I don't even care about the camera strobes and excited shouts suddenly surging around me. Thankfully, airport security is part of that tsunami, and I dash through the narrow gauntlet the officers create in the throng for me. Racing toward my peace in the storm.

Toward my hero.

"Velvet," he grates into my hair, some of his volume stripped by my collision into him. I don't think Reece minds. His answering embrace is a crush, and he tightens it until I'm a breathless mess. I pull away for air, but he's already tucked his head in, lifting a hand to brace my jaw and position me for the kiss I've craved over every inch of distance between JFK and here. By the time his lips sweep down, mine are already parted, longing for the hot and heavy thrust of his take-no-prisoners tongue. He doesn't leave me bereft. My mouth is filled with him. Assaulted by him. Sighing in utter bliss as he groans, sucking at me, before pushing in for more of my surrender.

Around us, cameras still shutter in a frenzy, and bodies collide as reporters jostle for the best angle of our mutual mauling. I'm beyond caring. As exhilarating as the last five days have been, they were four and a half days too long. We haven't been apart for more than five *hours* since we finally decided to make this interesting relationship work—emphasis on the *interesting*. But that term came with its own definition in the world of Reece, who'd revealed to me that his bad-boy-billionaire rep, while true at one time, had become the ideal disguise for his true identity as Bolt, LA's lightning-pulsed superhero savior. And the *oh, by the way* he piled on top of that? Just the small matter of the lunatic scientists who'd used him as their bioelectrical experiment to begin with and who were still hunting down their rogue Frankenstein.

Needless to say, our first few dates were slightly more eventful than grabbing a pizza and a movie.

But that's like another novel ago.

Right now, all I can think of is treasuring his muscular fullness in my arms, the powerful perfection of his mouth, and the feeling of his heartbeat next to mine again. Celebratory passion following what had to be the best business trip of my life.

The trip *he* made possible.

Thinking about it all—the phone calls he made, the emails he sent, the personal trips he took to shake hands with all the right people, to incite all the right kind of expediting—launches me to somewhere between giddy and euphoric. I funnel it all into my kiss, showing him exactly how much joy he's brought to every inch of my heart. He responds with a darker groan, twisting one hand into my hair and the other into my T-shirt, which sets off a new frenzy of flashing cameras and a new surge of ecstatic reporters.

"Sheez, Reece," one of them finally shouts. "Give the woman a chance to breathe."

He's answered by one of the women in the throng. "Well, if a girl's gotta meet her maker, that's the way to do it."

"Not before getting bolted in a big way," a new female quips. Or *is* she new? I pull back enough from Reece to glance her direction. Sure enough, it's Stall One Girl, now armed with a microphone and backed by a cameraman. My scathing scrutiny only incites her sorry-not-sorry shrug. Inwardly, I high-five myself for taking the icy professional path with her in the bathroom—not that it's made a difference, since she adds with a smirk, "And I do mean a *big* way."

Another reporter steps forward, seeming a little more on the sane side, until he taps his pen into the air and questions, "So what *does* comprise a Bolt-style homecoming for his best girl?"

"His *only* girl." Reece yanks me in tighter while correcting the guy, his tone edging toward censure. "And the rest of that's an irrelevant question because, as you all know by now, Bolt has taken an early retirement."

A round of groans is his instant reply. Some of them resound with disappointment, but the majority are expressions of skepticism, verbalized by the persistent pen tapper.

"Right. *Retired.*" A pen materializes in his *other* hand—imagine that—to assist his air quote emphasis. "Just like all his badass stunts were simply elaborate 'science experiments' used in a real-life testing ground."

"For which I've apologized to the mayor and made restitution to the city," Reece fills in. "None of the trials should have gone to the level of realism that they did, and for that I *am* regretful." His face takes on such somber lines, even I start to believe his ruse. "Of course, I'm also thankful. The DA has been lenient in not pursuing any charges in consideration of Richards Research offering to pay for all repairs to city property damaged in Bolt's escapades."

"Doesn't hurt that he helped put away some nasty bastards in the process," the reporter counters, supported by a round of nods from...well...just about everyone. "Including the creeps who tried to assault Miss Crist in the train station."

"For which Miss Crist is deeply thankful," I interject.

"Along with the other victims of the other crimes for which Bolt made the perpetrators pay—even though he isn't, and won't ever be, a paid law enforcement official."

I conclude by visibly squeezing Reece's shoulder, answered by his tender "yes, dear" glance. The moment sets off another flurry of flashbulbs, confirming we've done our job in convincing them the cover story is real. It helps that most of it is. I really *am* beyond thankful for what happened in the metro station a week after we first met, when Reece swept in and put down the scumbags who had me in a corner. He really did do it with nothing but six months' worth of martial arts and defense training under his belt, meaning the incident could've had a horrifically different result. And no, he's not going to attempt something like it again because Bolt's leathers *have* been retired for good.

The only thing the world doesn't know—or need to know—is exactly why.

"So." The declaration, issued from Stall Girl, all but lasers her question into the air. "What happens now, EmRee? Give us the scoop, you two. We've worked hard for it."

I grimace. "Paging understatement to the white courtesy curb."

She rewards my sarcasm with a cute wink, but isn't deterred from continuing. "Are we talking...what...a reality show? Maybe a scripted series? Endorsement deals? A book contract?" She tilts her head as if that one's rung a particularly loud bell. "Is that why you went to New York, Emmalina?"

Reece lifts one hand, almost looking like a Bible School Jesus about to multiply fish for the masses. "As stated in the press release from Richards Industries yesterday, which you all should've had time to read by now"—he hooks a brow her direction—"Miss Crist was in New York in her capacity as the supervising director of Richards Reaches Out, the new nonprofit arm of our company. RRO is focused on giving back to youth across the globe, especially in helping hardworking young leaders who haven't been given financial or social advantages to better themselves."

Another reporter sidles forward, bumping shoulders with Pen Tapper. "So you're actually contributing to social awareness beyond supporting the world's vodka industry, Richards?"

Rage clouds the edges of my vision. The prick is as smallminded as his gossip-rag readers. Can't they see that people can change when they really want to? That people grow up, man up, and want to take accountability for their lives? But the guy's smug smirk already gives me the answer, which should be my cue to summon my Zen side.

Impossible.

Thank God Reece has had a lot more practice with this shit, as he demonstrates with a diplomatic spread of his hands while offering, "Fair enough question, Quinn—but wouldn't you agree that turning over new leaves is a hell of a lot more interesting than digging through the worms beneath the old?"

The crowd buzzes louder as reporters order their cameramen to mark the time on their feeds. My man's zinger at the annoying Quinn will be tomorrow's leading soundbite—not that Stall Girl is going to rest on her laurels with that. Clearly, she's after juicier material here.

"So that's really just *it* for Bolt?" Her narrow face pinches into an accusatory pout. "We're not going to get the behind-the-scenes on those effects? The explanation of how your 'experimental' lightning pulses took down all those criminals—

and about how *you* survived all those showdowns?"

Reece flashes an indulgent smile. "Come, come, Blair. You write for *Silver* magazine. You know a good magician never exposes *all* their secrets. Everything we have to reveal at this point was contained in yesterday's press release. When Richards Research has something new to share, you'll all be the first to be informed. Until then"—he caresses my back, captivatingly possessive, inciting yet another burst of camera shutters—"I'm just a guy running a couple of businesses, dating the girl he's crazy about, and enjoying life in La-La Land."

He punctuates that by unhooking a couple of his shirt buttons, just enough to reveal the distinct purple and gold of a Lakers T-shirt beneath. A new round of laughter fills the air.

"Just like the rest of us, huh?" someone cracks.

"More than you think." I snuggle closer to Reece, hiding any tells about my white lie by turning my face into his chest. Ironically, it's the whitest fib of the bunch. Like them, Reece has good days and bad. He puts on his pants one leg at a time, struggles to tame his hair in the morning, and has true cosmic dilemmas about what to binge next on the Roku. They don't have to know that between all that, he's formed Richards Research as a front for keeping tabs on the whack-a-doodle scientists who call themselves the Consortium. Keep your friends close and your enemies on at least three different monitoring platforms.

And, oh yeah—between all that, be sure to pleasure your woman like the ever-charged battery you really are.

As *that* erotic thought heats my gaze, Reece's nostrils flare. His gaze drops to my mouth—for the two seconds before he crashes another kiss on me, hotter and deeper and fiercer than his first. My balance falters. My world spins. He's the rock in my storm, sheltering and crushing me at once, turning me into a helpless heap in his brutal embrace.

At the edge of the tempest, I hear the same reporter chuckle out, "Yeah. Sure. *Just* like the rest of us."

Without breaking our contact, Reece deftly turns, trapping me against the car and deepening our kiss. The mob of media, receiving our messaging loud and clear, starts to dissipate. They've gotten what they came for—and with this hotter-than-hell kiss, we've probably even given my bathroom buddy *her* story—and are content to let us be just another couple indulging pent-up passions after being apart for too damn long.

I'm home.

It resounds in my head as Reece rolls his tongue through my mouth, drenching my senses with his cinnamon taste, his smoky scent, his penetrating power. While it's been awesome to be the one driving the beat for the last few days, there's nothing like letting someone else lead the dance again. It's a sweet, calming harmony to the throbbing melody of my lust, grounding me in a way nobody else can. Yet, at the same time, tempting me to burn even hotter...

Which is exactly why I push at his chest, reluctantly breaking the seal of our mouths. "Mr. Richards." My protest is infused with my heavy pants. "If we keep this up, they're going to arrest me for man mauling in public."

My boyfriend slides out a grin that should be illegal in its own right. "How about mauling him in private?"

"*Now* you're talkin'."

He glides back by a step, fanning his fingers as if merely batting a bug away. The motion is a perfect disguise for the pulse he sends to the car, unlocking its two sleek doors, which rise up like wings.

For the first time, I actually focus on the vehicle—before vocalizing my resultant surprise.

"This isn't one of the babies." From the start, his nickname for his mini fleet of BMWs has always held a fond place in my heart. Even now, my invocation inspires a bigger grin from Reece before he issues an explanation.

"New kid on the block. A little prototype I'm testing out for Elon."

"A prototype," I echo, on top of the realization that aside from the license plates, the sleek cobalt car is devoid of any identification or branding. "For...Elon? *Whoa.*" Anyone gawking at the vehicle might mistake it for a cross between a Maserati and an Aston Martin. "It's a...Tesla?"

"You like it?"

"So far?" I reply as he helps me into the plush leather bucket of a passenger seat. "Oh, *yeah.*"

"Good," he answers with crisp command while sliding in behind the wheel with elegant athleticism. "Because the ride will be a few hours."

"A few *hours*?" I'm honest about my delighted surprise, my mind taking off with possibilities about his end game—though whatever he has planned, I really hope it involves him, me, and someplace with a *Do Not Disturb* sign. Between Richards Research going public and RRO making its debut, our schedules have made his superhero days look like a pleasure cruise. Still, I don't miss the Bolt days. Not for one damn second. "Guess it's a good thing I have bags already p—" I'm jolted by my own stunned gasp. "Hey! My luggage—"

"Is safe with Zalkon," Reece assures, reaching over to scrape his fingertips across my left thigh. "And on its way back to your apartment."

Blissful sigh. "Then I'm not worried." For my Valentine's Day gift, I'd asked Reece to hire Z as a full-time driver, valet, and go-to guy—and these days, I think *he's* thanking *me* more for the decision. The affable Armenian has become an invaluable gear in the logistical machine of our crazy life.

As Reece slides his touch higher on my leg, the tips of his magical digits take on a light-blue glow...and send electric thrills straight to the core between my legs. "I borrowed your essential toiletries from the suite at the hotel," he explains further, referencing the penthouse at the Brocade that's becoming more and more like my second home lately—especially because the second half of my Valentine's Day gift was a wall in the suite, newly redecorated with framed candid photos taken during the project that inspired RRO to begin with, at a Brocade employee's home, just a few miles away. "They're all in a bag for you."

I follow the backward jog of his head to find the small stow space behind our seats occupied by his rolling leather overnight bag and the gorgeous new Bendel train case I've been lusting after. After my soft squeal of delight and his cocky chuckle, I chill out enough to toss a wary side-eye. "You've packed stuff *other* than the toiletries, right?"

"Of course," he insists, only to tack on in a mutter, "Maybe not anything you can stroll out to the balcony in..."

"Oh, dear."

As I groan, he snickers harder—but takes my mind off pondering his wicked intentions as he accelerates onto the 405 and zips the sports car across to the fast lane. "Tell me about New York. I want to know all about the meetings. Are you feeling good about things?"

I twist in my seat, facing him more fully. Okay, here's a subject with which I can be comfortable for a while. "'Good' doesn't even come close." I'm gushing and I don't care. "Reece... this is all going to be so epic. You know your dad showed up yesterday morning for the meetings, right?"

"Yeah." His answer, dotted by the discernible tick in his jaw, is exactly what I expected. "That was...decent of him."

"Maybe because he's ready to believe the same thing about you."

He returns my soft suggestion with a hard grunt. "Or maybe he's just morbidly curious about *you*."

I don't demand clarification for that. He's already given it to me—though it wasn't such a secret, even before we met, and perhaps for years and years before *that*. I really have no definite idea of when Reece was relegated to black sheep status in the Richards fold, but instinct tells me it was long before he, Chase, and Tyce had even achieved puberty. With that kind of reinforcement, was it any wonder he grew up to be the family fuckup for so long?

A status he couldn't shake even after revealing himself as the world's real-life superhero.

"All right," I finally offer. "So what if he did show up just to vet me? At least he showed. And *stayed*. And even helped facilitate our call with India."

"India?" He lowers his brows until they're ducked beneath his sunglasses. "I thought they'd already turned the RRO concept down."

"They did." I gaze out past him at the modern white buildings of the Getty Museum up on the hill. "But your dad said he wanted to help us try again."

I give in to a soft smile, realizing how strongly Reece

resembles Lawson Richards. They have the same bold blade of a nose. Their gazes, though a few shades different, both become brilliant when they're challenged. And that forceful but graceful profile, speaking to the family's carefully documented noble heritage—and right now, taking me back to the crucial twenty minutes in which Lawson had become RRO's knight in shining armor.

"Hmmm." Reece breaks into my musings with his contemplative grunt. "Dad *is* good at international negotiations."

"He sure as hell was yesterday," I concur. "There was something about what he said to the reps about the program... no different than what we'd presented last week but just spoken in a different way, that made them really hear that our purpose is simply to help some of their most deserving students get a leg up, not to indoctrinate them." I pull my focus away from the memories, back to being all in with the man next to me. "I think it's hard for some people to realize that we really have no agenda but to help."

"Because nobody believes the world still possesses people as good as you."

"*Or* you." I lodge the argument as he finds my hand with his. "Don't glower. It's true and you know it, mister. Holy shit. Reece..." I shake my head as the hills of Getty View Park whiz by, covered in sage scrub and mustard flowers. "If it weren't for you, RRO would still be just a pipedream on paper, not a legitimate nonprofit getting ready to actually put our mission statement into action." I take a long moment to fill my lungs, certain I'll break down into happy sobs without the extra air as fortification. "In a few weeks, we're actually going to change the world for the better—and you're the reason why."

His attention doesn't sway off the road, but his grip meshes into mine with defined intent. "Because you're my more, Velvet."

Take heart. Insert into towel wringer. Forget turning the crank, because this man and the depths of his love have already done the job.

His confession pulls my thoughts backward, to the day when I'd first thought *he* might be *my* "more," as well. I hadn't known his full truth then, that he was actually Bolt the superhero disguised as your run-of-the-mill bad-boy-billionaire hotel mogul having some fun on the side with one of his executive team. Back then, we were just a couple of consenting adults with mind-blowing chemistry in the sack and nothing more...

"That's important to you, isn't it? Living...bigger. Having... more."

"No. Not having more. Being *more. There just has to be... something more."*

"There is. There is more, Velvet."

"Easy for you to say. You've already had more."

"Not yet."

"Not yet? What part of 'not yet' are you referring to? Swimming with the sea turtles in Tulum or skiing the Alps at Christmas? Or maybe..."

"You're my more, Emmalina."

He'd shown me that truth—that very afternoon, in fact—and so many more after it, as well. But no matter how explosive the sex, nothing told me how much I really meant to him until the Sunday he'd surprised me with a "field trip" to the home of a young engineer on the Brocade's team. Cal, a twenty-one-year-old who was raising his twin sisters on his own after their mother's unexpected death, had all the raw material to make his life better but not the time or financial resources to boost himself to the next level. After we'd spent the day helping repair and beautify his house, I'd found a part-time helper for the girls so Cal could get into some night classes and study his passion, Bio-Chem. And we'd gotten him into educational and career guidance to form five- and ten-year plans toward achieving his goal of a college degree.

He'd become the inaugural beneficiary of Richards Reaches Out.

The very same week Reece had helped me solidify a mission statement, a working budget, and an organization logo.

The week after that, he was helping me file papers and locate foundation office space.

He was giving me wings to be my own *more*.

The impact of the realization sparks the backs of my eyes with emotion I can't fight. "Reece," I rasp, unable to tame the quaver in my voice. "You *do* understand all the good you've already done here, don't you?"

We've cleared the Sepulveda Pass and the 101 exchange, meaning traffic's thinned enough for him to flash a polite smile. "Yeah, bunny. Of course I do."

"No." I grab his hand, squeezing it between my own. "You really don't." I tug again, waiting for him to look over once more. "In three months, we're going to be welcoming fifty kids from eight different countries to New York. They're going to get real-life, hands-on career experience and one-on-one mentorship from executives at every level of the Richards Corporation. Until now, every single one of these kids has thought their life wouldn't get any better than what it is now—

but worse, that they have no power to control that path. That they're trapped." A hard swallow takes over my throat. "That they can never be anything more."

A long, heavy breath leaves Reece. He twines his fingers tighter through mine. "The same way you once felt."

I don't give my answer in words. He doesn't need them. Even the intensity with which I work my fingers over his wrist and forearm isn't necessary. He already knows what I'm trying to say.

Yeah. The same way I once felt.

We travel another ten miles like that, until the urban outskirts of LA give way to the rolling hills on the back side of Topanga and Malibu, before I finally speak again. "We're doing really important stuff, Reece. Giving these kids one of the best gifts a human being can ever give another."

"Damn right." He pulls my hand over, smashing his lips atop my knuckles. "We're giving them hope."

I try to pull in my own inhalation—though it barely does me any good, since the man has, once again, deprived me of the ability to process air. And frankly, if given the choice to live on Reece Richards or oxygen, I'll be forced to tell the latter goodbye.

He slays me.

Gets me.

Sees me.

And yet still chooses to look over at me like some guy who snagged himself the perfect date for homecoming.

How have I gotten this lucky?

How come I still feel like Cinderella at that sparkling ball—looking to see that midnight was fifteen minutes ago?

So just in case...

"I love you, Reece Richards." I utter it with soft adoration, but the words are like a skin scratch compared to the sweet, deep wound he's dealt to my heart.

"I love you too, Emmalina Crist." And why does *his* declaration sound a thousand kinds of perfect—and flip a matching number of neurons throughout my body while activating *twice* as many misgivings in my brain? Things that *sound* like insanity but *feel* like wisdom...

If it feels too perfect, it probably is.

Happily-ever-after isn't free.

Books aren't their covers. And pretty pages often hide ugly truths.

I shake my head, freeing it from the images that invade along with the warnings. That always seem to. But why? They're senseless blobs, seen in my mind like lumps through frosted glass, which never make any sense beyond the dread they dump in my chest and the anxiety they prick into my mind...

Energy I will *not* allow to invade a perfect day like today.

I firm the resolve after we clear Ventura, where the highway rejoins the Pacific. Reece pushes a button that sends the roof sliding away, letting in the brilliant afternoon sun and the tangy ocean air. As we speed along, waves crash against beaches, wind breezes at wild grasses on the hills, and seagulls cavort in the air overhead.

I'm finding it tough to believe I woke up this morning in the Obelisk Manhattan, looking out the window at the Freedom Tower—but I'm *so* not knocking this scenery as Reece exits the highway at Calle Real and drives us beneath the distinctive white stucco entrance of the Bacara Resort. Within minutes, we're whisked by golf cart down the hill to a standalone villa with a private arched entrance through which I can already see the panoramic ocean view.

"Holy...*wow*."

My whole life, I've taken pains not to be "that" jaded Southern California girl—still, it's tough to get wowed-up about the ocean when it's ten minutes away every day. But the Pacific, from this particular Santa Barbara balcony, its whitecaps kissed by the molten gold of this California twilight...

It's a dream.

It must be.

Maybe I really *am* still back in New York, slipping in and out of subconscious fantasies before I fully wake for my day. Maybe I *do* want this particular dream to last a little while longer, especially because the pre-poured champagne is such a sweet sizzle on my tongue, mixing with the sea salt on my lips and the chocolate seashell Reece offers with a devastating smile. I bite dutifully into the candy, flicking my tongue out to catch the caramel that gushes from inside...and savoring how that induces him to spew a soft hiss.

Yeah. This dream is a keeper.

Slowly—because I'm definitely dreaming, I've missed him like freaking crazy, and I deserve this—I roam my gaze over his forearm before following the same trail with my mouth. Nibbling at his wrist. Sucking at his skin. Gently pulling his coarse hairs with my teeth until his hisses turn into throaty snarls. Relishing all those sounds as I turn, pulling him closer by the loosened tie around his neck, until his shirt is in my hands and I gain enough torque to rip it open, scattering the buttons. Loving his guttural "fuck" before he rips the ruined thing all the way off, along with his jacket. Loving it even more as he chucks the clothing behind, leaving it slung over the balcony rail, while ramming his beautiful body against mine.

"*Fuck*." I take the chance to fling the expression back as an amazed gasp while boldly exploring the sleek, sculpted lines of his torso. His perfect V of a form, so familiar yet so new. The little things are what memory makes fuzzy, even after just five days. The way his nipples tighten when I caress his hard pecs. The sharp rolls of his hips as I graze down his abdomen. The beads of sweat along his eyebrows as he struggles to hold himself in check.

"Christ, Emmalina." He fans the words, heavy and hot, across my forehead. "I've missed you."

I'm not surprised when he pushes me the remaining two feet back until I'm sandwiched between the wall and him. "I missed you too. So much that I dreamed about you."

"Oh?" His grunt is deep and low and arrogant. "And what was I doing...in your dreams?"

"Hmmm." I issue the sound as he reaches in, releasing the buttons of my jeans with swift, smooth twists. "A lot of stuff... like this."

He growls softly and plunges a hand down, skirting past my panties, until cupping my damp, trembling mound with his sure, sultry touch. "I'm not a man of ambiguities, Emma."

"No." How I manage to laugh it out, especially as he parts my lower lips and circles in a long finger, searching for my most sensitive core, is a mystery. "You...you certainly aren't."

"Then don't insult me with yours." With his other hand, he guides both my arms over my head before locking them there, his grip across my wrists. "Tell me what I did with you... in your wicked fantasies." As his mouth descends toward mine, he spreads heat across my entire face. "What I did *to* you."

Okay, I'm not laughing anymore. I'm barely breathing, for

fear that he'll stop bringing my body such consuming shudders and my senses the perfect plummet of surrendering to him... being filled and invaded and completely swept away by him...

Especially as he spills a sizzling snarl against my lips, hitches a knowing grin, and jolts my pussy with a shock of sheer electricity.

CHAPTER TWO

REECE

"Oh, my...*hell*!"

I watch her face as the words tumble from her lips—unable to tame the cocky chuckle that bursts from my own. "Oh, Velvet," I admonish. "I've already gotten a few good peeks at hell. *This* is nothing like it."

"Good to know." She nearly runs the words together before succumbing to more needy pants. "Just...just don't stop. Holy *shit*. Wh-What...are you doing to m-me?"

I smile down into her face, taking in every inch of her mounting desire. Primal victory fills me. The quivers of her lashes, the blooms on her cheeks, the sweet parting of her lips... All of it tells me how. "I fine-tuned a few things while you were gone."

Her gaze pops open, narrowing on mine with startling clarity. "You— You did *what*?"

I grin, cranking up the smugness. "Okay, it was more like... practiced. Taught myself some modulations."

"M-Modulations. To your *fingers*?" When I nod, she swallows hard. "I'm not sure whether to be excited or scared."

At once, her confession thickens my blood. It's heaviest inside my balls, which throb beyond the realm of blue—and not helped by the words I issue in reply. "What's wrong with both?"

Emma's pupils dilate. She inhales and then exhales, her breathing jumpy. "Is that what you want? For me to feel both?"

It's not the answer I expect but maybe the one I need. Now that Bolt is taking a break—perhaps retiring for good—it's been difficult to fight off some bizarre shit in my brain. Okay, maybe not so crazy for any other guy, but my entire life, I've never been "any other guy." As a kid, I was the family's signature troublemaker. When carnal knowledge became an actionable thing, I became the jet set's signature womanizer. For the last year, Bolt has been my hell-raising outlet—but in putting even him aside now, who am *I*?

Not Mister fucking Rogers, that's for damn certain.

But not the guy who's going to let the Consortium slink away quietly into the good night either. They're still out there, maybe *everywhere*, contemplating whose life they're going to fuck up next. Using Angelique La Salle and others like her to lure unsuspecting schmucks into their laboratory of horrors and then ruining *those* lives. And yeah, maybe ending a few. Hanging up Bolt's leathers doesn't suddenly preclude me from doing the right thing. The *necessary* thing.

Finding them.

And taking them down.

But Emma doesn't—and won't—know that.

Which has led me to dealing with a question I know nothing about.

Does she still want me, even without the danger high I once brought?

Thank fuck, the only answer I observe across her face is an unequivocal *yes*. Even better? For some reason I might not ever fathom, she's still, blatantly, all in on seeing my danger factor. Her body shivers from it. Her skin pebbles from it. Her chest huffs, frantic as a virgin in a horror movie, from it.

Ensnaring my attention downward by the second...

Wondering if other parts of her are just as clear about her fear. And needing to find out.

I slide my hand down from her wrists. Hook one finger, then two, into the V of her sweater, which aligns with the hammering pulse at the base of her neck. Revel in how that rhythm speeds up—just before I fire up the ends of those two fingers and cut them through her clothing like scissors of fire. With another flick, I decimate the center point of her bra as well.

"Oh, my God," Emma grates. It hasn't escaped my attention that her hands have remained where I ordered them, over her head against the wall, even though I've just undressed her from the waist up using my fingers like kinky lightsabers.

"Was *this* what I was doing?" I spread my fingers into the valley between her exposed tits, brushing lightly so all she feels is something like heightened static charges. "In your dreams... was I doing things like this to you?"

She shakes her head. Wets her lips. "Even my dreams weren't this good."

Another answer that exceeds *my* dreams too. "Good," I snarl, sprawling fingers completely over one of her breasts, letting the tiny charges fan out over her flesh as I take her mouth in a hot, open kiss. She groans into me and bucks against me, increasing the friction of my buzzing fingers across her engorged clit, especially as I push her hood aside and rub directly over her most vulnerable nerves.

"Reece!" She openly writhes now, nearly climbing me like a wildcat. Her head is tucked beneath mine. She rolls and thrusts her hips. "Holy *shit*, please!"

"Please what?" My taunt is quiet but serious.

"You *know* what." She angrily juts her crotch against my hand. "I need this. Damn it, I-I *need* to—"

"I know what you need." My tone broaches no argument and receives none from her lips—though she still combats me with her body, arching and lunging and gasping. "But I also know what *I* need."

"Anything." She lowers her hands to my shoulders, digging in her fingers to affirm her point. But does she have any damn idea what I'm about to ask?

I don't think so.

I step back, putting a few feet of distance between us, and hook my fore and middle fingers into my front pocket to hide their glow. I attempt not to think about what kind of hypocrite that turns me into in the eyes of karma, as I stand here with my fucking fingers in my pants getting ready to issue this kind of an order to my proud, kick-ass goddess of a girlfriend.

But I'm going to do it anyway.

Because deep down, I think—I *know*—it's what we *both* need.

"Go inside," I finally murmur. "Into the bedroom. Then take off the rest of your clothes."

An impish smile takes over the lush lines of her lips. "And wait for you in bed?"

I don't return her expression. I keep my own features on strict lockdown, even while pulling in a measured breath before expelling it with just as much control. "No. You'll wait for me on the floor. On your knees."

EMMA

I wish I could say this doesn't turn me on.

With any other man, it probably wouldn't. *Likely* wouldn't. It'd be thirty-one flavors of weird, slathered in an inch of uncomfortable and topped with a glob of whipped nerves.

But this is Reece. The man who's given me more. So *much* more. Most importantly, the *more* of himself. Of his heart and soul and life.

But not right now.

Not during any second of any minute since I've been back in California.

The conclusion is a clanging truth in my mind as I enter the villa's huge bedroom, where a four-poster king bed is centered on a blue and cream rug in a Spanish-style pattern. Capping one end of the rug is a built-in fireplace, in which flames already crackle against the logs. California or not, this is the Santa Barbara coast, so it'll be chilly tonight.

And there's my custom-made reminder, right on time.

Chilly.

It's the exact word to describe what I've been sensing from the man for the last three hours. On an afternoon when we should be plugging back into each other via every circuit we've ever connected together, a lot of those breakers are still dark and jammed. He's turned on the lights but not the heat.

He's the Reece I knew before he laid Bolt's mask in my hand.

Before I knew he'd been managing a hotel by day and saving a city by night.

Before I knew that on any one of those brazen Bolt missions, he might not come home—because the nutwings who'd turned him into a real-life freak were still determined to recover their exotic escaped test animal.

Before he'd finally realized he had to stop.

But what if he hasn't? What if, for whatever insane reason, he's put the leathers on again and isn't telling me? What if he's turning our reunion sex toward some kinky fun in order to disguise that fact? A blindfolded girl can't see battle bruises.

By the time I've written that full scenario in my head, I'm already on my knees at the foot of the bed. But fuming about it isn't an option because every molecule of air in the room changes as the man enters the room, shutting the door with a dominant *whomp*, though his steady stare never leaves my naked, trembling form.

He swipes a hand toward the entertainment console against the wall. At once, haunting synth beats fill the room like drops of nighttime rain. I hate him and love him at once for the selection. He knows all about my shivering attachment to this song by K.Flay. It's about beauty in blackness, salvation in silence, brightness in fading...

It's about how I feel when I lose myself in him. Am repowered by him.

Exactly what he's ordering me to do right now.

His stance says it, with his bare feet on either side of my knees. His body says it, the ridges of his abdomen flexing as I look up. His whole face says it, with his steely jaw and flaring nostrils. At once, my nipples turn into points. My limbs turn into melted arousal. My pussy turns into a needy puddle.

And that's just the start.

Because then he parts his perfect, full lips and states in a clipped, low baritone, "You're mine right now, Emmalina. Completely. Fully. You exist to please me...and I to please you." He cups my chin, fingers pushing at my jaw with defined command. "Your eyes say yes. Now let your mouth do the same."

"Yes." My own tone is nothing but a rasp. Dear God, how he spins me. And how I crave him for it.

He tightens his grip. "Say *all* of it."

"Yes," I whisper. "I exist to please you."

He curls his thumb up, rubbing over my whole bottom lip. "Good girl." Then he pulls down a little until my mouth parts for him. A quiet hiss escapes him. "*Very* good. Fuck, how you drive me crazy with this mouth."

Long seconds pass. The song throbs into a chorus. He keeps tracing my mouth with the pad of his thumb. I fight the need to get lost in his seductive rhythm, which would mean closing my eyes—but I must keep looking for even the smallest nick, cut, or bruise that'll give his ruse away. Yet as the minutes pass, that becomes harder and harder to believe. The only energy I receive from him is open, heated desire. The only darkness in his gaze is that of his mounting, consuming lust. He's a tangible presence in the very air I breathe, the atmosphere pressing in on me...

Fading me.

Encompassing me.

Giving me up to him.

The song thrusts on. Neither of us say a word, though as he shifts his other hand to the back of my neck, I already know what he wants. I move before his touch mandates it, pushing my ass off my ankles until I'm in an upward kneel before him...

With my face in front of his zipper.

I've never felt so mighty in my life.

Yes, here on my knees. Yes, at the feet of a man. But not

just any man. This is him. *My* man. The one who visibly shakes from the mere force of my stare. Whose abdomen clenches as my gaze roams upward, becoming a relief map of muscle and sinew. Who grunts with primal pleasure as he ensnares my uplifted hand and guides it toward the buckle of his belt.

Who parts his beautiful, sensual mouth on just two growled words.

"Do it."

Then three more, as soon as I've unlatched him, unzipped him, and set his erection free.

"Suck me, Velvet."

If he hadn't dictated it, I would have begged for it—from the second my sights landed on the milky drops at the top of his bulging shaft. What this man's special body does to *that* particular fluid... Let's just say that if the secret ever got out, we'd be stressing about him being hunted by more bastards than the Consortium.

But right now, nobody gets to have him but me.

And holy *wow*, has he been worth the aching wait.

His moan is music in my ears. His body is fullness in my mouth. His taste is everywhere in my senses.

As his essence seeps down my throat.

Then starts spreading through the rest of me.

Farther. Faster. Hotter.

I let my moan flow out, swirling in the air with his. I suck him more eagerly, like a junkie after her next hit. Maybe that's exactly what he's turned me into, but I'm beyond caring. I need more. The sparks of electricity in my veins are only the beginning of what he can do for me. The fulfillment he can bring to me, from the inside out...

More. Yes...please...more...

But suddenly, he's gone. He pulls away, his snarl buzzing the air in time to the swift violence of motion, leaving me swaying and gasping with a stunned gaze slicing up at him.

"Wh-What's w-wrong?"

Reece stumbles back by another step, shaking his head like the town drunk, returning my gaze with lust-clouded eyes. "Nothing. *Fuck.* Nothing."

"You don't look like it's nothing."

His jaw hardens as if I really have accused him of being the town drunk—which means I'm officially twelve kinds of confused. Thirteen now, as he shoves his pants to the floor and kicks them toward the corner. There's not a nick on his legs either. They're still just the flawless logs of glutes, quads, hamstrings, and calves that I remember—and adore.

So why is he still as cagey as a fenced-in palomino?

"I need to fuck you, Velvet."

Perhaps because he *is*?

"I'm here." I offer it with all the dedication of my heart— and yes, damn it, the chagrin of my mind. Have I really been mentally chasing him down for some stupid secret when the whole issue was just his unquenched lust? And if so, why did I let my doubts climb so far out of control?

There's an answer for that.

But that's not a victory that my past gets to claim today.

I reinforce that out loud by standing with hands spread to my sides in surrender while repeating, "I'm *here*, Reece. All of me."

He really seems to hear the words this time. The storm clears from his gaze, and his cheekbones take on harsher definition against his skin. "Good," he utters, jabbing his jaw my direction. "That's *very* good, beauty."

I don't answer him this time. His praise, verbal foreplay that could strip a nun from her habit, is clearly still an order too. I'm not left with any doubt of it as he paces back over, circling a finger in the air at the same time.

"Face down to the mattress," he growls. "And that sweet ass up toward me."

Inside, I melt. Through the room, the music gets louder. A new track starts. A new K.Flay song hits the air with a driving rock beat. The woman's defiant voice joins in, singing about her man being her citadel, her wishing well, the only high she needs. I whisper along as the drug of Reece's precome twines deeper into my bloodstream. I'm warm all over, languid as the setting sun outside but sharp and aware as the stars taking its place.

Especially when Reece moves up behind me, his cock sliding against the valley of my ass.

At once, every nerve of that crack, as well as the tissues throughout my pussy, spark to life. Quivering. Pushing. Swollen. Hot...

"Ahhhh!"

But then not hot. Drenched in slippery cold...a substance he spreads deeper into my ass...until his fingers guide the slick stuff to the tight opening between my cheeks.

Then all the way inside.

"Ohhhh!"

"*Velvet.*" His voice emulates the word, rough but soft, as I turn my head in time to watch him squeeze the lube container again. After a moment, my rosette is given a new bath of the cold fluid. My back tunnel is stretched to accept more of it, a strange contrast with the heat flowing through the rest of me. "Relax for me," he exhorts. "Get ready for me."

I bury my face against the bed again. He's being poetic, but his words might as well have come with a written decree and a court order. He's really going to do this.

"Ready for you," I snap. "You mean...back there."

More lube. More of his persistent prods. "I need to have all of you. I need to know you've given it *all* to me."

At once, he's stilled my squirms. Funneled my thoughts. Made me think, for a moment, beyond the uncomfortable thrusts of his fingers.

Instead, thinking about his voice.

About how his command has been given a new, pleading underline.

I need to have all of you.

All of me? How does he not know he already has that? Haven't I made it clear, over every day over the last three months, that not a second goes by in which he *doesn't* have me? Even when I was in New York, during every phone call and text and FaceTime conversation, he couldn't grasp that fact as truth?

In helping myself answer that, I'm unable to stop more of those initial suspicions from sneaking back in.

Something's changed for him.

And maybe not just over the last four days.

Maybe this trip simply provided the distance I needed to see it.

But whatever it is...he's made it clear what he needs to deal with the situation.

Damn it.

The same words tumble off my lips as he spreads my flesh even wider...and then nudges his hard tip at the tingling rim of that forbidden entrance.

"My beauty. *Oh, yes.*"

To my shock, the caress of his penis and the brush of his words meld into a jolt through my sex, coming to a blistering end in my clit. My body, tremoring from the aftershock, actually jerks backward, working his cock inside me another half inch. I cling to the bedcover, afraid to admit that I want more...but dear God, *I do*...

"Velvet. *Damn.* You feel so good already."

I yank in a shaky breath. "S-So do you."

But now, he doesn't return the tenderness. The potency of his lust, as tangible as the heat from the fire, breathes like a dragon in the air between us. The sound that rumbles from him is just as predatory and primitive, unfurling as slowly as the hand he hooks into the crevice between my leg and torso, securing my hips in place. He digs the grip in tight, securing me there...and pushing deeper into my back tunnel.

It hurts.

I moan.

He surges.

And moans deeper.

His fingers start to glow again. Their heat imprints my skin as he claims me with more of his cock.

Through the speakers, guitars grind. K.Flay wails about going higher, getting inspired, and never wanting to sober up. It's perfect. I'm drunk too. I must be. As Reece starts thrusting in full, hard strokes, I'm a pool of languid, lusty submission. Everything only gets better when he curls his other hand in, fanning those glowing digits against the strip of curls guarding my pussy. As his shaft claims new parts of my body, a new hum emanates from his magical touch...and he works every one of those vibrating tips through my throbbing, needy folds.

"Oh...*Oh!*"

"Yes. *Yes.*" He snarls it into the dip between my shoulder blades, slicking my back with his sweat, igniting my skin with his lips. "Take it, Emma. Take all of it."

"Yessss." My acquiescence is barely a sound as my body becomes his complete possession. He's breached me. Conquered me. Taken me prisoner in a kingdom of pleasure and pain and invasion and stimulation. High enough? Dear God, I'm beyond high. I'm on another plane. Existing for it. Accepting it all. I'm the willing vessel for his pleasure and the open conduit for my own. Entwined with having more of him. His cock, taking over my ass. His touch, the dictator of my arousal. His fluid, the life force in my blood. Every inch of every movement and every molecule of every breath is him...

My hero.

My lightning.

My love.

And now, in giant leaps of light and sensation, rapidly climbing toward another pedestal.

My release.

I know it, even as he lunges one more inch, stretches me in new depths. I reach for it, even as he moans and plunges again, doubling the agony of his entry. I scream for it as he slides his hot fingers through my folds and then fucks them into my other entrance.

I plead for it when he doesn't stop.

"Reece. *Reece!*"

He fits his face against the curve of my neck. Clamps harder to my hip, yanking my body back onto his with a brutal pace. "Don't ask me to stop, beauty," he croaks. "I don't know if I can."

I bunch the coverlet beneath my fists. "Don't you *dare* fucking stop."

His breath catches, but that's all I'll receive for an answering laugh. "Sweet beauty," he rasps. "My hot velvet bunny with her needy, wet pussy."

"Yes," I pant.

"And her tight, squeezing ass."

"*Yes.*"

He bites into my neck. "Do they both want more of me?"

"*Damn.*" I twist the comforter hard enough to tear it. "Yes. *More.* Please, Reece. Give me more!"

And somehow, in some miraculous way, he does. Piercing me so deep. Hurting me so hard. Robbing every thought from my head. Ripping every instinct and need from my body...but one. The yearning to give up the last piece to him. To come apart for him.

And I do.

Without warning, the explosion slams. I'm a thousand shards of sexual shrapnel ablaze at the same time, splintering until my mouth opens on a silent scream, as every membrane of my sex convulses and contracts and shudders and flutters.

I've been struck by lightning.

I'll never be the same.

For a moment, Reece freezes. Even his breathing is just shallow stutters, before he grates, "Fuck me. My *Velvet.*"

And then, he's no longer combusting the fire. He *is* the inferno, his fingers filling my womb with heat as he spills his come into my trembling back hole. And as he's promised, he doesn't stop. As his thrusts intensify, his double-sided burn is like a fresh match on my lust. I'm rocketed into a new orbit, coming for him again, this time managing at least a shredded shriek to give away my unrivaled, unending ecstasy.

But in gradual increments, it does finally end—at least for both of our physical selves. Reluctantly, I force my lungs to take deeper breaths, my heartbeat to consider the realm of normalcy. But even as Reece eases out of me and returns from a trip to the bathroom with a moistened towel, my senses aren't such an easy sell on the whole "normal" thing. I attempt to communicate that much with a weary glance at the man sliding up next to me on the mattress.

"Jesus. Wept."

I issue it with half a laugh, hoping Reece is able to decipher since there's no way I'm moving from my stomach-down sprawl for at least an hour. But my chuckle is cut short by my own yelp, as Reece smacks a possessive hand on my ass.

"Let him bawl." He smooths his newly normal fingers across my flesh. The cooler contact mellows the sting on my flesh into a delicious warmth. "This is still all mine."

A new shriek, as he embellishes by biting me there too. "Yo, Scrooge." I quip. "Don't you know sharing is caring?"

"Hmmph." He slides his lips up my back. "I share lots of things. The road. The elevator. Inspiring Twitter posts. Steak marinade recipes. Even cab rides, from time to time."

I visibly start. "Okay, whoa."

"Huh?"

"*You've* been in a real-life taxi cab?"

His casual shrug is the kind of charming most men have to practice. "In Europe. When I had no other choice. And probably too much to drink."

I fling up a hand. "You're edging on TMI territory, mister." Though the sketchy details and his averted gaze already fill in the unwanted blanks. Having "no other choice" means he was likely dragged into the cab by a woman—or two or three—even if "too much to drink" wasn't part of the equation. And though I fell in love with him knowing all this in full, thanks to "journalists" like Stall Stalker Blair, it's not something I'll ask him to reminisce about. I know he gets it—even right now, as he moves my hair away from my face and over my shoulder, continuing the pressure onto my scalp as a silent order to look back up at him.

"Hey."

His charge isn't just a cute greeting. I comply with the command, but not eagerly. "What?"

He traces my cheek with a thumb. "None of that is my life anymore, Emma."

"I know."

"Do you?"

"Yes."

"*Do you?*"

"*Yes*, damn it." I toss back an irked snip to his tight demand. "It's just that..."

"Just that what?"

Short huff. A longer sigh. "I'm just going to need lots more moments like this, Mr. Richards." My attempt at using the formality for levity is a failure. "Okay?" I add, attempting to backfill the awkward silence.

Reece frowns. Seriously, this lazing god, with his naked, nickless limbs covered in all that taut, tanned flesh, looks genuinely confused by my assertion. "Moments like what?"

"Oh, come on." I sit up straight, dragging one of the massive pillows over to cover at least part of me. I'm not bashful about my nudity—after the last half hour, the man's officially seen every crevice of my body—but the subject matter has definitely steered toward pillow-worthy discomfort. "I bet I'm the very first woman you've ever taken the anal sex cherry from." I cock my head. "Yeah?"

He jerks his head up, away from the elbow on which he's been angling. "Wait. *Fuck.*" He grabs my wrist and frantically peruses my face. "Are you...saying...that was..."

"Are *you* saying you couldn't tell?"

Another one of his effortless, gorgeous shrugs. "Most women play coy about it. Guess there's the nice-girl dirty-girl stigma."

"Most women," I mutter. "And oh, yeah. The 'stigma.' Of course, you know all about *that* too."

His gaze, which hasn't strayed a millimeter from me, also doesn't register comprehension of my accusation. "But...you liked it *so* much, baby."

"Duh." I really do bark out a laugh now. "Because it was *you.*"

"No." He makes me dizzy as he leans all the way over, cupping the side of my face. "*No.*" Then a little bit more, as he lowers a resounding kiss across my lips. "Because it was *you,* Emmalina."

And once again, he's dashed my determined plans into giddy girl dust. Just like that, he's taken my weird mix of qualms and doubts and self-skepticism, ground them up beneath the boulder of his love, and then rolled the stone away to let the sun shine in on my pulverized heart.

And in true giddy girl fashion, it sparkles.

And in true snarky girl fashion, I hope he's blinded by the shine.

But only for a few seconds.

Only long enough for me to roll over so *I* can initiate our next kiss. As our bodies mold tightly, I rejoice in his masculine taste, his dark-spiced scent, and his perfect, loving embrace. We tangle like that for a long minute, tongues dancing and limbs grasping, until he pulls back to let me take in his soft, adoring smile.

"Emmalina Paisley Crist, you're a goddess."

I bop his jawline with my fingertips. "And you're a dork." But I quickly turn my touch into a caress, grazing the irresistible spikes along his jaw. "But you're *my* dork."

He expels a long breath, nearly as if he's had a prayer answered, though his gaze turns the color of somber mist. "Don't you mean your glowing freak?"

"*Hey.*" I'm back to lightly smacking him. "If I'm not allowed the insecurity party, neither are you, buster. Besides"—I shimmy my crotch against his, adding a mischievous grin—"I think it's clear that I like how you dance a Friday night away."

His lips loosen with a spurt. "Disco down, baby."

"Oh, God." With my groan, I push at him a little harder. When he gives in, rolling to his back, I swing one leg over until I'm straddling him—and the erection that already surges beneath my suggestive rubbing. "I'm not sure about you, disco duck—but let's just say I never knew I liked dancing so much."

As he sprawls his hands over my thighs, clutching deeper to settle me more firmly on his shaft, he's got to be the most breathtaking male on the planet. At once, I yearn to lick his entire burnished chest. Suckle hard at his nipples until they're pinpoints against his pecs. Continue up to his taut jaw, tangling my hands in the decadent thickness of his hair.

"Maybe we should take another spin on the dance floor," he purrs with wildcat intent.

"Hmmm." I trail my hands atop his, letting my head roll

as tiny stars of sensuality spread out from my center. "Maybe we should."

"Only, this time, it's ladies' choice." He flashes a grin of faux innocence when I narrow my gaze. "I'm completely serious. Cross my heart, hope to die."

"Do *not* joke about that." I lean forward, capturing his wrists in my hands on the way down. "Not even a little."

His features soften. Only by a little, but enough to convey he's followed exactly where my mind has just gone. Back to the night he donned the Bolt leathers and sped to the El Segundo power station, lured by a false alarm that was staged by the Consortium and carried out by their key henchwoman in LA: Angelique La Salle, aka the ex-lover who'd betrayed Reece and dragged him into their clutches to begin with. The bitch had clearly been instructed to engage him in some kind of showdown, defeat him, and haul him back to their lab alive, but Mother Nature and Father Coincidence had other plans that night. A freak downpour and a downed powerline had nearly added up to a fried boyfriend when the ground itself became a charged electrical field, though ironically, the eruption saved Reece's life. Without it, he would have been Angelique's certain captive.

And what about the bitch herself? Surprise-not-surprise, the woman had survived the entire incident unscathed—at least physically. As for the gray matter beneath her insanely awesome supermodel hair? Way more debatable, since the woman had come trolling at my apartment less than a week later. Yes, in broad daylight. Yes, as her picture and stats were still being blasted across every news outlet, police scanner, and TSA checkpoint in the city. She'd slithered away after I chose to call her bluff instead of shiver in fear, but she likely didn't get very far. If the Consortium didn't execute her for the botch, she went underground to a place that probably makes her wish they had.

And that is *all* the consideration I choose to give Angelique La Salle tonight. Or any more thoughts of the six thousand ways she's betrayed and fucked up the man I love. Yeah, yeah, so there's the argument that he wouldn't *be* the man I love without the hell he endured in the Consortium's captivity, but I choose the old-fashioned response to that one. He was *always* this man, all along. With a little patience, love, and a few thousand dollars in therapy, he would've gotten to the same realization. Those lunatics in lab coats just took him there the quick and ugly way.

Reece's caresses pull me out of my silent anger. "No more jokes," he joins them in a murmur, stamping each syllable with searing sincerity. His gaze supports the message, the silver of his desire mixing with the gold of the sunset now streaming through the shutters and across the bed. "No more jokes," he repeats. "Just me, Velvet. It's all just me, here for you...always."

His declaration is like the sea beyond the balcony. Full of whispers and mist on the surface, surging with strength just beneath. I let the power of his ocean wash over me, pulling my passion higher, until I'm rocking my hips up and down, working the slick lips of my sex over every inch of his surging shaft. *Holy shit.* Electric come or not, I can't ever get enough of this man's cock. Some generous angel created him just for me, and I will forever be grateful—a fact I blissfully set myself to proving right now.

"Damn!" he grates as I dip forward, crushing my breasts to his chest and sliding more of my needy slit over his hot length. I run my hands higher, meshing our fingers. His thighs go taut as he starts lifting his hips, matching my increasing rhythm. "Christ. *Emma.*"

"Yes, Mr. Richards?" Threaded with my breath, my tone is a sultry tease.

"Let me into that perfect pussy. *Fuck.* Please."

His plea is my command—though I'm hardly going to *tell* him that. Instead, I work my hips against him in tiny circles, which soon sends us both into heavy breathing mode. We taunt each other with short, hot kisses as veins begin to bulge along his cock and an answering flow of arousal pulses from my core.

I want him.

I need him.

I spread wider for him...

As a cell phone notification slashes the air.

"*No.*" Reece's protest is nearly as violent as the buzz, which persists as I push up, lifting both hands.

"Well, don't look at *me.*" I giggle as he sits up, dragging hands through the tangles atop his head.

"Damn it," he grumbles. "I only had it set for important shit to come through but meant to turn the whole thing off once we got here."

I give his firm ass a light spank as he stands. "Well, you've been a little distracted."

"Most important distraction in my world."

"Yeah, yeah. You want some milk with all that sickening sugar?"

"I'll show you milk, baby."

There's no chance for me to get in a good comeback, since he highlights the point by swooping up from where he's yanked the phone out of his pants, only to lose his grip and watch the device shoot out toward me. I yelp as it lands on my bare stomach. I flip it over to hand it back to him—

But I don't.

I rear back, my new glare still glued to the screen—as well as the name of the person Reece has cleared for his "important shit." But the final bullet that shoots my heart down into my stomach? The actual message this "important" person has sent him.

"Mr. Richards?" It's quite possibly the first time I've ever sneered his name in derision instead of issuing it with respect... or desire. "Who the hell is 'Sally,' and *why* the hell does she want 'every inch of you' at 'the usual place' by midnight tonight?"

CHAPTER THREE

REECE

"Emma."

I'm not given an answer beyond the thrum of the freeway beneath the car—unless fury really can have a sound; in which case, she's blowing my eardrums out with the shit.

"*Emma.*"

"What?" Her bite is like a nail splitting wood. Appropriate, since I'm damn sure she's close to boarding up every square inch of herself to me now, and we've barely cleared Carpinteria.

"It's not what you think."

As soon as it's out, I have to swallow back the bile that comes up with it. Christ. I've become the cliché I always used to laugh about. Needless to say, I don't blame Emma for her sour chuckle.

"It must be that bad, or you must be that desperate." She turns her gaze out the window, but the ocean is a blanket of black. I clench my jaw, glancing at the reflection of her face illuminated by the dashboard. The corners of her eyes are tight. Her mouth is taut, telling me her own teeth are locked—and betraying the real driving force behind her anger.

Not hurt. Not sadness.

Fear.

Of what?

And the fact that I'm even posing the question illuminates how badly I've driven the nails into my coffin on this one.

"Fuck." I grip the wheel tight enough to squeak my fingers on the leather. "I should've been more upfront with you about this since the beginning."

Her laughter gains a new pitch. "You think?"

I push out a huff. "But RRO was taking up so much of your time..."

"Which was why you pulled the strings to get it up and running so fast? *Damn it*, Reece." Her outburst is justified as soon as I give her a culpable glance instead of an instant denial. "So...*what*, then? It was time to get me out of the way? Why?"

"*Shit*." Another measured breath. "Not 'out of the way,' Emma."

"Just too busy to notice you were up to something behind my back with someone named Sally."

"Not what you think."

"Stop saying that! You have no idea what I'm thinking!" She gathers up a knee, wrapping both arms around it before uttering, "Damn it. *I* don't know what I'm thinking."

"I think I have a few good ideas."

Her laugh is pure bitterness now. "This ought to be good."

I swallow hard. Fight the urge to reach for her. But even that won't narrow the real canyon of distance between us now. The gorge I've carved with my own actions. Only one thing will accomplish that right now. The honesty I still can't give her in full.

Maybe, if I give her what I can, it'll be a good enough patch on the wound. At least for now.

I have to try. No matter how ugly it gets.

Without taking my eyes off the road, I head in before I can

talk myself out of it.

"Dumbshit."

Her head snaps up. "Excuse me?"

"Dumbshit," I repeat. "That's what you called yourself at first, when seeing my phone back at the hotel. I'm right, aren't I? It was either that or some variation of it. Maybe pinhead. Or box of rocks. Or dipstick. Yeah, probably dipstick. You really like that one."

A beat. Another. I look over, unsurprised to see her dazed blinks. "I...really...what?"

"I know them all, Emma. Every awful thing you've invented to call yourself, thinking it'll help you atone for the sin of wanting a life beyond what you had in the OC."

"Excuse *me*?" She drops the leg. Pivots hard in her seat to fully face me. "I do *not* regret *any* decision I've made."

"Except when you have to explain any of them to your mother and father."

"All choices that led me to meeting *you*, remember?"

"Haven't forgotten for a second, sweetheart." I dare to hope the tender delivery will let me take her hand. I'm wrong. She's even more livid. The knee comes back up, this time joined by the other one.

"So that's what I did, huh?" she bites out. "Flogged *myself* because of a message like that on *your* phone?"

"Didn't say that." I lower my hand to the console between us. I'm not giving up completely yet. "I just said that was the beginning of your reaction."

"Ohhh, right," she returns drily. "Sure. The beginning. That led to...what? Come on," she prompts when I tighten my jaw. "Inquiring minds *do* want to know."

"Okay." I pull in a deep breath. Keep my eyes on the road,

though I can sense the continued intensity of her stare. "Like I said, you went for the dipshit self-label first but backed off fast because you figured it might be a work colleague or one of my direct-reports from the hotel. Yet after pulling up the profile and seeing there's no last name on it—"

She slices me short with a sharp huff. "I wouldn't go digging in your phone like that, Reece."

"Because you trust me?" I arch my right brow. "Or because you're afraid of what you'd find?" When she's eerily quiet, I dare a glance over—to read the confirmation of my second question all but tattooed across her gorgeous face. *Damn.* For all her taunts about my off-track claims, I've struck the very meat of her heart. Though I feel like crap about it, I take advantage of her distraction to finally land the handhold. "Velvet. You have full digging rights, okay?"

"Even when it comes to Sally?"

Despite the jab of the words, she doesn't try to get her hand back. Relief drives part of my ready reply. "*Especially* when it comes to Sally." I don't hide the severity of my next inhalation. "Whom I should've told you about the second I set up that profile in the phone."

"So why didn't you?"

Again, I reply with my truth. *All* of it. "I wasn't sure you'd understand me. Or even believe me."

She stiffens. "Why the hell wouldn't I?"

I firm my jaw in lieu of stealing another peek at her. I can't risk exposing any more of my fucking remorse about my past—and my fears about how it keeps haunting our present. "You moved to LA for the opportunity of a bigger world, not to fall for the planet's most prominent player. But he fell for you too, which made everything okay—at first." I pause, letting the truth of the words resonate—and hating that they likely do. "Deep down, you've been wondering when the paint will wear off the tiger and you'll learn he hasn't changed his stripes at all."

As I dread—and expect—there's nothing but a long silence from her side of the car. After the better part of another mile, she finally lifts her head and murmurs, "That's what you think *I* think, huh?"

I send an anvil of fuck-my-life down the length of my throat. "And I pounded the high score on it, didn't I?"

She draws in an audible breath. As she lets it out, I expect her at last to yank back her hand. Instead, she twines her fingers tighter against mine—before muttering, "Reece Richards, you are so full of shit."

So much for resisting the need to stare. Because now I do, with a jab of bewilderment, as she leans over until she's leaning on the console, nearly in my face with accusation.

"And now that we've gotten the easy excuse out of the way, why don't you tell me who 'Sally' really is and why *he* has you dropping everything like a criminal on the run?"

EMMA

"Damn it."

Reece's growl is an unnecessary embellishment. He's already given away just how much of his mark I've struck just with the strain of his shoulders against his shirt and the clench of his hands on the steering wheel. Those two elements alone turn him into a commercial for raw virility, but with the gleaming silver of his gaze, I'm beyond tempted to point out the next rest stop and suggest we screw away our frustrations.

But not everything can be handled the easy way.

Not all my anger can be simply screwed out of my head.

Not every hurt can be erased so easily from my heart.

As I work my hands against opposite elbows, nearly clawing myself to contain the wet stings behind my eyes, he grits, "How'd you figure that out?"

"That you really are as skittish as a criminal?" I chuff, implying just how transparent he's made *that* part. "Or that 'Sally' isn't the casual lover you'd want anyone to assume if they happened to be spying at your cell screen?"

He lets out a peeved bull snort. "You've really put all that together in the last half hour?"

"You're not in bed with a bimbo anymore, mister." I tilt my head. "But you're willing to risk having the world think that, aren't you? If even one intrepid photographer catches your phone screen from the right angle..."

"They won't discover a thing." His entire body tenses now. "Goddamnit, you know they wouldn't, Emma."

He leans over, again snagging my hand with his, but I yank free again in seconds.

Then scrutinize him hard—as the underlying truth of all this really hits.

This isn't about believing what he's already said. It's about questioning what he hasn't.

"But Sally is *somebody*." I gesture at the speedometer, reading twenty digits past the speed limit, and then out at the open highway in front of us. "You. This. Criminal behavior. I'm not imagining this, mister."

After a silence filled with nothing but his long inhalation, he says quietly, "No. You're not." A glance exposes the curious glint in his eyes. "But how did you know *she's* really a *he*?"

"I didn't." I lower my hands. Shrug quickly. "Until just

now."

"Fuck." He shakes his head as I free up a light laugh. "You're a minx."

"Wellll..." I seesaw my head. "Maybe just a minx with damn good instincts."

"And girl-balls as big as that ocean."

"And a body that drives you crazy."

"But a mind that drives me crazier."

His voice's descent into gritty seduction dips my body deep into molten arousal. I shift in my seat, gnawing the inside of my cheek to recheck my composure. *Damn it.* Pulling over for a quickie really *isn't* an option when one's boyfriend is attempting to break the land speed record for the Santa Barbara-to-LA run—especially when I'm still in the damn dark as to exactly why.

"You're not playing fair, mister."

The corner of his elegant mouth curves up. "Because I play to win."

His hands don't move off the wheel, though he might as well have slipped one under my dress and into my crotch. Dear hell, the man and his grin make me as wet as a schoolgirl pining for her hot science teacher. "And 'Sally' is going to help you win against...who?"

And just like that, he's back to driving the luxury car as if he's barreling a tank into battle. His face hardens into the same solid steel. "I'm not sure you want the answer to that, sweetheart."

Just as swiftly, my own mode shifts into a new gear. Goodbye, dewy schoolgirl. Hello, freshly pissed girlfriend. "Are you really falling right back into *that* game, player? Because the *last* round didn't teach you that I'm not falling for

ANGEL PAYNE

that bullshit?"

For a long second, I get no reply but a pronounced tick in his jaw. But just when I've resigned myself to spending the rest of the drive back to LA in thick silence, he gives the wheel a hard right and swerves the car to a stop along the shoulder in the darkness between Dulah and Ventura.

"What the—"

But then there's no time for breathing, let alone forming words. Reece surges into my personal space, star fire reflected in his gaze. No, I mean star *fire*, like exploding hydrogen and helium. "This isn't a fucking game, Emma," he seethes. "*Your* safety and *our* future are not fucking *games*, and that's exactly what I intend to let those bastards know, okay?"

"Those bastards who?" The words stammer from me right before their meaning finally wallops me. "Holy...shit." Now I'm the one forcing him to stay close, gripping the front of his shirt. "Are you...telling..."

He flattens a hand atop mine. Meets my gaze with more unblinking star fire. "We're going to do it quietly, baby. And carefully. You know what they say, right? Keep your friends close, but your enemies—"

"That idiot never had enemies like the Consortium!"

Assaulted by too many violent emotions at once, I let him go and lurch out of the car. The wind off the sea whips at my hair and pelts salt on my face, only making a minor dent in the heat of my fury.

Reece slams the door on his side of the car. "Damn it." His growl slices the air. "They're dangerous, Emmalina. To a lot of people besides just me."

"So you're deliberately declaring war on them?"

"*Not* war."

"Oh?" I stomp away as he approaches. The sight of the vast blackness beyond the guardrail is a perfect companion for my despairing senses. "What, then? Where, exactly, am I getting these semantics wrong?"

"It *isn't* war." His steps are determined crunches in the gravel. "We're doing it in unconventional ways. With opaque ops, small hits, and untraceable sabotage."

"Doh." I sweep up a hand, smacking it back down to my forehead. "Sorry. My bad. I must have missed the memo when terms like that *weren't* a bunch of fancy words for warfare."

He juts his jaw. Plants his hands on his hips. "War takes participation by two or more parties."

"Riiight." I drop my head, nodding hard. "So you're just terrorists, then. Is that it?"

He throws up his arms. "*Christ*, Emma."

"He's not going to help you, Reece. Not after those assholes own you again."

"That's not going to happen."

"Why?" I whirl back around, stabbing the accusation of my stare into him. "Because you're hiding it better this time? Because you still 'got a guy'? Is that who 'Sally' really is? And if the Consortium gets wise to him, you think they won't be able to trace all the subterfuge back to you anyway? You really think the cheerleader call signs and the coded texts are going to throw off a bunch of geniuses who've mastered electronics so well they're using it to alter human beings?" When he doesn't say a damn thing to any of that, the backs of my eyes become furnaces—though fury is no longer the accelerant. His silence has now sparked my bone-deep fear. "*Damn it*, Reece. Do you seriously think the entire world is going to take Richards Research at simple face value now? *Hey, look everyone. There's a receptionist in the lobby and real lab stuff in the building.* Sure. Okay. Nobody's going to doubt that shit isn't exactly what you say it is *now*."

With disarming grace, he covers the two steps remaining between us. With unnerving calm, he pulls me into his arms. "But shit *is* exactly what we say it is." He meets my glower with steady conviction. "The lab is fully functioning, Emma. We *are* doing legitimate research there. I can say that to you with certainty because *I'm* monitoring every damn stage of it."

"What?" I don't sugarcoat my surprise. "And *you're* the resident science geek now?"

He rocks his head back and forth. "Well, yeah. It's been somewhat of a hobby my whole life." His lips quirk, hesitant and awkward as my frown deepens. "In college, I actually minored in bioscience management, thinking I'd expand the Richards portfolio into hospitals and research centers for modern disorders."

I shift back, feeling thoughts line up like dominos and then tumble perfectly into one another. "And now, you're doing just that—only you're researching the cure for your *own* disorder."

"Ahhhh." His mouth softens back into a smile before he presses a kiss on my nose. "See? I *do* love you for more than your sexy-as-fuck body."

I ignore his obvious bait, instead chasing the bigger conclusion. "And if you discover a way to reverse what the Consortium did to your blood..."

"Their 'disease' will be rendered as obsolete as polio."

A thrill bursts through me. "They'll be destroyed."

"Yeah." His nostrils flare, working with the elements to turn him into an even more alluring sight of primal beauty. "They sure as hell will be."

I fight off the urge to kiss him. Barely. A rush of perplexity helps, hitting me as fast as the excitement did. "Okay, so why not focus everything on that?" I challenge. "Why all this extra bullshit?" I push my forehead into the dip between his pecs, blasting a harsh huff against the muscled contours. "You're poking the bear in all the wrong ways—and he has big fucking teeth."

"Yeah?" His comeback is too flippant for my comfort, but I let him drawl on, "Well, a bear that's busy digging thorns out of his ass is less dangerous than one pillaging the forest."

My shoulders sag. "Good point," I mumble.

"*Damn* good point." He tugs me closer, resting his chin atop my head. "Especially because we likely won't reach any kind of research breakthrough for a year, *if* we're lucky and *if* we keep the rockets at full burn." He dips his face down, pushing a heavy breath into my hair. "And that's three hundred and sixty-five days too many if you're strapped to a steel table at the mercy of a whack job with a one-eighty IQ."

His utterance ensures I gain a few pricks of my own to contend with now—luckily not in my backside. But every one of them jabs at my psyche, bringing new understanding to his crazy actions. "The ones you had to leave behind," I finally murmur. "At the lab in Spain."

In the chest beneath my ear, his heartbeat intensifies. I swear I can hear the ache in every thump resonate.

"I wasn't the one who deserved to get away, Emma." When I attempt to negate him, even with a soft shove, his grip turns to iron and his stance stiffens to stone. "It's the truth, goddamnit, and I refuse to add pretty filters just to make it easier to look at." He swallows hard. "For whatever reason, I got the means to get out of that hellhole—though every day since then, I've truly wondered why."

Only then does he pull back, but he keeps me close by grasping the sides of my face. His touch pulses at my hairline, hot and urgent. And the starlight in his eyes... *Dear God.* It's the beautiful stuff this time. The glimmering, mesmerizing, take-my-breath-away light, making my chest hurt because of its resplendence.

At last, with the same mix of sorrow and tenacity, he speaks again. "So yeah, baby, I'm going to poke the damn bear. I'm going to stab that fucker if I have to. As hard as I can, as much as I can, in any way I *possibly* can—until *everyone* is free from those fuckers."

His promise turns the star fire into energy throughout his body. The brilliant force of it makes me wrap my arms around him, hoping some of that cosmic-level faith will rub off—because right now, all I can think about is the bear getting tired of the jabs at its ass and turning around to take out its tormentor...

Reece's arms enfold me tighter—once again, seeming to reach into my brain and see every doubt and fear still lingering there. With another fervent kiss against my hair, he whispers the exact words I need to hear.

"It's going to be all right, Emma." His promise matches the unyielding force of the waves that crash and pummel the rocks twenty feet away. "This time, the Consortium doesn't get to win. However that happens, however long it takes...*we won't let them win.*"

✦

Ninety minutes later, as Reece leaves the Tesla's keys with the Hotel Brocade's valet and starts walking me across the lobby toward the executive offices, those words keep resounding through my head.

We won't let them win.

Sounding worse now than the first moment I went ahead and pushed the repeat button on it.

However that happens...

Sounding more stupid by the second.

However long it takes...

No. Sounding like complete lunacy.

Which, officially, must make me the world's worst girlfriend. I mean, what woman *doesn't* want her man to declare words like this? This is the stuff of dreamers and fighters and heroes. Of Braveheart and Superman and Maximus the Gladiator...

Who are all fictional.

And still ended up dead.

Meaning it's time to dig myself out of the YouTube tunnel of despair and get back to loving my real-life dreamer fighter hero—who has, uncannily, never fit the role more than in this moment. With his hair a wind-tossed mess, his shirt and slacks casually rumpled, and his trendy glasses emphasizing the gleam in his eyes, he's like Clark Kent checking back in at the *Daily Planet* as we clear the back security door into the hotel's executive offices. One big difference, though? Nobody in this place has gotten over the bombshell Reece dropped on the world three months ago—or is ready to accept the new "reality" we're still trying to float as fact.

Accordingly, as soon as we enter, everyone on the nightshift team seems to emerge from nowhere with giddy enthusiasm.

"Well, well, well. Lucky us. The Bolt God himself."

Annnnd some are a bit more jubilant about it than others.

As Reece endures a hearty handshake from Wade, my onetime workmate with the grin of a Cheshire cat and the humor of a frat boy, the rest of the night crew quickly crowds in behind him.

"Mr. Richards." Fershan, his wide eyes contrasting with his skin, doesn't emulate the handshake. Instead, trembling in blatant hero worship, he leads each comment with a llama-like extension of his head. "It is a grand pleasure to see you again."

"You as well, Mr. Bennett." Reece turns, noticing the new face in our midst: an eager-eyed thing with a spray of freckles across her nose and a knowing tilt to her heart-shaped mouth. The woman is a stark contrast to my friend Neeta Jain, with whom she's entered—though her girl-next-door vibe possesses a distinct worldliness, especially as she ogles my man.

Seriously. She's ogling.

"Mr. Richards." She strides forward on ankle boots that add six inches to her petite frame and extends a slender hand. "My name is April Levine. I'm Miss Crist's replacement." She adds, practically touching her lips like some starlet who accidentally let a nipple slip, "As the Guest Satisfaction Manager, of course."

"Ah. Sure." Reece is either *that* out of practice about picking up a woman's innuendo or more focused on his meeting with "Sally" to care. "Nice to meet you. Welcome aboard."

"I've been a big fan for a while," she croons while they shake hands. "I read and notated the articles you wrote for

Return on Investment two years ago and even have Team Bolt T-shirts in four different colors."

"Yeah?" To my shock, Reece grimaces. "Well, I was a dick when I wrote that piece, and those T-shirts will make nice bathroom cleaning rags for you now. But the good thing is, now *is* now, and you're part of a team building a great future for this hotel. Granted, you have huge shoes to fill"—he tucks me against his side—"but with Neeta's guidance, I have every confidence you'll do well."

Neeta's flawless skin usually doesn't give away blushes, but pride beams from her elegant features as she murmurs, "Thank you, Mr. Richards. That is truly appreciated."

"Oh, she *is* wonderful." April meshes her fingers and crosses one foot over the other, going for the whole fashion-ad-pose-as-social-filler angle. "I mean, the way she can upsell the suites is textbook *wow*."

"That it is." Though Reece's clutch on my waist tightens to the point that I yelp. "Baby?" he asks, swooping down a concerned gaze. "You all right?"

"Dandy," I mutter, tightening the corners of my return glance. "We were just in the car for a while, and nature calls, so if you'll all excuse me..."

With perfect timing, the penthouse's express elevator arrives in response to Reece's summons, its doors parting on a whisper. Reece joins me in dispensing our quick goodbyes, and then we're both silent until the lift carries us about three floors up—

The moment we break into simultaneous laughter.

"You can just call me Mr. Textbook Wow from now on," Reece chuckles out. "Is there a T-shirt for that one too?"

I give in to a fresh giggle, leaning against the rail next to him. "You sure you even want to know? Though Mr. Return on Investment definitely has a catchy ring...to..." But my declaration is consumed by *his*—a long, wet, lingering, tingling mesh of his mouth to my mouth, his body to my body, his heartbeat against my own...his erection surging at my slit. We bite and suck and thrash at each other, at once consumed with what feels like a mutual craving to climb inside each other, spiking my blood to fevered intensity and swelling my clit with hot, tremoring need...

Which all gets a hideous ice bath as soon as the car is filled with the most irritating *ding* since the brass call bell was invented.

"Fuck." Reece drops his forehead against mine.

I smile and bite my lower lip. "Sounds like a damn good idea to me." Except I'm not the one with an appointment that had us hauling ass in a custom Tesla to get back here. An appointment I have *no* damn trouble distracting him from, as he grabs one of my thighs, hitches my foot up to the rail along the elevator's short wall, and then loops my other knee over his shoulder as he falls to his knees before me.

"*Fuck.*" His echo heats the panel of my panties, awakening my entire pussy like a blast of summer sun.

"As I said..." My ass cheeks constrict. My throat is parched. My nipples are puckered. "*Damn* good idea."

"You'd like that, wouldn't you?" With a fast sweep of his finger that peels away the satin covering my sex, he nearly obliterates my control with his sultry breath and his teasing touch. "You'd like me to get inside you right now, with my fingers or my cock..." He interrupts himself with a hum, working those magical fingertips over the outer petals of my sex. "Either would be fine. Perhaps *both* would be."

With slow, tiny circles, he closes in on my trembling, fiery center. Everything south of my waistline trembles, and I buck my hips at him almost as a Pavlovian response. Dear sweet *hell*, what this man does to me...

Enrages me. Enslaves me. Engulfs me. Entrances me.

"And you too." I gasp it out as he starts those perfect little swirls again, holding my flesh hostage to his touch, binding my mind to every erotic nuance of his voice. "Dear God. *Reece*. You too, okay?" I slap at the elevator walls where he has me cornered in more ways than one. "Please. I need...I need your cock. Pounding inside me. Coming inside me." And now, none of this is about being his diversion. It's about being his completion.

Needing it...

"Then that's exactly what you'll have, sweetheart..." He rises, skimming my hips and waist as he goes, stretching his arms until his heated fingers thread with mine and his bold, sure mouth teases the top curve of mine...

For all of five seconds.

Before he pushes back, visibly fighting for his own control, knocking his head back against the wall as he reaches over and slams the Door Open button.

"Just as soon as I get my ass back up here."

For a second, I don't move. I *can't*. "Wh-What?"

He drags a hand through his hair. Like *that's* going to calm my lust? "I'm sorry, baby. You know I am. But as soon as I get done with this damn meeting..."

"Right. The meeting."

"Goddamnit, Emma. This isn't just another stockholder or vendor I can push off until—"

"You made that clear before getting me out of bed in Santa

Barbara."

He watches as I somehow force enough strength back into my legs to support my weight again. "So that's how you're going to be?"

"Because that's how you've *already* been?" My shredded panties fall to my feet. I kick them at him with a sharp flick. "Don't give me gorgeous and confused, Mr. Richards. I know it's worked for you in the past, but let's call this one as we see it."

He sucks in an audible breath. Doesn't move his hand from the button. "And how do you see it?"

I fold my arms, not backing down from his scythe of a stare. "The primeval act as an insurance policy. Making sure you've got me hot and bothered enough so I'll wait for you in the cave like a good little bitch."

"Is that what you really think?"

I don't surrender my stance. Even through the squirm-worthy silence that takes over. If I don't move from the car, he has to stay here and deal with me. With *this*. With the fact that he might as well be sending me off so he can go put on the lightning boy leathers and face down a hoodlum or twelve. He's evoked the same visceral terror in my blood and disgusting fear in my heart. "I have no idea why you're even bothering to ask," I mutter. "Because apparently you already know what I'm thinking. And, for that matter, what information might be useful for me to know and what's convenient to hide from me."

With a sound of raw frustration, he abandons the button and resorts to flipping the red emergency stop. "Damn it, Emma," he bellows over the clanging alarm bells. "I'm trying to protect you!"

"No." I flinch back. "You're still trying to be a fucking

superhero. Only I'm not some fluttering damsel in distress, Reece. I'm the woman who loves you." I repeat, in a shaky mutter, "God help me...I'm the woman who loves you."

He drops his arms. Coils his fists. "Then be the woman who trusts me too."

I mirror his stance. "Then be the man who lets me in."

With timing that couldn't be any worse—or better, I suppose, depending on the viewpoint—his phone trills in his pocket. He doesn't reach for it, and by now we both know why.

"I have to go, sweetheart."

"I know." My retort is just as stiff, matching my backward steps out of the car. "The cave needs to be tidied anyhow."

As I mutter it, the elevator doors start to close. Reece jams a hand into the opening, retracting them. "*Emma.*"

I hate myself for being compelled by the sandpaper in his voice. And after my head is lifted, by the aching gray of his eyes. "What?"

He steps out. Presses the long, tapered fingers of one hand to my cold cheek. "I'm fighting for us."

I compress my lips. "Then let's fight *as* an *us.*"

His eyes slide shut. I get the feeling I've said the best thing and the worst thing in one fell swoop.

But definitely not the thing to change his mind.

He slides away from me, pushing back into the elevator with a face stamped in determination and a stance stiffened by pure purpose. "I love you, Emma Crist."

"Fuck you, Reece Richards."

In the silence following the descent of the elevator, I stalk into the penthouse's living room and plunk my purse and Bendel next to the luggage Zalkon delivered from the airport. I plop onto the couch with a heavy sigh, struggling to listen to advice from my heart. Sagacity that's been passed down along the ages.

Don't go to bed angry.

It's so trite but timeless, even Mom likes saying it. But what about when one's man is a superhuman with electric blood, in denial about his world savior complex? Worse, what happens when one knows he doesn't give a crap about the fame and fortune of that gig? That his devotion truly stems from a moral calling to set the world right?

To get trite again, his tortured heart and his burdened soul are both in the right place. He's just not inviting *me* to that place.

I wrestle—okay, throw down a WWE match—with the rumination, even as my exterior starts a weary shuffle to the kitchen to seek out my favorite moping buddies. With a glass of milk, a peeled banana, and a glob of Nutella to dip it in, I hunch over the table in the breakfast nook, fighting not to feel like the girl who wasn't invited to hang at the mall after school.

Like Lydia always was.

Lydia. The thorn in my side but my greatest inspiration, rolled into one athletic, vivacious, and totally sweet package. Yeah, my sister was always everyone's first pick for those fun excursions...

No.

My spine becomes a ramrod as I drop the banana. It splats into the brown topping, as much a fresh mess as my thoughts. There *were* times that 'Dia got cold-shouldered from the mall too—because the politics of girl packs make Washington, DC, look like *Sesame Street*—only I never really noticed much because my sister didn't care.

My sister, for all the ways she loved embracing the Orange

County shimmer-and-shines, would *never* accept being reassigned to cave duty.

If she didn't have an invitation to the party, she'd just write herself one.

I take a big swig of my milk and swallow it before repeating to myself, "Just write...your own invitation."

As I murmur the last word into the stillness of the kitchen, there's a loud vibration from back in the living room. It's coming from my purse, still on the floor next to my other bags. I scoop my phone out and smile at the picture of the caller. "Miss Neeta Jain, as I live and breathe."

"Miss Emmalina Crist." My friend's voice, like a verbal version of a *sari* from her native land, is colorful but graceful. "Is this a bad time?"

I let my sigh fill the line. "As much as I wish you were talking to my voicemail right now because I was too busy with other things, I am one-hundred-percent free to speak with you."

"Oh, dear." There's a soft swish, lending me to think she's tossing her hair over her shoulder. "That's what I thought, though was pained about it." One more meaningful pause. "Reece came back down so fast after you two went up to the penthouse. To be honest, we weren't expecting to see you two at all. He informed me he would be out of town most of the weekend after picking you up from your trip."

"Yes, well..." I inject a dark huff. "The plans changed."

"Have you two quarreled?" She adds in a rush, "And I have no right to know if you do not wish to speak about—"

"Oh, I *do* wish to speak." I pace across the room, gazing out over the city through the floor-to-ceiling windows. The twinkling light carpet is restless tonight, as if fighting against the hot winds that got angrier after sundown. I couldn't think of a better companion for my mood as the Santa Anas whip their heated fury around the sides of the building, making the windows moan. "But more than that, I need some actionable intel."

"Information?" Neeta drops into a gleeful whisper. As much as Wade and Fershan are addicted to video rogues, thieves, and gorgons, this woman is a sucker for a good spy adventure. "I'm your inside girl, Emma Peel." The second she uses her favorite nickname for me, invoking one of the most badass female spies of all time, I know I've got her on board.

"And I'm your grateful one." I'm sincere about it. "Because I'm about to pull you down a rabbit hole so deep you might beg for the nearest exit back out to the looking glass." I wait for several beats, ensuring the words have a chance to sink into her. "Or, I can limit your involvement to the basics, and you can stay saner and wiser. Think about it hard but not too long. Even seconds aren't expendable right now."

"I'm in." Her commitment is instant and eager, which means she heard everything I said but the most crucial part. But as I've just said, pretty square-on with the summarization of things, even seconds can't be wasted right now—a concept the woman herself embraces at once. "Just call me Alice—though as long as it's understood I'm the edgy, ass-kicking Alice from Wade and Fershan's video game, not the idiot blonde. *Not* that I don't have my favorite blondes."

I use my laughter for a little bolster while retrieving my running shoes from my luggage. "All right, then, Edgy Alice. Consider yourself forewarned."

"Good enough, Emma Peel. I'm on my way up."

"Uh-uh," I rebut. "I'm on my way down. And while I'm

handling that, you have some pop-up homework."

She breathes in like a kid being given lunch money for the first time. "Do I need to memorize a secret alphabet for our decoders?"

"Ahhh...no." I want to laugh again, but she's really that intent.

"Wash off my body lotion so the wiretapping tape will stick?"

"Whoa. Still no."

"Practice flipping off the safety on my gun?"

"You have a *gun*? And *hell* no."

Her sigh is laced with frustration, but her voice is still eager for adventure. "So what *do* you need?"

"Information."

"Oh." And the kid just lost her lunch stash. "Well, all right. If it will help. But I truly don't know much about her yet, aside from the information on her CV."

I wince, hating that I already know the subject of her comment—and worse, that I allowed my claws to show that clearly when April played so obvious-and-desperate with Reece. *Don't get under the bridge with the trolls. It ruins your shoes.* It's a nugget I inherited from Mom, who sometimes isn't *all* about keeping up with Newport Beach optics.

"And I'm sure her CV is impressive," I issue. "But Miss Fresh and Freckled can do her cute little dance far away from my radar."

"That's the spirit!"

I almost envision Neeta's fist pump, which I accept as a needed bolster. For the plan I have in mind, it's going to be needed. "I need to know about Richards Research," I declare. "Well, specifically about their building."

"What about it?" Confusion clouds over her enthusiasm. She knows I'm well aware of all the obvious details. The building is a newer Richards Enterprises purchase, bought for a steal in the Los Angeles real estate market because of the property's age—but because it's just three blocks away, the potential to the corporation can't be ignored. Much to the city's relief, Reece chose not to demolish the building but to restore it to its forties-era glory. Though the top floors of the twenty-story structure are still under construction, Richards Research has already gotten comfortably settled into floors one through ten.

"The hotel is housing a lot of people traveling into town for research, right?" I dive right in, alerted by the heavier whirs and grinds of the elevator gears. Once the car arrives back up here, I might lose her when I board the lift. "So, is there a 'back way' they use to access the building? Maybe something not so...monitored by a million cameras?"

Neeta releases a knowing hum. "Where someone could walk in, perhaps accompanied by someone with a key card, and not be detected right away in the security office?"

"Something *exactly* like that."

"Hmmm. Yes." There's a distinct squeak. The woman enjoys playing mogul at her desk when she can but refuses to get her executive chair oiled. "Perhaps something like...a direct-access tunnel."

She finishes with a chuckle—maybe because she's just watched my jaw plummet past her office window.

"There's a *tunnel* between the Brocade and Richards Research?"

A new laugh. "You think they were just attracted to that place's history?"

At the moment, I'm not concerned about the *why* of the acquisition.

Only about fighting off the onus that I'm really about to exploit the hell out of it.

By spying on my own boyfriend.

The elevator arrives with ideal timing. No more time for second guesses or guilt. "Put on some shoes you can get around in," I direct Neeta. "As in, sprinting if you have to."

Through the phone, I weather another loud squeak of my friend's chair—right before her triumphant little snort. "*Now* you're talking, sister."

CHAPTER FOUR

REECE

I've enjoyed working with Sawyer Foley for several reasons. He's quiet but laser focused, literal but intuitive. And the best part of the whole package? He's prettier than me, which means nobody in the lobby of the Richards Research building even notices I'm here, waiting next to the coffee and magazine kiosk, as he strides over and pretends to read the morning's issue of the *Times*.

"Where the hell have you been?" His charge seems disembodied, a ferocious bite that doesn't match his casual pose, board shorts, and form-fitting short-sleeved rash guard. Ink that matches the dark-blue of his shirt extends down both arms—a dragon on his left bicep and a wolf dominating his right. His legs are free of tattoos but dark with tan. Sun streaks are rampant in his mop of dark-blond hair—and that "mop" shit isn't a metaphor. The stuff cascades everywhere, almost making him look out of place in the corporate lobby. Only in California.

"You remember the part where I told you I was taking my girl to Santa Barbara?" I snarl back.

He flips a couple of pages. There's a cologne ad on one with a guy who could be his doppelgänger. At least I now know what he'd look like cleaned up. "So...what? You came back and then screwed her anyway?"

"Wouldn't you like to know?"

"Not particularly."

He shoots out the retort so fast, I go for the obvious conclusion. "Hey, whatever floats your boat. Love is love."

"And business is business." He slides the magazine back into the rack and turns a glance out the window. "And the day is burned, so let's not do the same to the night."

Without waiting for a reply, he scoops up a pack of breath mints, tosses a five on the little counter, and doesn't wait for change, thanks to the three secretaries exiting the elevator and eyeing him like the token surfer boy in a *Magic Mike* review. All three of them stop as he strolls into the elevator they've just exited. As the doors slide shut, I watch him pull out his phone and single-thumb a message.

Two seconds later, *my* phone vibrates with an incoming text.

> *12th floor. Right turn off the landing.*
> *Keep going until the plastic ends.*

"And the crow flies at midnight," I mutter beneath my breath while swinging a careful gaze around the lobby. There's no other way to ward off the strange current that sprints up my spine, as if picking up on a similar frequency from the air itself. The energy races back down below my belt, reaches under my ass, and grabs me by the center of my balls. *Christ.* I'm usually the one emitting this kind of shit, not enduring it. The only other time I've been on the receiving end of a zap like this? The night I first met Emma. When she stepped off the elevator in the penthouse, bringing me that report...stepping toward me like a bunny toward a wolf...electrifying everything in my body...

Changing my whole damn world...

But not now. Not here. Thank fuck.

Shaking off the random scrotum jolt as being anything from an energy surge in the building to my body's own greed from thinking of Emma, I stride into the other elevator and jab the button for the twelfth floor. The sooner Sawyer and I get this business handled and done, the sooner I can actually get back to my woman and sate that hunger.

And damn, do I plan to have a feast.

Yeah. That's *exactly* what I'm going to do. I fill the elevator car with a long, low growl as I contemplate how many times I'll be able to make her come for me, her gorgeous cunt spread as my continuous banquet...

The peal of squeaking gears slices into my fantasy. While the city's historical society might worship us for updating the vintage elevators instead of replacing them, I make a mental note to order that they're tuned not to *sound* like it.

At least Foley knows I've arrived. And, as I hook a right off the elevator landing and push through makeshift walls of long, hanging construction plastic, he knows I'm a good fella about following orders—even if I don't like or understand them.

"What the hell?" I grouse after pushing through the last layer of the plastic bayou and making it to where Foley leans against a small ladder, gazing out over the sea of moonlight and streetlights. Behind him, a single lightbulb on a stand still seems a ghostly sentinel, not easing an inch of the pressure my gut's endured since he dropped his text bomb this afternoon. And yeah, I mean bomb. The verbiage is our encoded version of *drop everything you're doing and get your ass here,* but now that

I've done so, I'm growing weary of all the *Mission: Impossible* tactics. "You couldn't do this in the lobby? The entire building is private."

"Yeah? You really think so, eh?" He side-eyes me. Bastard even has me aced in *that* pretty-boy department. His gaze is that mossy-grass kind of green, lending his stare a piercing memorability. But I didn't hire him for his eyes. "While I was waiting for you, three delivery guys were buzzed in through the front door. The security guards changed shifts. Dude at the newsstand ordered a pizza. That's five not-so-private intrusions on your lobby in just under two hours."

I hired him for reasons like that.

Nevertheless, I growl, "Shit."

He jerks up a shoulder. "Don't stress. You're not operating an FBI field office or anything—though even when I was a G-dude, we needed good pizza instead of the cafeteria mystery shit." He grimaces. "Though why *your* guy ordered from that rat hole down on Fig instead of Papi's, I'll never understand."

I pace over to the window. "You know, I'd love to get poetic with you all night about downtown pizza joints..."

"No, you wouldn't."

"Yeah. Okay. I really wouldn't." A fast flip of balance has me facing him again. "So let's get on with it so we can both go back to our Friday night plans."

Foley snorts. "In what universe do you think I get to make Friday night plans, man?"

"I'd start up the violin, but what I'm paying you will buy an orchestra."

"Good point."

"Now that we're on the subject of good points..."

"Smooth," he comments on my segue, pushing away from

the ladder. "You have game, Richards." Though his demeanor remains beach-bum cool, there's no mistaking the thumbtacks beneath his tone. My observation is confirmed when he moves to jab hands into his back pockets but takes them out a second later, flexing his fingers wide. "And now I'm going to request you keep walking that cool-boy line—while keeping a very open mind."

Well...shit.

"Why?" I poise my own hands at my sides, forming two half fists next to my thighs. If I have to punch the wall, I'm ready. "What have you learned?"

"This isn't about what I've learned." Weirdly, Foley continues his little stroll. "It's about who I've found." He pushes through another wall of plastic perpendicular to the forest through which I just walked, revealing a door to office space that's already been installed. With a minimalistic jerk, he twists the knob. The panel creaks open, cracking the air with way too much haunted house vibe for my liking.

Especially as a creature from my darkest nightmares appears in the doorway.

Not just a monster.

The monster.

Looking like she's just stepped out of my phantasm again. Her white-blond hair is styled in the same seductress waves. Her sex harpy curves are again poured into long leggings, with a tight black top allowing no guesses about her bra cup size. The only difference between now and when she led me to hell—*twice*—are her shoes. Gone are Angelique La Salle's man-killer stilettos. Now she wears functional black boots that consume half her calves. They're even a little dirty.

Perfect.

Because when I throw her into the wall instead of punching it with my fist, there'll be no stress about the mess.

Excellent plan.

I don't think twice. I don't think at all. I've already thought long and hard about what I'd do if fate ever brought me this moment. The first time, I squandered it away. I'd actually deluded myself, thinking Angelique had come all the way to LA to clear her soul and make amends. Instead, she'd run a shell game on me much worse than the first, and I'd nearly paid for my gullibility with my life. Of course, I wondered how she hadn't paid for it with hers—but that detail didn't matter when she resurfaced days later with Emma in her crosshairs.

Now, she's firmly in mine.

And I couldn't be more fucking giddy.

Until I take two steps and am ramrodded to a violent stop. *Shit.* For being a good twenty pounds leaner than me, Foley is deceivingly mighty. His hair tumbles into his eyes, now gleaming as bright as lasers, as he shoves me back into place with an economy of motion.

"Whoa, cowboy."

I bare my teeth. "Fuck you, Foley."

Angelique has the audacity to bite her lip, feigning contrition. Are those *tears* gleaming on her eyelashes? "Listen to him, Reece. Please."

"*You.*" I lunge at her again. "Shut. Up." Then again only to be held back harder. Foley's wrapped himself around me in a demented version of a bro hug, planting the ball of his shoulder into the gap of my ribcage. "Let me go, Foley. I swear to God, you're going to be eating your own balls—"

"Nom nom." He's unnervingly oblivious to my rage. "But you'll still be watching me scarf them up from right back here."

"This is *fucking* ridiculous." I fight him, tightening my fists, ready to deflate one or both of the man's kidneys. Foley only intensifies his hold. "She's got you whipped, doesn't she? Well, I hope her pussy is worth the price you're paying, asshole!"

"*Reece!*" Angelique jumps her plea to heights I've never heard. Goddamnit, I almost believe her desperation. "*S'il vous plait. Je vous en supplie. Arrêtez!*"

"Stop? Seriously?" I spear her with a damning glare, making the rest of my meaning clear. Just because I've never heard her sound so desperate doesn't guarantee my mind won't twist it—and then it does. She's the bitch who betrayed me. The Consortium's temptation trinket. And from what I remember, which was a hell of a lot in a hell of an ordeal, she wasn't doing so with a gun to her head. "I don't *fucking* believe this." With the profanity, I let my wrath take over—at least enough to pulse through my hands and blast Foley off me like a spider monkey on an electric fence.

"Well. That makes two of us."

The comment lands on the air so unexpectedly, I wonder if my mind has channeled Emmalina into this mix as a coping mechanism for my sanity. But after taking in Angelique's dropped jaw, backed up by Foley's stunned stare, I whirl and confront the disgusting truth.

I'm standing in a bog of what-the-fuck between the bitch of my nightmares and the goddess of my dreams.

"Christ."

Foley snorts. "Not sure he'll be much help, but if you say so..."

I silence him with an energy pulse to his Adam's Apple—without my stare faltering from the woman I'd love to snatch up and throw over my knee right now.

"Emma."

I stomp forward, but she halts my charge with a furious lift of her chin. Only then do I notice Neeta, key card still in hand, which explains the *how* of their intrusion. But that's not the most important question at this point, which I issue at full growl.

"Why the hell did you follow me?"

A weird sound spurts from her. Not a sob, but sure as hell not a laugh. "Why the hell do you *think*?"

I raise an admonishing finger. "Velvet..."

"Do *not* go there." Her returning jab goes for flesh, stabbing my bicep as viciously as a punch. With the added impact of her pale-pink fingernail, I'm certain she's out to break skin. "You do *not* get to do 'Velvet' right now."

"Fuck." It's becoming a favorite word tonight, for all the wrong reasons. "It's not what you think, okay?"

"Oh, God." Her high laugh is like a wineglass shattering in my ear. But that's not the driving pain in my mind. That agony comes from understanding every ounce of her reaction—and the justification she has for clarifying it in biting syllables. "Well, *that's* original. Haven't heard it for at least a couple of hours...since we dropped everything and raced back here from freaking Santa Barbara." As if someone's smashed the glass in *her* ear, she jolts. "We...raced back here...for your precious... *Sally.*" She rivets her glower onto Angelique. "Shit. *Sally.* Was I that naïve? That stupid?"

"No." Foley, thank *fuck*, steps around me. Gone is his Malibu Ken ease. He approaches Emma with posture I didn't know he was capable of. "*I'm* Sally."

Neeta, who politely stepped a few feet away during the Showdown at Richards Corral, mumbles nearly beneath her breath, "Hel-*lo*, Sally." Her lips quirk bashfully, leading me to believe Foley rewarded that with some charming smirk or wink.

"Sawyer Foley." He extends his hand toward Emma. Though the move is professional, a new tone in his voice makes me battle the craving to beat his arm down. And the rest of him. "I've heard a lot about you in the last month, Miss Crist."

Emma returns the greeting but jerks out of his hold as soon as she can. Her gaze has turned the shade of icicles. "Then you've probably heard that I don't like being out of the loop, Mr. Foley—especially when the loop includes people who work for batshit rogue scientists fond of seducing and then kidnapping their live experiment subjects."

And this is the moment—either the worst or best call of the night—that Angelique picks to step up too. Every pore in my body pricks at the same rate Emma's tension heightens, an impression exacerbated by the fact that in the past, I'd been used to hearing Angelique before seeing her. Damn her for choosing now to go high utility over fashion. "Emmalina," she intones with equal practicality. "I know this is strange for you."

"Strange?" Emma wheels on her with deceiving calm. "'Strange' is when the four-oh-five is traffic-free at six p.m., okay? 'Strange' is when I can go to the dry cleaners without three photographers snapping my dirty clothes." Her veneer starts dissolving as she takes another step toward Angelique. "*This* isn't strange, *Angie*. This—*you*—are creepy. And scary. And infuriating. And disgusting. And—"

"I want to help."

Well. Angelique always did know how to deliver a good shocker.

I'm just not sure whether this is good shock or a complete

disaster. Emma appears mired in the same strange dilemma, mute and gaping as Angelique swings a gaze as fortified as a sword made of green steel.

"I...want to help." Her second assertion is even firmer—but that's where Angelique's surety ends. The woman has, for all intents and purpose, willingly stepped into the noose of her accusers. "I know there is no logical reason to believe me, but I mean it. With every bone in my body...and crack in my heart."

Silence.

A long, uncomfortable one.

Until Foley draws in a grimacing breath and utters, "Damn it. I don't want to believe you."

"But you do." Emma's features bunch up in a similar way. "And so do I."

Fuck it all.

I believe the bitch too.

But I'm not ready to give Angelique the courtesy of the spoken concession. The woman should be damn glad I haven't picked up the phone and called every law enforcement agency in the state on her deceitful ass—no matter how huge a dose of contrition she's gulping down now.

"Out with it." I watch her eyes as I issue the order from tight teeth. The feat isn't easy, but if there's any bullshit about her game, I'll see it at the edges of those emerald depths first.

Fortunately, the woman's smart enough to know that too. She's so clear about it, she doesn't blink while ticking her head to the left. "Front pocket," she tells me. "Photograph."

Foley obliges with the honors of fishing out the picture. It's cropped into an oval and the edges are frayed, as if the image has been pulled out of a frame. In the picture, there's an Angelique I barely recognize. She's makeup-free, her hair thrown up into a carefree ponytail. She looks about sixteen—and I almost believe it's a picture from her adolescence—but that's before taking in the rest of the image and the man she's got in a tight clench. Her head is tucked against his broad, burnished chest. One of her hands is molded to the top of his shoulder, tangled in strands of his long black hair. The guy's eyes are dark and unreadable, but his full, roguish mouth holds the entire truth of the picture. It's so indisputable, my gut accepts it before Angelique even speaks it.

"I loved him. And then they killed him."

During the last of it, her voice cracks. And her eyes finally close.

But if she's lying about this, I'm the Duke of Wales.

Which also leaves me—all of us—in one hell of a mire. Foley's the first one able to translate that bewilderment into words, returning the photo to her with a flick of his stiff fingers. "When did this all go down?"

Angelique still doesn't open her eyes. "I met him two-and-a-half months ago. After the Consortium called me back to Spain."

"After you failed to recapture Reece that night at the power plant." Emma doesn't mask her protective fury, giving me hope that this situation isn't the train wreck of my instincts. If she's still angry, she's still feeling something. I can work with *something*.

Angelique looks back at Emma like Hester Prynne proudly brandishing her *A* in the village square. "I was ordered back to the Source to receive punishment. Yes."

"And the Source is...what?" Foley asks.

"Their central hub of operations." Angelique's gaze flicks to me. "Where everyone begins their empowerment."

Against my will, my own gaze slams shut. As if someone's shaken loose a hive of memory, voices and images pelt my mind from all sides.

Do not fight it, Reece.

You, above so many others, have been chosen for this.

You will be better for this. Launched beyond your wildest dreams. Flown beyond your highest peaks.

You will be a force among men. A beacon among mortals.

Freed. Enlightened. Empowered.

And I thought her appearance would be the worst of the nightmare-coming-to-life thing today.

Somehow, by clenching every muscle and ordering myself to keep breathing, I fight the images back to a dull roar—long enough to wheel back around and utter at her, "And they gave *you* a taste of 'empowerment'...didn't they?" Her hitch of breath is all I need for corroboration. "They hooked you up with just enough juice to get you addicted—and ensure that if you had to fight me, you wouldn't lose. Maybe they even thought I'd be intrigued, getting to spar with someone who was like me. Maybe they thought I actually harbored feelings for you, and they told you to use that allure to get me back."

As I lay it all out, Emma circles forward—and peers at the affirmation across every tormented inch of Angelique's face. "Oh, my God," she murmurs. "They thought *all* of that?"

Angelique meets her scrutiny without flinching. A new look crosses her face, seeming oddly like admiration, before she replies, "They simply did not anticipate...you." Her lips tremble. "Frankly, neither did I."

"And they punished you for the oversight." The conclusion is supplied by Neeta, infusing it with the sadness none of the rest of us can muster. I'm not sorry about that, but nor am I proud of it.

"Dario was the one assigned to discipline me." As the whisper leaves Angelique, she strokes a finger over the picture still cupped in her palm. "Instead, we fell in love."

Foley huffs. "And things were hunky-dory until someone discovered that he wasn't really punishing you."

For a long moment, she's completely silent. And frozen. I brace for the moment her reaction breaks through, manifesting itself in a tremor that claims her whole body and a sob that consumes her whole throat. But just one. As soon as she's finished, the woman is like a rebooted robot and back to being the same sleek unicorn I chased through Paris and Barcelona nearly two years ago. *A lifetime ago.* She straightens, smoothing a hand down her Aphrodite hair, gazing as if to suggest we all take a nap before snazzing up to hit the hottest new club in town.

"Those cocksuckers need to be taken down."

That's definitely not a call for clubbing.

Neeta, who's heard far too much now to be shooed away and looks ready to handle the responsibility, eyes her up and down before venturing, "And we assume 'the cocksuckers' do not know you feel that way?"

Angelique arches one perfect brow. "Not one fucking particle of it."

"You sound sure of that," Foley comments.

"Because I am," she returns.

"Because you've *convinced* them." Neeta edges closer as she says it, the perception in her voice matching her tender steps. "As soon as they killed your lover—"

"Dario." Angelique bites it out. "He has a name, and it's *Dario.*"

"As soon as they killed Dario." Neeta barely misses a beat. "You realized the only way to exact real revenge on them was to remain one of them."

For the first time since she entered, some of the regal starch leaves Angelique's posture. *"Oui."* She dips her gaze so much I'm able to note those *are* real tears on her lashes. "To plead at their filthy feet for mercy...and accept the full punishment Dario never had the heart to dispense."

She finishes by lifting her head once more—though her action doesn't stop there. She flows a hand up, like a ballerina reaching for the floodlights—

Giving none of us warning about the sight that comes next.

As she digs her fingers into her hairline and pulls violently at the stuff.

As it all comes away in her hand, revealing the burnt moon landscape that is now her actual skull.

As she hurls away the wig, mutely enduring all four of our stunned gasps.

As she reveals, with a re-braced stance and revitalized glare, the extent of her own "rebirth" at the hands of the Consortium.

It's hell trying to find my voice—but the next words in the room must come from me. Whether I like it or not, I'm the only one here who can halfway comprehend what could have caused her entire scalp to resemble a black, mottled, foreign planet.

"What...did they..."

The woman's chin shudders. Her hands ball into fists. "This is the next phase of their experiments," she finally grates.

"Now they're playing with brain matter." I push out the

words she clearly cannot. The explanation that populates her horrified memories. My reaction is violent and visceral, feeling like I've been tossed into a funhouse filled with condemned clowns—only the clowns are us, and the circus is forever.

And with that recognition, I know I'm the last one to save her—or even comfort her.

Like the selfish bastard I am, I'm already mentally running. Turning and walking away, my steps full of lead and my mind full of ugliness, to the salvation I've been granted in my own hell.

To my beauty...

Who has disappeared.

And for once, gives me reason to thank fate for the creaks and echoes in the old elevator shaft.

Allowing me to sprint toward the compartment into which she's just dived and ram open the doors just far enough to jump in with her.

EMMA

"What the hell?" I punch out the words instead of him. But not in fury. I'm not mad.

What the hell *am* I?

Confused. *Beyond* confused. Frustrated. Way beyond that too. Upside down, and not in a whee-yay carnival kind of way.

My chaos worsens as Reece pushes into the elevator and corners me.

"Seriously? Because you want to repeat *this* bullshit, too?" I seethe it out before he consumes my personal space, stealing the very air in my lungs with his mix of smoky cologne and musky man. And sex. Sweet *hell*, I still smell our lovemaking on him too.

"Emma." He breathes it into my forehead.

"Get away, damn it."

"*Emmalina*."

"Get. *Away*."

He acquiesces when I resort to pummeling it into him—but as he backs off, one palm raised, he sneaks out his other hand, stabbing the button for the roof before I realize I never punched in a destination of my own.

Because if I had, it wouldn't have been the roof.

Where he'll have me captive, at least for a few minutes.

Damn it.

As gears and pulleys groan around us, he emphasizes the T of his torso with both hands on his waist. It's a stance he usually shuns, hating how it spotlights the superhero stereotype, but right now, I don't think he's concerned about optics or public image or projecting any other message but one.

"We have to talk."

That one.

I grit my teeth and raise my chin. "You know how bad an idea that is right now?"

He folds his arms, making me wish for the T again. The lightning-level determination in his gaze aside, the dual slabs of his forearms are a force of nature in all the most alluring ways. *Shit*. Why does he do this to me, even with his damn forearms? It's not fair.

Nothing about tonight has been fair.

And the situation only looks like it's going to get worse before it gets better.

"Fine, then. We *need* to talk."

"About what?" It spews more brutally than I intended.

Maybe I *am* more pissed than I think—or maybe it has something to do with being taken hostage against my will. Frankly, I'm too fed up to analyze the situation. The facts appear pretty fucking clear already. "Should we talk about the fact that you rushed the foundation's ramp-up just to get me out of the way so you could play spy games with Sawyer Foley? Or about how those machinations now involve Angelique La Salle, who's pretty impossible to hate anymore thanks to the self-sacrifice-despite-a-broken-heart thing?"

"Which I learned about just when *you* did." He drops his arms and looms in tight again. "She made her grand entrance exactly thirty seconds before you and Neeta arrived." His softer tone is rough with sincerity, which only tightens every knot in my stomach. "*Velvet.* I was just as stunned to see her as you were."

I jab both hands at his chest. "You still don't get to go there with the 'Velvet.'"

He nods and then pushes right back in. "But you believe me."

"That still doesn't make any of this all right."

"I'm sorry."

"Neither does that."

"You want Angelique out of all this?" The elevator's opening doors help punctuate his offer. "You just say the word"—he brushes back, letting me barrel past him out the open doors—"and she's gone. I'll tell Foley to send her back to wherever he found her. Or wherever *she* found *him*. It doesn't matter."

"No." I tug a strand of hair off my face as the hot night wind hits me. Here, twenty floors up, the Santa Anas claim free rein, though their stunning effect on the scene before me can't be denied. The rooftop, in the midst of being converted into a garden, is a vast wonderland of shadows and light as trendy LED bulbs sway on suspended lines overhead. "It *does* matter." I stomp over to an oval-shaped chaise lounge with a wicker overhang that's keeping the large throw pillows from being blown into the modern fountain about fifteen feet away. Cushions from some of the other couches haven't been so fortunate and are now soggy sentinels in the fountain's glowing ripples. I give the lumps a glance of commiseration while plunking down on the thick foam cushion. "It matters a lot, and we both know it."

Reece lowers next to me and fits one of his large, firm hands around one of mine. "Nothing matters more than you." He squeezes his long fingers in as the gruff words spill out. "Or more than the heart you've given to me." He turns, dragging me close. "Christ, Emmalina. *Nothing.*"

I burrow against him, treasuring the haven of his form as the wind whips around us. "Well, my heart is going to be irreparable if those monsters get their hands back on you and start playing electric Parcheesi with your brain."

"Parcheesi?" His shoulders shake from a chuckle. "Do I want to know where *that* came from?"

I join him in the mirth, adding a fast shrug. "Family board game night. Used to be a thing, when Lydia and I were kids. 'Dia was damn good at that one too. She's scary-smart at strategic skills. But that was all before—"

"Before what?" He hasn't shirked on his attention—and sees the change in me before *I* even realize it. "Before *what,* Emmalina?"

A new shrug. Not as carefree this time. "Before everything changed. You know. Dad's hot job offer. The grand new house.

The fancy social life at the country club."

Which had entailed both Mom and Dad getting really *social...*

Baggage that's already been dragged too far out of my closet tonight.

Which also doesn't escape Reece. Which he also already knows and doesn't like one damn bit. Which he tells me, in no uncertain terms, by whipping his hold from my hand to my wrist the second I try lurching back to my feet.

"No way, Velvet." He stresses the endearment, clearly knowing he now can. "You don't get to stomp off with all your eggs still pretty in the basket after forcing me to break all mine."

"*Forcing* you?" Indignation makes it possible to at least gain my feet—though with his grip still locked to me, I have to lean over to spit out the rest. "I haven't *forced* a damn thing here, mister. Not tonight, and not in the last three months— which, by the way, is all I've asked you the courtesy of being real with me about."

His lips part. His nostrils flare. "Now I'm just asking the same from you."

"I *have* been real." I finally twist away, pissed to the point it burns my vision, and the bastard sees it with his usual damnable insight. "I've given you nothing *but* my reality!"

He tilts his head. "Oh?"

"My *past* is not my reality, Reece."

"Ohhhh, beauty." A grating chuff. "Who's the one full of shit now?"

The rage at the edges of my vision, fueled by the fear at its core, becomes a full cloud across my sight. The stuff flows through me like a furious centipede, straight up my arm and into my hand.

Smack.

I slap him so hard, it stings back to my elbow. The pain unlocks my soul's Pandora's box, and every emotion I've been stuffing there all night—especially since that stupid Parcheesi memory—comes flying out with vengeful glee. I'm hurt. I'm confused. I'm lost.

I'm at the country club mixer, watching Mom flirt with Dr. Evans in one corner and Dad make the moves on Mrs. Whitler in the other.

I'm in the break room at the Brocade, watching Angelique kick the crap out of Reece on a TV monitor.

I'm pushing through a plastic wall within punching distance of that bitch, catching her in the act of making new moony eyes at my man.

And now I'm standing here, whacking the hell out of him myself, letting the tears come because the pain of freeing them is less torturous than the hell of keeping them in. At the same time, I battle to breathe past the weight in my chest, the one that always precedes how I have to cope and deal and resign myself to this whole damn onslaught.

Alone.

Only...I'm not.

Not by a longshot—though the certainty of Reece's kiss takes a few seconds to blaze past my numb lips and into my whirling mind. Not that I'm complaining. Not that I don't slam into him with a soft sob, gripping his neck as I give in to his ruthless pull, letting him kiss me for another ten seconds. Then ten seconds more as he slices his tongue inside my mouth. Then...

Then I don't care. Seconds, minutes, hours, days. Time is the last damn thing my senses care about as his passion wraps around me, his electricity surges through me, and his embrace finally yanks hard enough at me, demanding my full surrender.

And I tumble.

Figuratively. Literally.

My desire is an upended whirl, my balance a nonexistent mess, as Reece sweeps me back down to the chaise, pushing me all the way against the pile of cushions in the furniture's protected grotto. There, as devil winds flow over the city around us, my own wicked rogue brings gusts of fire to every enlivened nerve in my body, every racing electron in my brain... every pulsing inch of my pussy.

I writhe and moan, tangling my hands in his hair, watching with amazement as his energy mixes with the wind, making his thick umber strands glow with golden light. The lust in his eyes forms a decadent contrast, his gray pupils turning as silver as a wolf in the moonlight. But the most beautiful color he brings is the deep blue of his fingertips, lapis magic against the stars that seem to dance on the wind above the downtown buildings. With those luminescent points, he grazes down my neck, into the V of my neckline, stealing hot sweeps beneath. Soon, my nipples are tingling and erect for him.

"My beautiful velvet bunny." He grits it as a promise, kissing me just as deeply and fiercely. When he pulls away to ply the curve of my jaw with his masterful mouth, the fire of his touch permeates my chest, dictating me to give him the rest of the tears in my heart. "Damn. *Damn.* You drive me so crazy."

I spurt out a watery laugh. "Yeah. That's me. The walking, talking, boyfriend-slapping freak show."

He centers his lips over mine again. "Oh, yeah," he growls. "But you're *my* freak."

Another rickety chuckle. "I should hit you again for that."

"You sure should." He enforces the point by using his knees to spread mine. "Because then I'd have to hit back."

It's innuendo, raw and rough—and my libido responds in urgent need. A moan escapes me as I spread for him, giving him space to slam his crotch against mine. At once, my sex is a pool of lava. My thighs are achy and shivery. My limbs are ropes of stimulation, wrapping around him beyond my control or care. I just need him closer, tighter. Around me. Inside me.

I...*need*.

"Oh, God!" I wonder why my shriek seems a visible burst on the air, until realizing it is. The energy of it, riding the static-charged air, has collided with the electricity flowing off Reece and transformed into a miniature firework between us. I'd actually be enchanted with the sight if my roaring blood isn't commanding my attention directly toward the pulsing, pounding center of my body.

"Fuck." Another brilliant spark as Reece growls it out.

"Do it." Another couple of fireworks, whisked off into the night, and I don't care. I widen my legs. My dress is already hiked around my waist from the friction of our desperate dry humps. My clit is engorged. My sensitive channel is flooded. I can't take the waiting any longer. I'm a lighted fuse. A charged ion. A star needing its supernova. A girl needing her superhero. "*Do it*, Reece. Please!"

He raises up, parking his ass on his haunches. With grunting fever, he unfastens his pants. With a darker snarl, he shoves them down his hips. I watch, licking my lips, as his swollen penis fills his hand. *Holy shit*, he's so beautiful. Everything between his balls and tip is already aglow, his cobalt veins beating hard against his strained flesh.

As he strokes himself, my pussy clutches at the air. As he

leans forward, notching his hard mushroom to my entrance, I shudder. As he feeds the first inch into me, I scream and clutch at his shoulders.

"Tell me." He punctuates it with a hiss when I dig my fingers in, marking his shoulders with deep grooves. After retaliating by biting hard into my bottom lip, he dictates in a hoarse snarl, "Tell me exactly what you want, beauty."

Right now I'll recite the damn Gettysburg Address if that's what he wants. But thank God he's not after that. The throb of his cock and the voltage in his eyes supply it to me with heart-halting clarity.

"Hit me back." My supplication is thick and guttural with lust. "Damn it, Reece. *Please.* Now!"

He angles tighter over me, snaps up his hands, and grabs me by my wrists. He pins me against the pillows using the same hold, his fingers sliding against the bottom bones of mine—

As he rams his body into mine.

"Oh!"

Hitting me back.

"Shit!"

Pounding me deep.

"Yes!"

Possessing me completely.

His cock is hotter, fuller, bigger than I remember—and *damn*, does he know how to use it. Like a vigilante possessed, he drives into me with strokes that make our colliding flesh sound more like pops of gunfire. As if the night notices—perhaps it does—the wind borrows our carnality for its fury, the city rushes and honks and screeches around us, sirens careening on the buildings and airplanes scraping the sky, their frenzy climbing as ours does. The tumult growing as he does. The violence throbbing as I do.

The life overflowing...as his does.

"God. *Damn.*" Reece's words are more claws in his throat than sounds on his lips, rushing against my neck as he rams deep and then stills inside me. I gasp and writhe as every drop of his essence pours in, drenching my womb in electric heat—

And knowing very well what that means for me.

Within seconds, I'm coming apart from the inside out, an orgasm drenching me in ecstasy and light and fire and forever—but at the same time, engulfing me in frustration. "Let me up," I croak, fighting the shackles of his grip. "I need to hold you."

He only snarls with more primitive fury, filling my ear with his heavy breaths. "No. You need to take me."

"Damn it, Reece!"

"*Take it,* Emmalina." He rolls his hips, working his cock deeper inside, sliding his pelvis along more of my pouting clit. "Take. It. *All.*"

And unbelievably, he's groaning again.

Giving me all of himself again.

Filling me with his come again.

Turning me inside out again.

But this time, I don't entertain a single thought of resisting his hold. What the hell *is* thought? I'm only light and noise and sensation—and a hot, relentless wind brought by the devils but turned into heaven by this incredible bolt of a man. In seconds, I'm incited to fresh tears and then whispered words that even the gusts can't rip from us now.

"I love you, Reece Richards."

"Not as much as I love you, Emmalina Crist."

It feels so easy to contemplate bantering back. Not just easy. Natural. It's what we always do after making love. Yeah, even the monkeys-in-the-wild stuff we just blew each other's toes off with now. Hell, *especially* in these cases. Sarcasm, just like normal couples, brings the illusion that we're a normal couple too. That for a few minutes at least, we can face life's shit and conquer it with all the stuff everyone else does.

But we're not everyone else.

A recognition that hasn't relented its hold on my psyche— or my heart—even now.

That I might have been able to forget for a few minutes, to the point I seriously wonder if my toes *have* fallen off. No woman should be allowed to experience such mind-bending sex. From tonight on, even my two-hundred-dollar vibrator will be demanding therapy for its inferiority complex.

But it's not the answer.

It can't be turned into *our* answer.

The resolutions must take a one-two punch on my composure if Reece's sudden tension is any indicator. "Hey," he prods softly. "What is it, Bunny?"

With as much tact as I can muster with my dress still around my waist, I push up onto my elbows. "I think...we really do need to talk."

"All right."

He splits my heart open with his tenderness as he pulls out and then gives me room to right myself. At the same time, he tucks his own shit back in, wincing a little as he zips back up. When we're both reasonably decent, he remains facing me on the chaise, holding both my hands in his—with a massive case of trying-not-to-freak-the-fuck-out stamped across his features.

"I all but issued you an ultimatum about this," he mutters. "So I guess I deserve what's coming, right?"

"*Wrong.* Reece—" I tighten my fingers against his, compelling him to keep looking at me. "Oh, hell. You couldn't be more wrong. *Why* should you have to slam me with an ultimatum to get me to open up to you? And why should I have a hundred walls up about that—other than the fact that I had to sneak around to find you here consorting with Angelique?"

"Damn it." He stabs his free hand through his hair. "We weren't *consorting*, okay?"

"I know." I yank that hand back over, pressing my cheek to his palm. "*I know.* But I can say that with my lips and even believe it in my heart...but right now, I can't trust it with my soul."

He jerks his hand away. Dips into a stillness so surreal, he begins to scare me. In a rasp as barren as the wind, he charges, "You don't trust me?"

Now I'm the frozen one—dunked in so much terrified ice, it hurts. The only relief, if I can call it that, is the hot sting behind my eyes. This is, without a doubt, one of the shittiest ordeals of my life. Knowing I'm the one making him so stiff and quiet, stabbing him with icicle after icicle of heartache...

Heart*ache.*

Not heart*break.*

The perception couldn't hit with better timing. It lends the strength to assert, "I trust you, Reece. About so damn much. More than anyone I've ever met or anyone I've ever known."

A stiff inhalation flares his nostrils. His lips twist as if he's eaten something nasty. "'About so much,'" he spits back. "But not about everything."

"You don't trust me about everything, either." The chill isn't going anywhere now, claiming me with ruthless spikes as I watch the truth also take over his face—and am mesmerized by the sight. *Damn it.* Like frost across a mountain landscape, only anger brings out some of the most beautiful parts of his features. "And how can you, when I refuse to open up to you?"

I reach for the fingers now glowing with the steel blue of his rage instead of his aroused aqua. "We need to work on things, Reece—but at the same time, I know we really can. I also know that I love you enough to try." I press a soft kiss to his knuckles. "We both have to do some digging. We have to push past our fears enough to be safe with each other beyond just diving into the sheets together." A new kiss, this time lifted and bestowed on his dour lips. "I love you, Mr. Richards. You're my superhero because you're an incredible man and an astounding human being, not just a hunk who turns my pussy to magma and then knows exactly what to do about it."

He grunts softly. "Well, gee. Now that you put it *that* way..."

"Right now, there's no putting it *any* way." I keep his hand nestled in both of mine, using the leverage of his arm to scoot closer to him. "I just think we need some time."

"Time." His chest rises and falls with the force of his inhalation. "You mean...apart, don't you?"

"I mean in places where we can't easily think about getting naked, horizontal, and primeval with each other, yes."

"And you've already formulated a plan for that."

It's my turn for the long breath in. "Sort of. I guess." *Shit.* All the words, until now, have sounded okay in my head—but now, actually talking about acting on those lofty promises... stepping away from the precious cocoon of us... Well, *now* I know what scary really is. "Thanks to your influence, your dad has approached RRO about throwing a small but chichi fundraiser dinner next week in Manhattan."

More of the eerie silence from Reece—joined by a tension that makes me wonder if honesty has really been the best call in this instance. "Well, no shit," he finally says, a small grin twitching his lips.

"Yeah." I issue it with conviction, quirking a smile of my own. "He's proud as hell of you because of the foundation, Reece. I know he really wants to help in any way he can."

He snorts softly. "Well, he's sure as hell figured out that the quickest way to my soft side is through you."

"And maybe *his* soft side is *you*." When he gives no discernible reaction to that, I forge ahead. "Anyhow, there's a lot to prepare for with this thing, on top of all the student applications we're going through, as well as ramping up marketing and getting the New York office organized." I press my hand over his heart and give him the steady certainty of my stare. "They really could use my help."

"Okay," he says slowly. "When?" The tightness in his own gaze vanishes in the wake of his fresh gape. "*Now?* You want to go now? For *a week*?"

I firm my chin. "I'm not deploying to the Middle East. We can FaceTime every day. As a matter of fact, we'll need to. We can—"

I stop short as he pushes away. After rolling to his feet, he finally snaps, "We can what? Pretend you haven't put an entire fucking country between us in the name of emotional intimacy?"

For a few seconds, I don't move. When shock finally releases me from its chokehold, I blurt, "Again, I'm not proposing a sabbatical in Antarctica. I'll only be in New York, doing valuable work that *you've* made possible..."

"Which you just returned from doing for five damn days

barely that many hours ago!"

I return his glowing glare with a jerk to my own feet. "Time you had no trouble filling with 'Sally' and Angelique!"

"Christ." He wheels away, dragging both hands through his hair. "Are we back *there* again?"

An extra-strong gust rips across the rooftop, scooping up the abandoned chaise between us and tipping it over. The pillows that were just our launch pads to sexual heaven now cartwheel across the patio. A couple of them end up in the fountain with their cousins, rapidly taking on water and turning into directionless blobs.

I hate how much I commiserate with them.

Even worse, I hate the soft croak of my voice, as I gaze once more to the man on the opposite side of the upturned couch.

The other side of a valley that's suddenly too damn wide and too disgustingly dark.

"I have no idea where we are, baby."

But I know I refuse to be too scared to find out.

CHAPTER FIVE

REECE

"Mr. Richards?"

I jerk my head up, breaking out of the stupor in which Emma plays a starring role. Since it's nearly lunchtime in Manhattan, I try to imagine what she's doing—not that the online gossip sites won't provide me with that answer within a few hours, as they faithfully have for the last week, along with the typical speculations about why Emma Crist has been seen out and about in one of the world's best cities for young, hot bachelors.

Bachelors who don't bring baggage like radioactive come and global savior issues.

Guys able to return her texts with more than one-word answers.

Men capable of giving her a normal life. Movie dates. Lazy Sundays. Board game nights. Kids. Stability.

But she never wanted that. She wants you, *asshole. And now she's taking the steps to strengthen things with you.*

But did she really have to do it from three thousand miles away?

"Mr. Richards?"

I shake my head, focusing fully on Neeta—who's clearly on the fifth or sixth take of the summons. "Yes. What?" I stand

and move out from my desk, steeling myself against the sounds of kids' laughter from the Brocade's newly installed soft-materials playground.

She never said she wanted kids.

She only said she wanted more...

"I'm sorry," I amend, plastering on a polite smile. "What did you need, Miss Jain?"

"Not me, sir." She extends a file folder. "What *you* need, yes? The weeklies?"

"Ah. Of course." I straighten my tie while taking a fast glance at the overall numbers. According to what I see, the Brocade has kicked ass and taken names in our comp set for the fourth straight week. Dad will be pleased, and I don't fight the warmth in my chest at considering that.

Which leads, of course, to wondering if Dad has seen Emma at all in the last three days. According to the gossip gurus, she's only lunched with coworkers and other nonprofit movers-and-shakers. Doesn't mean he couldn't have stopped off at the Richards Reaches Out offices to go over plans for the "intimate" dinner that's now grown to over two hundred confirmed invitees...

"How are you getting settled in down here?"

Neeta's formal but conversational tone brings welcome relief from my brain's newest tangent. In the second I take to respond, one of the toddlers outside holds up a plastic superhero figure and shows it to his friend. The second kid reaches over and yanks the head off the toy. Both of them scream in unfiltered laughter.

"It's been good to come out of the clouds," I admit with a wry grin. "In more ways than one, obviously."

Neeta, having succumbed to a chuckle at the boys' antics,

extends her laugh. "Well, Wade and Fershan couldn't be more thrilled you're walking among the mortals."

"Even though I've retired from being *im*mortal?"

"As far as they're concerned?" She dips a serene nod, assuring me every secret to which she was exposed last week will stay at that status. "Yes."

I copy the nod, tacking on a new smile—full of gratitude. "It's good to have you around, Miss Jain."

"So your girlfriend likes to tell me, Mr. Richards."

Fate is on my side today. Another serendipitous segue, one I'm not going to waste. "How's...she doing?" I grind both knuckles into the top of my desk, failing miserably at the by-the-way-just-a-nonchalant-question thing. Because of that, I decide to go for the meat anyway. "I mean, how's she *really* doing? Not the bullshit I can get from five minutes and fifteen Google hits."

The woman nods once more, this time in deeper understanding. But just as she threads her fingers together, clearly stalling while composing a reply that won't betray Emma, her whole face transforms. Her mouth pops into a perfect O—just before Sawyer Foley bursts into the room.

"Dude." He heads straight toward me. Gobs of beach sand mark his wake, though he's wearing khakis and a reasonably white Henley. He's also run a comb through his hair, though it was probably just a sprint, which explains why the executive office day assistant rushes in right behind him, her face painted in anxiety.

"Oh, my God," she exclaims. "Mr. Richards, I'm so sorry. I tried to stop him. He just ran in off the street. I thought the police were doing more about the crazies in this area. He says it's life and death—"

"It is," Sawyer growls.

"It's all right, Joanne. Please put Mr. Richards on DND and shut the door on your way out." Neeta forms the words my mind can't process. Not since the words "life and death"—igniting every electrified cell in my body in sudden dread. My instincts are sound. No way would Foley come exploding in here like a half-crazed beach rat, looking as if he's about to expose a hellmouth under the hotel, without serious justification.

The same conviction turns his gaze to amber neon as he stops directly in front of me. "This won't wait for the bat signal, man."

I dip a tense nod, letting it serve as my approval. "What do you have?"

For all the urgency of his entrance, he darts an uncertain glance at Neeta until his obvious recall of everything she already heard Friday night. "A new dispatch from Angelique. A fucking scary one."

I fight off the sensation of every nerve ending getting stripped by dull blades, finally gritting, "She's back in Spain already?"

He shakes his head. "She'd been assigned to stay here, in LA—until she received new orders this morning."

The harsher jut of his jaw inspires a matching tension in mine. "Orders for what?"

"To get her ass to New York." Foley's mouth thins to a razor's edge. "Along with every other domestic agent of the Consortium. They've been told they're needed in Manhattan in four days—to send an important message to an 'escaped angel.'"

Forget the stripped-wire nerves. Every one of them is an

exposed tip of pain, giving rise to the screams of my senses—
as Neeta's stunned whisper serrates the air. "Four days? The
night of Emma's fundraiser."

IGNITE

PART 5

CHAPTER ONE

REECE

Zoom.

From superhero to stalker in less than forty-eight hours.

And damn proud of it.

Every word of the conviction is a fire in my chest as I shake rain out of my hair and walk into the Midtown Manhattan apartment I'll be calling home tonight. Yeah, and probably a few more nights to come.

I refuse to think I'll be here longer than that.

Denial is a valuable attribute in a stalker.

Yeah, I've learned that at the speed of light too. Or, if I'm going to be glib, at the speed of lightning.

Okay, screw glib—because I've arrived on this island fully ready to bring the real goddamn lightning. The thunder too, if my hand is pushed. And holy fuck, does part of me want to be pushed. The part, entrenched in my gut like a fucking tumor, that metastasizes a little more each morning of my life. In those few seconds before the relief of consciousness, I'm back there again. Still strapped to a table in a lab, in the middle of an unmarked warehouse, in the middle of a Barcelona suburb, in the middle of the hell called the Source.

The Source.

It has a name now—though that knowledge hasn't made

anything easier. I'm still assaulted by crippling memories, followed by the same furious irony. Where's the karmic payback for whackjob scientists choosing to name their lair as if it's a spa retreat? Further, where's the eye twitch *I* should be battling because that information came from the woman who handed me over to the Consortium in the first place?

And that's when more of the irony sinks its teeth in.

Because right now, Angelique La Salle's intel is all I have to trust. All I *must* trust. Yeah, even if it all turns out to be lies and the bitch is just leading me back into another trap that will land me up on another lab table.

Because not believing her would lead to much worse results.

Not worse. Unthinkable.

The Consortium catching Emmalina in their crosshairs. I'm not putting it past the bastards—as smart as they are heartless—who are now aware she's the key to chopping me short at the balls. *More* than aware.

So yeah, underestimating them would be as stupid as ignoring them—and I haven't shirked on either account, despite how doing so has me here in a rented shoe box off Eleventh instead of checking into a two-k-square-foot penthouse at the hotel I own up the street. But this is me doing my damnedest to give Emma the "space" she demanded while keeping her safe from those crazy cocksuckers at the same time.

Threading moral needles is also a good trait in a stalker.

Especially when dealing with a band of scientific deviants who gave up ethics for legacy and never bothered to deal with the shit again. Yeah, the same posse who kept me captive for six months while the whole planet thought I was still just being an irresponsible prick. They even covered up my imprisonment by making strategic withdrawals from my bank accounts.

Letting them heap trash on my reputation was one thing.

Letting them think they can touch one hair on my woman—let alone plan some sort of violent vengeance at one of the biggest events of her life?

Not. Acceptable.

Which is why I'm now here, dripping and clenched, staring at the Hudson River through rain-spattered windows and struggling to take just one breath not fried by impatience and dread. But knowing I'm going to fail. Recognizing there's only one thing that will heal this burn. Seeing her again. With my own eyes. Hearing her laugh, watching her smile, rejoicing that she's in this world...making it a better place for everyone lucky enough to know her...

So, yeah, kids. I'm sure as fuck owning this stalker shit.

"Shiiiiit." Sawyer Foley's drawl cuts into my internal seethe. The guy adds a low whistle to it while walking in, dropping his duffel bag as if he's tossing down his surfboard after catching a set of Malibu breakers. His appreciative gawk continues as he takes in the clean lines of the décor, custom-designed to emphasize the space via track lighting, custom blonde woods, and cream-colored furniture. "*This* is your idea of slumming it?"

I turn around with two scuffing steps. My hands are still jammed in my overcoat pockets. In the right one is a wadded napkin and the last chunk of the protein bar I forced down during the flight from LA. In my left is a more significant package. A velvet box, all but burning my palm...

Needless to say, having to answer Foley is a fucking godsend.

"I said it was going to be small," I murmur. "Not a slum."

But it was the best Neeta Jain had been able to find in Midtown West with a night's notice—and took her working through the night to do so. Asking the task of the woman, a member of my leadership team at the Hotel Brocade in LA, had been uncomfortable but necessary. Roping anyone else into our small circle of knowledge wouldn't be dangerous just for them. The more who know our secret, the more links we must add to the chain for finding and dismantling the Consortium—and doing that is already going to take a strong-as-fuck chain.

"Yeah, well..." Foley strolls back in from the first of the place's two bedrooms and whistles again. "I like the way you travel, Richards."

"Rule," I correct. "Reilly Rule, remember?"

"Yeah. Right." He draws out both words with a narrowed glare. "Though I want to know how you got the cool cover name, and I got the wiener one."

"What's wrong with Felix Faegan?"

"Besides the fact that it sounds like a wiener?"

I laugh. Not long and not loud, but I do. Despite the fact that Foley always speaks like we're in a surfing movie, with the flowing locks and physique to match, he and I have adapted okay to each other. *Adapted.* I won't call it friendship. I may be a charmer in any social situation into which I'm thrown, but beneath the wit, I'm still a wary asshole who grew up second-guessing everyone who wanted to have a relationship of any kind. Emma is the only one who broke all my molds.

And continues breaking them.

The truth of it can't be more vivid than now. Leaving "Felix" to struggle with his wiener issues, I round the corner into the bedroom I've claimed as mine and crouch in front of my own luggage. The smaller bag has been designed with custom compartments to accommodate high-powered surveillance goggles, a camera, several types of listening devices, and a sizable black box covered with more switches and lights than a gamer's dream den.

Without hesitation, I grab the goggles and camera and transfer them to a smaller satchel already containing a black ski cap and more protein bars. I haven't had an appetite for anything else since Foley barged into my office back in LA bearing the information bombshell Angelique had just relayed to him. The intel that had exploded my world with a couple of huge epiphanies.

One: Six months as the Consortium's lab rat didn't come close to teaching me true fear.

Two: Sometimes, stalking really is totally justified.

Despite what the expression on Sawyer Foley's face is telling me.

"Daaannng." The guy peers into my bag, shaking his head like he's about to watch me lick a flagpole in the snow. "You still think this is the best play for keeping your woman safe, huh? Playing creeper spy on her?"

Token grunt. "And your own plan would be what, Einstein?"

"Oh, I don't know...actually telling her what's up, maybe? Including her on the new intel...since it directly affects her?"

"News flash, Sally." I toss in his radio code name for ironic fun. "I'm not on the woman's VIP list right now." I'm probably not on Emma's *cleaning crew* list right now. Not since she learned that even though I retired from public duties as Bolt, I've been working in secret with Foley to maintain watch on the Consortium—and yes, if the occasion presents itself, to penetrate even deeper into their defenses. And one day, if we're lucky, to break out the rest of the victims who haven't gotten as lucky as me. Who are still being violated on a daily basis in the name of those lunatics' grand plan of turning human DNA into rechargeable battery matter.

"She's a smart woman." Foley's statement isn't just steady with confidence. It's soft with admiration. I clench my jaw, choosing to ignore the latter—for now. "She knows the grittier parts about your life now, man."

"If you mean having to deceive the media, our friends, and our families, then yeah. But in this case..."

"When she found you hanging with the coo-coo ex after deep-sixing the romantic stay-cay?" The guy scores points for his sincere grimace. "I *am* damn sorry about dropping that nuke on you, man."

I lift a dismissive hand. "You kept Angelique under wraps for good reason. If you'd asked about bringing her to the meet-up last week, I would've told you to go deep fry your dick."

"Valid life lessons, the FBI version. Better to ask forgiveness than permission."

"Couldn't have said that better myself." I roll out a full smile before firmly patting the satchel and slinging it over my shoulder.

Foley facepalms himself from the figurative corner into which I just painted him. "Fuck."

I clap him on the back. "Too slow, gotta go. Sucks to be you, dude."

He scrubs a hand over his stubbled jaw. "So you're really going to do this? You're that convinced Emma's not even close to forgiving you now?"

"Why do you think we're staying in this dump instead of a penthouse at the Obelisk?"

He drops his hand. Shuts his eyes. "A dump, he says." A new snicker bursts on his lips. "Dude, just a couple of hours with the blueprint *you're* working from..."

I copy the chuckle, transferring the box from my right pocket into a more secure place inside my trench. The action is doubly beneficial, since I have the chance to check the same compartment for the key card that'll get me into the office building across the street from the Hotel Obelisk, where Emma *is* staying. "You're hammering with a new crew now, Sally."

Foley cracks his neck and tosses a wry grin. "In that case, hand me the nails."

"I'd prefer it if you handle the Stingray unit."

"*Modified* Stingray unit." He grits it out, dropping his volume. "Though I'm sure that won't stop the right people from throwing us into some deep holes if they learn we even have this bad boy."

My new shrug couldn't be bolder about not giving a shit. "At the moment, my concern is for one *right person*, okay?"

Foley grunts while scooping the surveillance box out of its compartment. "Bad guys of the planet, beware the dude with billions to spend and electrons for blood."

As he disappears back out into the living room, I whisper for the ears of the universe only, "And a woman in charge of his soul."

Only the universe has to know the full truth of it too.

That it's not just confirmation...but supplication.

That I'll gladly keep admitting that Emmalina Crist commands every corner of my mind, heart, and spirit, as long as fate works with me to take down the bastards who want to end her life.

⚡

Ten minutes later, we're tromping down Eighth, heading into a vicious headwind as well as the downpour it's brought into the city. Though the weather's a polar opposite to the sunshine and balm we left behind in LA, I've never been more grateful for a storm in my life. Beneath my black knit cap and upturned trench collar, I'm just another poor sap having to get around the city in the muck, not my usual existence as one of the world's biggest paparazzi magnets.

The weather's got people so distracted, they don't even notice how the drops from above are performing a fun acrobatic show of their own when they hit the charged airspace around me. Poor Foley's taking the brunt of that action, as most of this atmospheric pinball game pings and hits him instead.

"Guess there was no need to take a shower this morning," he finally mutters, rain spurting off his lips.

I snort, owing him at least the semblance of humor.

After we pace across a subway grate, weave around a newspaper stand, and then dodge three umbrellas, we're finally walking at a proximity allowing me to speak freely again. "So... you *do* notice it."

Foley side-eyes me. "Notice what?"

I return the look. "It's all right, man. You can say it." I swirl a finger at the drops still popping off thin air, as if I'm the fucking Starship Enterprise with its deflector shields up. "It's like I'm wearing a body condom of ions. Not exactly a state secret."

I hope the joke will relax him a little—since we left the apartment, the guy's been crawling with as much tension as me—but he just grunts again. "Are you really talking to me about 'weird,' dude? You do remember when you were first checking my creds, and I mentioned a little something called six years with FBI special cases?"

"Right." I smirk. "Special cases like a guy who changes the polarity of the air *and* can fully charge your phone with a good finger job?"

At last the laugh. But just as fast, a sober head shake. "You have no idea, Reecy."

"*Reecy?*"

"If I have to be Sally and Felix"—he pauses and thrusts his neck like a cat ready to hurl a hairball—"then yeah, *you're* Reilly and Reecy."

The next second, I don't care if he calls me Engelbert. Or, for that matter, Mouth Breather—which is what I am now that the ocean of umbrellas has parted, opening a clear line of vision to the multi-use commercial building we're headed for. It's a straight shot across the boulevard from the Obelisk, the iconic hotel my family has owned for nearly twenty years. I've seen this view in thousands of ways since my childhood—but I've never had it scorch every nerve ending in my body, making me blink and growl, fighting back a fog of dread like this.

Because it's never included the scenario unfolding on the sidewalk fifty feet ahead.

"Yo, dickface. Where's the ghost?"

Foley answers his own wisecrack with a violent *unnggh*, relaying the sentiment from my own gut. Laying eyes on a ghost would be a hell of a lot better than what I witness now.

The building in which Neeta's helped me lease an empty office is also home to a gym, from which my girlfriend and another female have just exited. The sight brakes me in place, jolted as if it's been a decade instead of a week since I last saw her. No. It's like the first time I met her, when her presence on the air was just as significant as mine and she'd sent my senses to another galaxy of comprehension, a cosmos of zero gravity. I'd been terrified of her effect on me, with her angel blond hair and her honest enormous eyes, and even that little sway to her hips, betraying the vixen beneath the seraph...

Yes, from the start, she'd possessed the power to unhinge me—as she does now, stopping and turning as someone bursts out of the gym, calling for her to hold up.

Not just any someone.

She and the mystery woman are joined by a guy.

And goddamnit, does he have curb appeal. Biceps on top of his biceps. Neck as thick as his head, but the face on that head belongs on a Russian prince. He's the fucking love child of brawn and beauty.

And he's touching my woman.

He encases the top of her shoulder with a beefy hand and adds a flashy movie-star smile, uttering something that makes Emma laugh. Her workout buddy is also all giggles—until she steps out of Emma's sightlines. As soon as she does, pretending to smooth the bloodred hair that's already pulled into a ballerina bun, her charm falls away. She replaces it with a calculated stare, shooting that scrutiny up and down the street before zooming it back to the Russian prince. He acknowledges her cue but is smooth and subtle about it, even during his casual follow-up. While laughing at something Emma's just said, he "shuffles" two steps to his left, even farther into the rain, compelling Emma to follow.

A fist forms in my gut. Then two more at the ends of my arms. "What the fuck?"

Foley turns, pressing against my side. "*Easy*, tiger."

"In another life," I snarl. Despite my raised hackles, I force myself to keep breathing—and to keep looking at every nuance of every movement the prince and his partner make. "Something's not right, damn it."

"Course it isn't," Foley mutters. "There's a side of beef making a play on your girl. Good news is, he's probably not the first to try it, and Emma's a smart woman."

I shake my head. "He doesn't worry me." I mean it. In another lifetime, that might've been a different story, but I don't have time for jealousy right now. Not with the apprehension now clutching more than my belly...

"Then what? Well, fuck."

Foley's first two words might as well have been *you're paranoid.* Then the last two? *Okay, maybe you should be.* Especially when it's clearer with every passing second that the prince is just the distraction for Emma. The one assigned to keep her engaged, with his patrician smile and courtly charm, while Madame Blood Hair performs the crucial tasks.

Of what?

What the hell is their game with her?

Thank fuck, Foley finally hops on the bandwagon of belief too. "*What* is going on?"

I'm not able to answer because Emma peers up the street, brow furrowed. I duck into the shadows created by some construction scaffolding, yanking Foley with me. Have I gotten too close? Can she feel me here, even half a block away? The charged awareness between us has only strengthened over the last three months, though we've never even wanted to test its range. There's a distinct possibility that she can already sense me, even from this far.

A distance that suddenly feels as wide as the Atlantic

Ocean—

As the air is ripped by a screech of tires.

And the roar of a gunning motor.

And a massive *whoosh* as a giant box on wheels barrels past us, flashing red and yellow strobe lights, its back end fishtailing wildly...

Before it hops the curb, taking out a dozen potted cypress trees and a fire hydrant...

And continues on the sidewalk straight toward Emmalina and her friends...

"Friends" who suddenly join hands and jump out of the ambulance's path, leaving Emma in the middle of the sidewalk like a hundred-point bonus hit for the driver's kill points...

Meaning I'm left with no fucking choice.

With a low growl, I let the familiar lightning pour through my veins, charging into my limbs with barely controlled energy. As it heats and sizzles, it already starts frying away my jeans, Henley, and knit cap. Thank fuck for the downpour and the necessity of having to wear a leather trench tonight. As if not having one would stop me now. There's an ambulance racing down the sidewalk, and it's about to take out the love of my life. I'll do this shit naked if I have to.

Those assholes picked a bad night to mess with Bolt's woman.

CHAPTER TWO

EMMA

In a flash, so much is different.

A flash feeling too much like a lightning burst.

One second, I'm savoring Mother Nature's override on New York's typical magnetism—a second in which the bite of the wind and the slash of the rain are more powerful than asphalt, steel, and neon—and joking around with Ashley and Luke in a post-workout endorphin high.

The next second, the two of them are gone. *Whomp*ed away by the new lightning on the air. But I'm not too stunned to figure this part out. The blast hasn't come from the clouds overhead. This electricity is from a singular source. A distinct force. An intruder who knows every damn way to explode my senses. Every last force to lock me into his sensual tractor beam.

Every mile I've flown across the country to escape it.

To get away from him.

To finally get some clarity about him. And yeah, I've actually been gaining some headway on the whole thing...

Until now.

Until he crash-lands back in, electrocuting every molecule of the air, warping every thought in my head. And yeah...waking up every tissue between my legs. Dear God, especially that. I'm actually embarrassed with how my body zings to life for him, my atoms surrendering him my electrons, my circuits needing his switches.

Damn him.

I suck in a breath, needing to scream something that'll convey that, but suddenly realize how thoroughly he's turned my world upside down. I mean, everything *is* upside down. My vision is filled with his legs, my thighs are clamped by his arm, and everything whooshes by, wet and confusing and upended. The man has zoomed in from out of nowhere, hauled me over his shoulder like a caveman bagging a saber tooth, and electro-pulsed his way across the street before I can even contemplate a scream.

But I think about it now.

Then more than think.

"God*damn*it." I get in a couple of whacks to his kidneys before he finally stops. "I swear to all fuck, Reece, if you don't put me—*ahhh*!" I start kicking—well, try to—the second he lands a solid *smack* on my ass. "What. The. Hell?"

I shriek the last of it as he spins around, making the world go by in a crazy panorama courtesy of the one-sided mirrors that form the Obelisk's front lobby wall.

"Did you see where they ran?" Reece shouts.

"Did I see where *who*..."

That's when I choke to a stop, having nothing to do with being turned into his human serape. Again, I look into the mirrored windows. *Really* look. The scope of the scene hits me. The crowd gawking on the sidewalk, well clear of the fire hydrant that's been busted open into a geyser. The broken pottery, downed trees, and collapsed canopies. The astounding absence of any pedestrian injuries...or casualties.

ANGEL PAYNE

The comprehension that I could have been one.

And there's my proof, in the form of the ambulance that's now wrapped around the light pole Luke was just getting ready to lean on.

"Oh my God." I squirm hard enough that Reece is forced to set me down, though I'm toasted so badly by dread, I grab him by the forearms to stay upright. "Luke," I gasp. "And Ashley. Holy shit, they were right next to me. Are...are they—"

"No." Reece's snarl makes no damn sense. It seems connected to new tension that started the second I mentioned Luke. "They're not dead because they're not there."

"Huh?" I gape across the street, looking for the distinct dark heads of the friends who have been so kind to me this week. Trying to figure out why Reece is referring to them like a pair of parasites...

"Hey." The hail comes from a guy who's run up the middle of the street, which has already been blocked off by NYPD. After a couple of seconds, I recognize him. The sun-streaked hair. The eyes an arresting green somewhere between moss and grass. The hang-ten vibe mixed with antsy energy. Sawyer Foley, Reece's new partner in the secret quest against the Consortium. I'm not as surprised to see him here as I'd expect. But nor am I shocked about Reece's appearance, either— an admission that should probably come with a little more gratitude if I'm correctly interpreting the evidence across the street.

Holy shit.

If Reece hadn't been here, would I be crushed between the ambulance and light pole right now?

Considering that answer brings on an icy shudder, I wait for the gratitude to sink in—but it doesn't. A thousand needles of fear replace the icicles almost at once. The pain worsens as I watch the exchange between Foley and Reece.

"Hey." Reece practically grunts it. "Did you see where they went?"

Foley shakes his head. "Small matter of a rogue ambulance got in the way—but with any luck, maybe they jetted back inside the gym."

Reece swings back toward me. Before he speaks, I interpret the question in his eyes. "There's a parking lot out back." I point across the street. "Just a small one for employees, but you can access it through the—"

"Alley," Foley finishes for me, his voice jacked with eagerness as he spins and sprints that direction. "On it!" he shouts, dodging the police cruiser that's just pulled up.

"Stay here." Reece commands it in a new growl while easing me onto a bus stop bench—and damn it, raining fresh shivers over me in the doing. But these are worse than the others, since fear isn't their only instigation. The arousal sweeps through with merciless speed, making it impossible to think about moving another step, let alone escaping into the hotel. My limbs are liquid. My mind is a mess.

Focus, damn it. Just a little.

But I'm not sure that dictate is a wise move, either. Re-honing my attention on the incident brings a slew of disconcerting details. The way Ashley encouraged me to cut my workout short just because it looked like Luke was wrapping up at the same time. Then Luke catching up to us with a lame excuse about wanting to talk protein powders. I'd thought I was helping a couple of friends hook up...but right now, examining the angle of the ambulance against the pole... It was a dead-on slam. The truck didn't just randomly hop the curb. That driver was gunning for us.

For *us*? Or just for me?

I don't want to confront that answer, but Ashley and Luke really aren't anywhere to be found for corroboration.

Did they really escape the accident just in time? *Did they know this was going to happen?*

Answers I've only just begun seeking are now rushing in fast as Reece beats the police to the rig and hauls out the driver by the scruff of his neck. As soon as the guy stumbles into the light, I'm able to get a full view—and despite the rain and blood cascading down his face, I let out a horrified cry.

He's big, burly, rugged, and dark. Just like Luke.

Exactly like Luke.

The wonder twins detail doesn't escape Reece's observation either. From all the way over here, I can still hear his gritted "Fuck," which he repeats as soon as the cops wrestle the guy away from him. But when they're too busy handling the legal stuff and going PC-gentle with the cuffs and Miranda rights, Reece emerges from the scuffle with the guy's wallet in hand. By the time a third officer realizes he has it, Reece has gotten an extended look at the contents—resulting in the scowl that takes over his face.

A look thrown right back at him by a fourth cop. Followed at once by a grinning gawk.

"Hey, you guys!" His yell is a hundred percent Jersey boy. "Check it out! We're on Team Bolt tonight!"

As soon as his proclamation penetrates the crowd, the throng doubles. Shouts and *whoop*s punch through the rain, instantly turning the whole street into something more than a crime scene. It's about to become a full press event, and nobody's composure foretells that better than Reece's—

though I doubt anyone but me can see how he forces down his fury in order to throw up a wall of charm, crime-fighter style.

"Damn straight," he says, letting the Jersey boy haul him into a gruff handclasp. "And believe me, I'm glad the Big Apple sent its finest to help figure out this mess."

"Oh, yeah!" One of the first two officers throws a hand up for a hearty high-five, his cell already out for the necessary follow-up selfie. "My man, Bolt! We're at your service, broheim."

"As I'm at yours." Reece claps the guy's shoulder. "And you know, actually, I'm not really doing the Bolt thing anymore. I was just here as a normal civilian, and—"

"A normal civilian?" The cop spurts with a laugh so hard, I can smell the coffee on his breath from where *I'm* standing. "A *normal* civilian, the guy says! Ha!"

"Well, anyhow..." Reece braves his way through a civil smile despite the coffee-breath air freshener. "As a regular bystander, I witnessed the whole thing, so if you want to follow up with any details about any of it, just ask the staff here at the Obelisk to contact me. I'll be in town for another few days at least."

"Another few days." I'm unable to silence the mounting fume beneath my echo or its eerily effortless follow-up. "And just how long have you *already* been here, Mr. Richards?" Since that part's so easy, the rest of my message can get injected to him through a glare. *Were you lying through all of our texts and calls and FaceTimes? Pretending to comment on the LA "heat," when you were just getting it off the weather app? Pretending I'd woken you up at five, when you were already working on your second cup of coffee—or even already spying on me from God knows where?*

"Well, that's incredible news." The first cop's declaration, two decibels short of a bellow, makes it impossible to get deeper into my seethe. Though that's probably a good thing. The guy's cheek isn't exactly what my mood needs right now. "What, you taking a break from tofu burritos and spray tans? Deciding to *enjoy* your retirement the real Manhattan way?"

Reece joins their laughter, making me glad I don't have to. He's so believable that even the glance he throws back over to me is, for all intents and purposes, a portrait of bro-time fun—making the invisible meaning he pierces at the end of it, meant for me alone, even more maddening. And electrifying. And arousing...

"Yeah," he drawls out, even cocking half a smile. "Something like that."

Jersey Boy, who's been helping his buddy out by snapping a few more shots with his own phone, suddenly frowns. "So what're you doing out here on a night like this, helping pull dipshits out of the muck?"

Reece inclines his head, confirming the validity of the question. He finishes the move with a new nod toward me. "Because *this* dipshit almost took out my most high-value target."

"Holeeee eff." The smile disappears from Cop Two's face, leaving only a stunned stare. "Uh...you okay now, miss? You need medical attention, or an—" Just in time, he realizes that offering an ambulance might be like extending a blanket in a sauna right now—though I'd gladly offer my freezing nipples for either. Fortunately, Reece reads every syllable of that thought and even seems to sympathize for a second—but as a second shiver rolls over him, my curiosity rises. And my concern. How much of his bioelectrical charge did he have to use in speeding in to save me? I've only seen his bloodstream crash after significant bad guy battling type stuff, but he swore off all the heavy-duty fighting months ago...

Or so he told you.

I hate the nagging voice but compel myself to listen.

He also assured you he was only "monitoring" the Consortium. That going after them would be a fool's game, and he didn't want to play on that board anymore.

I drag in an aching breath as Reece assures the cops he'll get me any necessary medical follow-up before he starts walking back to me. At the same time, I force myself to look at him through the lens of the next hard truth.

He told you all of that even as he had Sawyer Foley waiting in the wings, helping him formulate a plan to infiltrate the Consortium at their "Source"—using intel they got with the help of Angelique La Salle.

Angelique.

The woman who's already fucked her way into his circle of trust once. Who turned around and used that trust against him in the most despicable way possible...

And that, I'll never be able to accept.

But *that's* the thought that gets me back to my feet as Reece approaches. And go rigid as he steps in, sliding a steady hand around my waist. And keep my lips clamped as he dips his head toward my ear. And command myself not to cave as he whispers my name like a parched man thinking he's found an oasis.

And attempt a professional tone as I quietly answer him, "I guess I owe you some thanks."

He stops an inch above my mouth, the corners of his own taking on sexy twitches. "Which I'll accept in a number of forms, little bunny."

I flatten my hands on his sternum in order to set him back by a few inches. "Yeahhh, you see, that's just the thing." I shove him harder. Fortify my glare with equal ire. "Bunnies aren't supposed to wander into the doghouse."

$$\lightning$$

"Dog house?"

I have to give it to the guy. Even on his sixth repeat, his incredulity hasn't waned. Does he really not get it, or is he trying to wear me down? Either way, now that he's decided to follow me in through the Obelisk's side door, past the bar mitzvah cranking into full swing in the ballroom, and right into the empty—*thank God*—ladies room, it's time to set the man straight.

Easier said than done.

And as long as I'm going for clichés, maybe absence does make the heart—and other body parts—grow fonder. And for that matter, wetter. And hotter. And...

Holy hell.

I'm just going to admit it. I'm a full-blown ball of horny as he twists the latch on the main restroom door, locking us in here. I drop my gym bag as he paces forward, warping the air by a thousand more molecules with each step, until he's looming over me with all that soaked, thick hair and that chiseled, stubbled jaw and those lightning-crackled eyes...

"Okay, *wait*."

I get in a relieved breath as he heeds me, though his sudden jerk backward rustles his trench enough to release tendrils of smoke, smelling like someone fried a computer draped in a sweaty T-shirt. I'm not making that up. One, the electrical stench speaks for itself. Two, after years of scooping Lydia's tennis clothes into the bathroom hamper, I know *Eau de Sweaty T-shirt* like the backs of both hands. Fitting reference. I lift them both, flatten them to his chest, and then shove him far enough away so I'm unable to maul him inside three seconds, smell or no smell.

"First things first," I say, nodding to myself in encouragement. "I *do* owe you proper thanks...for whatever the hell that was out there. So, thank you." When all I get in response is a pause of unnatural stillness, I dare a glance back up. He's still looming, only now it's with barely reined tension and gorgeously terse features. "Annnnd the customary answer for that is..."

"Not what you're going to get from me right now." The smoke winds its way into his voice as he shifts toward me by imperceptible inches. He's closer but hasn't encroached enough to validate more pushback. Not yet. *Hustler.* "I'll have my moment once you have yours."

And just like that, I'm back to needing a sky full of rain—or at least a throat that hasn't turned to a desert—as his statement settles its double entendre right between my legs. I'm not even readjusted to the man's carnal force field yet, and now this? And damn it, the hustler knows it too. Is even well into enjoying his quiet, arrogant gloat about it.

Fine. The bastard wants my "moment"? He'll have it.

"Cool." I manage a devil-may-care shrug before letting my hands fall. Blithely, I pivot toward the mirror. It's a big risk, since I catch a glimpse of the heat flaring even higher in his gaze now, but if the last three months have taught me any ruling paradigm about Reece Richards, it's his need to prove he's evolved from the man-slut who used to walk into the ladies' room with a woman for only one purpose. Maybe two, if his date had hit up her supplier that night. If he's that eager to prove it, maybe I'm that keen to help him.

"You do have my gratitude," I reiterate—while stripping out of all the drenched workout clothes above my waist, including my tank with its built-in bra. "But you've also earned yourself about a thousand new warning sirens too, buddy."

And yeah, maybe I've pilfered a play from the hustler handbook—a move well worth it, just to bask in the glow of his lusty stare. "Warning sirens about what?"

He grinds out the last word so hard, it fills in his silent subtext. He doesn't like *buddy*. Not one damn bit. Beneath the rising temperature of his gaze, I'm not sure I like it anymore, either.

"You know damn well what." My body betrays my enjoyment of the game with its pronounced goose flesh and pebble-hard nipples. Still, I'm coherent enough to find a dry T-shirt in the bottom of my bag. "You were there just when I needed you tonight. But why were you *there*, instead of where you *should* have been?"

Deep furrows appear between his eyebrows. "Excuse the hell out of me?"

"Stop it." I brace both hands on the sink and glower at him via the mirror, fury making me forget all about my shirt. "You know damn well what I mean."

"Where I *should* be, no matter what, is protecting *you*, Emmalina."

"And you couldn't do that from LA, where I asked that you stay?"

The furrows vanish from his forehead and reemerge as

deep brackets at the corners of his mouth. "And where I *did* stay, until—"

"When?" I turn, folding my arms, fully aware I'm probably turning temptation into complete pain for the man—but too pissed to care. "Until *when*, Reece? During all the FaceTimes with those 'palm trees' behind you and the early mornings when you said even five a.m. was bearable because you were talking to me..."

"All of which was true." He snaps it from locked teeth.

"And I'm supposed to believe you...why?"

"For the love of fuck." He whirls, spraying water all over the place with the swish of his overcoat, and dives a hand through his hair. "So this is the way it's going to be from now on? You want a copy of the charter flight record from Teterboro, proving Sawyer and I landed just three hours ago?"

"Considering Sawyer himself was a complete secret from me until last week?" I rebut. "Might not be a bad idea."

He links his hands against the back of his head. "And you still think that was a deliberate deception," he utters. "Just like him recruiting Angelique as a double agent."

Suddenly, it's easy to slip the T-shirt on—though nothing about the move helps to cover up the raw exposure of my heart. Or the vulnerability of my self-esteem...and all its ugly cracks. "At least I now believe it was actually Sawyer who did the recruiting," I mumble. "Or whatever the hell it was."

"Thank God." He lets his arms fall like his fingers are made of lead.

"Yeah, well, that still doesn't mean I like her having access to the Bolt Brigade clubhouse. Double agent still means *double* agent, mister."

He turns back. Not all the way. Just enough so he can slant

his head over again, piercing me with a silver laser stare. "She turned over the intel that brought Foley and me to New York."

I rock my head, putting movement to my sarcasm. "Just in time to save me from the crazy ambulance driver."

"Well." He turns a little more. "Yeah. But—"

"Convenient timing," I snip. "Don't you think?"

His head seesaws toward his other shoulder. "Ah. *That's* the angle, then. *You* think Angelique set up all that insanity to go down tonight in order to gain our trust?"

"No. To gain *your* trust." It emerges as nearly a sneer, and I'm just fine with that. "Seeing as how she can't use her pussy as leverage anymore." But just speaking the words is like taking a hammer to those cracks in my confidence, breaking them open into gaping wounds. I have to force myself to mutter the follow-up, actually afraid of what the answer will be. "Or...can she?"

As soon as I spew the words, I want to haul them back in. I brace myself for Reece's anger—or worse, his laughter. How can I doubt his devotion by even a drop after the man has already declared it before the world? Thinking of the answer yanks the hammer back out, pounding at my dignity all over again.

But this isn't some doting little Bolt babe we're dealing with. This is Angelique La Salle, owner of the magical vagina that led Reece to his original ruin. Is my love enough to keep him from getting caught in her spell again? And how the hell do I prevent all those thoughts from traipsing their way across my face now?

I don't.

Damn it.

I know it with horrifying clarity as my temples throb and

my lips twist. I'm a thousand kinds of messed-up about this, expecting things to get even worse as soon as Reece lets loose with that laugh or that fume...

Though neither comes.

Through another long moment, just more silence and stillness—even though he continues to hover, subjecting me to the potency of his stare and his clean rain smell and his mighty, beautiful body...

Until he's not hovering anymore.

He's kneeling.

My fierce, headstrong, hulking hero of a boyfriend has dropped to his knees on the bathroom tile in front of me, keeping me fixed in place with his hands at my waist and his face pressed into my stomach, spreading warmth through my entire center as he finally speaks again—in a grating whisper.

"There's only one pussy on earth I worship now."

As if his words haven't demonstrated his meaning, he drops his face lower...then lower still...until...

"*Oh.*" The syllable shudders from me as he scrapes at my workout tights with his teeth, moaning like a starving man at the very core of my body. Beneath the Lycra, every tissue in my sex swells and sizzles and shivers, and I lurch my hips, needing more of his illicit attention, already imagining his mouth on me, inside me...

Oh...him.

Oh...this.

Oh...us.

Oh...*yes.*

It echoes in my head because I'm powerless to give him any other answer. Because every channel in my system is dialed into him, and every frequency in him is tuned for me.

I know it. I feel it. I revel in it. I'm lost in it. This is what we're made to do together. To create together. To ignite together. It incinerates my inhibitions. Torches every logical thought in my head.

This is why I had to get out of LA.

To get lucid from the fever dream of him. To break free from exactly this. To try to figure out how to do this "relationship" thing with a man with fingers that hold the power of the sky and thread the mental needle about putting my trust in him—if I can. Because isn't trust a thing of equality? And how equal can I be to a creature like him?

But at the moment, do I really want to push the issue? *Can* I?

Screw the issues.

And for that matter, screw perspective.

Right now, I need to forget. To dream again. To have the dream of *him* again. Of *us*...

Reece's growl is a toe-curling interpretation on the same message, electrifying everything south of my waistline as he drags the top of my pants the same direction. The skintight fabric sticks to my wet skin, making him work for the prize. His fervor makes me feel like a carnal reward—a succulent fruit he's unpeeling, dripping with juices for him to devour...

Until he gets so consumed with stripping me, his trench coat loosens and falls away from *him*.

Revealing that underneath the leather duster, the man is nearly as naked as the day he was born.

"Reece." My jaw plummets. "What the..." Shock rips the rest of it from my throat. Clinging to a few—*very* few—of *his* bare, wet muscles are the *remnants* of clothes, as in half the collar of his Henley, one thin strip of his pants, and the tops of his socks, looking like burnt curly fries bursting from the tops of his calf-high boots. The other threads scattered along his frame—which I'm more than aware of as he rises back to his full height—won't even roll up into a decent lint ball.

Not that I want him covered in lint balls right now.

Dear God.

Not that I can even imagine anything else against his rippled, burnished skin...except me.

A resolve the man doubles, then triples, as he drops his hold from me long enough to let the duster fall all the way to the floor.

There's still enough moisture on his body that the leather keeps clinging to a few places, like his taut ass and formidable thighs. Not that I regret getting to appreciate the view—until turning my face back up to recognize that the bastard is noting every second of my diversion and is unafraid about letting me know. If only his new smirk weren't so damn cocky...or the surge in his cock, now sliding against my trembling cleft, wasn't so huge and hot...

"Saved a damsel tonight," he rasps, his lips against my temple. "Just wasn't planning on it, so the leathers weren't handy. And Bolt blasts verses cotton and denim?" He moves back in, grabbing me by both thighs in order to hike my ass all the way up onto the counter. "Guess which side won?"

At first, I'm only able to reply with a serrated sigh. His lips along my face...his fingers against my skin... They infuse me with so much heat and light and awareness, I'm temporarily stunned. Has it been only one week since I last knew this magic? Was consumed by this connection to him? But neither of those are the most burning question on my mind. "So...wait. You just happened to be strolling out on Eighth Avenue, in front of this hotel, when that ambulance jumped the curb?"

He pauses long enough for me to feel his silent contemplation. Angling his head up by a few inches, he wets his lips while still gazing at mine. "In a matter of speaking? Yes."

"In a matter of speaking." I fight to get at least a prick of are-you-fucking-kidding-me into it. "Which means, essentially, you're a damn stalker, Mr. Richards."

More of his lip-licking—which would start bordering on disgusting if this man's lips weren't as decadent as a Renaissance painting. "In a matter of speaking...yes."

I don't want to concede how aroused *that* makes me either, but I'm helpless to ignore it. In his subtle Reece way, with his shameless, audacious nakedness, he's attempting a weird form of *détente* between us—at least right now. And with what he's doing to my body, I'm not sure my mind has the capacity to resist.

"Stalker." I repeat it with more definition, my arousal spiked by his brazen acceptance of it. "That's on top of being a pervy flasher, you know."

One of his brows spikes up. "Ah. Is *that* what you're calling it?"

I meet his mischievous smile, raising the game by one ruthless nod toward the door. "I could probably make kidnapping stick too."

"Probably." Though his voice is a wry mutter, the lust across his face speaks a different story—as well as the efficient tug he gives my left shoe, getting it off my foot before freeing the rest of that leg from my tights. With my thighs physically free to spread for him, he steps in and does exactly that. With our bodies now fitted from head to crotch, he brings his face close again, letting ferocity take over his beautiful features.

"But you moved to the big city for the excitement, little bunny."

My lungs stop as his feral growl works its way through me. When I release my breath again, it's mingled with the hungry heat puffing in and out of *him*. "Which means I have to learn to play with the wolves?"

"No," he grates. "No playing." He hitches his hips, teasing at my quivering entrance with his thick erection. "Just fucking."

Oh. God. Yes.

As the words spill through my mind, my head falls back and collides with the mirror. The scrape of my hair on the glass is a perfect companion to the claw of need in my pussy. Reece's cock swells too, his throbbing veins caressing my labia. I hold my breath, knowing he's close to spurting precome. Just a few drops of his scalding milk on my clit, and I'll be able to—

I scream as the lightning of the orgasm slams. Reece sucks the sound down with the mash of his lips, blending in his ruthless groan as he invades me completely with one brutal thrust. It hurts, my body not accustomed to taking in his size, but I welcome every harsh, hot sting of the agony, recognizing how my world is righted even as my sights careen.

We kiss hard and screw harder, the smacks of our bodies drowned by hundreds of voices shouting a deafening version of "Hava Nagila" from across the hall. With his grip still cupping my ass, Reece digs his fingers in, searing the insides of my cheeks with the lusty glow of his fingertips. I groan, abandoning myself to the consuming heat as he starts pile-driving my body onto his, impaling me deeper with every savage stab.

This is twisted. Insane.

I'm still mad at him. Maybe even more than I was before. He really is the fucking wolf, sweeping back into my forest and dragging me off by the fur into his lair—and goddamnit, even making me like it. No. This is more than liking it. This is craving it. Drowning in it. Wondering how I got by for a whole freaking week without it.

Wondering, even now, how I'm going to give it up again.

Not a great moment to even toy with that dilemma—as Reece releases one of his hands from my body to slam his palm to the mirror, impacting it so hard that I'm stunned the glass doesn't shatter. His entire arm flexes, precluding the surge of pressure into his cock by just seconds, before he drops his forehead to mine and snarls hot words against my lips.

"*Emma.* My Emma."

Then, there's no more room for anger. Or insanity. Or anything but him, in a fast and fierce flood, pouring himself into me. Jumpstarting every nerve of me. Igniting and enflaming and filling me, until every spare inch of me...

Is him.

And for that perfect second, in the chaos of his passion and lightning and fire, I'm completely at peace.

All the doubts vanish. All the distrust melts.

All the world goes away.

And in that space, I'm finally able to find courage.

It's not that I don't know what the stuff feels like. I've accomplished a lot of courageous things—many would argue falling in love with a guy nicknamed Bolt was one of them—but none that felt as significant as this.

None that required trusting that same man.

Really trusting him.

With truths I've never told anyone in my life before.

With truths I can no longer withhold from him. Not if I'm asking him to keep on loving me and trusting me with *his* truths.

Oh, God.

I barely realize I've whispered it out loud until more words spill out afterward, full of the sighs that turn them into strident pleas. "Here goes nothing."

CHAPTER THREE

REECE

I have to face the inevitable. Fate has bashed me between the eyes with it.

Heaven's soundtrack isn't angels on harps. It's a ballroom full of people yelling "Hava Nagila." And instead of a white silk robe, all I have to wear is a few shreds of torched clothing along with my shitkickers. And the whole place smells like bleach and bathroom potpourri and rain-drenched skin. And sex. Some of the best sex of my life. Yeah, in a damn bathroom, in the middle of New York, without even taking my boots off.

That's because none of the outside details matter.

Only she matters.

Only she makes this huge of a difference.

To everything...

Now, I just have to remember how to do a few minor things, like thinking and talking, and then I can ask for her phone in order to buzz the Obelisk's kitchen. My own cell, stowed in an inside pocket of my trench, is likely cooked worse than my clothes after the zero-to-ninety sprint tonight. Can't say the same about my appetite. I'm ravenous, but that won't last for long. With any luck, Cindy's heading up the kitchen tonight, and she won't blink twice when I ask her for a priority delivery of her killer lasagna with a Bundt cake chaser. I love

Cindy's Bundt cake.

Though the next second, I'm tossing the cake dreams into a mental trash can. And yeah, damn it, the lasagna longings too. All the energy of Emma's rasp suddenly weaves through my mental fog and goat-hooks the center of my chest.

"Velvet?" My own voice is sandpaper, not a surprise since I've just damn near emptied every drop of moisture from my body into hers. "You okay?"

"Yeah." But as she lifts her hand to my chest, her features tighten. "No. *God.* I don't know."

"Sssshh." It's more a sibilance than a scold, leaving me as I glide my own touch up her backside and around to her waist once more. "It's all right. Take your time." I catch her stare with a roguish wink. "I really didn't fly all the way across the country just to do this—though it was a damn nice fringe bennie, woman."

Luckily, she doesn't belt me for that—a move she could probably get away with, considering my physical battery's nearing its redline after letting Bolt the Badass *and* Reece the Lover run wild over the last hour. But she's also not chortling in amusement. The tension around her eyes and mouth fortify the impression.

"I have to tell you something," she murmurs after another thick pause. "It's...it's not easy. I think...maybe...I'm even ashamed, though I have no idea why."

Hell. This is considerably more than just "something." So much so that letting her confess it while flattened to a bathroom vanity and my dick still twitching inside her is out of the fucking question. With a decisive huff, I slide out of her body. At once, my system screams its disapproval of the move. I grab the counter as my body temperature plummets, steeling myself as the walls spin.

"Oh, sheez." Emma pops to her feet and seizes one of my arms. "Baby, are you—"

"I'm fine." I try lightening up the growl with a dark snicker, but it just sounds like I've downed one too many shots of Stoli—and not in the good way. "It'll be over in a second." *I hope.* Sometimes, my drops last for thirty seconds. Other times, it's been three hours. Fortunately, the room realigns as I turn and prop a hip against the counter. "And damn it, what do you have to be ashamed of, Emmalina? With *me*?"

I deliberately bite out the questions. The last thing the woman should ever be, anywhere near me, is ashamed. My goal is to make her world the opposite. Free and safe and confident and joyful. And yet right now, none of that claims her face, her posture, or the mutter with which she continues speaking.

"There's a reason why I freaked out on you," she says slowly. "Back in California. About Sawyer, then Angelique."

I tilt my head. Study her intently, from the way she worries her bottom lip to the nervous skitter of her gaze. "You mean, to the point that you bugged out of the entire state."

She starts rolling her workout tights back up over her thighs and hips. "Well, yeah."

"Bugged out on *me*."

Her head snaps up. Her gaze flashes turquoise fire. "A penalty you partly brought on yourself, mister."

"Affirmative." I dose it heavily with my contrition. "You should have known about Foley from the start. I'm sorry."

"And Angelique?" She folds her arms, pursing her lips so hard it's adorable.

"Is a necessary asset for us right now." It's businesslike because, unbelievably, I'm already fighting new pressure in my balls. *Fuck*. How can one woman possess the power to do this to me even with my gas tank damn near empty? "One *I've* had as much trouble accepting as you, okay?"

She folds her arms. Kicks at the floor. Finally mumbles, "Okay. Whatever. Fine."

"Now who's the one going private chat with the honesty?"

"All right, so it's not fine. And I'm not happy about it. But do you want me to try getting over myself to support you here or keep skipping down my hideous path into the forest of possessive girlfriends?" She tacks on two seconds of an agonized grimace before hunching away. Well, *damn*. Karma's been a funny but profound bitch this week, having just brought us both back to the same place: confronting our uglier sides and working to get past them for each other.

Maybe now we can accomplish that *with* each other, as well.

I push off the counter and press myself to her, running my hands along her rigid shoulders. "Possessive *is* kind of sexy."

"Said no normal man, ever."

"Normal hasn't spoken to me in nearly two years, Velvet."

Though she yields to that truth with a tiny glance back, there's no more change to her posture. I rub the lengths of her arms, hoping to stroke some reassurance into her, but the woman remains stoic and stiff and silent. Weirdly, the hush provides the few seconds I need to pull at a mental thread. Though I hate the place it's unraveled to, this beautiful, brave woman has just shown me that necessary isn't always fun and honesty isn't always comfortable, but love is always worth the pain.

So I drag in a deep breath, delay releasing it as long as I can, and then finally utter, "Who was he, Emma?"

She peeks back at me again. This time, it's with a couple of nervous blinks. If I haven't hit the target on her truth, I've come damn close.

"He...who?"

"The one who took your trust and stomped all over it." When the muscles beneath my fingers strain to the point of trembling, I revise my estimation. I'm not just close to her target. I've landed a bullseye. "You fell for him in—what—college? Maybe even high school? And he was...let's see... probably captain of the debate team. Maybe the future business leaders. Or maybe, if you were busting way outside the mold, the water polo squad." I step quietly to the side, threading my fingers with one hand of hers, and lean against the partition between two stalls. Now, I can at least see her profile—and something tells me I'll need the insight as I wade into her deeper emotional waters. "You wouldn't fall for a cliché like the star quarterback or the lead guy in the play." I weave lightness into my tone, immediately observing that I've struck the target's center again. "But he was driven and determined and just amazing enough to fascinate you and then to capture you." I wrap my fingers tighter around hers. "Right before he broke you."

My effort at the connection isn't enough. She twists her hand free before backing away, her head and shoulders low, until her backside bumps the counter again. As soon as she's there, it's as if a switch gets thrown. In place of her cowering stance and furtive glares, there's a lioness rising to full height, head rolling as if she really is about to let loose a roar.

Instead, her lips curl on a droll rebuttal. "Wow. You really figured all that out on your own, hotshot?"

Every inch of my psyche bellows at me to stomp over and

kiss that sass out of her—if only that's all her issue was. But I see right through her, and it doesn't take a mountain-moving effort. I see through her because I have damn good reason to. "Figured it out and locked it up, sweetheart. A long damn time ago."

It's my last sentence that ushers the sheen of tears into her eyes. "Because *you* were that guy."

"To more Emmalinas than I can remember." I swallow hard. Funny how penance tastes like glass. "To more than I want to admit."

Her face pinches as she rests with that for a long moment. Okay, "resting" isn't the right verb. Wrestling. That fits better. So does struggling. And yeah, maybe mourning—though that's not going to change my mind about refusing to sugarcoat this shit. Do I hate going into this much detail with her about my past? Hell yes. But lying to someone is easier than wiping my own ass. I can do it for days. I *did* do it for years. She's worth more. She's worth the truth. She's worth the hard.

She's worth me sucking up my pride enough to quietly pace across to her and scoop a gentle finger beneath her chin. And yeah, she's worth using my other hand to thumb away a lone tear down her cheek before I softly ask, "Who *was* he, Emma? What was his name?"

Now, she gulps—though her effort to get even that accomplished is rough. Rough breaths puff in and out of her nose. Her lips quaver but still part and allow her to offer up one word of answer.

"Dad."

EMMA

The moment is nothing like what I imagined. I'm not drenched by sudden catharsis or soaring on clouds due to my suddenly unburdened soul.

I'm only standing here, watching a storm's worth of reactions cross Reece's face. The plummet of his brows over a gaze gone dark as thunder. The defined tick in his hardened jaw. The clench of his teeth, so white in contrast to his dark, heavy stubble.

"What in *hell* are you saying?" His voice has dropped to the territory of low but lethal, scorching to the very marrow of my bones like flames in logs. Because of that, I discern every thought behind it, as well as his growing intention to fly back to California and Bolt-pulse my father into the Pacific.

"Not what you're probably thinking." I wrap both hands around the one he still has raised to my face. When he forms a fist beneath my grip, I push my cheek against it, coaxing him to stand the hell down. "Seriously, Reece. Let me explain."

"I'm listening."

By tiny increments, he relaxes the fist. By matching increments, I let myself breathe. How I still believe the man is going to stomp out of here and take out a wall or two without thinking, even though he still stands here in nothing but his burnished skin and that ominous stare.

"I...I still love my dad, okay?" I jerk a quarter turn to the right, just enough so I can drop my gaze to the molding on the bathroom's wainscoting and not a penis that would earn the man serious flow if he ever auditioned for the male strip revue up the street. "He's just a different guy than the man who was my king when I was a little girl. And before you ask, I know that nobody's father can be their perfect Prince Charming forever. I knew it long before..."

"Before what?" Reece supplies when I descend into a fidgety silence.

"Everything," I rush out, giving myself something to do by tracing the patterns in the wainscoting. The Obelisk's décor theme is marketed as *Nuevo Egyptian*, and I roll my finger over stylized lotus blooms while force-feeding new words to my lips. "Just...everything."

"Everything how?"

His tone is less growly, lending me the courage to keep talking. To speak things I've never said aloud to anyone before—not even Lydia. Shit—*especially* not Lydia.

"Life, I guess." Easing into it with the noncommittal flair, complete with a *fuck-whatever* toss of one hand, isn't working one damn bit. "As soon as Dad landed the job at Telson, everything changed so fast for us. At least that was what it felt like." I shrug, using the motion to pivot back around and slump against the wall. "One week, we were ordering pizza and wings for board game night, and the next we were at the country club's regatta gala, learning how to gracefully bite into crostini loaded with caviar."

Reece snorts. "Quick answer. You don't."

"No shit."

"I hate caviar."

"And I just fell a little more in love with you."

His snort turns into a smile. Small but sultry and lined with just enough intent that I'm sure he's going to kiss me. *God,* I want him to kiss me.

Instead, he prompts, "So you were all in zero-to-hero mode."

Shrug. "That's one way of putting it."

"And your dad...really got into being that hero."

A caustic sound escapes from between my teeth. I nod with the same intent. "Two for two, champ. Nice job with the crystal ball."

He shakes his head, loosening thick damp strands across his forehead. The hair doesn't diminish the impact of his sad gaze. "No sorcery. Just life experience. I spent a lot of afternoons at our own country club in New York watching the exact same thing." From his own lips, he copies my acerbic *tsk*. "Funny what power and money do to people. Funnier still when they get it in a big rock star rush. They think *all* the privileges of a rock star come with the package too...especially the naked groupies."

That officially takes him to three for three—a home run, if I give him credit for the pain lobbed right into my heart. And while it's been ten years since that summer and I've grown into an adult who realizes my parents are as human and fallible and, yes, forgivable as anyone else, that little keystone in my core will forever be worn away. That innate trust in the world will be eternally tarnished.

I fight my way out of the mope by rubbing my hands along opposite shoulders. A chill has set in again, and I don't delude myself about its source—or my need to truly get the hell over it. "Well, nobody's perfect," I finally state. "And it's not like I didn't need to learn that lesson sooner or later."

"Not like that." His snarl is just a rasp of sound but consumes the air with its violence. "Not from your own fucking father!"

"Okay, sparky. Whoa." I reach out, grabbing him by the wrists. Fortunately, he slackens the tension right away, and I'm able to slide my hold down, flattening our palms and meshing our fingers. "It's water *way* under my bridge, okay? And for the record, Dad wasn't the only one who had groupies." I actually suspect Mom might still be keeping a few under the radar but wisely decide against sharing that little fuse with my walking bomb of a boyfriend. At least for the moment. "And I'm not dredging it all back this way because I'm suddenly in a space to dissect it. I'm doing this for you, Reece. Period." I tug on him a little, bringing his gaze up to meet mine as I finish in a whisper, "You need to have this piece of the puzzle. You deserve it."

When I tug again, he moves in with quiet purpose. He releases my hands to brace his on the wainscoting behind me, making me the filling of a sandwich between the polished stone wall and his harder, sleeker body. "I'm not sure I'll ever deserve anything about you, Velvet," he confesses. "But I'm thankful for this and the bravery it took for you to give it to me."

When he fills in the last few inches between us, taking my mouth beneath his with tender impact, my bloodstream races and my senses spin. Sometimes, his softer kisses incite the most gigantic riots inside me. Now is definitely one of those times. I don't hesitate to prove it by fastening my arms around his neck and opening my lips wider. *Take me. Dear God, please.* Reece moans as if I've begged it aloud, plundering every corner of me with his decadent, demanding tongue—but after invading me for just a few seconds, he pulls back with a reluctant growl.

"What is it?" I get it out between taking gasps to recover the air he stole with that incredible kiss. "Reece?"

He pulls in a strict breath and anchors my face by forming an *L* with his hand against my cheek and chin. "Your honesty deserves my reciprocation."

Awkward smile. "I'm not sure whether to be thrilled or

freaked about that."

Another deep breath raises the plateaus of his shoulders. "Well, you're not going to be thrilled."

"*Shit.*"

He allows me to duck down and then swoop free of him. When I reach the end of the counter and spin back around, he's at least still looking at me—which provides weird consolation despite my solid case of freaked. "If it makes you feel any better, I said the same damn thing."

"The same damn thing when?" I charge. "And why?"

Annnnd forget the consolation. The new tension in his posture thoroughly sees to that. "When Foley barged into my office in LA," he explains. "Looking like he'd just hauled ass in from a zombie apocalypse."

I straighten, not bothering to hide my bewilderment. "Why?" Picturing the tanned-over, Zenned-out Sawyer as anything above a three on the stress scale is impossible.

"He'd just met with Angelique—who'd given him the real mother lode of intel that put us on the plane here."

And yes, *freaked* has turned out to be the most useful word of the day. At least of this hour. I use copious amounts of it to finally stammer, "Wait. *What?* But—"

But what? My mind hits replay on our conversation so far. I instantly assumed that Angelique had forewarned them about the runaway ambulance—right before accusing her of orchestrating the whole accident as her ticket into Team Bolt. But if she'd really been on the level and really *had* told Reece about the incident...

"Holy crap," I blurt. "You...you weren't wearing your leathers tonight." My confirmation comes in the form of six-feet-plus of rippling sinew and lustrous skin braced before me into a pair of black shitkickers and crispy noodle socks. "Which means...what? That the ambulance thing was really just an accident?"

Reece helps me out in the focusing-on-business department, scooping up his trench and sliding it on. "Right now, that's an unknown," he states. "But we're going to move on as if it wasn't—and that the Consortium chose to try it as a replacement, or even a prequel, for the original hit they're planning."

I'm grateful for the counter now, supporting the weight of my stunned sag. "The *original* hit? On what?" Comprehension snakes its way into my belly—then sinks its fangs in. "No. Not on what. On *who*."

On me.

As the fastest, most painful way to get to Reece.

"Shit," I blurt.

"Yeah." Reece closes his overcoat with a sharp cinch of the belt. "*Shit*."

"When?" I issue it quickly before my resolve gets acidified by my bile. "Where?"

Reece nods. His jaw hardens in a clear commitment to the rip-the-bandage tenet. "Night after tomorrow," he supplies.

"The night of the gala?" Now I grip the counter—tempted to rip the whole thing off the wall. "Holy. *Fuck*. The night of the gala."

And that sure as hell answers my question about where.

I wave my hands in front of the sink sensors. When that doesn't work—because who except a contortionist gets it right with these damn things—I pound a fist at the porcelain bowl. As soon as the faucet turns on, I scoop as much water as I can and drench my face. Then again. And again.

"Emmalina."

He's come up behind me to murmur it. *Bad idea.* I rise up, throwing an elbow backward. I don't mean to hit him, but I do, and the beautiful man just takes it—and the next two—with barely a flinch. I can't decide whether to scream at the ceiling in frustration or spin around and drench him in my sobs of rage. My boyfriend is a superhero, meaning I can use him as a punching bag whenever I damn well want. But my boyfriend is a superhero—meaning a gang of loon factory scientists are intent on turning one of the biggest events of my life into their freaking battlefield.

He cups my shoulders from behind as I sag against the counter and watch forlorn drops plop out of the spigot. "We haven't even validated that the threat is real yet," he says quietly. "My first concern was just getting here to make sure *you* were safe. But Foley's working on it with some trusted contacts at the bureau, and if he discovers anything substantial, we'll ensure that RRO still gets the money it needs to—"

I silence him by cracking the towel. The snap hits the air like a whip. In the ringing silence it leaves behind, I utter through my teeth, "The *money*?"

The syllables sound as insignificant as they are—as meaningless as the dollar signs are to the RRO event. But going on from there, trying to explain what this is all really about, is going to come up just as short. He either gets it or he doesn't. He either sees that the growth of the event, from twelve to fifty to two hundred in just a few weeks, isn't because of him or me or his dad. It's because of passion and heart and people who believe in this...who believe in these kids. RRO's "blind application" process—shielding the applicant's name, ethnicity, and gender from the acceptance panel—has given us a first wave of apprentices from so many corners of the world, including a lot of US cities. The fundraiser, featuring video interviews with all those kids, is going to be the official start of all their journeys. Their launch into their *more*.

It's a hell of a huge message to ask a man to read just by looking at my face—but as the Almighty likes to remind me, in a moment like this, I haven't given my heart to an ordinary man. Reece Andrew Richards shows me that stunning truth with the new compulsion of his hold, fitting as perfectly around my shoulders as his presence fills my heart—and his commanding murmur brims at my ear.

"You really want to throw your party, bunny?"

I press back against him, hoping he sees and feels that—caviar crostini be damned—I really *am* more in love with him now. "It's not *my* party, Reece. It belongs to the kids we're going to help. And the staff. And all the vendors who have donated so much because they believe in this..."

Again, I stop because I'm daunted. There's too much to say and no good starting point to go in.

And yet again, the man of my heart conveys that I don't have to.

While dipping his head in to press his lips to the special spot just behind my ear, he wraps the perfect cords of his arms around my waist. With equally unwavering confidence, he murmurs against my neck, "Then that's what we're going to do. Now, you've just got to add fifty names to the gala dinner count."

I jerk in his hold before piercing a stunned stare at him via the mirror. "*Fifty?*"

"My security team will have to eat, Velvet—especially because they'll know if anything happens to you, they'll be snacking on their own balls for dessert."

CHAPTER FOUR

REECE

"Woooo. Somebody's leveled up to special snaz."

Foley puts the cherry on top of that by "kabooming" his hands and then adding the requisite sound effects. Without breaking concentration on fastening my cufflink, I grunt to acknowledge the compliment. Well, what I assume was one, especially because he's decked out in a similar ensemble to mine—"similar" being a loose term. He's got the basics of the tuxedo just fine and has even tamed his hair with the styling product I ordered him to use, but I doubt the battle will end with equal success if I attempt to nix his Chucks instead of the formal Prada loafers that were sent over from Yuziki's shop. I'm not even thinking about going there about his pocket square, either. If the guy needs his parrots-and-tequila pattern to stay focused on shit tonight, then parrots and tequila it shall be.

Because I *need him* focused tonight.

I need *everyone* focused tonight.

Especially the fucker staring back at me in the mirror.

I issue the same mandate, more or less, while giving myself another once-over. Beyond the apartment's windows, a boat on the Hudson sounds its horn, a forlorn sound in the showery night.

As if my nerves need any more help in the doom and gloom department.

Foley, picking up on my fresh tension, leans against the doorjamb of my bedroom before asking, "So tell me again why you decided to stay here instead of the Obelisk for the last two days?"

I toss a taut glance. The man's savant-level aptitude for details, a trait I'd slotted in his "plus" column when first meeting him, has come back to bite me in the ass in the last seventy-two hours. From the second I'd walked back into the apartment after leaving Emma at the hotel, he'd quirked a salacious grin, knowing exactly how she and I had filled the hour after the ambulance incident. But he'd been surprised when I didn't grab my bag in order to return to Emma's room at the Obelisk, a confusion he's been stubborn about sustaining, even now.

"Because if that fucker in the ambulance really was in cahoots with the Consortium, it's best that they think my last contact with Emma was our spat on the sidewalk after that shit went down." I yank at my bow tie hard enough to communicate the rest of that to him with the nonverbal stuff. That the tension in my fingers is a direct correlation to the strain in my cock—and that the torment has been unchanged since my body was reminded, in Biblically perfect detail, how thoroughly it craves hers. "As far as they've been concerned, we argued and then Emma shoved me."

Foley's eyes narrow. "And once you were inside the Obelisk, *nobody* saw you two making up?"

"Nobody." Giving even that answer brings back the memories, heavy and hot, of how Emmalina and I mauled each other in that locked bathroom—which of course, Foley also takes comprehensive note of.

ANGEL PAYNE

"So you haven't any more time for *additional* make-ups?" he pesters. "No nooner she's sneaked you in the back door for? Little happy hour special, maybe?"

As I said, not a direction I didn't expect—so I stop on my way back out to the kitchen and pivot to confront his suggestive smirk. "Did NYPD ever get back to you? Tell you anything more about aggro ambulance guy other than the fact that he magically made bail the morning after the accident?"

Quiet aggravation sneaks across the guy's face. "No."

"Then why would you think I'd endanger Emmalina by sneaking back into her bed, knowing the Consortium might be watching?"

He frowns, clearly caught between perplexity and pissed-off. "Then why are you going to be publically at her side tonight, knowing they're *likely* watching?"

Again, not a query I didn't expect—but am actually gratified to field. After rooming with the guy for a few days, I know Foley likes approaching most of life from Margaritaville. Sometimes, especially on a night like this, it's good to be reminded that his cocktails are really laced with nails, and if pressed, he won't hesitate to use his surfboard as a lethal weapon.

"But we don't know that either, do we?" On the sparse chance I'll get an eleventh-hour answer to that, I scoop up my phone and swipe through the updates. Not one message or text from Angelique's code name, Alain, or from the six guys Foley hired on to track the woman, as well as her claims about the Consortium's "special plans" for the Richards Reaches Out fundraiser that starts less than an hour from now.

My woman's event.

The official start to her helping out so many people across

the planet.

Meaning that if they really do fuck with it, the Consortium will be earning themselves a special place in hell—into which I'll provide a personal escort.

"No." Foley's response, though coated in gloom, affirms how he'll be happy to help me out with the task. "We don't know that, damn it." He shifts as if his tux is too tight, though the garment has been custom tailored for him. "And I'm sorry about that, man."

I slice out a stunned stare. "Why?"

"Because my guys are usually better than this." He huffs. "*I'm* usually better than this."

"You think I don't know that?" Now I'm looking for a way to offset my awkwardness. "I didn't hire you for your sparkly wit or dreamy hair, Foley. You're fucking good at your job. But the Consortium...they're good at theirs too. Far as I know, the 'Find the Loony Scientists' app still doesn't exist."

He hikes a thigh onto an arm of the sofa. "That supposed to make me feel better?"

"That's supposed to drag your head out of your ass." I betray the snark gods by giving the words an amiable overlay. "So if *feeling better* helps you to do that, then have at it." I conclude by shoring up my stance, feet at shoulder distance and stiff arms at both sides. "Long story short? I need your A-game tonight, Sally."

The guy breaks into a smile. "Then that's what you'll get, Reecy."

I spread my arms, palms out. "And if Angelique's fed us crap intel, we'll know soon enough."

His head cocks a little. His gaze narrows. "You almost wish that were the case, don't you?"

"*Almost?*" Probably doesn't take his savant skills to notice this one. "You want the PC answer to that one or my ugly truth?"

One side of his mouth kicks up. "Which one do you think I'll rout out anyway?"

Fucker. "Fine," I grumble. "Truth is, it was shitty enough to worry about the woman even after she disappeared off the grid."

"After that crap went down at the El Segundo power station," Foley states. "Right?"

"Not exactly." After my defined punches on both words, he grunts in surprise. I go on. "A few days after that, she popped back up—at Emma's apartment."

"The hell?"

"Yeah, well..." This time, I go ahead and free up a chuckle. "I wasn't happy about it either. But by that point, I had a tracker on Angelique and arrived just in time to watch my girl go Xena-battle-mode all over the bitch."

Foley tosses his head back on a full laugh. "Are you freakin' serious?"

My smile is warm with pride. "Completely. She was only missing the bustier and the Chakram."

He shakes his head and stares at his feet, now crossing them at the ankles. "That woman of yours is..." He rubs at the back of his neck. "Well, she's something else."

"Yeah." I don't hold back my subtle growl. "That woman of *mine*, Foley."

He raises both arms, palms up. "Heard and acknowledged." After waiting a long second to be certain I've registered that, he murmurs, "So...what happened then? And how are you alive to tell about it? Or is getting in the middle of a girl fight really *not* like being tossed into a velociraptor pit?"

Though I'm not done with my tension about his wistful goo-goo face for Emma, I volley, "I didn't have to go there. Fortunately, Angelique knew when to cry no joy and slink off with her tail between her legs."

"And so you were able to keep tracking her."

"Of course—until the signal suddenly vanished. It was the day after I went public about Bolt, and she was at the international terminal at LAX, so I assumed the Consortium had called her back to Europe and ordered her to ditch her SIM card before boarding the plane. When my guys in Barcelona caught her on airport cameras there, I couldn't turn the page on that chapter fast enough. Didn't even stop to celebrate the knowledge that she was likely going to be punished or killed for failing to recapture me."

"Which explains why you and Emma are conflicted about having to reopen the book on her again."

"Oh, we're not conflicted." My voice is as cold as the glass through which I peer. There are whitecaps on the river now, making me glad I ordered the Obelisk's bell desk to reserve the hotel's Escalade for Emma's transportation tonight. Since the sun went down, the storm has gotten scarily stronger. "We're both damn clear about this. We're trusting Angelique because we have to. Period."

Behind me, I hear Foley uncrossing his legs and then pushing back to his full stance, measured but purposeful about his moves. "Because a leopard really doesn't change its spots, then?"

The insinuation—it really can't be called much else—is the rope that twists my attention back around. "A leopard that raises a little hell on a few club crawls is a lot different than one who lures a chunk of prey into the laboratory to have its DNA altered."

He dips a diplomatic nod. "Outstanding point, Team Reecy."

I'm not sure whether to laugh at him or seethe at him. He can't be *trying* to piss me off, can he? Especially after his not-so-stealthy fan club meeting for Emma. But a thorough assessment of the man reveals no hidden snark. Maybe his agenda, whatever it may be, just has to be added to the list of mysteries for tonight.

A list that seems to just get longer as we head down to the street and I open my phone to the car service app—only to be interrupted by a voice I haven't heard in a long damn time. Not since just after college, when I was summoned back to New York for the requisite Richards family rite of passage—Dad's "what are you going to do with your life now" speech. But the speech was preceded by the ride. And the ride included the man with the voice of a motorcycle gang leader but the face of a closet computer programmer. Not a thing has changed about that in the last seven years.

"Reece Andrew." Nothing has changed about Angus's insistence on using my full name, either. From anyone else, the familiarity would be odd; from the odd man who's stayed in my father's employ the longest, it's just part of the charm.

Charm I couldn't be further from expecting tonight. I communicate as much when I stop short right in front of him and the stretch Bentley he's brought. *Dad's* stretch Bentley. Ignoring how Foley plows into me from behind, probably making us look like the black tuxedoed versions of *Dumb and Dumber*, I grunt out, "Angus. You're...here."

"Good evening." He tips his cap and straightens his glasses, though the growl still makes me wonder if he'll conclude by shooting off my kneecaps.

"*Why* are you here?"

His high forehead, outlined by the smooth comb-down of his mouse-brown hair, develops a couple of furrows. "To take you to the gala." When I don't register immediate understanding, he continues, "The Richards Reaches Out event? Over in the East Village? You *are* attending, yes?"

"Yeah." My confusion nearly turns *that* into a question. "I mean, yes. I am."

"*We* are." Foley's assertion isn't much better for hiding bewilderment. He peers at Angus like the guy is a shapeshifter and only needs a second to morph into the wolf he actually sounds like.

"Yeah," I toss out. "I mean, we are." A fast hand fling arced between the two men. "This is Sawyer Foley," I offer. "A new business associate."

"A pleasure, sir." Angus dips over from the waist now. "Angus Colfe, Mr. Richards's head driver."

"Mr. Richards." Foley nods with his puzzle-putter-together look. "As in, *Lawson* Richards."

"Correct, sir," Angus offers. "I've been in his employ now for twenty-six years." Which makes Foley's face pop back to eerie shifter-seeking mode. Angus doesn't even look thirty. Still, that's not the strangest thing about all this—an anomaly I refuse to be silent about anymore.

"Which means he rarely lends you out to anyone," I mutter. Then, even more quietly, "Least of all, me."

Angus discreetly pushes his round glasses up on his nose. "Your father has had the opportunity to reconsider a few policies in his life lately."

"Yeah." I lift a wry grin. "*Lately.*" Like, say, over the last three months—since I told the world I was the guy behind the adventures of Bolt, the people's superhero. *And* did it in the name of true love—in a ballroom filled with some of the most influential corporate players in Southern California. *And* followed that doozy up by bringing him the idea for the Richards Enterprises nonprofit arm that's a corporate publicist's dream.

In short, the dots are easy enough for a six-year-old to connect.

I'm good for the Richards bottom line again.

Bringing another simple-enough-for-a-six-year-old recognition.

After all my years of trying to reconfigure the boxes of my world—everything from coloring on them to pissing on them to completely decimating them—the answer to my dilemma with the damn things was right in front of me all along. They just had to be zapped with a little lightning.

Granted, I had to *become* that lightning...

Which, as I climb into the Bentley after Foley, actually brings on a laugh.

While Angus reacts with a wide smile, open curiosity takes over Sawyer. "Is the rank and file allowed in on this particular yuk yuk?" he drawls.

I settle back into the leather seat, gratefully accepting a tumbler into which Angus has poured two fingers of Macallan Rare Cask. As Foley accepts an offer of the same, I supply, "You know all the bullshit about thinking outside the box?"

"Of course." He punctuates that with a groan, appreciating his first sip of the top-shelf whisky.

"Well, my parents have box seats *inside* the boxes."

"But now you've burned the boxes." As soon as I confirm his direct hit with an arch of brows over the rim of my glass, he snickers. "Which is turning tonight into an interesting piece of irony, then."

As we pull out into traffic, I stare through the window at the passing kaleidoscope of fluorescent and neon lights, seemingly animated in their own right due to the punishing wind. "If my father's twisted olive branch is the most 'interesting' part of the evening, I'll take it."

Foley takes his time with another sip of whisky before speaking again. The care he's taken with the words permeates through to his tone. "You give any thought about the reason behind why the old man's playing nicey-nice?"

"Don't have to." My reply is just as steady. "Apparently, he's stopped in at RRO several times since Emma and the team set up the office." Just mentioning her name brings a smile to my eyes before spreading to my lips. "My woman is a walking magic spell, Foley. Seems that even a stiff-nuts like Lawson Richards isn't immune."

Foley cocks his head back against the butter-soft leather and regards me from newly hooded eyes. "So you owe the little sorceress a giant thank you."

"Excellent idea—in theory." I rest my snifter on one knee, tapping on the glass with a finger. "Execution just might be a little tricky."

His features tighten on a frown. "Things are still really that tense between you two?"

"It's complicated."

Which, if turned into a meme, would edge at breaking the internet. But it's impossible to make the statement and *not* remember its inspiration—the moment in which it had sunk

ANGEL PAYNE

into Emma, after I didn't flinch about it for an entire minute, that I was completely serious about RSVPing for myself and fifty disguised operatives for the fundraiser. For two seconds— but only two—she'd smiled sweetly. It had taken her two more to pivot back around on me and then another two to tuck her hand between my legs, angling in to twist my balls. Not hard, thank fuck—but hard enough. Reaching that sweet spot just beyond ruthless flirtation but shy of turning my sack into a demented version of lightning in a bottle.

"Comfortable, Mr. Richards?"

"Not particularly, Miss Crist."

"Then you don't want to know what I'll do if you and your 'team' screw up my fundraiser based on bad intel from a woman I trust as much as a fairy tale hag."

Like the second in which she'd finally let me go, I grunt hard and indulge a quick glance down. Okay, everything's where it should be. Though the move's unnecessary tonight, since all my leathers have been built with structural reinforcements around my junk, Foley nevertheless catches the look and pieces it with my statement to draw a halfway accurate conclusion of his own.

"Shit." He emphasizes the word by drawing it out.

"Breathe." I take another swig of the Macallan. "It is what it is, okay?"

"With all respect, fuck the breathing," he mutters. "And *fuck* 'it is what it is.'"

"Well, it *is*." I toss in a growl to keep this from descending into a bad comedy sketch. "And like it or not, it's what we're dealing with tonight."

"You mean what we're being forced to accept tonight." He downs the rest of his whisky in one gulp. He grimaces from the burn but swiftly turns it into a fierce grunt. "An operation we're walking into nearly blind, burning your money on fifty fucking operatives—"

"I have the money, Sally. *Breathe*."

"—who don't know shit about when or where or how or *if* these bastards will strike—"

"Because these bastards are the fucking Consortium."

"—who have no intel about what they look like or what they'll do—"

"Are you listening to me?"

"I've been *trying* to listen to *them*, damn it. To *find* them. To learn even one goddamned detail about them for the last three fucking days, and—"

"*And*"—I grab a handful of ice from the sideboard and hurl it at him—"as I've already told you, they're the fucking Consortium."

"Which makes them *what*?" He openly fumes while picking ice chunks off and tossing them back, one by one. "Freaking gods?"

"No." I lean forward, elbows on my knees. "It makes them...*them*." I slam my glass into the circular holder in the side console. "They're just good at this shit, man."

"Well, I'm better."

"I know."

"I'm good at my job, damn it."

"I *know*, Sawyer."

He halts his ice hunt. Using his given name—his first, at that—succeeds in slowing his roll just short of dragging out his full résumé. It doesn't stop him from pushing out another fume before muttering, "But now you're going to give me more crap about how it's only been a few days since Angelique handed over the intel, and—"

"Foley, they hid me from the whole world for six *months*."
After the Bentley glides another three blocks with no sound
but pounding rain on the roof, I finally add, "We know what we
know. It'll have to be enough."

The glower he unfurls makes me suddenly understand
how Yoda felt when Luke refused to believe he could raise the
star speeder from the swamp. "And what if it isn't enough?"

"It'll have to *be* enough." Oh, yeah. I'm feeling small,
green, and really warty now. "But with any luck, we'll be sitting
around in the kitchen in a few hours, stuffed on prime rib and
tiramisu, and wondering how many more bad cover songs the
band has until their next break."

That does the trick—however that can be defined. With
a defined eye roll, Foley toasts me with the last of his whisky
before muttering, "From your lips to God's ears, dude."

I lift my glass in time to join him in his toast, draining
the last of my Macallan. My strung-out nerves barely feel the
alcohol's impact. The whisky does, however, help in reining
back the laugh I'm tempted to throw back now. *God's ears?*
Since when did God even pretend to care about all this?
Yeah, there was a time when I thought He did—or at least I
wanted to, during the initial weeks of my captivity, when the
Consortium was running me through their first batteries of
diagnostics and tests. I was still a naked, shivering, drugged-
out prisoner, unsure what procedure was going to come next.
I kept begging God to just get me through the next evaluation.
Then the one after that, and the one after that, and the one after
that. I promised that if He gave me the strength to endure, I'd
summon the will to keep on living.

Until the bastards started the electric infusions.

And death had sounded like a better idea every day.

Nevertheless, I survived that purgatory. *Without* God's ears. Without God's care. Without God's help.

And tonight, if I have to confront every soulless freak from that mire again, I'll gladly do so. Because so help me God—and any other deity who cares to show up *this* time—if any of those bastards so much as sniff at Emma's *shadow*, they'll answer to a fury *they're* responsible for. A power I've honed and evolved and strengthened into a force so potent, the world now calls me *super* for it.

And the *hero* part?

Well, Bolt *is* officially retired. And what good is retirement if a guy doesn't live it up a little? Some men choose to join an exclusive golf club. Others buy a Corvette and go for hair plugs. I like the idea of a little electric fusion basket weaving. Using the intestines of a few Consortium minions.

The fantasy holds such appeal, I almost hope the bastards do truly show up. *Almost.* I've come prepared. Every part of my tux has been designed to tear away for the leathers I'm wearing beneath—but even the chance to take a small chomp out of the Consortium isn't the most important priority tonight. The most outstanding priority for *all* my nights.

Nights in which I now sometimes actually dream instead of battle nightmares. Nights that turn into dawns I actually greet with a smile. Nights that aren't clichéd metaphors for the midnight depths of my soul, because that soul now has the light of living with a purpose. The best purpose of them all. Loving—and protecting—the woman who was created for me.

And damn it, that's what I'm going to do. Whether she likes it or not.

CHAPTER FIVE

EMMA

"Wow."

It bursts out of Lydia as we reenter the main event room from the kitchen after having checked on how the meal prep is going. During the half hour in which we were meeting with Yuri Lane, the hot new chef-on-the-block who's donated his culinary genius for the party, the event crew has had the chance to turn down the work lights, turn up the party lights, and cue the DJ to get some jazz in the air prior to the band's first set.

But surely there was another element they added to the mix at the same time. Some fairy dust.

Gone is the basic, blank East Village warehouse space. In its place is the incredible embodiment of everything I wanted to communicate with the only theme that felt right to pick for tonight's party: *Dreams Do Come True*. The entire space already has a dreamlike quality, with the high ceilings and exposed ducts softened by stretched spandex sails in different shades of blue. Lighting effects that look like constellations are projected onto the new-age "sky," from which silver light filaments dangle to support suspended centerpieces over each round banquet table. Each custom-designed three-dimensional Native American dreamcatcher measures four feet across and is adorned with Swarovski crystals, glittering feathers, and bountiful bouquets of live flowers. Each dreamcatcher's theme is made even more distinct by the matching hues of the linens on the table below. But the room is kept from being a thematic train wreck by strategic accents of gold elegance—the cutlery, the Chiavari chairs, the foundation's logo embossed on the white Lucite dance floor...

I'm finally able to answer my sister, though the muttered words don't feel like mine. "Wow is a good way to start." The whole scene is like a dream, far more beautiful than I imagined everything turning out. I almost want to yank my brain out of my body just to comprehend it all—but that would mean giving up the wonder of getting to wear this princess-worthy gown. Yeah, so I was never one of *those* girls, even growing up ten minutes from "the kingdom" where "princesses" were featured in twice-daily parades, who felt the need to dress in miles of lace and crinoline. But this dress would turn even Hulk Hogan into one of those girls. The thing is a production, starting with eight layers of nearly sheer gossamer on top of a cage skirt that's rigged with thirty battery packs, powering nearly four hundred blue LED lights. So yeah, the dress glows. Literally. There's a similar process beneath the fitted halter bodice, which is given more definition from silver piping that matches my silver ballet flats and swirl-shaped hair combs.

Yeah. Princess. And even taking a few seconds to enjoy the whole thing before remembering that I've got to actually be in charge a little here. Maybe more than a little.

Right before wondering if I'll even have anything to be in charge *of*...if the intel from Angelique is right...

"Hey." Lydia brings a friendly shoulder nudge along with the prompt, tilting her head over to peer at me with shining sky-blue eyes. The party lights glint in her curls, picking up the natural strawberry tints in her blond. "You're not going to throw up on me, are you?"

"No." I gently elbow her in the ribs. "Not on *you* directly..."

"Oh, stop," she chides. "It looks wonderful, Em. Everything's going to be great. Now relax."

"Easy for you to say." And now I really *am* tempted to throw up—with no easy pink medicine to help with the issue, either. And now I'm officially stuck between one *ugh* and another. If Angelique has been on the level about wanting to help us, then her intel is solid and the Consortium is planning some "surprises" for the party beyond a few hospitality baskets and a couple of piñatas. But if nothing happens tonight, Angelique's fed us the information for another reason, and I can't ignore the obvious explanation for that. My boyfriend's glamorous ex wants to sink her elegant claws all the way back into Reece.

Nope. All the pink medicine in the world isn't going to help with this one.

"Hey." Lydia wraps me close as I clutch a hand to my gut. "What are you talking about, goof? You *really* need to look around. Can you believe what you've accomplished? The food smells great, and the band's warming up, and the silent auction is ready to go, and *you* are the most stunning belle of the ball I've ever seen."

"Says the tennis-diva-gone-glam-goddess in her own right."

She pirouettes, showing off the gold and cream glimmer of her frothy bell skirt, matched by the sparkly tassels on the scarf designed to fill the scoop cut ending just above her backside. "This *is* a pretty kick-ass look, yeah?"

I duck a glance down to her rear. "Literally or figuratively?"

She waggles her brows. "Are you saying I have a nice ass,

sister of mine?"

"Not that I want to get in the habit of checking out your backside, but yeah."

"Well, one of us has to represent in the Crist Girls sassy-ass department. *You've* worked yours right off on all this." She leans in to give my shoulders a solid shake. "But now it's time for you to *enjoy it*, okay?"

I let my head loll around like a bobblehead on a crazy taxi dashboard. "Gaaahh. Okay, okay."

Though Lydia ceases the shaking, she doesn't move her hands. Her grin remains impish. "Whoa. Was that *my* sister indulging in a moment of *silly*? Who are you, and what've you done with Emma?"

"Shut. It."

"Whew." She rocks on one heel, backhanding her forehead. "*There* you are. For a second, I thought I'd have to fire up the search light and have them activate the Bolt Jolt over the skyline. If it looked that good over LA, then it'll be epic over—"

"Wait." I slice one hand through the air. "Activate the *what*?"

Her gaze narrows, tighter than before. "Oh, man. You really don't know what I'm talking about, do you?"

Slow grumble. "Okay, if this is a set-up, you're doing a bad job of it. And don't even *think* about getting it on video, missy. So if you're pulling out that phone for any other reason than—"

She flips her phone around, exposing a new image on the screen, and I forget everything I was about to say in favor of words that fit the moment much better.

"Holy...shit."

It's a view of downtown LA from what looks like Union

Station. I recognize the mission-style buildings, as well as the top of the Olvera Street bandstand—but in the night sky over the sleek towers in the distance, there's something more than just the glam glow of La-La Land light pollution. A beam of high-intensity white light, originating from somewhere in the middle of the downtown labyrinth, angles up toward the stars, stamping the sky with brilliant light...

In the shape of a lightning bolt.

"My friend Sadie was at an early celebration for *Dia de los Muertos* on Friday night and took the picture," Lydia explains. "Someone turned it on around six. Wasn't on for long, but isn't it the epitome of epic?"

I'm not sure she wants my stomach's answer to that—especially as its new twist illuminates what my head's already figured out. "Friday night," I repeat, attempting to keep my dread from it. "Around six."

Which meant it was nine o'clock here.

An hour after Reece yanked me free from the runaway ambulance.

Not a coincidence. I'm sure about that much. But why? The incident hadn't been a huge secret. The throng of lookie-loos in front of the Obelisk, all taking as much footage as their cells would allow, had guaranteed that much. By the time the eleven p.m. news broadcasts aired that night, speculation about "Bolt's emergence from retirement" already took up the A and B programming blocks, but that's nothing new for the gossip media. They pull that shit even when Reece just carries bags for me at the farmer's market or obliges with fans' requests for poses in the Brocade's lobby.

So is the Bolt Jolt just another fan proving their devotion with a big splash—or is this something else? Some*one* else?

Someone in cahoots with the nutcases Angelique has warned us about...who might be lying in wait around the corner even now, waiting for their moment to strike *tonight* because Friday was a bust?

And damn it, why am I in such a restless hurry to find out?

Aside from the fact that two hundred of New York's A-listers will be walking through the entrance within the next half hour? Oh, yeah—just *that* little nibble of a factoid...

"The epitome of epic, eh? Gee, Lydia, if I'd known you wanted to talk about me, I would've lingered longer at the bar."

And of course, of all the A-listers to make an early arrival...

"Well, Reece Richards, as I live and breathe."

And of all the sisters to play coy with the one man who's got me tied up in a thousand different knots...for a matching number of reasons...

"Here I am." The smile in his tone matches the one spreading across his lush mouth, which seizes my attention as if I've never beheld it before. No, it's worse because I know all the tantalizing tastes of those lips and all the wicked things they're capable of doing in return. My fantasies are only intensified by his groomed stubble, defining the angles of his jaw in all the most alluring ways. At least he's not subjecting me to his special brand of hair porn too. The trademark Reece waves are tamed beneath a lot of shiny product—for now. But none of it captures my attention like the affectionate wink he gives Lydia, all because he knows how much I appreciate his efforts to be friends with her, just before he adds in a sarcastic drawl, "Oh yes, it's me. In person. The Jolt inspiration himself."

"Oh, my God," I mumble.

"Oh, my *God*," 'Dia cries out, even earning us perplexed glances from the catering servers congregating against the opposite wall. "You saw?"

"Yeah, well..." Damn it. Even his nostril flare is beyond sexy. "No good deed goes unpunished."

"Or unthanked." Lydia rushes to him with a loud swoosh of skirts and then turns on the turbo hug, yanking him close with gusto. "And here's at least an installment payment from me, Bolt-a-matic."

"Installment?" Reece counters, layering a *pssshhh* on top of a grunt. "No way, girl. You're paid up in full." Despite the assurance, his face stays unexpectedly stern. "Though call me Bolt-a-matic again, and we may have to talk new terms... Princess Purple Pants."

For the first time in the last three days, I succumb to a full laugh—as Lydia jumps back like Reece has hit her with shock paddles. "How do you know about..." She jerks a glare at me. "How does *he* know about..."

Reece leans over, cupping his hand as if to share a secret, though tells her in a stage whisper, "*Pssst*. Boss-level life hack. Beware the guy who's sharing pillow talk with your sister."

A grimace takes over her gawk. "*Pssst* yourself, buddy. There's this thing called TMI. Learn it. Know it. Especially the *sister's pillow talk* part. But for the record, painting my pants purple was a *brilliant* idea—and I'm sure Barney the dinosaur would've agreed if Mom hadn't deep-sixed my plan to ride the bus into LA to show him."

"I was rooting for you too, Dee Dee." Using my exclusive endearment for her, formulated during the pants-painting days, comes with a diplomatic spread of my hands. "Of course, I was only *three*..."

Reece succumbs to another soft laugh while dropping his forehead onto a couple of fingers. "You two aren't the small-dreams types, are you?"

"Says the guy standing next to the girl in a glowing dress?" Lydia counters. "Who probably powered that whole thing by plugging his finger into—"

"Oh, God." I bathe her in blue light while swooping a hand over her mouth. "Remember that little thing called TMI, sibling unit?"

"But if that *wasn't* a thing here..." With matching speed and his damn ninja grace, Reece has invaded the space behind me. "Where, exactly, would my 'charging finger' get plugged—"

"*Stop.*" I land my hand on the middle of his chest as Lydia lobs a high laugh.

"And that is *so* my cue to leave." She steps away with another saucy swish of the bell skirt. "Besides, I hear a martini calling my name."

I glance at her. "Don't you have that big regional match next weekend?"

"La, la, la, la. Can't heeeaar yooouu."

"Of course you can't," I mutter as Reece circles around until he's directly facing me. "Which is why you'll be the death of me one day, *chica.*"

He snorts, but the sound isn't a laugh this time. "Well, speaking of things *not* being your death tonight..."

Without altering his stance, he extends an arm and moves two fingers in a directive motion. From the shadows at the perimeter of the room, a man takes shape. At first, I'm able to only gawk at the guy—until I realize there are a lot more like him, barely noticeable in all-black, modern-day ninja wear, stationed around the room. But that's just part one of my amazement. The second half comes as the man approaches, as silent as the darkness from which he's emerged.

"Emmalina Crist, meet Drake Gregor—point man for your fifty bodyguards tonight." As he turns to address the solemn, slender man, he slides his arm around my waist. "Gregor, this is the most important person in the room tonight."

The guard dips a fast nod. "Roger that." To me, he gives an even faster acknowledgment. "Ma'am."

"Mr. Gregor." I repeat the nod since Gregor doesn't even look down at my extended hand. "Errrmmm...those are impressive moves," I offer. "So which side of you is begotten from the ninjas? Mom or dad?"

"Neither, ma'am. I hail from something better. Scottish Highlanders."

"Whoa." I issue the reaction soon as his quiet brogue registers. "No shit."

"Thanks, Gregor." Reece taps his head back toward the shadows. "As you were."

"Affirmative." The guy returns to near-invisible status on steps more stealthy than his first approach.

"Wow," I finally manage to stammer.

"You okay?" Reece tugs me tighter, his mouth flattening and his brows hunkering.

"Yeah." I nod. "That's just...intense. If I didn't know he was there..."

"Exactly the point." His expression relaxes, turning even sexier as the DJ throws on a sultry warm-up song. Reece takes advantage of the moment by using his hold, still on my waist, to pull me into a full dancing position. Still, I dart a couple of glances around his shoulders just to make sure my eyes aren't really deceiving me.

"Incredible," I mutter. "And how long have they all been here?"

"Since they turned down the lights and made it easy for us. When you and Lydia were back in the kitchen."

"Not that we would have noticed, even if we *were* out here."

"Ahhhh." Now his lips lift into a devastating smirk. "Honorable mistress of the party begins to comprehend the ninja way."

When he steps away enough to give me a brief bow, hands pressed in prayer pose in front of him, I spurt out an enchanted laugh. The mirth, along with the knowledge that fifty men under his command are literally watching every square inch of the room, succeeds in disintegrating my tension—at least for one moment.

Well, *most* of the tension.

There's still plenty of pressure building between my legs, adding to the ache that hasn't gone away for the last two days, now rising in direct proportion to his masterful nearness. And his smoky cologne. And his touch, rubbing at the valley of awareness at the small of my back, as he pulls me close again. And, *oh yes*, even the confident grace with which he leads our romantic back-and-forth to Lana Del Rey's hypnotic croon.

To ensure I keep my own balance, I raise my hands to his shoulders, where my probing fingers find the distinct ridges of his leathers. Holy shit. *Now* I'm really done in. He's like a multi-layered man candy bar—a meaty center of Deadpool dipped in a delicious coating of James Bond. But the truth it leads me to is shaded by a thousand shades of mortification. Realizing he's come prepared like this, to face danger head-on for me, is the headiest part of my custom Reece aphrodisiac. It turns my voice into a dreamy murmur as I force words to my throat, attempting to balance the dizzying effect of his stare on every hormone I possess.

"Are there any girl ninjas on your bitchin' Bolt squad, mister?"

That unsettles his gaze for a couple of seconds. "Not tonight, if that's what you mean," he says carefully.

"You should consider it. In the future."

"Perhaps I will." His voice stays steady. He holds me tighter. "In the future."

"Yeah. You should. I mean, *I* could even be—"

"No."

"What?"

"No."

"Why?"

He kisses me into silence. Firmly. Ferociously. And for another incredible moment, the world drops away. In spite of the man's no-girl-ninjas rule, he's the only thing on the planet, in the cosmos, that matters. As our mouths mesh and mold, I bask in his passion and power and desire...in the bond that makes all the insanity worth it. That makes *him* worth it. The truth that finally, fully, feels right in my spirit...that, ironically and maybe even stupidly, I came all the way across the country to try to "find" here, in my solitude...

Only to realize that solitude wasn't the answer.

That what I was running from...wasn't him. That what I'd thought was a slip in our trust...wasn't.

That the only thing we'd lost...was this.

The compulsion that bound us to each other in the first place.

The pull, dictated by fate itself, that we're both beyond controlling.

The need beyond mere attraction. The connection beyond

lust. The energies that fuse our spirits and our souls, turning us into something pretty damn incredible. Yes, even beyond *EmRee*—though when naming us something that sounds like a ring from the land of fairies and wizards, maybe the press saw what we hadn't yet.

Our magic.

Why did it take me until now to see it? To realize that when the universe gives out something as amazing as this, a girl doesn't kick it in the teeth by running away from it, damn it.

She grabs on.

She holds tight.

Just like Reece and I do now, twining both hands into each other's.

She beholds it. And she's grateful.

Just like this amazing man does with me now, refusing to rip his stare from me.

And yeah...she would also make sure fate hears her gratitude—just like *I* do, with a throat clogged in thick emotion. "Thank God for *you*, Reece Richards."

A smile blooms on his lips. Its warmth is clearly born from places deep inside him. I'm given a good hint about those places as the broad plane of his chest heavily rises and then falls. Though the action doesn't produce words from his lips, they're already there for me—in his eyes. The silver-gray depths are fortified by the same determination and adoration they possessed two nights ago, giving me the safe emotional space in which to share the ick-factor stuff about Dad and Mom and the country club's version of "member initiation." In return, he'd given me exactly what I needed: his own honesty, despite its supreme difficulty. The disclosure about Angelique's intel regarding the Consortium—more importantly, about their plans for wreaking havoc somewhere in New York tonight. Well, their *supposed* plans. Which may or may not include *this* event...

Who the hell am I kidding? It's *Sunday*. Even in the Village, there aren't a lot of bumpin' New York parties begging for a group of batshit Dr. Moreaus to crash. If the Consortium is really going to "play" somewhere in the city tonight, they'll fuck with Reece in the doing.

And that means fucking with me.

Though I try to hide how I suddenly feel like an ant caught beneath a magnifying glass, the man sees right through my ruse. He releases my hands in order to band a stronger grip around me, despite how his voice is the textural opposite. He caresses me in verbal silk as he murmurs, "You are the most beautiful thing I've ever seen, Emmalina."

Well, what do you know. Ants can blush too.

I drop my head, encouraged that my silver shoes aren't shiny enough to capture all the blood rushing to my face. "Very nice job, Mr. Richards. Using flattery to deflect stress." I add a wry *tsk* to the crack. "Just wish I could tell you that it actually works."

"That so?" His dark slice of a tone is surpassed only by his decisive grasp beneath my chin. He uses it to compel my whole face up, to confront the blades of determination now defining every square inch of his beautiful face. *Holy shit.* It's moments like this, when he's nothing but raw man and concentrated lust, that, unbelievably, make me most afraid of him...and of what he can do to me. If the lightning fizzled from his blood tomorrow, this would still be how things are between us. Potent. Powerful. Terrible. Incredible. "Because I wouldn't know."

"Wouldn't know...what?" I'm lost in the pull of him,

struggling to remember even my own name at the moment.

"About flattery." The edges of his own words are frayed, like pesky afterthoughts to what he's feeling. "Because this *isn't* that," he utters. "This is my truth, sweetheart. My soul. The core of me, Emma...that *you* rule. That you will always rule." His eyes hone tighter on me. The gorgeous twists of his mouth compress into a strange line. "What is it?" he finally utters. "You don't believe me?"

"I *do* believe you." And with that whispered confession, it's impossible to keep all the clichés of my reaction at bay. My gown's bodice isn't just glowing anymore but a victim of my heaving breasts. I moisten my lips. Stab my teeth into my lower lip. "Can't you tell?" I rasp. "I'm a walking cheesy romance chapter here, and that's only the stuff you can see from the outside. You think I'm doing all this on purpose, mister?"

From my periphery, I'm acutely conscious of him watching all the reactions I just mentioned, plus the "surfacy" greetings I now wave to some of the party's early arrivals. He waits, with nearly eerie silence, until I'm able to turn fully toward him again—and then moves in, with deftly sensual skill, and tucks his lips against the curve of my ear.

"Only the stuff I can see from the outside?" His hands, now framing my waist, tug me closer toward the formidable frame of his. More of his perfect aromas surround me. The starch in his shirt. The luxury pomade in his hair. The crispness of his soap. "That implies lots of...stuff...on the inside," he prompts. "Like what, little bunny? The pulse of your sweet, tight tunnel? The clench of your willing pussy? The wild race of your incredible mind, as your body surges to catch up with your fantasies?"

I slide my hand farther up his shoulder until my fingers collide with his neck—into which I dig my fingertips. It's only fair play, since I'm now biting my lip so hard, I'm shocked there's no blood. "*You*, Mr. Richards, are a wicked, wanton, evil man."

"Guilty as charged, Miss Crist." He lets a hiss erupt from his teeth as I make deeper scores into his neck below his collar line.

I make sure he continues to feel my touch as I work more fingers inside, over the neckline of his leathers. "Oh, yes. Very wicked. And very, *very* naughty."

I deliberately stamp the last of it with more serious accusation. In return, his posture stiffens. "So you expected me to show up tonight without being prepared to protect you?"

"Of course not." I thread my fingertips up to play with the silky ends of his hair. I want to paw a lot more—and would dare any red-blooded woman to resist doing otherwise. "I just expected you to show up in leathers that weren't my favorites."

Now he gets a turn at looking like the verbal shock paddles have hit. "You have...favorites?"

"Yeah." My tone implies the *duh*. "And *this* is the set."

He's still dazed. "I didn't know you had favorites."

I seesaw my head. "Yeah. I have favorites."

"But you hate all my leathers."

"I don't hate *any* of your leathers, Reece."

He huffs. Pretty loud. "But—"

"I don't hate your leathers. It's kind of hard to hate head-to-toe black leather, especially when it's custom-fitted for *this* body, okay?"

He preens. Just a little. Clears his throat before shooting back, "So why—"

"I don't hate your leathers," I reiterate. "I simply hate what you've had to *do* in those things, and I *really* hate it that you've come prepared to do the same thing tonight, but I don't hate the damn leathers."

His smirk is immediate. And sexy as hell. "You even have favorites."

Soft laugh. "Yeah. I even have favorites."

He doesn't surrender the smile. Or his hold. "Does that mean you have favorites of other things too?"

"Other things?" I wish my puzzlement came off as more authentic—but his seductive tone doesn't make that possible. The best I can do is a wide stare with batting lashes and getting out on a giggle, "Why, what 'other things' do you *mean*, Mr. Richards?"

"Hmmm." He vibrates it into my neck while nuzzling the sensitive valley beneath my ear. "Maybe you need a demonstration, Miss Crist."

"Maybe you're right." My sigh accompanies that one, feeling just as right as the words themselves...

Until it's cut short by a quip from an all-too-familiar source.

"Sheez Louise. Cute took some crack tonight and pooped these two out."

My fuming groan is mixed with Reece's laughing snort, meaning he earns the first jab of my glare. "You know you're just encouraging her, right? And that as my big sister she knows a thousand *more* ways to torment me?"

His laugh gains a lusty edge. "Bet they're not as interesting as *my* ways."

As I debate whether to shut him down or let him prove that, hopefully shutting *Lydia* down, she dares to let out another long giggle—that's joined by a heartier laugh. And once more, a recognizable sound.

All too recognizable.

Shit, shit, shit.

In horror, I realize *that* part spilled out of me too—while attempting to untangle myself from Reece's arms, keep my bodice respectably in place, and plaster on a respectable smile for his father. Nothing like a multitasking fail. Fortunately, the man from whom Reece gets his arresting gaze and proud stance is already chuckling at my profanity dump and slanting a lopsided grin he probably called his "Billy Idol sneer" in his younger days. The man's still attempting to pull off the Idol spikes with his cropped light-brown hair, buzzed short on the sides but pomaded on top with something probably called The Stiff Stuff or Hold Me Tight, Baby. I have to admit, the 'do was an eye-popper when I first met him, but with his take-charge personality and his prominent features, the hair is a natural fit for him.

"Cute took some crack." He wags a finger at Lydia, smirking wider. "That's a good one, little Lydia. May have to steal that for the next time *this* one shows up at the front nine in her newest designer togs." With a telling snicker, he ushers forward a woman with hair more closely matching Reece's color, her trim figure outfitted in a dark-violet evening gown that perfectly brings out her sea-green eyes.

"Mr. Richards." I step forward, leaning in to exchange light air kisses with the man in his trendy, shawl-collar tux. "Thank you for coming tonight. It means the world that you're here."

"Well, it means the world that you included us." Though he continues to smile, his gaze narrows with meaning. "But if you don't start calling me Lawson, lectures *will* be in order."

The second that's out—actually, for the ten seconds

before *that*—I can physically feel the rise of Reece's tension behind me. But the human nuclear reactor isn't going to sway me, especially with his dad trying this hard at familial détente. "Well, I happen to enjoy your lectures"—and it's the truth, because the man is smart and I've actually learned a few things from them—"but tonight is for fun, so you win, *Lawson.*" I turn to the woman who's been filling the time by keenly studying me. "And you must be the woman I've heard so much about." I extend a hand. "It's so nice to meet you at last, Mrs. Richards."

"Theresa," she insists, returning my smile with a gracious one of her own and resembling Reece even more in the doing. "But please, call me Trixie. All my friends do."

"Of course, Trixie." On any other woman, the name might teeter dangerously close to being paired with a roller derby queen, but Trixie Richards's refined style would turn even the word *shnozzle* into something regal and gorgeous.

And as long as we're on the subject of regal, the sound of a pair of steps behind me brings on the royal resonance, despite the nuclear cloud that's towed along for the journey. With his hands at my waist and his jaw in my hair, Reece intones, "Mom...and Dad." I feel his courtly nod against the top of my head. "You're both looking well."

"Thank you, Reece Andrew." Lawson dips an equally respectful nod. "As are you." With the rise of his head, there's a discernible difference to his chiseled face...factors I've certainly never seen there before. Deeper crinkles at the edges of his eyes. And an energy inside those eyes, full of emotions I can't interpret. I only know that beholding them adds a layer of emotion to my chest and throat and makes me want to grab Reece and force-fling him at the man. A fast glance to Trixie ensures she's on the same page. Even Lydia finally picks up how Reece is vibing the man and swoops back in with her can-we-fix-it-yes-we-can gusto.

"Heeeyyy. Why don't we all grab a drink before the masses converge on those poor bartenders?"

"I'd love a drink," I pipe in, meaning every word.

"Oh, me too," Trixie adds.

Reece doesn't give up an inch of his tension. "I don't think—"

"That's an excellent idea." Lawson, taking his lip tilt to full "Rebel Yell" status, even nods a few times as if the song plays in his head, spurring him on. I join Trixie in a laugh at the behavior, since we both recognize it as normal, but it's not her or me for whom he reaches as we all walk to the nearest bar, themed for the night in a wraparound material of gold prismatic shapes, backlighted so it glows. It's a perfect descriptor, since I feel like personally glowing—beyond the gown—when Lawson wraps an arm around Reece's shoulder, saying something too quiet for us to hear. Whatever it is, I approve, since it elicits an instant laugh from his son.

"Emmalina?" Trixie's query yanks me out of my musing. "Everything okay? Is the dress zapping places it shouldn't?"

Lydia leans in to quip, "Or where Reece *should* be?"

"Oh, my goodness." Trixie covers her titter with her gloved hand.

"You're being kind." I smile at Reece's mother and stab a glower at my sister. "But fortunately, I don't have to be—especially when it seems my sister left her filter behind in California."

By this point, I've dug into my clutch and pulled out my phone, turning it into a perfect spanking paddle for Lydia's toned backside. As she yelps from the smack, Trixie succumbs to another giggle. "It's all right," she tells us with a carefree wave of a hand. "Really. I have *two* sisters, and to this day we'd never dream of kidding with each other like that." Her mirth ebbs into a wistful sigh. "If video killed the radio star, then country clubs killed the humanity of every trust fund kid in the eighties."

Instinct prompts me to find Lydia with my gaze—where, in the ocean-blue depths of her own, I confront a surprise that *wasn't* one of the twists for which I've tried to prepare tonight. The bond to what Trixie's just said. At least the important parts. The stuff not really requiring a trust fund or an eighties adolescence to know. The murder of a kid's soul, country club style.

Holy crap.

She knows about Mom and Dad too. She's been carrying the exact same burden on her heart, all these years...

We're going to talk. The message broadcasts from her face at the same time I send it out to her. For a moment, I'm tidal-waved by warm emotion. Though I hate the understanding that's brought us here, I feel more connected to Lydia than we've been in years. She's grown into a pretty cool person—making me hope our talk won't consist entirely of bonding over our parents and their secret lovers.

The wave jostles me back to the moment, as well as the initial reason I pulled out my cell. While punching up my camera, I murmur to Trixie, "I'm hoping to lock down this memory forever."

She scoots closer, looking at the shot of our men that I've lined up from behind. On the screen, Lawson and Reece stand together at the bar, leaning toward each other, their bold profiles illuminated from below by the luminescent bar top. I wait for one more second as Reece keeps explaining something to his father and Lawson nods in return, listening intently. I need to savor it for myself before capturing it with a click.

"Ah!" Trixie exclaims as soon as I get the snap. "What's the expression they use for those? No filter needed?"

"You're exactly right." I grab her by the hand and hold on tight, letting the burn of tears brim at the corners of my eyes. "But filters really aren't needed when dreams are coming true."

Trixie swallows, clearly wrestling with some sap of her own. As she pulls in a long but happy breath, she shows off the dimples that Reece inherited, along with the uncanny ability to pull her emotional shit back together while continuing to look a hundred kinds of fabulous. "What do you say we go and be a part of that dream too?"

I scoop my elbow through hers, basking in the jubilance of my grin as Lydia completes the chain on Trixie's other side. "I say that's a damn fine idea."

CHAPTER SIX

REECE

"All right, all right, all right. Is everyone on the party train now?"

Dad's newest pop culture reference has even Mom on the verge of a reactionary groan, but she holds back with a fast eye roll and a wink my way. I smile in return, admitting to a strange wash of bashfulness. The last time she looked at me with such gushing affection, I'd been a boy—before my teens and my rebellion had hit, before my college years and *that* rebellion, and then the grim acceptance, somewhere along the line, that I'd simply become the official family screw-up. And though it's true the Brocade has been shattering sales records, my parents are too seasoned to be swayed by a few glowing accounting ledgers. Another force has entered their galaxy, hitting with enough brilliance to alter their very orbit.

Not just the sizzle of a Bolt.

The bright perfection of a star.

A star named Emmalina.

It's easy enough for me to identify since she's altered my own heart's trajectory, my entire life's course. And I realize it like an epiphany brought by high-end acid—only even better because I'm going to actually remember this—that this is where that route has led. That destiny, in its grand and crazy sagacity, laid out every single step of the path that brought me to this moment. With a long, deep breath, I acknowledge that higher wisdom, using the pause to send out a silent message of my own.

I hear you. I see this. All of it. And I'll remember it.

I promise.

"Hey." The star in the glowing dress hooks an arm around mine, becoming an ideal addition to my reverie. "Everything okay, hot stuff?"

I loop my hand around hers and then buss the top of her head. "Everything couldn't be more perfect, sweetheart."

Dad strolls forward, purposely taking center position in our little gathering—to which Foley has added himself within the last minute, stepping in next to Lydia with a drink that sprouts a yellow paper umbrella. Unsure those things are even legal in the Village, I keep my horror a secret and refocus on Dad.

"Everybody have a libation?" he asks, sweeping a confirming glance around the little circle. "Ah. Excellent. Because I have an interesting announcement...that will deserve several toasts."

A glass of Scotch is passed from the bar to a cocktail server and then to me. A quick sniff confirms it's the same high-end Macallan that Foley and I enjoyed in the limo. I look up in time to see Dad watching my small smile of approval and nodding my way with the same worldly endorsement.

In that split second, another revelation slams.

The old man didn't send the limo to get us as an olive branch.

He'd sent it as a real show of respect.

Respect that grows in his demeanor now as he follows

through on the nod by pivoting completely in my direction, raising his own tumbler of the amber liquid. "It gives me pleasure beyond compare to tell you all that of the twenty-three hotels in the Richards Resorts portfolio, the Hotel Brocade of Los Angeles led the pack in third-quarter statistics on every front. Occupancy, RevPAR, overall earnings, guest satisfaction, and even *employee* satisfaction... Son, your property led the entire pack."

I sure as hell hope the universe doesn't have another epiphany to drop now, because I'm too dazed to notice and too happy to care. But oddly, feeling too guilty to join everyone else as they take their congratulatory quaffs.

"Dad." I move forward, meeting my father's open admiration and fighting the sensation that I must be dreaming and that, any second, the dream will change, turning everyone into chimpanzees staring at me in my underwear. "I couldn't think of a better place, or way, in which to be told this—but I'm going to hold off on taking this drink until I can enjoy it with the whole team back in LA." I look back to Emma, who gives my decision a teary-eyed, if adorably awkward, thumbs-up. "I didn't work half as hard as they did for this honor. They deserve to celebrate it too."

I'm not surprised to end the statement by holding my breath. Despite whatever new "thing" he's attempting to do with his hair, "Stiff-Nuts Richards" has more than deserved his nickname from me in the past. If he laughs and calls me a sappy wuss now, then he does. I've been through much worse in the last couple of years.

"I had a feeling you'd say that, son."

Annnnd, here it comes.

"And actually, I'd hoped you'd say that."

Annnnd, just as I thought—

"Huh?" I recover with a frenetic shake of my head, hoping the marbles on my brain's puzzle board are knocked back into their correct slots. "I— I mean, excuse me, sir?"

Dad smiles with so much empathy, I wonder if he's been bingeing *Family Ties* in his old age. "A good leader knows when to make all the right decisions," he states evenly. "But a great leader empowers his *team* to make those decisions."

With more emotion washing over her face, Emma says to him, "Well then, your son is the greatest of them all, Lawson."

"A truth I couldn't be happier to agree with, my girl." The smile he gives her is an equal gift to me, and I hope I've dug my senses far enough out of their haze to show him so, even as he clears his throat once more, sliding all the way back into his shell of Richards Corp's CEO. "Which leads me to a picture-perfect segue—in which I can confirm, to all of you and to the world, that the rumors are true about Richards Resorts opening a new flagship property in the heart of Paris, France." With Emma's happy gasp as accompaniment, the man closes the gap between us and reaches to clap a hand to my shoulder. "Naturally, I want my best man to lead the opening of that hotel." He pauses for a second, as if making sure his meaning has sunk in—probably a good thing, since *I'm* not entirely sure it has. "Will you do it, Reece?" he asks quietly. "As my personal emissary?"

I'm still stunned into silence. Which also might be a good thing, since the women are happy taking over on event commentary now. As their *oh my God*s are woven in and out of discussion about every perfect thing about *la Paris*, my mind fixates on every astonishing—and amazing—and terrifying—impact of Dad's not-so-little bomb.

He wants to move me up to the family's version of the Big Show.

As his emissary.

One of the most significant steps of my life.

In the city where Angelique La Salle first led me to my biggest downfall.

The daze doesn't leave me, even as the crowd thickens and the gala shifts into higher gear. It still hovers as we take our seats for dinner, meaning the pumpkin soup and hand-baked bread may as well be toddlers' snack puffs. The synchronicity of the comparison isn't lost. I'm suspended in limbo like a kid, feeling like I've been invited to eat at the adults' table but unsure what's in half the dishes or which utensil to use with them. Which is fucking ridiculous because I *know* how to eat, damn it. If I use a steak knife on the butter, doesn't it work just as well? All the circumstances of tonight happen to serve up *that* answer the best. Why am I sitting here, battling imposter syndrome about leading a staff of housekeepers, butlers, engineers, and marketing execs, when Foley and I are, at this very second, responsible for a small *army* of highly trained spies, soldiers, and—

A clatter breaks into my consciousness. The sound of silverware dropped onto china.

My bread plate.

Onto which I've just let my soup spoon fall.

Out of my stunned, motionless hand. Which matches the rest of my body, now covered in sheets of shocked ice, as my gaze races down one entire wall of the room. Then the other. Then back again, unwilling to believe what I see.

More bizarrely, what I don't see.

"My men."

I grit it out with vicious emphasis on both syllables. It makes the server for our table pause, almost overfilling Dad's wine glass. It also stops Emma midsentence during a conversation with Lydia. She turns from her sister just as Mom pivots from Dad, wearing nearly the same mix of confusion and worry on her face. "Reece? What're you—"

"The men." I jerk my head Foley's way—where his answering gape ensures that my nervous system is headed for another iceberg. "Where the hell did the men go?"

EMMA

It all takes just ten seconds.

From a paradise of a night to its freakish, hellish opposite. Ten seconds.

I cling to the counting as if my life depends on it. My sanity sure as hell does. Whatever I'm calling sanity at the moment.

It takes two seconds to interpret what Reece's query to Sawyer actually means. One more to realize that they're both clueless about the answer. Then, as I peer more carefully into the shadows around the room—one more second—so am I.

In the next three, both men lurch to their feet.

In the three following that, with all the lights in the room flung back to full power, the full scope of hell is revealed.

Ten seconds.

Before screams erupt across the room—as the downed members of Reece's team are revealed, bleeding and moaning right at the stations in which they were first posted. Okay, *most* of them. Five of the ninjas, still dressed in their black jumpsuits but now sporting Zorro-like masks that cover everything but their mouths and chins, team up to control the crowd's panic.

A sixth and seventh have been assigned only to Sawyer and Reece. The pair orders them to sit against the wall, making short work of zip-tying their hands and ankles.

After two seconds of seeing them like that—of seeing *Reece* like that—my protein bar lunch and tonight's champagne threaten to rush up from my stomach. I force the sick back down as one of the Zorros strides to the center of the stage. In a corner behind him, the five members of the band have collected into a trembling huddle.

"Ladies and gentlemen." He stretches his hands out like an evangelical preacher. "We apologize for interrupting your meal, but let's face it—a lot of you were glad we stopped these guys from the blasphemy they were committing on that Journey song, yeah? No?" He sends a snarl across the throng. "Ah, come *on*."

Under the table, 'Dia fishes for my hand. Her clench is painful, but I'm grateful for it. She gives me a life ring in the midst of my nerves, nausea, disbelief, and fear. I seize her just as hard in return while becoming severely aware of everyone's eyes on me, which would be the case even without the glowing dress. That's what comes along with being the name at the top of the program.

A program of an event that won't be taking place now.

An event that's become a disaster—because I refused to listen to Reece. Because I shut down on him the second he said he was delivering *Angelique's* news. And because of *that*, pulled the same emotional trigger that had shot us in the knees to begin with.

I'd cut off all my trust.

My trust *in him*.

Now, because of that, nearly fifty men have been seriously

wounded—*oh my God, don't let any of them die!*—and Reece is one of their bound hostages, a situation providing me with another bizarre distraction from my own terror. With eerie ease, my mind finds its sole remaining tunnel of logic and quickly sets up a base camp of questions there.

Why are the Consortium's minions settling on binding Reece with basic plastic ties?

Why is *he* putting up with that treatment?

How did the Consortium recruit so many traitors from Reece's handpicked men?

If they really wanted to get to Reece, why haven't they just hauled him out of the room and then shot the rest of us?

I'm saved from having to contemplate any of the answers when a sharp movement from across the room makes everyone gasp. Karcher Crawley, the magnate behind one of the country's biggest hamburger chains, has punched to his feet so fast that his chair clatters behind him.

"Cut the crap, you filthy hooligans." The man's castigation is as in-your-face as his chain's TV commercials.

The Zorro on stage cocks his rifle to one shoulder. "Ahhhh. A fool with some *cajones*, after all." Tilts his head with blatant arrogance. "What can I do for you, Gramps?"

"Besides fucking off?"

"Karcher!" A woman dressed in a cream sheath encrusted with crystals and pearls yanks at his elbow. "Please, dear!"

Crawley snorts as if she hasn't spoken. "You can spare the cocky theatrics and tell us what you want, assholes."

"Hey." One of the gunmen, stationed nearby on the floor, pumps his rifle while approaching them. "*Language*, man. There are ladies and sensibilities present."

"Sensibilities?" Mrs. Crawley barks it with twice the

venom her husband brandished. "Don't you dare stand there and preach about sensibilities, you animal!"

The rifleman halts. Dips his head to an acutely curious angle. "*Animal?*"

"You weren't concerned about my 'sensibilities' when you killed those men!"

"*Killed?*" The dispute comes from Zorro Number One, who leans over the lip of the stage with a glower that refreezes my blood. "Whoa. Hold up that garbage truck, Trashy Trudy. We're thieves, not murderers—though my friend Mr. Happy Stick there does enjoy picking himself off a kneecap or two when it comes to mouthy sons of bitches." As he backs off the edge, he grabs a microphone stand and swivels it out, Mick Jagger style. "Show 'em, Happy."

At that, the next seconds go by like horrific hours.

I'm conscious of the single rifle shot, cracking the air like a steel fork on a cement egg, setting free a yolk of screams and panic and terror. My filter is fuzzier as Karcher Crawley goes down, blood spattering across his place setting as he does. His wife shrieks hysterically, slumping to the floor next to him.

After that, my mind is like a window in a windstorm, flapping open in harsh spurts, letting in only glimpses of clear comprehension...

"Stay calm, stay calm..."

"...will all stay alive if you obey us..."

"...put everything into the bags we pass...watches, necklaces, rings, phones..."

But when the collection bag is dumped in front of me, I only stare at it. I'm as frozen as a heathen in church, clueless about what to do. Though terror has turned my limbs into ice floes, there's another force at work inside me, breaking up the frozen sheets into useless chunks.

That force is rage.

Raw. Pure. Potent.

Spurring a voice from deep in my gut. A voice that screams with such a shrill pitch, the glass in the window of my consciousness is completely shattered.

This isn't right. This isn't fair.

My senses roar with it, fighting my *common* sense, turning me into an unwitting rebel for its relentless cause.

Its *stupid* cause.

If I get myself shot because of an obstinate devotion to justice, Reece will take out half of New York's power grid, not to mention every one of these assholes. If I think having a superhero boyfriend is hairy, it likely pales next to having a convicted murderer boyfriend.

"Hey." The prompt comes with a painful jab at my shoulder, but the barrel of a high-powered rifle isn't supposed to feel like a love tap. Though my mind recognizes the full reality of that truth, I stare up the long tube with a strange sense of wonder, as if the broken glass on my mental window has started reflecting prisms. "Hey," the gunman barks again. "Glow-and-Blow Barbie. Your jewelry and cell phone. In the bag. Now."

I blink a couple of times but still don't move.

"Em," Lydia grits out. "Damn it. Listen to him!"

"No." The objection is nearly as shocking as the gun still aimed at my face—considering its mind-blowing source. But sure enough, Lawson Richards pushes forward, arms propped on the chair arms behind him, as if he's ready to bust into Billy Idol throat kicks at the bastards. "Stand your ground, Emmalina. You *know* who has your back now."

I can't help but peer hard at him. Stand my ground? Like this is a *choice* I'm making?

"Fuck it to hell, you wankstain." Another member of the Zorro posse rushes over—though not without his frustration giving away his thick brogue, making me nearly swallow my tongue. "That fucker is right. You *do* know who has her back, don't you?"

The "wankstain" flips the end of the rifle away from my face. Peers at me with beady-eyed interest before drawling, "Hold up. I *do* know her."

He chuffs his friend's way, giving me the perfect chance to study him closer. *Damn it.* I was too busy fighting all the butterflies Reece first brought with him to pay too much attention to any part of Gregor's face, let alone just his jaw and neck. Aside from the distinctive brogue, I wouldn't be able to tell him apart from anyone else in a police lineup—until now, when I really memorize the man from the nose down. Blunt chin, thin lips, and hair the color of watered-down beer, from what I can tell of the strands he hasn't tucked up into the head covering.

"Yeah, *yeah,*" the gunman exclaims. "I got it now! She's banging that guy. He's in all those Hollywood gossip rags my old lady buys. Used to be some hotshot playboy, and then he came out as Bolt, but then he *wasn't* Bolt..." He shakes his head. "Yeah, whatever. Now he's just some uptight suit." As he sidles a little closer, the confused twist on his lips gives way to a slimy smirk. "I bet he has enough flow so this little one can take care of her hot little bod, though." He shoves Lydia's chair away so hard, it tips over—but when I instinctively lunge for her, he stops me with a hand at the base of my neck. "Where *you* going, baby?" he murmurs. "I mean, maybe I'll let you keep your own stuff...if you want to barter something else, instead..."

"Billy." Unbelievably, I'm thankful for the ringleader up on the stage now, growling at his distracted mutt. "What the fuckin' hell?"

"Jesus, brother. Take a chill. I'm just having a little fun." Wankstain Billy steps back but repositions the rifle so the barrel catches on the dip in my dress's bodice. As he pulls, the fabric gives until my nipples are nearly exposed. "Who wouldn't want to know what it'd feel like to be inside the pussy where Bolt has been?"

As soon as the words slither out of him, time gets another readjustment—only on this round, everything's sped to double tempo instead of slowed down.

First blink—the gun is gone.

Second blink—so is Billy.

Third and fourth blinks—watching the guy squeal from where he's been hoisted, ten feet up and bouncing atop an invisible electric pulse as a second beam throws a pair of zip ties around his wrists and fuses them shut. Only then is he released, and he crashes down in the spot from which Lydia's just risen. Wankstain Billy now finds himself with a five-inch stiletto in his crotch.

"So much as sneeze," 'Dia purrs, "and your little olives will be the garnish for my next martini."

I refrain from joining in her delighted giggle to spend blinks five, six, and seven whipping my head around—

To have blinks eight, nine, and ten consumed by my joyful gasp. Then my conflicted tears.

The majority of my emotion is pride. The stuff deluges me, welling and spilling at the sight of my amazing man stretching to his full height after retracting the pulse with which he took

Billy down. As he rises back up, Reece shrugs off the last pieces of his convertible tuxedo while sweeping his attention to the front of the room. His boots scorch the cement floor as he swings that direction too. His profile, now embellished by a huge chunk of his hair escaping the pomade, is defined by undaunted fury and inescapable purpose.

So yeah, I'll admit it. Blinks eleven and twelve are wasted on a moment of pure lust. That's before the tears take over. The other fraction of my emotion, backed up by the awful stabs in my gut, as full realization blares in my conscience.

Ladies and gentlemen, Bolt has officially left retirement.

"Fucking. Hell."

As if my supposition needs more endorsement, the snarls from the ringleader do just that.

"Should've thought about that before your dog got off his leash." Reece backs up the riposte by flinging one of his hands like there really is a dog leash in it—if leashes came in lengths of electrical pulses that extend over fifty feet and can lasso a grown man on the first try. But maybe they do, since the Zorro on the stage howls like a German Shepherd that's had its chew toy snatched away. And then Reece yanks his arm back, toppling Zorro onto the stage. "Shame, shame, shame," Reece growls, crackling the air anew as he adds a second electrical pulse, using both the tethers to drag the asshole down the stage steps. "This is New York, buddy. You've *got* to clean up after your dog."

"Fu-Fu-Fuck y-y-you!" The guy's baritone comes out in jarring pieces as he bounces down the steps, though his defiance becomes a girlish squeal as Reece flings him against a catering cart, burying him in at least twenty-five bowls of pumpkin soup. He continues whimpering as Sawyer—fried

ANGEL PAYNE

zip ties clinging to his legs—swoops in to hogtie the jerk using
lengths of catering cellophane. Thankfully, Sawyer pulls out
more of the stuff to wrap around the asshole's mouth too.

"Holy crap," Lydia breathes.

"R-Reece?" Trixie stammers.

"Fucking. Amazing," Lawson utters.

The exclamations hit the air as Reece whirls to confront
new adversaries: the pair of Zorros who originally bound
Sawyer and him. The jerks yell like Apaches on the war path—
until Reece slashes his arm sideways, turning the air itself into
one hell of a cock-blocker. Both the criminals endo over the
barrier, groans cut short as they splat to the floor. I succumb
to a guilty laugh, along with the rest of the room, as the party
guests at the nearest table swarm the asshole pancakes and
keep them subdued until Sawyer can make his way over with
the industrial-strength cellophane.

But the levity is short-lived. The last members of the
Zorro posse, Gregor included, have now realized just how
fucked their life choice was for tonight, and are scrambling to
get out while they're still ahead. Hoisting the bags of loot they
have managed to collect, they race for the building's rear exit—

Until four white-blue lightning spears sizzle over
everyone's head and then dip and stab straight into the fleeing
crooks.

All four of them are halted midstride, impounded in place
like kids who've played in the sorcerer's yard and been caught.
The long-distance Taser charges, courtesy of my boyfriend's
four outstretched fingers, haven't even rendered them
unconscious. They're standing. Breathing. Even talking, if
their terrified whimpers qualify as that. The only thing they're
not doing is moving.

Once more, my tablemates all react at once.

"Holy *shit*," Lydia chokes.

"*Reece?*" Trixie repeats.

"Un. Real." Lawson looks ready to pump a fist.

This time, I add to their commentary. "That's...new." But regrettably, it doesn't make my old emotions easier to handle. The second half of why tears still brim from my eyes and roll down my face. Along with the pride that swells from watching my man kick bad guy ass, times seven, in just as many seconds, there's a new admission I have to face. A fact that's as real as the wizardly ways he channels the air in this room—in front of two hundred gaping witnesses.

Bolt really *has* left retirement.

And won't be able to return again.

The chaos in the room only becomes a crazier storm as the cops arrive on the scene. Their entrance, perceived by some in the room as more bad guys instead of good, incites a new round of screams. As soon as that's over, a fire alarm gets tripped because the catering staff were forced to abandon their positions before food prep was complete. The stench of burned steaks tangles with the odor of toasted electricity, especially after Reece releases the four near-escapees into NYPD's custody.

Somehow, I manage to push to my feet—only to be tackle-hugged by my sister, who looks energized and terrified at once. After her mouth opens and closes a couple of times, she finally blurts, "That was *epic*!"

Seeing that 'Dia and her endorphins have temporarily fascinated Lawson and Trixie, I seize the chance to sprint to Reece—and am glad I have. Before I get to his side, he's reaching for me. Once I'm there, a slew of alarming observations hit.

He's whiter than the wall. Breathing like a winded bull. I swear I can hear his teeth grating the enamel from each other.

But none of it prepares me for what I confront in his eyes. *Holy shit. His eyes.*

"*Reece.*" I can barely raise it above a whisper. "Dear God..."

He shakes his head, silencing me. Which is probably good, because if I speak much more, I'll scream for a paramedic. Not that they'd be much help. What kind of diagnosis would they treat? His pupils are nothing but pinpoints. And his irises—his lush, mesmerizing, gorgeous gray irises—are now stripped of all color. Surrounding them, in the parts of his gaze that should be white, are areas that resemble plasma balls that pulse with blue lightning in time to his breathing.

As more first responders fill the room, he starts to sway. Then the tremors start. He clenches his whole body to hide them, but since I'm now jammed into the crook of his arm and halfway supporting him, there's no way I *don't* feel them.

"Wh-What do you need?" I plead it while bracing my hand to his chest. "Should I get the paramedics here now and—"

"No." He all but seethes it, his nostrils pumping. "No paramedics."

"All right. Then I'll make them transport you to the hosp—"

"No!" He grabs the side of my face. "Lights. Needles. Exam tables. *No hospital.*"

"Then *what*?" My voice breaks as my heart cracks. He did what he came here to do—kept me and every person in this room safe from the hit Angelique foretold—but at what cost? His powers? His sanity? His *life*? "Please, Reece," I rasp. "I don't know what to do. I don't know what you need!"

With a ponderous grunt, he pushes closer to me. Gathers

me close with one hand digging into my shoulder and the other twisting my hair so tight, several hair pins pop out and ping across the floor. They dance on the cement like a bunch of mocking fairies, and I instantly want to murder them.

Until Reece bores his gaze into me, surreal and violent. Then clutches me close, almost kissing me with his guttural plea.

"You. I need *you*, Emmalina."

CHAPTER SEVEN

REECE

Before the words are finished on my lips, I pray that she understands. That she sees why I never showed her this side of Bolt. That I wasn't just afraid of how *she'd* react—but because I'd never had the courage to fully face it *myself.* Who wants to think of themselves as a human electrical generator with no place to spill the rest of their freak show power surge? As a mutant who's just routed the bad guys but is now a disgusting gargoyle in his own right, ready to take off someone's head because his blood refuses to stop boiling...because that blood starts to collect in the worst place in his body? In the most painful pair of receptacles...

And yes, thank *fuck*, she knows that part. More incredibly, she understands it. I see it in her urgent nod and feel it in the way she wraps a hand to the back of my neck in return and as her gaze flares from her own swell of awakened lust. As much as I crave to kiss her, I don't. Just the effort of being this close to her, feeling her breath on my face and inhaling her honey-sweet smell, is nearly enough to unravel the few threads of self-control I still have left.

"Okay," she whispers after a few seconds that feel like five fucking hours. "Okay. I understand." With her other hand, she grabs the side of my face. "Just hold on for me another minute, baby, okay?"

Unbelievably, I manage to nod without fully mauling her. Christ, she smells so good. And the glow of her skin above the gown's glowing bodice... My mouth waters, thinking of how good it must taste...

"Hurry," I growl as she drops her hand into mine and twines our fingers—but that's the only command I'm capable of. Fortunately, she knows that too. With a loud *shoosh* of her skirts and a needy groan from deep in her throat, she starts yanking me toward a narrow stairway to the left of the kitchen doors.

"Em!"

We both stop, gritting mutual profanities, as the distinctive voice whips through the rest of the chaos. But Emma doesn't turn. *Thank God.*

"Not now, Dee Dee."

"But the police have a billion quest—"

"I said *not now.*"

The ferocity in her voice has to be one of the sexiest sounds I've ever heard. Coupled with my unique view of her ass, even buried underneath the five billion layers of tulle and lights and crinolines, I'm half a second away from breaking my promise to her. I can't hold on. My blood is screaming like a thousand lusty savages, and my nerve endings are the innocents they've just scalped. I'm raw. Raging. An electric storm trapped in a man's body.

Where the hell is she taking me?

And for fuck's sake, how much longer will it take to get there?

Around a tight corner to the right. Another to the left. Past two rooms holding shit that looks like Christmas decorations and wedding props, until a closed door appears before us. There's a security pin pad on it, and when Emma frantically punches in the code, it buzzes with infuriating denial.

"Shit!" she mutters and then forces down a calming breath.

Her second try yields an approving ding that has to be the *second* best thing I've heard tonight.

We tumble into the room, a dressing area from the looks of the wardrobe bags, accessory trunks, makeup satchels, and hair product strewn everywhere. Not that I notice or care about any of it, beyond making sure I don't knock Emma into something dangerous as I whirl her around and claim her mouth in a harsh, ruthless, tongue-filled kiss. She parts for me with a feral whine, stabbing her tongue out to be used, sucked, laved, and dominated by mine. At once, our passion spikes like some damn fire plume from a rock concert, searing us both until we're breaking apart, gasping for air past the consuming flames.

But I'm only getting started.

I need more. So much more.

Emma sees it. Knows it. As I step back toward her, I even wonder if the damn woman has climbed inside my mind and foreseen my intent, with her back arching so perfectly as I descend both hands, my electrified fingertips slicing open the front of her bodice.

She gasps.

I groan.

Her bared breasts are ripe fruit beyond compare. Full and firm and succulent, each centered with a beautiful, puckered areola supporting a strawberry-colored nipple all but begging to be touched. I lift my hand, half my mind already feeling her flesh warming beneath my palm and seeing her tight peak getting redder as I pinch it...

Until the glow of my fucking fingertips pierces my entrancement.

And I grit out a new curse before dropping my hand into a fist.

"Reece." She moves forward, grabbing at my arm.

I resist, releasing a low growl.

"*Please.*"

I drill a damning look down at her. She's defiant, pushing in until her chest brushes mine. "I need to fuck you, Emma, not brand you."

My words bring new heat to her gaze. Her nipples pebble against my chest. "What if I want both?"

Fuck.

She had to go there. And even though my brain expected her to, my traitor of a body didn't. Just the thought of really doing it, imprinting her silken skin with my burning touch, my balls become time bombs, my cock their throbbing fuse.

I resist the lure the only way I know how. By gripping the tatters of her bodice, twisting in tight, and using the torque to spin her around, facing away from me.

"You don't always get what you want, Velvet." As I snarl it, I lift her voluminous skirts. She lets out a soft yelp, the vehemence of my move propelling her forward over the armrest of an overstuffed chair.

"Wh-What about...what I n-need?"

I've sliced away one spine of the dress's crinoline cage. As my fingers sear through another, I utter, "*That* can be arranged."

The light strings attached to the huge contraption begin

to sputter and die—though now I'm capable of providing my own light in the hunt for my ultimate treasure. In addition to the glow from my fingers, there's a luminescent drop at the tip of my newly freed dick. I groan while peeling back more of my leather fly, working my balls away from their tight cage, as well. Dear *fuck*, this feels good.

But not good enough...

"Bend over farther, Velvet. Your head against that cushion. Your ass raised toward me. That's it. *Yes*, damn it, that's it." One quick snap of her pretty lace panties, and I've got the view of so many of my fantasies. The creamy globes of her ass, parted a little so I can glimpse the slick pink flesh of her perfect core, its folds starting to pulse in time to her hot, breathy sighs.

"God*damn*," I grate, simply looking on as her mounting lust sends more blood to those perfect, pouting lips at the entrance of her most erotic triangle. It's all full and slick and ready for me—and Good Christ, what all that desire has done for her tangy, torrid scent. *Fuck. Me.* She's the pheromone that's been custom-mixed by the angels for me, and I send them a fast, fervid prayer of thanks while breathing her in again.

I finally shudder from the olfactory force, weakened to the point that I fall forward, smashing my lips to the back of her neck. Emma's answering cry is guttural, primeval, and perfect, to the point that I fight the craving to enter her for the payoff of simply savoring her. Just for a few...more...seconds...

"Holy *fuck*," I growl against her nape.

"Holy *shit*," she whimpers at the same time.

"Velvet," I rasp. "Your *scent*." I add my tongue and teeth to the assault on her neck, celebrating every note of her responsive mewl. "I swear to God, I can taste your sweet cunt just by smelling you."

"Yesssss." Her hiss is more air than volume as she dips her head to give me better access. I shove aside more of the tulle in order to align my hips directly between hers, tapping at her soaked folds with the swollen head of my cock while I continue to suckle her, taste her, bite her, mark her. The entire back of her neck, as well as the curves of her shoulders, are covered in my ravenous teeth marks. Breathtaking. Incredible.

Mine.

Mine.

"Oh, God." She moans it as my precome begins sprinkling into her tunnel. "Reece. *Fuck!*"

The filthy word springs from her on a scream due to the brutal bite I sink into the top of her spine. Beneath me, her whole body convulses and shakes. Around my cock, her channel tightens and floods. And holy *fuck*, how good it smells. As I fill myself with her essence, more of mine fades away. A haze takes over my control. Primal. Pure. Thunderous. Dangerous. But in the midst of the storm, I still hear her voice. A high cry, paced in time to the carnal call of her body.

"Damn it. *Reece.* I need it. Give it to me!"

The storm inside provides me with her answer. Another bite, though into her hair this time. A brutal twist of my head, making her gasp in pain and arousal.

When I release the strands, I bash my mouth against her ear. "This isn't about what you're given," I tell her in a snarl. "It's about what I'll make you take."

The very next moment, I show her exactly what I mean.

With my cock, slammed deep and hard inside her cunt.

With my thrusts, showing no mercy or softness.

With my come, spilling in a torrent that dissolves my Emmalina into wild, free screams.

Fortunately, as I fuck her through second and third orgasms for us both, the cushions of the chair serve as an ideal muffler for her cries—which, by the time we reach the third completion, have actually turned to tears. As soon as I've returned to normal—whatever the hell that means when shit applies to my biochemical state—I pull free, step around, and fall into the chair, pulling her down into my lap along the way.

"My love," I murmur into her hair as the rest of her emotion spills out. "My life." I stroke her hair back from her face, kissing her temples in soft intervals until she's spent.

I love you so much.

I want to vocalize that too, but a wad of emotion clogs my own throat as soon as she lifts her face, smiling at me through her adorably mussed makeup. Even now—perhaps especially now—with her mascara turning her into a raccoon and her cheeks tracked with her eye shadow, she has to be the most beautiful woman I've ever seen.

We hold each other's stare like that for several minutes, simply attempting to wrap our minds around the enormity of our emotions, before she finally speaks again.

"Thank you, Mr. Richards."

I crunch a frown. "For what?"

"For all of it." She states it as if telling me two and two equal four. "For finally showing it to me. What it really does to you."

I deepen the scowl. "Because it's *that* stunning?"

She rolls her eyes at my sarcasm. "Because it's that *real*." She lifts a hand to my face, where she strokes the corner of my right eye with the pad of her thumb. "Because you trusted me enough to let me see it."

Finally, I get her point. After I took down those assholes

who barged into the gala—my fury at Gregor and my fear for her turning into a double whammy for the grand Bolt light show—I was so far gone into the residual surge, I thought there was no choice about what she saw or didn't see. But there had been. I could have run—could have gotten out of the building, found some secluded spot in an alley and rubbed one out for the cause—but I hadn't. I'd stayed. I'd let her help me instead.

I'd trusted her. With all of it.

No matter how terrifying it had been—and shit, now that I replay every one of those minutes, I realize that it *had* been—I'd let her see all of the pain this time. All of the beast. The monster I'll never fully be rid of.

Yeah, he's still there. Still lurking inside, though tethered and mellow now, even as a deep thrill wraps the length of my spine while I lean in, kissing her deeply once more, our tongues gently swirling as our heartbeats throb in tandem.

When we finally pull back, neither of us goes very far. Still savoring her taste and reveling in her scent, I smile and murmur, "No more secrets, little bunny."

Her answering smile is slow and sweet...and sexy as fuck. "No more secrets *ever*, big bad wolf."

We kiss again, even doing the tongue tip tango, but I'm confused when we part. There are new furrows in her brow, and they're defined and deep.

"Emma?" I communicate the rest of the question in my incisive tone alone. *What is it?*

She pushes out a determined breath. Squares her shoulders a little. "I'm so sorry that I ever doubted you, Reece. About what happened tonight. About what you *told* me would happen." Her gaze falls. "And all I did was torque your balls and threaten you about ruining my stupid gala, and..."

I use her tearful pause to jerk her face back up, drawing her in for another kiss by clamping two fingers to her chin. "*Not* a 'stupid gala,'" I dictate. "An event you worked tirelessly for to benefit an organization you care deeply about—and for good reason." I stretch out my fingers, sending them along her jaw in strong, reassuring strokes. "An organization that is *still* going to do so much for so many. I promise you that, Emma. I'll work with my father on this. Between his contacts list and mine, we'll make enough calls to the right people so that RRO can keep running for years to come." I stop, blinking in befuddlement when globs of tears brim in her eyes again. "Is... is that okay?"

She bursts into a teary laugh. "You amazing dork. It's better than okay." Her new kiss is fervent and salty and perfect, confirming I've definitely instigated the good tears again. "And it makes me happy, beyond belief, that you're willing to partner with your dad on it too."

Fast shrug. "I didn't say that part would be the easiest."

"But not impossible," she asserts.

"No." I force a smile. *Fake it till you make it.* Hopefully, the adage will prove true now more than ever. "Not impossible, thanks to you."

She shakes her head. "I'm just the door girl, Mr. Richards. You two are the ones who have to walk through now. And I truly believe you can."

I slant a sardonic grin. "So two dicks walk into a bar..."

A giggle tumbles out of her. "Oh, *dear*."

"And say, 'What do you have that'll reform us?'" I'm on a roll now, despite her pressing fingers over my lips. "And the bartender says, 'Hold on, I'll go get Emma...'"

"Who has her own shit to work on, thank you very much,"

she cuts in, pulling her hand back. With knuckles curled against her temple, she clarifies, "Because if you're going to work on stuff with your dad, I hereby promise to attempt civility with Angelique." Her eyes drift shut, as if she can't believe the words have truly just left her. "Her intel was, after all, valid."

I gaze at her for another long moment, overwhelmed with a bizarre mix of emotions. There's love, of course, but I'm certain that's been around since the moment I met the woman. The rest of it is what guts me now. The depths to which I admire her, respect her, even realize how much I can truly learn from her. My commitment to get along better with Dad, especially after his offer from tonight, is like a puddle of strength compared to her new pledge about Angelique.

"Well, I don't think she's expecting you to invite her out for mimosas and pedicures, sweetheart," I murmur. "But it's clear we'll *all* have to learn to work with her and trust her, at least when it comes to learning the inner workings of the Consortium and the Source." As all the uncomfortable implications of that clearly settle into her, I pick up her hand in mine and reverently kiss every one of her knuckles. "We'll take it one day at a time, my love. Days—and nights—in which I plan to show you, in no uncertain terms, how thoroughly *you* have taken over every square inch of my heart, my body, and my soul."

"Hmmmm." Though her reaction starts out in *we'll-see* skepticism, it turns into a *show-me* sigh as I continue my kisses over her wrist and along the inside of her arm. By the time I close in on the curve of her elbow, Emma's using her free hand to dig into my hair and coax my mouth back up to hers. We groan together as our lips meet and our tongues mate, the heated union soon turning into a torrid embrace. Arms tangle, hands seek, and moans encourage until my woman rears up and twists around, planting her hips on either side of mine. I growl my approval, keeping my arousal centered in my cock in order to clamp her thighs, guiding her clit in a slow, rolling ride along the length of my cock, as I finally secure my mouth over one of her gorgeous breasts...

Until one of her hips meows.

My suction on her flesh is popped free as I give way to an extended grunt. "What. The. Fuck?"

Emma's giggle is *not* what I want to hear—nor is her funny fumble into her dress, no matter how tantalizing her breasts look as they bounce along with her motions. After another three meows, she finally pulls her phone free.

"The damn dress has lights *and* pockets," I grumble. "Sure there's not a snack dispenser somewhere in there too? I'd like some Funyuns, a Snickers, and a martini, please."

"What the hell?"

"I know, I know. Funyuns and martinis? But trust me, the salts really complement each other..."

"No." She throws up a distracted wave while peering at her phone. "Dee Dee says I'm needed downstairs right now. Some kind of issue the cops are having with their report."

I rake a hand through my hair as she backs off and fully stands. "Yeah. That makes sense but doesn't. She can tell them everything you can in terms of what happened, but your name is still on all the paperwork."

"Of course." Her voice is tense as she shimmies completely out of the big gown—well, what's left of it—and digs into a nearby suitcase for a pair of leggings and an oversized T-shirt from her favorite Broadway musical of the moment. "And, to be honest, as crappy as this timing is"—she gives my exposed cock a forlorn glance—"I think I want to talk to them too."

I join her in issuing a silent apology to my erection. Talk of cops and incident reports would normally be just the pin to pop my bubble of arousal, but not right now, with the woman standing there in clothes that can be more easily shucked than the damn dress—with no bra or panties on underneath.

Think harder about the cops. Big dudes in sweaty uniforms, wanting nothing but the facts.

Though in this case, I'm not sure those guys are going to believe it. Even *with* a room of two hundred witnesses.

Which circles us around to the subject now at hand.

"Why?" I respond to her assertion. "There won't be any statements they'll be cleared to give you until after they book all those bastards and read them their Mirandas."

"No. That's not it." Emma lowers into the chair in front of the room's large vanity table. The bright lights around the top and sides of the mirror are still on, turning her eyes the color of Caribbean waters as she grimaces at the makeup collage on her face. I don't move, hoping my dick will still be open to cooperating in a few minutes, though just by studying her expression in the mirror, I'm exposed to the new direction of her thoughts.

Probably because they've already been at the back of my mind too.

"You're wondering why a sophisticated group like the Consortium sent such a ragtag operation to disrupt your event."

She pauses, makeup wipe on her chin, to stab a glance at me via the mirror. "How the *hell* do you climb into my mind so freaking easily?"

"Same way you crawl into mine, Bunny." I wince while

beginning the torture of stuffing my balls back into my leathers. "But right now, let's just say great minds think alike." One testicle in. *Fuck.* Do I really have to do this? "And the same thing isn't making sense to me either."

She finishes wiping her face in the time it takes me to ease the second nut into the leather. From the corner of my eye, I watch her battle back a giggle.

"Baby," she says gently. "Should I wait for you?"

I grit my teeth. Hard. "Go," I get out, wondering how my dick will speak to me again after what I'm about to do to him. "This'll be easier without you here."

"Yes, sir." Her voice is laced with mirth, though her steps are respectful as she rises and approaches, a goodbye kiss already in her eyes.

"Raincheck, Velvet." I whip up a hand, palm out, as the fucker between my thighs already jerks with fresh blood. "*Please.*"

It's the green light on Emma's giggle, finally tumbling off her lips despite how she tries to mask it with a hand. Unbelievably, despite the raging boner still making my world a miniature hell, I find my own chuckle joining in, mixed with the sound of her calling back up the stairs, "I love you, Mr. Richards!"

"I love you, too, Miss Crist," I whisper back. "God fucking help me, how I do."

EMMA

Where are you?

After tapping out the text to Lydia, I again scan the

dwindling crowd in the main event room. I'm standing next to Sawyer, who's talking to a huddle of four cops who have assured me they don't want to talk to me—yet. Four more men in NYPD blues, as well as a trio of official-looking guys in baggy suits with badges on lanyards around their necks, are still walking through the ballroom and dropping little numbered evidence flags.

After five minutes with Sawyer and the uniforms, I truly wonder why they told 'Dia they needed me down here so fast. I almost wonder if they'll want my statement at all, since Sawyer is giving them more details about the incident than I could hope to remember. But as Reece just said upstairs, in all his erect and awesome glory, my name *is* on all the paperwork.

Just thinking of my superhero stud fills me with a million hot prickles accompanied by twice as many screaming hormones, all but ordering me to run back up to the attic dressing room and maul that magnificent cock of his all over again. But other instincts are niggling too. Something's off about Lydia's texts—and now I'm anxious to find her and grill her as to why.

I wonder, with a number of sister-wise intuitions, if she wants to talk about Sawyer. On more than a few occasions tonight, I caught her giving the man surreptitious head-to-toes—which might be, as far as I know, the only "base" she's ever been to in her life with *any* guy. So if she's gonzo interested in the surfer spy guy, that alone could explain her cagey behavior.

Finally, there's a new meow from my phone.

Out back. Near the kitchen entrance. I
need to talk to you. NOW.

Soft chuckle. "Ohhhh yeah, sister. You've got it bad for Mr. Fine Foley."

Hold on to your panties. On my way.

Now that I'm not hindered by fifty pounds of glowing tulle, I make my way easily across the room and out the kitchen. A warm smirk spreads across my lips as a variety of one-liners fly across my brain. With as much hell as 'Dia's given me over the last three months about "snogging the superhero," it's going to be such sweet revenge to get in a good opening dig about her infatuation with Sawyer.

But the second I step outside and see Lydia again, the fire in my smile fizzles. And the warmth in my blood drains.

As I take in her tear-streaked face. And her widening, terrified gaze. And the way she holds her hands behind her back...

"Dee Dee? What's—"

"Em!" Her voice is only a gasp. "Don't come any—"

A hand slams over her mouth. A hand covered by a sleek white elbow glove—on the arm of a woman I recognize from the gala. She's older, which made me believe she was a friend of Lawson's when I saw her earlier, but now I realize she's not a fucking friend. She's the dark-eyed, evening-gowned bitch who's got my sister cuffed from behind and who now uses the cellophane gag trick on Lydia too...

Before hurling her inside one of the catering company's vans.

Instantly, I have to resist doing two things.

Screaming.

And vomiting.

Neither is going to help me make headway with this eerily calm monster, who, ironically, has also brought the cosmic keystone, raising up all the strange chunks of tonight that haven't made any sense. Suddenly, the whole bridge is there, connecting Angelique's intel with the near-joke of a heist that those morons almost pulled off.

Almost.

Because they were never meant to really accomplish the crime.

The mass stick-'em-up was nothing but a smokescreen. For this. For what the Consortium really had planned all along.

As my mind wraps around that sickening knowledge, I square my shoulders. Raise my chin. Meet that bitch's stare without blinking or shirking. Making sure she knows, without any second doubts, that I'm memorizing every inch of her face—and that if I make it out of this ordeal alive, there won't be any location on the planet she'll be able to hide.

But right now, she holds all the damn cards.

And because of that, I keep both the bile and the scream from rising in my throat.

And because of that, I rein back my stance. Hating every inch of the motion but somehow compelling my body to give her deference. Respect she does *not* deserve.

"It's not my sister you want." I stun myself by managing it with no wobbles.

The bitch in sequins curls a small sneer. "You are correct."

"And it's not even *me* you want, is it?"

The woman cants her head, angling her face into the alley light until I can almost picture how she looked as a younger woman. She was probably just as worldly and lovely as Angelique, only in a darker, Salma Hayek kind of way. Now, she's nothing but angry angles and gaunt desperation, even as she returns in a murmur, "You...have uses. Perhaps even beyond what we have first conjectured."

Uses.

Beyond what we *have conjectured.*

She's Consortium, all right. And she has me nailed to her evil pinboard like a rare butterfly—that she's willing to do some desperate things to keep. If I want to survive this—if I want *Lydia* to survive this—I have no choice but to stay still and look pretty.

"All right," I utter past dry lips and a thick throat. "Then if it's me you want, it's me you now have. Just...just set my sister free. She was just in the wrong place at the wrong time. You have no reason to hold her."

Madame Butterfly chuckles in full now. "Oh, *querida,* I have *every* reason to hold her."

"Goddamnit." My terror explodes into furious tears. "You *don't!*" I lunge for her, only to be wrenched back from behind. A beefy male arm swings around to engulf my neck, chin, and mouth, restraining me and muffling me in one move. Still, I scream, "Let her go!"

Butterfly hikes her skirts and jerks her head, apparently instructing the henchman to get me into the van too. "Get in without any more fuss, Miss Crist, and we will discuss it."

For one more second, I debate whether to fight. I can probably get a meaty bite into this asshole, which would earn me a few seconds to scramble free and scream like my life depends on it.

And maybe it does.

Because while I'm sure the Consortium won't kill me, they are clearly, definitely pondering plans for me that go beyond being bait for Reece.

But they won't even give Lydia that consideration. She's expendable. A pawn. Not even a butterfly on the board.

I know my choice now.

Because the truth is...I have no choice.

IGNITE

PART 6

CHAPTER ONE

REECE

"Fuck!"

It's at least the thirtieth time I've bellowed the word in the last five minutes. As if I give an actual shit about keeping count. Nothing matters right now except pulling a clue, *any* clue, from the ninety seconds' worth of grainy video footage that Sawyer Foley has managed to isolate from the feed off the cheap camera mounted over this building's ramshackle service entrance. But as of right now, at the end of the fifteenth replay we've given the footage, there's nothing more than the basic facts about the incident that has turned one of the best nights of my life into the worst nightmare of my existence.

Foley freezes the frame. If only the same could be done to my horror, rage, and despair. But it all plays on like an endless loop from an eleven o'clock newsfeed covering a crappy accident on the interstate, sensationalizing the carnage of my soul over and over and over again.

Still, I force myself to push back from the little office's corkboard wall, watching a thumbtack give up the fight against the force of my punch, falling to the floor along with the motivational words it was holding up: *Jolt it Like Bolt.*

Fucking wonderful.

I stomp back over to the desk where Foley is seated and

rivet my gaze on the screen of the computer connected to the security camera. In a low growl, I order, "Play it again."

At first, Foley only throws back a deep rumble of his own. "Damn it, dude. You really think we'll learn anything from the sixteenth play as opposed to the fifteenth?"

"Play it again."

"But the sooner I can send this to my buddy at the New York bureau office—"

"Play. It. Again."

I mean it. There's something I'm missing in the footage, and I'm as sure of it as the lightning still crackling in my blood, no matter how thorough a struggle it is to keep my synapses charged at this high level. Ninety minutes ago, I was accessing the blood cell batteries to put down a gang of thieves who'd used my own security force to infiltrate the charity fundraiser organized by the love of my life, Emmalina Crist. Forty-five minutes ago, she and I were dealing with the resultant power surge to my system in my favorite way of all: screwing each other like there was no tomorrow.

Now, there really is no tomorrow.

Because while I was jamming my dick back into my leather "superhero" suit, she'd come back downstairs in response to an urgent text from her sister—whom we now watch in our sixteenth replay of the footage from a security camera that had to have been bought off the back of a truck on Canal Street. Despite the crappy quality, it's easy enough to recognize Lydia Crist, still dressed in her frothy gown from the gala, which is the only similarity shared with the young woman who joked around with us all before the evening took a fast train to Shitsville. Lydia enters the video feed with her wrists already bound behind her back, her shoulders shaking from sobs, clearly pleading something to the statuesque woman who strolls into the frame with her.

"Who...are...you?" I grit through my teeth while scouring my memory bank for the connection to her. She's dressed in a long, beaded dress, meaning she was a guest at the fundraiser, though the only person I focused on in that room was Emma. That means this woman, now blithely tapping a message into a phone—likely Lydia's, and likely the urgent text that coaxed Emma out of my arms—is someone I've met before. But where?

Is she one of Mom's friends? No. Too young.

Another New York society wife? Perhaps a climber who successfully maneuvered her way into spoiled second-wife status? No again. She's too slick. Almost as if she doesn't belong here.

A light bulb forces its way through the chaos of my brain.

That's it.

She really *doesn't* belong here. Because she's not from here. Or anywhere else in this country, for that matter.

Meaning this whole clusterfuck really *is* becoming my worst nightmare.

"Wait." I clutch Foley's shoulder while barking it. "Freeze the frame." I scour the screen with my stare, tearing it apart pixel by pixel, letting another violent snort escape from the piss-poor quality of the picture.

"What is it?" Foley grills and then adds when I'm still silent, "What do you see?"

"I don't know," I mutter. "Yet."

But now I know I *will* see it.

And when I do...

"Advance it another couple of seconds," I murmur. "Again." A new search, then a fresh growl. "*Again.*"

After that, Foley learns my cues enough that the demands aren't necessary. We watch, frame by excruciating frame, as Emma comes onto the scene, dressed in the sweatshirt and leggings she'd thrown on after I destroyed her gown in the throes of our lovemaking. There's a slight scuffle, and the mystery bitch flings Lydia into the van. Though Emma's entire body flinches as if about to launch herself at the woman, she checks herself, complete with strained shoulders and clenched fists.

Good girl.

My silent message goes out to her from the middle of my soul, as it has during the previous replays. My hands ball against the top of the desk, but I force myself to keep watching the other woman, noting every millimeter of her mannerisms as the video advances, frame by agonizing frame. What the *hell* is so familiar about her? All the most notable aspects— the femme fatale stance, the appraising stare, the ruthless red sneer on her lips—are persistent nicks at the edges of my memory, though nothing digs in hard enough to penetrate recognition.

Until the bitch tips her head.

On a replay in normal speed, the movement was likely nothing more than a glitch of motion—a subtlety meant to economize time they were rapidly running out of. The grimace the woman succumbs to, lasting no longer than that frame, confirms that much. But it takes her longer than that to swing her head back down—and in that moment, with her neck still stretched, I finally see the image that clicks into the lock of my memory.

"Stop." Every muscle in my body works to get the word out. "Right. There." As Foley jams on the pause button, I lean forward without blinking. Frozen. Fixated.

I slowly raise one hand, pointing to the area of the woman's exposed ear.

"Shit." It's an extended sound on Foley's lips. "What *is* that? The bitch in beads really hiding horns under that mane?"

I expel a harsh breath. "That's ink."

"*Shit*," Foley repeats, standing and peering closer for himself. "You're right. That's a tatt. But with this craptastic video quality, I doubt we'll be able to figure out what that shit is."

"We don't need to." I straighten. "I already know." Just as my mental key finally turns, unlocking an avalanche of memories—making me realize exactly why I'd kept them so tightly sealed.

She'd been there.

That night.

She'd been there.

When the thugs in white had strapped me down, stripped me naked, and injected me in a dozen places. She'd stood there, stroking the hair from my face, murmuring to me like a Spanish mother to her child...words of calm and comfort and pacification, while my veins were ignited with agony and my mind felt like a transformer ready to blow.

She'd been there all the other times, as well.

To the point that every time she returned, I knew the experiments were about to intensify. The torture was about to get worse.

"*Richards.*" The prompt is so impatient, I realize Foley's likely on his third or fourth attempt. When he adds a sharp snap of his fingers, I'm sure of it. As soon as I refocus, he charges, "So you *do* know her?"

I incline my head. "If you mean like a rat knows an insane scientist, then yeah." I gaze once more at the monitor.

"What the hell does that—"

"It's a scorpion." I get to the point because the metaphor isn't worth explaining. *You're not there anymore—but Emma just might be if you don't pull your shit together and help Foley work the sole clue you have to this thing so far.* "The tattoo is a scorpion," I elucidate. "And what we're seeing there is the tail. The rest of it disappears under her—"

"Hairline." Foley issues the conclusion in a deep, jarring growl. The apprehension isn't eased when he studies the monitor as if beholding his own revealed ghosts. I watch with an extra resonance to my blood as the guy's face is overtaken by violent angles. "The tattoo extends around her head, because at one point, she had to shave it all off for the inking."

As his tone gets thicker and tighter, so does my posture. "And how the hell do you know *that*?"

A rough swallow takes over his windpipe. "Because I know more than I want to about the Scorpio Cartel."

Now *I* want the chance to indulge that gulp. But I don't. I can't. Past the desert my throat has become, I growl, "Excuse the fuck out of me?"

"Excuse granted." Sarcasm is the guy's way of working around his stress. I know him well enough to figure that out by now. But the explanation does nothing for the dread taking over my senses. "*Fuck.*"

Especially when his voice dips to new octaves to snarl that out.

While ordering myself to pull in a full breath, I stab a hand back against my skull. "Okay. Just for giggles, let's get this straight. You're talking about *the* Scorpios? The scumbags who have people bought off in nearly every major transportation hub and police force in the world? Who, because of that, dominate the globe in moving illegal drugs, guns, jewelry, art, women..."

My larynx clutches on that as the implications of my words completely set into my psyche. Through the shit soup of a silence that follows, I wait. And wait. And command myself not to hurl what little contents my gut contains at the moment.

Finally, Foley utters, "Yeah. *Those* assholes."

I wheel away from him and punch the wall hard enough to topple the corkboards.

After it all crashes to the floor, I finally spit, "Fuck."

"About sums it all up." Foley turns back toward me with a scuffing step. "How the hell do *you* know that bitch?"

I let my head fall between my shoulders, which are now as stiff as I-beams. "Remember what I said about the insane scientists?" After he lets his grunt suffice as a yes, I growl, "Well, I was that one's favorite lab rat."

"The fuck?" Another scuff. "You mean, when those Consortium bastards had you on lockdown in Spain?"

Flimsy nod. "Yeah."

"But it took you this long to recognize her?"

I lift a burning glare. "Can *you* readily remember every cocksucker who tortured you?"

The question is a jump out on a limb. While the guy's never openly shared, the faint scars on his legs and the marks he attempts to cover with his "groovy" wooden bead bracelets have had me wondering about what his life was like before the FBI experience for which I hired him. Foley doesn't strike me as being ex-military, but a person who's been through trauma can sometimes, somehow, sense it in another. And yeah, my

Spidey sense has often pinged high with him.

"Got it," he finally mumbles and then turns away before plummeting heavily back into the desk chair. After another long pause, he finally grates, "Jesus."

"You really think he's listening?" I stab back.

"So the Consortium...and the Scorpios..."

"Are so tight in bed together, they don't need lube," I snarl.

He has no sarcasm, even of the darkest slant, to fire at that one. The truth I've just declared is too glaring. Too huge. Too terrifying. It doesn't just demand our silence. It robs our abilities to create any worthy sound or reaction other than our mutual mental Novocain, wondering when the numbness will wear off and the reality will set in.

And hurt like hell.

Like now.

The moment I compel my stare back up at the monitor, my senses scream again. To behold the image now, with the bitch of my sickest horrors that close to the essence of everything good and right in my world, brings on a pain in my heart unlike any torment I've ever known—even as that witch's helpless lab rodent. Only now, as a peculiar afterthought, do I realize that I never even knew the woman's name. Not that the detail will subtract one fucking drop of the pleasure I'm going to get from killing her with my bare hands.

The resolve is galvanizing. I'm back in motion, lurching from the tiny office next to the kitchen back out into the main ballroom area, which I behold with eyes much different than my glower of twenty minutes ago. Don't get me wrong. I still see the East Village space that Emma called "trendy" and I called "seedy," and I still fight the urge to throw my head through one of the walls as punishment for not insisting she relocate this thing to one of the eight Richards-owned buildings in the city. I still see the two hundred Chiavari chairs that I want to snap into kindling, and I still see the two hundred bowls of unfinished soup at the now-empty place settings because all the guests have gone.

I still battle the dark ache in my chest, mourning the loss of my woman's dream.

No.

No, goddamnit.

Not lost. Just...delayed.

I refuse to believe anything differently. I shove aside any intuition or feeling that contradicts that certainty, totally focusing on the bizarre hope behind the horrific conclusion that Foley and I have just reached. It's a strange goddamned silver lining, but I'm shooting at the damn thing with every logic-bearing laser in my arsenal.

With that in mind, I spin back on the guy once he emerges from the office behind me. "Enough wallowing. Now let's figure out how to use this to our advantage."

Foley stops, strangely looking as if he's about to bust out on the comedy act. "Use...this?" he challenges. "To our *what*?"

I shoot back an equally caustic glare. "Come on, Mr. Expert-on-the-Scorpios." I tap at his temple. "Access it. Use it, goddamnit. What are they doing? Where are they taking the girls? What's the MO in a situation like this?"

Now Foley does laugh. Not hard and not loud, which makes me wish for either in place of the mirthless grunt he shoots before pushing past me, hands laced at the back of his head. "What, in any conceivable universe, makes you think the Scorpios are dumb enough to have MOs?"

While my muscles absorb the bitterness of his tone,

clenching in any way they can, I shake my head hard, refusing to let a single dart of that energy take hold where it counts. "Fuck that," I snap. "They have to have patterns. Even small ones. If *you* were working for them—"

He spins back around so fast, his face so virulent, that I'm already cut short. "I don't work for those goddamned animals, and I won't ever pretend that I do." Just as viciously, he stomps toward the stage area of the room, where the police are still dropping evidence flags like E.T. with Reese's Pieces. I follow him, not giving myself a second to grimace about the fucking metaphor, but am halted short when he stops again, tearing off his tux jacket and hurling it across a table with an unintelligible curse. "The MO is that there's *no* MO, okay?" He fetches his jacket, now dripping in cold pumpkin soup, and wads it up. "*You* don't find the Scorpios. The Scorpios find *you*. And only where they want to find you and when."

I'm about to walk around the table and square off against him with at least three different ways of expressing why and how I refuse to acquiesce to that, when my pocket begins to play a song. "Superheroes" by The Script.

The song Emma personally picked out as her identifier on my phone.

The song gets louder in direct proportion to Foley's shrewd look. I ignore him, homing in on the part of the song Emma always loved the best. About a hero who's stronger than he knows, and from that, his heart of steel grows...

From the strength in that heart, the one she's taught me to believe so thoroughly in, I press the green answer button on my cell. Yeah, even knowing she's not the one who's calling. Even knowing that for all my chitchat with Foley about torture, I haven't begun to know the true meaning of the shit until now.

As soon as the line opens, I take a verbal lunge. Yeah, making the first move is the suckiest strategy, but rational thought and I said bitter goodbyes the second I watched the first loop of the security feed.

"What do you want?"

There's a hitch of a female's breath, as if my malevolence has found its way through our connection. I can only hope. At last, a voice like dark syrup oozes back at me, "Reece. Darling."

"If you mean the guy who's going to greet tomorrow's sunrise with his hands around your neck, then yeah, 'darling' works."

Her petulant huff fills the line while raw fury swells my blood. "Now is that any way to speak to your creator...*Señor Bolt?*"

"Sorry," I rebut. "I missed Frankenstein's TED talk."

Her syrup spins into a light laugh. "*Ay.* You were never this funny in the lab, darling."

"Sorry again. I was a little busy being turned into a fucking one-fifty-watt freak."

"But have you not heard? Freaks are all the fashion now. And as for fucking..." Her mirth turns sultry. "I would like to think that some pleasures are worth waiting for."

I twist my lips, fighting a fresh coil in my stomach along with the deeper, darker memories her words bring. Being braced on a steel lab table, my arms and legs bound, surgical lights blinding me to the outskirts of the room. Her voice, in that tone, ordering the technicians to increase the wattage to my groin. Her heavy sigh as my cock responded in kind...

I thrust the images away with a jerk of my head and a savage rumble in my throat. "Well, I'm done with waiting, bitch. State your demands, and let's get on with it."

Despite that I already know what those ultimatums are going to be.

Despite how I understand this could all end up with me being back on that damn table soon.

Better me than Emma.

Dear God...anyone but her.

Nothing solidifies my intention more than the cheeky *tsk*s that come through the line, each stabbing the severe truth back into my psyche—this demoness still holds all the fucking cards.

Or does she?

"I have a name, you know," she murmurs, with at least half of her confidence replaced by irritation. I turn and pace slowly back out into the alley, free of the echoes of the main event room. If that *is* a fissure in her composure that I hear, I want to be ready to pick at it. Stab into it. Make the monster bleed.

"Yeah?" I counter, purposely injecting my tone with a low—and false—note of lust. "And I think you're mistaking me for someone who cares about it."

"Faline." She blurts it nearly immediately—and definitely desperately. I want to rejoice and recoil at once. My instincts are right. She wants me but not just for what's between my legs. "You may call me Faline." She's back to the Spanish sun croon. "Why don't you start practicing now so you can say it clearly when your lips are between my thighs?"

When every rat in New York grows a brain and turns into an Uber driver.

It fits. I have a strong commiseration with the rats of the world right now. To that end, it gives me more than thorough pleasure to drawl into the phone, "Just tell me where and when you want this to go down, bitch."

Now I'm walking a line. Might just have toed too far

over the thing, if the heavy breathing from Faline's end is any indication. Either that or the woman gets *very* turned-on from men jerking on her dominatrix chain. Neither matters to me, because ultimately, I have what she wants.

Me.

But damn it, *she* has what *I* want—and fuck it if her silk scarf of a laugh doesn't clearly lay that out.

This is going to be a head-to-head battle of two monumental wills.

And I have to keep my shit together enough to stay one step ahead of the bitch.

Like right now, as Foley walks out with pen and paper in hand, pointing at the phone in my hand. As Faline continues loving the sound of her own laughter, I instantly interpret what the guy needs, and I scribble Emma's cell number onto the pad. I look up long enough to catch Foley pulling his hands apart, thumbs and forefingers pushed together, in the universal sign for "string it out." I nod on the outside but groan on the inside. I'd like nothing more than to never hear this woman's voice again.

"Well, well, well. You *are* a fun one, aren't you?" she husks, dragging me back into the swamp of her energy. "Maybe having you back in the fold will be good for more than just a little recreation."

"You're just figuring that out now?" I'm rudderless about how to sound. Foley's useless for feedback, having already returned inside. His head is bent into his own phone, hopefully on a direct line with one of his spy-world contacts across the country. Getting triangulation on the call might be our fastest route to Faline—and even if Emma isn't with her, it'll be a start in the right direction. Well, a better one than the knowledge of the Consortium's connection to the Scorpios. "Did you really just commit the biggest mistake in the book when it comes to me, Faline?"

She sends out a sound like a purr and a hum. "And what might that be, Reece Richards?"

"Believing everything you read about me."

"Ah. *That* mistake." The purr-hum again. "Well, then. It shall be enjoyable to separate fact from fiction. Maybe you'll give me a pleasant surprise."

I spin, crunching loose pavement, as if the action will help me keep a grip on the buttons of this conversation—fastenings that *her* tone is clearly twisting free. "I'm full of them," I babble, grinding to a new stop as if that'll also mute my urgency. *Christ.* The last time I was this nervous talking to a female, I was twelve and hoping to cop a feel up Amanda Ogden's sweater after I took her to the Manhattan Cotillion's winter formal. "Surprises, you know. As if anything surprises you anymore?"

Fuck. This shit is staler than the cookies they served at that damn dance. And there's *a lot* more on the line than Amanda Ogden's nipples. But the rule has to hold true, even for a bitch like Faline. Get a girl to start talking about herself, and—

"We shall see about that too, won't we?"

"About what?" At *last*, a line I don't have to work so hard for. "Fact, fiction, or you being surprised by either?"

"As I said"—and suddenly, she's biting my head off as if I said her ass looked big in that train wreck of a beaded gown—"we shall *see*, Reece Richards."

But worse than her snip is the new noise in my ear.

The false placidity of a dial tone.

"Shit," I choke out, only to roar it again at full volume. I barely restrain myself from hurling the phone down the alley.

"Hey!" Despite Foley's bulldog bark, his presence gives me some needed calm. Not a lot but enough to realize that if he's taking the time to be pissy about my rage, he's got actionable news. "We got it locked down." He holds up his cell. "Em's phone is at Teterboro. Now whether she's anywhere near the damn thing—"

"Let's roll." I bite it out fast, not only because every second is precious right now, but if I start moving again, I'm likely to overlook the need to question him why my woman is suddenly "*Em*" to him.

Helping in that distraction is the arrival of a couple of black Escalades that screech to dual stops after barreling up the narrow back road. My nerve endings are naturally called to alert, until Foley walks to the driver's side of the front truck and smacks palms with the driver in a classic *mano a mano*, missing everything but the shoulder bump. Before they're done, Foley motions me over with a jog of his head.

"Took the liberty of calling in the cavalry, in a manner of speaking," he explains, motioning toward a guy who looks like he should be blown up fifty feet high over Times Square in nothing but his underwear, despite the black turtleneck and flak vest in which he's now dressed. "This is Sergeant Ethan Archer. We do sets at Malibu or Venice when he's in LA. And, oh yeah—he also dabbles a bit in Spec Ops from time to time."

"Army," the guy says in answer to the curiosity in my stare. "Out of JBLM, Washington State." He smiles and extends his hand. "Nice to meet you. Most of the fuckers in here will be calling me Runway. Feel free to do the same." He cocks a thumb toward the second row of the car, where a couple of lean-muscled guys wave their hellos. One looks descended from real ninjas, despite his angular Asian features being surrounded by spiked hair the color of an eggplant. The other has equally chiseled features but thick ginger hair and grins as if he's about to file a report for his Hollywood interview show.

Foley pivots around, pointing at the next Escalade. "You might know pretty boy number two back there."

I walk a couple of steps before laughing as recognition hits. "Dan Colton?"

The CEO of Colton Steel, also a contender for underwear-over-the-Square placement, leans his tawny head out and beams a movie-star smile. "Hello there, sir. Understand you have need of some guys who know what the hell they're doing?"

"Which completely qualifies *you*," Foley cuts in. "As long as you don't take the labels off the foot pedals."

"What the fuck?" I mutter as the two men flip joking middle fingers at each other. "Ohhh. Wait a second." I narrow my gaze back at Dan. "You used to be a G-man too, yeah?"

"Yeah." He smirks Foley's way. "CIA. Showed this choad a few tricks when we worked a few overlapping cases."

"Yeah," Foley retorts. "Just as soon as *I* showed *him* the basics, like how to turn on a computer."

Colton throws him another mocking glower before tossing back his head to beckon me over. "Yeah, yeah, whatever. Let's do this. Time's burning." He nods a silent *you're welcome* to my grateful glance before calling out, "Hop in down here, Richards. Kane's riding shotgun"—he nods toward the dark-haired hulk of a guy in the passenger seat—"but the back seat's clear, and we brought flak jackets for you and Folic Acid there." He gives my leathers a fast but professional assessment. "But since we're already giving *you* a gold star for coming to class prepared, you can use the drive time to brief us all on a secure channel. We'll be locked and loaded once we hit Teterboro to get your girl."

"Fucking. Perfect," I answer instantly.

"Just as long as 'Folic Acid' hits the skids right now," Foley mutters while we break into a jog toward the rear Escalade.

"What?" I counter. "You prefer Sally?"

He rolls his eyes. "Thousands of dudes doing this dangerous spy shit across the globe, and *I'm* the one frontloaded with the lame call signs."

I'm tempted to one-up him on that. *Just try thinking about getting through orgasms that feel like your dick's been jammed in a light socket.* But right now, I really am like a rat in a lab maze, unable to comprehend anything beyond the route in front of me and the walls around me.

Walls with gears I can hear turning every minute, cranking their confines tighter in on me. *Tighter.*

But I trudge one foot in front of the other. Then again and again. To the end of the row, then around another twist. Inhale, exhale, repeat—no matter how hard it feels to live another minute without her.

To think about her in the captivity of those fucking bastards...

Another step.

Another turn.

Another breath.

Praying she'll be at the end of the maze.

And if Faline is there with her?

All the better.

As I yank my bow tie free and strip off my formal shirt to replace it with a Henley and a bulletproof vest, I allow myself to affirm it with a low growl. I don't mind that the sound burns every inch of my throat. I don't even mind that the fire spreads lower, through my chest, claiming every rib like napalm through a forest. The fury is perfect. My purpose is seared on my conscious—and its promise blazes in a savage snarl from my lips.

"Your rat's grown out his teeth, bitch. And now he isn't afraid to use them."

CHAPTER TWO

EMMA

"It's time for you to spill, sister."

It's the first time I've ever heard Lydia speak those words with something other than a snarky grin and a matching wink. The difference between that and this fear-tinged growl are like soft jazz and punk rock—and right now, I seriously wish I could flip the channel back to sappy saxes and crooning clarinets.

Yeah, and I also wish my backside were parked on something other than a concrete floor that might as well be a slab of ice. And that I'd put on my *Phantom* sweatshirt instead of my *Waitress* T-shirt before answering Lydia's text. And that I'd managed to snap two coherent thoughts together once I *had* found her, trembling and bound and terrified, at the mercy of thugs obeying the orders of a woman who makes Lucrezia Borgia seem like Twilight Sparkle. That I'd been able to think of any other option than obeying the bitch with just as much blind stupidity. Even if I'd thought it through to leave behind some kind of clue for Reece...

Reece.

My chest squeezes as his name echoes through my heart. I let my eyes do the same while knocking my head back against the storage room's wall, but only for a fast second. Only long enough to let a silent scream tear through me, soaked in the anguish of imagining what he's enduring right now—a pain I felt from the moment I got into the van next to Lydia. As soon as my dread soaked down to my knees, making me fall into the seat next to my sister, they'd rammed the door shut behind me with a horrifying *whump*, not only locking us into the car but flooding my system in pure fear. The goons hadn't even had time to bind me yet, but I didn't even think of moving. I'd been helpless. Paralyzed. Terrified that if I even breathed, they'd injure 'Dia—or worse.

I wince from just recalling the moment—and the long minutes that went by after that, in which I was too terrified to gather even one pertinent fact about the city streets on which we drove. I would've had time too. This crew was smart about the getaway, immediately slowing to match the pace of traffic from the moment we emerged onto the main roads. They turned the vehicle into just one of a thousand in the Village, even near midnight on a Sunday. When NYPD sped by, lights and sirens at full wattage and wail, they hadn't even slowed at the sight of a catering van making its way across town. As the sirens had gotten fainter, my spirit had sunk deeper—then even deeper still—into the mire of one awful revelation.

This feisty damsel-in-distress stuff is *no* effing fun.

The declaration, while stemming from despair, gives back a weird blessing to me, the form of much-needed fury. *There's* the strength I need to straighten my posture and reopen my eyes, despite knowing the sight that'll rip me open again when I do.

My sister's terrified face.

Correction. This feisty damsel-in-distress stuff is impossible.

If fate needs another chance to drive that point in deeper,

it's when I struggle to give my shoulders a break from their tension because of my bound wrists at the small of my back. The motion makes me squirm, and I'm immediately alerted about the hugeness of *that* mistake when my full bladder aches for relief.

"Damn it."

"What?" Concern replaces 'Dia's fear as she wiggles closer. "Are you all right, baby girl? Are you hurt? God*damn*it. If they've hurt you—"

"I'm fine." I push it from between locked teeth. Going for any other option would have me succumbing to the stings behind my eyes. *Lydia.* Always my fiery, plucky, protective big sister—even now, when she's been captured, kidnapped, and entrapped by the Asshole Dumpling Gang, and I'm the reason. Even when she's shivering just as badly as I am and her arms and hands probably hurt worse. Holy shit. *Her arms.* The instruments of her profession. The powerhouses of the winning streak she's been on, even earning her the attention of a few potential sponsors.

Okay, screw the damsel in distress. *Plot twist.* I'm now one pissed-off princess.

"You don't sound fine." Lydia mutters it as if we're simply out for lunch and there's too much mayo on my sandwich.

"I'm *mad*, okay?" I let all my frustration dump into the words, knowing 'Dia already hears and understands the dread that's driving it. I just wish my wrenched heart and fried nerve endings did. They crumble just enough to let hot tears well and spill, and I instantly duck my head to hide the awful weakness. "You...you shouldn't be here. You shouldn't be tied up like this, miserable like this, because of something you have nothing to do with. As soon as those piss buckets had me, they should have let you go. I should have *made* them let you go. Now, you're caught in the middle, and—"

"Okay, *stop*." She's close enough now to jab her knee into my thigh. Hard. "Every day, people get dragged into circumstances they have nothing to do with, okay?"

I jerk my head up, side-eyeing her. No. Side-glaring her. "*That's* your tack for making me feel better?"

"What?" she rebuts. "The truth?"

"God, I hate it when you're practical. *Ow.* Hey!" The last of it punches out as she knees me even harder.

"And I hate it when you're melodramatic."

"Excuse *me*, Vivien Leigh?"

Her turn for the side-glare. "Fiddle dee-dee, wench."

I give her a dismissive eye roll before jerking my head a little higher. Sweep my gaze up and over the concrete ceiling from which a long lighting fixture hangs, its fluorescents illuminating several steel shelves filled with hundreds of boxes. A mind-boggling sea of numbers is stamped on the end of each box. At the back of the room, tucked into the space between the shelves and the wall, are a couple of leather bucket seats, as well as some crescent-shaped control panels outfitted with enough switches and levers and lights to put the *Starship Enterprise* to shame.

"I'm not melodramatic," I mutter. "I'm realistic."

"And *that's* supposed to make *me* feel better?"

Soft snort. "I have to pee."

"Thanks for *that* reminder too." Unbelievably, she's able to push to her feet without using the wall for leverage, wobbling but keeping her balance on her four-inch heels. And once again, my sister flabbergasts me. I'm in padded flats and my feet are already screaming. Lydia's in the latest Louboutins yet struts like a queen toward the back of the room. "Maybe they have a spare potty hanging out around here," she calls. "Hell, I'll even take a dismembered airplane crapper right now."

"Airplane?" Her comment whams me with so much adrenaline, even I'm able to surge to my feet in two seconds. "Holy shit, Dee Dee. I think you're right." I'm close enough to read the small print from several of the boxes. "HF antenna. Landing lights. Engine sync switch. Spoiler lever." I look back to her, unsure what to do with my new recognition. "So..."

"They've got us stowed at an airport," she finishes, dropping into one of the spare seats. "Likely Teterboro, which is why we don't hear anything. They have a noise abatement rule in the middle of the night."

I drop into the seat opposite her. "Says the girl who paid attention to pillow talk when she was bonking a pilot."

She twists her bow-shaped lips, which are still a flawless shade of some bold red. "You and Reece are determined to give me the squeebs about the pillow talk thing tonight, aren't you?"

As soon as his name leaves her lips, my chest twists more painfully than barbed wire on a zombie hunter's bat. I don't even try to hide the resulting wince. "Right now, I'd give both my nipples for a chance to share *any* pillow talk with him again."

She draws in a harsh breath. "Sorry, baby girl. I didn't mean to..."

"I know you didn't," I return. "But if you really want me to start talking, then that means bringing him up, doesn't it?"

She replies with a stretch of silence—unless the gears whirring in her head can count as legitimate sound. That hum is followed by the click of inevitable conclusions notching into place.

"So," she finally utters, already sounding stunned. "He really *does* have"—she shakes her head, eyes bulging wide—"superpowers."

I let my head fall back again. The headrest of the old seat is a hell of a lot better than the wall, though that doesn't make this part any easier. "Yeah. He's really and truly...enhanced."

"Enhanced?" she laugh-sputters. "Em, your boyfriend shot *lightning* out of his fingertips and took down seven bad guys by himself. He's...he's like Voldemort, with a nose. A really nice nose. And better biceps. And that *hair*..."

"*Behave*." I stab out a finger but keep my head lolled.

"But honey, his hair needs its own Snapchat."

"You want the whole story or not?"

"Yes, ma'am." She pushes her knees together and digs one stiletto heel into the floor, biting her bottom lip in an expression that's uniquely hers. At least *I* don't know anyone else who can say *I'm sorry* and *fuck you* with the same glance.

After a long inhalation, I finally lift my head and fully meet her gaze. "So the story we've been telling the world isn't exactly true."

My sister's nod is swift but accepting. "Meaning there's no Richards Research that's exploring energy displacement and maneuverability?"

"Well, there *is* a Richards Research. And all the bio-electric theories *are* part of its research." I lean forward a little, copying her compressed knees, beyond thankful that it helps pacify the bull sitting on my bladder.

"Only that's not everything they do."

She says it with another serious nod, and once more I emulate her. "The company provides a front for what Reece is really up to."

"Which has something to do with that bitch in the bad frock and her nasty-ass goons?"

I groan, dropping my head, as we dissolve into mutual giggles. "Speaking of bitches, nothing south of my waist agrees to speak to you again."

"And I care about *that* part of you *why*?" Before I can summon a decent comeback, she prods, "All right. Moving on. So...Reece and these assholes have some unfinished business..."

At first, I field that by teeter-tottering my head. "Depends on who you ask."

Her gaze narrows. "But Reece has formed an entirely new company and put a false story over on the whole world, just to cover his connection to this group."

"'Connection' isn't quite how I'd phrase it."

"Okay. Enlighten me." Only my sister could lean back like that, still in cuffs, and look as breezy as if she's asking me about the bad sandwich again. "How *would* you phrase it?"

A perfect answer bursts at once to my mind, but I take another beat to really consider it. Realizing my first instinct *was* right, I give up just one syllable.

"War."

Well, that succeeds in melting Lydia's chillax. She sits forward, her gaze turning the dark Atlantic blue that at once tells any observer about the depths of her concentration. My sister can don a lampshade and nail a night of beer pong with the best of them, but when she decides it's time to get war-room serious, Pentagon generals would probably tell her to lighten up.

"War," she repeats, her tone just as businesslike. I can't say the same for the heavy rush of a breath she pushes out after that, as if *she* just ate the bad sandwich and is about to be sick from it. "Because...these are the bastards who made him that way?"

I spare her the doleful nod. She reads it in my gaze already, in the awesome way sisters have of doing those things. "They call themselves the Consortium. It sounds daunting because it is. Though on paper they're just a bunch of scientists with some crazy ideas about the next stage of human evolution, their devotion to it is nothing short of religious zeal."

Her nose wrinkles. "You mean like a cult?"

"I mean like a bunch of genius lunatics with a lot of effing money to play with."

She gulps. "So, a dangerous cult."

Once again, I debate the information I should share with her—until realizing what she already knows is a giant slab of *holy shit*. Adding some catsup to that order isn't going to change the weight of the patty. "You remember, almost a couple of years ago now, when Reece went on that party boy bender for a few months? How he was seemingly at every rager from Ibiza to London, even when the travel details didn't make sense?"

Lydia shrugs. "Don't know anyone on the planet who wouldn't. It was a little surreal."

"Because it *was*," I fill in. "Surreal, I mean. Actually, it was *un*real. All of it."

"Huh?" But after I supply the rest of the story, about how the Consortium manipulated existing images of Reece and then fed them to the press to create the illusion that the world's favorite bad boy was sowing wilder oats than usual, all while they were pouring liquid electricity into his veins, the expression on my sister's face quickly mutates. Confusion.

Astonishment. Shock. Horror. Then outright fury. "Holy. Fuck," she finally murmurs. "No wonder Reece wants his ten pounds of flesh from those monsters."

Heavy sigh. "If only it were that simple." I jog my chin up, trying to find at least a little sarcasm to work into all this. "Vendettas can be mellowed with a few trips to a good therapist."

Lydia's stare intensifies. "But there's *more*?" Then her eyes bug wide again. "Holy shit. There really is more, isn't there? The ones who didn't make it out, like him. *Wait.*" She keeps the gawk wide. "How *did* he make it out? *Wait.*" And, unbelievably, she stares with more awe. "Crap, crap, crap. He escaped somehow, didn't he? And Maleficent and her crew did *not* like that. And now they want him back."

The whole time she speaks, I do nothing to dispute her. Now, after a long sigh, I finally answer with a knowing nod. "Now you know why I called it war."

With terrifying timing, the word on my lips acts like an ignition switch on the air.

At once, every inch of concrete around us seems to tremble from a distant blast. Then a not-so-distant one. Even through the thick walls, we can hear shouts, bellows, and the thunder of hustling feet. Lydia and I add our own frantic steps to the mix, jerking out of the seats as if we synchronized the move.

"Shit." Fear drenches her voice again.

"About says it all." My attempt at a deadpan is a miserable failure.

"Wh-What's going on?"

I shake my head, indicating I'm just as clueless, but keep the rest of my assumption to myself.

This is either really good or really bad.

When the beep of a key card precedes the sudden sweep of the storage room's door, I hate how my mind takes a turn for the latter—and how that instinct is confirmed when the Salma Hayek doppelgänger strides back in, her old lady gown replaced by a black turtleneck, skintight pants, and red thigh-high boots. She looks over us both from head to toe. After a second, she sniffs and jogs her head. I'm baffled about what that means, other than the fact that I now, officially, feel like a slab of meat.

"Follow me," she commands. "It is time for you to serve your purpose."

As 'Dia and I huddle together, jabbed forward by the barrels of her henchmen's rifles, my sister rasps frantically, "What the hell does *that* mean?"

I manage a quick shrug but again keep quiet about the follow-throughs. Because the truth is, I have a pretty good idea of what she means.

We're being used as bait.

And now, as the bitch has anticipated, Reece has arrived to bite on it...

A scenario that, no matter how many different ways I run it in my head, is going to end up with somebody getting hurt.

Somebody I love.

War isn't hell.

It's worse.

REECE

"Well, that's one way of saying hello."

Foley's derogatory drawl has edges as sharp as the glass doors I've just blasted apart with the sweep of my hand, removing the barrier between the lobby of the Teterboro luxury jet company and its adjoining hangar. I roll a glare his way, but only for a second. "Did you honestly think we could *Zero Dark Thirty* this? You told me yourself that locking down Emma's phone was painfully easy. Now we're here, with this place lit up so bright everyone on fucking Mars can see it."

From the front seat, Big Guy Kane twists his head with a deep grunt—the first sound he's made since his muttered greeting when we first got into the truck. "Sorry, Folic. Point goes to Bolt on this one." He swivels his sights back to the front window. "These bastards all but rolled out the red carpet."

Foley fumes to the point of being audible about it. "So we're supposed to take them up on it, then? Give them exactly what they want?"

"What they want is me," I counter while retightening the straps of my vest one more time. "And if that's what it'll take to get Emma and Lydia out of their hands..." I meet his gaze steady and straight-on. "Then yeah, we give them what they want."

A grating noise comes from the radio wedged into the console between the front seats. With our secure line still open, I feel confident that every man in the other vehicle has just clearly heard my directive—for the ninth time. Nevertheless, Runway's voice crackles over the line, "Roger the prime objective. That being said, are we cleared to take first position?"

Colton, Kane, and myself swing our gazes to Foley. He nods, flashing me a fast glance of appreciation for the respect, before barking, "Affirmative. Time for the pretty boys to break out the ugly sticks."

Before he's finished with the direction, Archer has surged

out of his Escalade, along with the two impressive soldiers from the back seat, whom I now know as Mitch and Alex. They take up defensive positions, automatic rifles on shoulders, behind the truck's big doors. Through the open channel, we can hear their newly roughened breaths. They remain like that for the better part of a minute, deceivingly still. We're close enough that I can observe the minute ticks of their heads while studying every inch of the building before us.

Like them, it's a ruse of calm. I know it so completely because I can feel it. Because I know it. I feel and know *her.*

"She's here." I declare both syllables like I'll die for them, because I will. I don't stop to question the surety of it, pausing for just half a second to consider what it truly means. Two years ago, I'd go to movie premieres where pretty heads on big screens spouted this kind of shit, and I'd laugh in derision while secretly checking my texts. Now, I know I may not leave this airport alive—and I'll willingly pay that price if it means Emmalina lives. "She's here," I repeat after several seconds' worth of Foley's inaction. "And she's freezing. And furious. And terrified." And yes, I'm as sure of all that as the breath I use to testify it. "And I'm going to go get her."

The last line leaves me as a command from which I do *not* plan on backing down. I just pray to God—and yeah, I take a second to really follow through—that Foley and his wall of belligerence are ready to get on board with the plan.

"I'm coming as your cover. Kane, you're with us too."

Well, what about that. Prayers sometimes do make things better.

The three of us swing out of the car and fall naturally into a walking triangle, me at the top with Sawyer at the left corner and Kane on the right. With measured but quick steps, I lead the way toward the blasted-out lobby.

Halfway there, I'm hit by a fresh flood of sensations. Bone-chilling cold. Logic-stealing dread.

And heart-halting panic.

Fuck.

"Velvet," I utter. "I'm on my way."

My steps turn to stomps as I accelerate to a full run. I'm not above sending up another prayer, this time in gratitude, for the two men who keep pace with me without question, their feet making simultaneous crunches across the field of glass, until we're all the way inside the building.

But there's not a sliver of movement to greet us in the lobby either. The desks, all sleek white marble and custom steel accents, are all empty and tidy. A smooth jazz track plays through hidden speakers, glossy saxes and synthesizers backed by ocean waves.

New deception.

But coupled with a new hit of connection to Emma, it's not amusing anymore.

It's beginning to just piss me off.

"Faline!"

I push so much of myself into the roar, the air shudders.

In my periphery, Kane's balance falters by a couple of inches. "Well, damn," the guy murmurs.

"Now you know why I said he didn't need a gun," Foley utters.

There's another long pause of cool sax and ocean sounds before a woman's voice—*her* voice—singsongs through the air. "Darling! You made it!"

I roll my head and shoulders, releasing sparks of tension down through my arms and legs. Though the ends of my fingers start pulsing with blue light in time to my heartbeat, inciting more terse profanity from Kane, I'm not lighting up the night like normal. The drain of putting down the thieves at the gala, along with the terror of realizing my worst enemies abducted the love of my life, have turned my glow sticks into blue fireflies.

And if anyone should know that with glowing clarity, it's the bitch who laughs softly at us from...

Where?

Faline's provocative chuckle is everywhere and nowhere, seeming to dance on the air molecules themselves, taunting like we've blown on her giant, wicked dandelion. I show her exactly what I think of her poisoned spores by huffing hard at the shit and barreling forward, only to be stopped short by iron grips around both my biceps.

"Goddamnit." I wrestle against Foley and Kane, unable to stop despite knowing the insanity. My battery's already low, and I need the remaining charge for Emma.

Emma.

The second that truth—my only truth—sinks in, I sag and fall back. Then howl again, in place of zapping them both back out to the trucks. "I've had enough of this witch's games!"

"So have I, man." Foley wheels around, probably guessing my craving from the overall rise in my temperature, even through my leathers. "Believe me, *so have I*. But tearing half-cocked into a place this size would be an exercise in stupidity, even if you were operating at full juice." He gives my arm a brutal shake, ordering from between his teeth, "You already know this, damn it." He eases off on the hold as soon as I let my head plummet, abhorring the scraps we're being made to follow like starving dogs, including how I can scent Emma's

ANGEL PAYNE

dread on the air with freakishly canine sensitivity.

Until the poisoned spore laugh floats out through the air again—interrupting itself only to croon, "Half-cocked? Oh, no, no, no. We cannot have that kind of nonsense, can we, Reece Richards?" Another noxious giggle. "You were *always* my full-cock man."

"Shut up!"

As soon as Emma's scream slices the air, I jerk free from Foley's hold. "Emma!" I thunder back, using that same hook in my heart to be guided toward a door behind the check-in desk. Locked. Like that fucking matters. With a swipe of one hand, I *whomp* the whole thing off its hinges and stomp across the slab before it's even done falling into the hallway beyond. I barely register Foley's frustrated mutter and Kane's impressed growl, all my senses consumed with the growing heat of her in all my fibers. The rising certainty of her in my psyche. The swelling connection to her in my spirit...

Including her terror.

"Reece!"

The same shit her cry is dunked in now.

"Emma?"

I clear the long passage in two seconds. At the end, there's another door. I blow it clear without bothering to check the lock. Just beyond, a wide stairway—but unpassable due to the pile of discarded plane parts stacked on top of it.

"The fuck?" Kane skids to a stop at my right shoulder. "Who uses a stairwell as storage?"

"They don't." Foley, leaning over from my left, shakes his head. "This was put here on purpose—to slow you or to test you."

"Makes sense." Kane takes in the heap of tangled metal

piled at least five feet high by twenty feet long. "Can't see any cameras, but that doesn't mean they're not watching."

I grunt, acknowledging what they're both trying to say. No matter how it's phrased, the end result isn't changed. We're still rats in the maze—and the cheese is still on the other side of this fucking mess.

I ball my fingers into fists and the heat builds beneath them, straining my veins and shrieking through my muscles, until the pressure pops and sizzles and ignites. When I extend the digits again, they've become electric blowtorches.

"Showtime, motherfuckers."

CHAPTER THREE

EMMA

I feel him before I see him. Bright as a star inside my mind, sizzling as sparklers in every drop of my blood. I jerk from the force, knowing every drop of the savage agony he's suffered while searching for me.

But now that he's almost here, I force myself to shout the most hideous words I've ever fired at him.

"Don't do it, Reece! Stay away, damn you!"

Because no matter how this shit goes down, 'Dia and I won't be leaving this situation alive. And damn it, I'd really prefer my last mortal sight not to be the man I love more than anything trapped by the bitch I hate more than everything.

"It's a trap! God*damn*it, Reece. Listen to me!" I shriek it with my mind as much as my lips. Cram the alarm into every shred of my thoughts and every beat of my heart. *Listen to me, you effing dork. Nobody is going to win here, okay? Faline won't allow it. But damn it,* you *need to survive. You need to live— because you need to take down these filthy bastards in every form they exist.*

But the shithead, in all his stubborn glory, isn't listening. As the booms and screeches of colliding metal grow louder through the hangar, I understand why I can't even sense his desperation anymore. He's focusing too hard. Diverting every spark of his energy toward getting in here.

Stop! You stubborn shithead, you need to stop *right now. This is exactly what she wants you to do. Don't you get—*

With a crash that hits the air like a shockwave, a door to the hangar's catwalk flies off its hinges. The steel slab teeter-totters on the railing for a second before tumbling fifty feet and hitting the floor with a deafening clatter.

And then there's no more trying to stop him.

Because he's here.

Damn him. He's here, already making my lips twitch into a smile and my heart race in pure lust, despite the really disgusting circumstances of this whole thing. Can I be blamed? I almost want to scream that too. *Look* at him, with the wind in his hair, the fire in his fingers, the lightning in his eyes...

"*Faline!*"

And the rage in his voice.

"Holy *shit*. He's *pissed*." Lydia scrunches closer to me—if that's even possible, considering we're trapped in a nylon net like a pair of almonds in an oversize wedding favor. Only there's no cute birch reception tree to support us here. We're dangling from a hook attached to the end of an airport catering vehicle. The only reason I'm so sure about that is because something Italian must've been transported in there last, and my stomach constricts just from getting to smell the savory mix of tomato sauce and melted cheese.

Somehow, I push out a dark laugh. 'Dia's understatement, joined to the recognition that I'm suspended in front of a luxury jet's engine and can only think about pepperoni pizza, have made the humor inescapable. Still, I follow up the chuckle by muttering, "Yeah, he is. And that's exactly what I'm afraid of."

But I'm alone in the feeling. From the second Reece

stomps out onto the catwalk, joined by Sawyer on one side and Rambo's long-lost little brother on the other, the surge of hope in my sister is palpable. There's not a hitch of trepidation from Reece and his wingmen, either.

His wingmen.

Holy shit. My boyfriend now has support troops.

But nobody's all-out confidence freaks me out more than Faline's.

The woman appears in the plane's passenger door opening, still dressed in the black and red cat-bitch outfit with a smug smile draping her bloodred lips. Though she's yanked her hair into a ponytail, she still looks like airbrush art from a fanboy needing to jack off to a mashup of Black Widow and a Rio beach babe. Seriously, I wonder how the armed goons pacing the floor below us aren't sloshing through their own testosterone puddles by now.

"Darling!" she gushes Reece's way, opening her arms like a gameshow model showing off the jet for a showcase package. "You made it at last. And my oh my, looking so handsome too. Now I know why the VIPs always come late."

As soon as she stresses that last verb like an orgasmic moan, I clench every muscle until the whole net shakes. At once, Lydia jabs me hard with a shoulder.

"Breathe, baby girl. *Right now.*"

"Even if it means imagining that bitch being violated by five kinds of farm animals?"

"You'd subject those poor animals to a trauma like that?"

I release my rage through a violent snort. "I hate her, 'Dia."

"Well clearly, so does your man. So focus on him and help him defeat her disgusting, perfect ass."

I don't reply to that out loud. But inside my cracking heart, there are still words. So many things that I can still feel. *Oh, Lydia. My incredible warrior of a sister. The angels will be stronger with you in their number. I'll just do my best to keep up.*

I wish to God I really could let it all tumble out. And let her label me melodramatic again. And wish, for once, it was really true.

I'm not melodramatic. I'm realistic.

And there, in its sucky purity, is the truth of right now.

That even if Reece hands himself over to the bitch—and he will, because he shares my sister's conviction about a "dignity among assholes" code at work here, like "honor among thieves" only crazier—that the witch on the stairs is really going to let 'Dia and me walk out of here despite how we now know her first name, her distinctive tattoo, and her astonishing immunity to camel toe.

That's *not* the reality here.

And believe me, how I wish I could jab my head into the same dream in which Reece and 'Dia are living and really see things otherwise. But I believe that within the next fifteen minutes, I'm going to be dead.

Dear God, just not by the method I think Faline's planning...

But that hope's busted too. In the very next second. The moment the woman steps to the top of the passenger stairwell and sweeps one hand high enough for the pilot to see—

And the turbines of the engine we're dangled so close to now rev to life, powering the massive fans that suck in the air they need for flight.

And anything else that gets too close to the massive blades. Like a pair of human almonds trapped in a demented wedding favor.

"What the hell?" Lydia sobs it close to my ear, and I lean into her with eyes tightly shut. It's the moment I've dreaded. She's tumbled out of the dream and into the glare of the truth. We're going to die tonight. Faline is prepared to make that happen, probably in several different ways. I just pray Reece will do something to ensure it isn't *this* way.

"Stop!"

His drawn-out bellow, though barely audible over the engine's din, is still discernible. I finally trust myself to look—and breathe—again, as the engines fade and then click off. But only in this moment do I realize that the engines haven't been the only machinery that's been in motion over the last minute. Faline's go-ahead to the pilot also served as a high sign to the driver of the catering vehicle—who's nudged the whole rig, including Lydia and me in the net, forward another couple of feet.

"Holy shit," Lydia rasps. Then continues to whisper the words as a pacifying mantra, even as Reece's roar takes over the air again.

"What the living *fuck*?" He doesn't move from his location but visibly quakes from the effort of holding himself back. Silently, I try to lend him my dwindling strength. *Stay there, Reece. If you hit the floor, her minions will corral you.* "News flash, Faline," he proclaims, stabbing a finger toward Lydia and me. "You kill them, you don't get me."

Her petulant sigh vibrates on the air—and grinds the diplomacy off every nerve in my body. "*Ay, papi.* You were so much more fun with a plastic bit in your mouth and a needle up your cock."

"Shut. Up." Reece's growl is a bizarre piece of comfort.

Another wire of connection back to him. I pull in a deeper breath, feeling a little stronger. Maybe a drop braver. *Maybe.*

"*Mierda.*" Faline wrinkles her nose and examines her nails. "And now you are just being a grumpy prick."

"Who's finished with your goddamned games," he snaps, curling bright-blue fists around the catwalk's railing. With a longer snarl and a tsunami of a glare, he snaps the metal like a toothpick. He rips the two pieces out of their riveted moorings and hurls them aside but doesn't bother to watch as they're embedded into the hangar's thick steel walls. "Tell your man to lower that net and set the women free," he orders. "Only then do you get me without a fight."

Faline runs her fingers along the rail at her side, clicking her nails in a sadistic Morse Code. "I do believe I will already get you without a fight, darling."

Sawyer pushes forward like he'll be the next to snap the railing in place of the woman's neck. "So you *were* behind that joke of a robbery at the gala."

Faline rears back, one hand splayed on her chest. "Now, *that* is not very nice. My boys worked hard on coordinating all that. Well, *bah.*" She dismissively waves the same hand. "It was needed entertainment. East Village or not, the event was a bore. But a means to an end, I am afraid."

"And now you have that end." Reece braces his stance wider. "So let's get on with it. Free them and take me."

"Nooo!" I've been a quivering ball of tension, fighting to hold the scream back, but the cold words of this brutal bargain, on *his* lips, are too much to bear. "*Damn it*, Reece!" My tears, terror, misery, and fury spew with it. "Do *not* be a dumbass about this! You have to carry this fight on. *You.* You're the only one who can!"

His shoulders, weighted like they each support ten elephants, rise and fall. He rumbles, without altering an inch of his glower, "Faulty argument, Velvet. Because I'm not me without you."

I drop my head and watch my tears splatter against the tops of my knees. "With all due respect, Mr. Richards, *fuck that.*"

The retort is no sooner out of my mouth than a peeling laugh pours out of Faline's, and she tosses her head back before rolling her sphinxlike gaze between Reece and me. "You know, Alpha Two," she finally croons to Reece, "you chose very well for a mate. I do like her."

I whip my head over, knowing the admiration in her assessment should petrify me worse than her disdain. But rage is my new best buddy, and the trooper doesn't let me down now. "You know what, *Fart*line? Fuck you too."

The wench's lips twitch, hedging on writing off my insult with another chuckle, until most of her henchmen beat her to the punchline. As soon as their snickers start, her smile disappears—and the edges of my mouth hitch up in matching measure. The woman may have bypassed the curse of camel toe, but I managed to twist her panties anyway. If only for one second...

"Oh, yes, Reece. She *is* special." But only the words are an accolade. In her voice and in her eyes, I'm subjected to unfiltered venom—and unbridled violence. "And how fortunate for all of us, yes? It makes the observation that much more...*special.*"

With her emphasis on the descriptor, she twirls her hand again in the air. At once, the jet's pilot complies—along with the catering vehicle's driver.

One second.

The comprehension screams through my brain, fate's twisted joke on me now, as Lydia's wail fills one of my ears and the engine's torrent is a demon in the other.

One second.

For even Lydia's voice to be drowned by the relentless *zeer* of the revving turbines and whirring fans.

One second.

Which brings the crazy discovery that at the height of personal terror, there's a strange, accepting kind of peace. As my hair whips forward, sucked by the strengthening intake of the mighty fan, my mind breaks through a nauseous ozone into a numb outer space that I take a moment to treasure...

Knowing it's about to be stained with blood and pain.

Then the darkness of forever.

REECE

One second.

The words slam through my psyche like something meaningful. A realization. An epiphany?

No. A surrender. *Emma's* surrender.

She's ready to die.

For me.

Because of me.

As I drop into a crouch on the landing, I give myself only one moment more to crash her misguided mental party—with words that seethe from my clenched teeth but originate from the whole of my screaming soul.

"Not. Tonight."

And then there are no more seconds.

No more time for delays or games.

No more limits on what I must do. What I *have* to do. No matter what the cost.

I dig my psyche into that purpose before forcing it down inside myself, past the red lines of my reserves, to the dark, vicious places that have been depleted several times over tonight—until I force them back into the light. Ram their charging ports with new charges. Flood their anodes and cathodes with a power I've embraced as limitless.

The magnitude of loving an extraordinary woman.

I'm steady in that purpose now, even balanced here on just the pads of my fingers and the balls of my feet, like a sprinter on invisible blocks—that overlook a forty-foot drop. But that distance is barely a scratch on my conscious and a nonfactor in determining the course my actions must take. I only see the space separating me from the most important target in this room. The bundle of two terrified women, across the field I have to clear before they're sucked in and slashed apart.

"*Not.*"

I summon the voltage to my legs.

"*Tonight!*"

I push out my war cry as I punch the new thrusters inside, launching me off the ledge...

Through the air.

Farther.

Farther.

Until I collide with the net with such force, it swings on the hook like a cocoon in a hurricane.

As Emma and Lydia scream, I fight to do three things at once.

Redirect the charge in my blood back to my fingers.

Wrap both arms inside the net to avoid getting sucked away myself.

Find some kind of voice so I can snarl at them, "It's me. It's *me*, damn it. Stop biting!"

"Reece?" Even hoarse from terror, my woman's voice is the most beautiful music I've ever heard. But there's no time to savor it now, despite the tears and kisses in which she drenches each joyful repetition. I only have enough time—and strength—to grit out a terse command in response.

"Brace yourselves, girls. Ride's not over yet."

The second the electrons fill my arms again, I swing one high and wide over my head and burn a clean slice through one of the cables holding the cocoon up. It hurts like a motherfucker, and I glower at the thick black line across my fingers, knowing I'll slice them all clean off if I go for the second cable with the same hand. Not that I particularly care about the things, except for the service I still need from them in getting Em and Lydia all the way out of here.

With a snarl worthy of a Wookiee, I switch hands and finally get the second line severed. I hang the hell on as the three of us plummet toward the floor. A couple of feet before we hit, I twist in order to cushion our fall.

"*Oof!*"

Despite my exclamation, the impact wasn't as nasty as I expected. Good thing too, since Faline's already shrieking at her men to hustle their asses and surround us again. But the circle they're supposed to form around us is more like a sad crescent, thanks to Foley's last-minute-but-badder-than-badass battalion. Thank *fuck*, half of the Consortium's goons are already wounded or motionless, though I hardly pause for a "Kumbaya" with Archer, Mitch, and Alex, who are still bringing their finest *G.I. Joe* game as they work on the rest of the assholes. I join them, pulsing back any dickhead who dares to approach the girls, until Kane reappears in front of me with intention in his stomps and steel in his stare.

"Let's do this," he growls. "Colton's got wheels right outside that door." He nods toward a corrugated roll-up about ten feet away. So close but so damn far. "You pulse where you can. I'll cover the rest."

I nod and then growl, "Charged." I raise one hand to show him the neon rods of my fingers, their glow emphasizing the black burns across the knuckles. "And ready." I lift the other, which forms enough light to reflect off his near-black eyes.

"Fuck." He dips a fast nod. "That *is* cool."

I don't answer him this time. No need to. The girls are my first and sole priority. I roll back toward them, grunting in approval as they kick off the last of the netting, but then wonder why their moves are so clumsy. Did Faline have them drugged? Holy fuck. Are they injured?

Handcuffs.

The observation is a relief. This, I can handle.

While jabbing my pinky at the key post of Emma's cuffs and then at Lydia's, I use the pause to dictate to them, "Listen to me like I've got a gift code for free shoes." I jog my head toward the roll-up. "I'm getting you out of here right through that door—but until we're out, you both stick to me like tree sap. Got it?"

Wordlessly, they nod as one. Damn good thing. The three of us need that unity. *Right now.*

As soon as they cast off their cuffs, I roar one word.

"Go!"

The sprint to the door is the longest journey of my life,

including my escape run from the Source. Though that flight was longer by a quarter of a mile, fleeing the Consortium's grip didn't include turbofan jet engines, flying bullets, a dozen soldier-grade profanities, and one screaming banshee in red stiletto boots.

But we're there.

And the door is rolling up, freed by the jolt I've just directed at its lock.

And we're ducking beneath it, keeping low as we clear the final five feet and tumble into the Escalade, Colton yelling things from behind the wheel that I can't hear. But there's a hell-yeah smirk on his movie-star lips, so I'm positive a bullet isn't about to rip up my spine.

If only I didn't already feel that way.

The agony gets worse as Lydia slams the door right before Colton hits the gas. It's a mass riot in my system, a million renegades rushing my blood and a million more overrunning my nerve endings, combated by only one soft whisper. But holy God, what a rasp. What a voice. The perfection of strength and sibilance I've battled so hard to hear again. *So hard...*

"Oh, my God. Oh, my God. Reece. *Reece,* baby. Can you hear me? Open your eyes, you big dork. Please. Oh, *God.*"

"Hang on!" Colton again, his shout drowned by screeching tires. The whole vehicle swerves and jostles. A groan fills the air. Male. *Fuck.* Has Colton been hit?

"It's okay. It's okay. It's okay." Emma's frantic murmur, vibrating in my ear, supplies my answer. The groan was mine. The next one belongs to me too—a long, uncontrollable eruption, as more guerillas join the relentless rebellion in my body. I've driven them too far with my dictatorship. The revolt has begun. The revolt is violent.

Worth it.

"It's okay, baby. Stay with me, Reece. Stay with me!"

"Yeeee haw!" A new blare, this time of elation and definitely *not* mine. As Colton bellows again, the truck clears some kind of bump, bouncing like a carnival ride. "We're out—and we hosed those cockmunches!"

I groan again.

As pain sears every inch of me.

Worth it...

"Reece? *Reece?*" Emma's not whispering it anymore. I comprehend the shriek in her voice but can barely lift a hand to her forearm, grazing my touch over her silken skin. "Holy shit. What happened to your hand? *Reece?*" Her lips brush my forehead. Her tears soak into my scalp. "What have those bastards done to you?"

With another miserable moan, I coerce my eyes to open. The depths of her gaze, liquid as fantasy lagoons, are already waiting. Though it hurts to smile, I can't help myself. Though it hurts even more to lift my fingers all the way to her cheek, I do that too.

And though I can't comprehend my parched throat being capable of sound, two syllables fight their way up that arid tunnel anyhow—in the pair of sparse seconds before the insurgents completely take over and plunge me into blackness.

"Worth. It."

CHAPTER FOUR

EMMA

Worth. It.

The words echo in my head and my heart even twelve hours later. As the day grows longer, I can swear the reverberations get louder.

The not-so-crazy justification?

I keep wondering if they'll be the last words I ever hear him speak.

The not-so-paranoid backup for *that*? Every damn memory of the last twenty-four hours continuing to assault my mind. His heroism at the gala. Less than an hour after that, his magic in giving me the cosmic triumvirate of orgasms. Less than an hour after *that*, his mind-bending moves to leap—literally—to save Lydia and me.

But at what cost to himself?

At what drain to his system?

"Damn it, Reece." I mutter it past tears because I abhor every answer my psyche conjures for those questions. And because *he* has no answer, lying so still against the pillows of his bed in this apartment where he and Sawyer have been holing up since getting to Manhattan. At least that's the conclusion I've come to, since I broke my own rule about clingy girlfriend stunts about three days ago and finally jabbed his private number into a phone-finding app.

But worse than the admission of doing it is the confrontation of exactly why.

Once I'd learned he'd chosen to stay at a rented place around the corner from the Obelisk instead of at the hotel itself, had I been touched that he chose to give me the space I'd requested when leaving LA? Had I considered that it was probably killing him to leave me alone despite suspecting the Consortium was hatching a plan to get to him through me? Had I even tried to think how excruciating it was for him to watch me from afar instead of being directly by my side to protect me?

No.

Because it had been easier to be irked with him than face all the terror that comes with loving him. If I wrote off his alpha wolf behavior to overreaction and testosterone, I could at least get some things accomplished—because the alternative was crippling.

Having to deal with thinking about all of this. Watching him in a room that's too damn silent. Holding my breath as I peer for signs of his. Every other second, swaying from the flood of relief when his chest rises and falls.

His chest, still so pale.

Upon which his arms are crossed...and end with his limp, burned hands...

I blink against the fresh burn behind my eyes and force a sketchy breath in. My exhalation is just as unsteady.

"Hey." The utterance comes from Sawyer, who's suddenly appeared by my side. I feel my brows pucker as I struggle for orientation. I didn't hear him enter the room, let alone cross it to get to me.

"Hey." I curl one hand against my sternum, wordlessly ordering my heart back beneath my ribs. That's not the easiest thing once I register the peridot intensity of his gaze. "What is it?" I rasp, following my gut instinct. "What's wrong, Sawyer?"

"Nothing. Really." He has to underline the second word when I flash disbelief at the first. "I'm just worried about *you*."

He lifts a hand to cup my shoulder. Strange alarms clang in the back of my psyche, and I step away. "I'm fine," I mutter, rubbing my upper arms with opposite hands.

"You're *not*." He remains still, but I scoot back a little more anyway. "Have you been off your feet at all since we got back?"

I return my stare to Reece—and discover the brief break did me well. I'm able to behold him with fresh eyes. To notice how the burns across his knuckles have faded to dark cobalt. To watch him take deeper breaths past lips that are regaining a little color. Dear *God*, his beautiful lips...

"I'm fine," I repeat.

"And he's going to be, as well." Again, the soothing tone. Again, my instinct's odd reaction. But this time, I shake it off. The man stood by Reece through the entire hell back at the hangar. In truth, Sawyer helped save my life too.

"Thanks to you." I swivel my head, letting my gratitude pour into my gaze now. "I haven't had a chance to thank you, Sawyer. For...everything."

He shakes his head, guiding my attention to the damp blond hair playing at the tops of his T-shirt-covered shoulders. He's probably recently showered. "Skip the lip service, Emma. You can thank me by taking care of yourself."

"Sure." I manage a cooperative smile. "Just as soon as—"

"No. *Not* 'just as soon as.' *Now*."

No more smile. "Damn it, I'm not leaving him."

"And I'm not asking you to." He folds his arms. "You'll be in the next room, eating the pizza slice that has your name on it. While you're doing so, Kane can come in and keep an eye on Sleeping Reecy here."

After just digging in my heels, my spurting giggle feels wrong—but at the same time, all kinds of right. If Sawyer's seeing enough improvement in Reece to go for the snarky bro-time insults, maybe it's all right to recharge my own strength while I can. The tiger in my tummy is a persistent reminder that it's been nearly empty since this time yesterday—with its newest rumbling timed perfectly to the entrance of the straight-from-a-video-game soldier who helped Reece get us the last ten feet from the hangar to the Escalade last night. He's slightly less scary now in his plain black T-shirt and matching workout pants—but only slightly. The man is a dark brick wall of don't-fuck-with-me.

Sawyer sweeps a hand between the two of us. "Kane Alighieri, I'm pleased to introduce Emmalina Crist. Emma, this is Kane. We met...well, a while ago. He's been a trusted friend for a very long time."

"And I know firsthand why." I push a smile past my nervousness and extend a hand. "And because of that, I think I owe *you* huge thanks, too, Mr. Alighieri."

Kane's hand literally engulfs mine. "Not necessary, ma'am. But you're welcome all the same." Short grunt. "And quit with the 'Mr. Alighieri' shit, or we *will* have problems."

"Back at you with the 'ma'am' shit," I volley, though add a wink.

"Understood." There's no wink, nor a shade of any matching mood, to his reply. As he pivots and marches toward the easy chair in the corner, he dictates, "Go get yourself some grub. If your man bats an eyelash, I'll holler."

"Thanks, Kane."

I follow it up by tiptoeing over to give Reece a soft kiss through the stubble now turning into a beard, before following Sawyer out into the area where the kitchen, dining area, and living room exist in the same open plan. There's a small laundry room off the other side of the kitchen, and a doorway off the dining area leads to what looks like basic office space.

While wandering into the kitchen, I spot a second bedroom through a door that's slightly ajar. Passed out horizontally across the bed in there are Dan Colton and another guy, whom I remember in sketchy spurts from the hurried dash we all made between the parking garage and the apartment. I never got the man's name, though he's easy enough to distinguish from Colton in nearly every way possible. Where Colton is ginger and lean-muscled with a trendy corporate crew cut, the second man has nape-hugging waves of jet-black hair and muscles like a lumberjack. They've both cast off their boots and shirts and look to be slumbering like the dead. They're joined in dreamland by my sister and another guy from the rescue team—I think they introduced him as Alex—who are vying for the snoring award on the longer of the two couches, heads on opposite armrests and blankets tucked under their chins.

The only person who's still awake out here is the fighter I know as Mitch, now wearing a black sweatshirt and jeans as purple as his hair. As he rolls out of the easy chair and starts strolling over in the same smooth move, I admit to being bummed by the apartment's small size. Watching the guy's fluid grace is like having a front-row seat to a Cirque show.

Mitch refills his water from the dispenser in the fridge's

door while I load up a paper plate with antipasto salad and two slices of cheese pizza. As my hunger roars with louder vengeance, I sneak a few globs of left-behind cheese and barely suppress a blissful moan. Manna from heaven.

The pizza itself is just as perfect, classic New York style, with dough as soft as a cloud and tomato sauce probably made from scratch. There's no taste on the planet like a slice of New York pizza, not even in Little Italy back home. I'm beyond tempted to just plant my face and suck up the goodness as fast as possible but mush my hands between my knees while waiting for Mitch to sit as well. Sawyer, who's pulled out my chair for me, seems content with nursing a bottle of beer.

"You're not having any?" I inquire him anyway.

"Already did," he supplies. "Right after we got back here and settled in, I ordered food. We've been taking turns on watch duty. I had first shift."

"I've already eaten too," Mitch explains, sliding into the chair opposite me and stabbing at his helping of the salad. "I'm just a pig."

"You also annihilated at least ten thousand calories saving my sister and me, so you're allowed." I send over a smile before digging in myself. Another moan vibrates my throat at first bite of the Italian meat, cheese, and veggies. Damn, it's delicious. The LA adage is that food is better at the beach. I'm sure that was coined by someone who'd never eaten after escaping a lunatic bitch and her cutthroat Scooby gang.

"Hope that goes for the rest of us." The black-haired guy from the bedroom mumbles it while plodding into the room. He stops to extend a long-fingered hand. "Good morn—" He glances at the oven clock. "Errr, afternoon. Don't think we've officially met. Ethan Archer."

As I return the greeting, I split a bigger smile. "Morning, afternoon, or midnight, you're still a hero. I'm not sure I'll ever find any words or any way—"

"Then don't." One side of his mouth hitches up. "You're alive. Use the gratitude to pay it forward, which I understand you were already doing before those pissheads wrecked the night." He turns for the kitchen, peering over the pizza selections that are still left. "Besides, it was kind of fun. And everyone got out alive. Annnnd the statue for ass-kicking goes to...*usssss*."

As he embellishes that with a roar-of-the-crowd sound effect, I widen my gawk. Sawyer, noting my bewilderment, chuckles. "Try to cut Archer some slack. He's married to a Hollyweird stylist, and some A-listers are her clients."

Archer grunts. "I've been living *awards season* for three months now, and it's not happening for three *more* months."

"Hold up. Can we get back to the 'kind of fun' part?" I dart my stare between both of them now. "*Kind of fun?*"

Mitch inserts himself back into the discussion with a soft laugh. "We know that sounds insane from where you're sitting, but keep in mind that between Sawyer and the five of us, you had nearly seventy-five years of top-shelf spy-guy experience on that op last night."

"Truth." Ethan pumps a fist with one hand while popping a beer with the other, which doesn't help my confusion one damn bit. Sawyer, who hasn't stopped scrutinizing me with an odd kind of attention, comes at once to my rescue.

"I think what they're trying to say is, none of us went into this thing as greenhorns, Emma." He tilts his head, contemplation taking over his face. "You know how some guys like to go shoot the Banzai Pipeline or drop out of a helicopter to ski down some face in the Alps? Well..."

Seriously? I communicate as much with my bold side-eye. "You telling me Faline and her stunt were your version of the Alps?"

"Yodel-leigh-hee-hoo," Ethan deadpans.

"You all could have *died*."

"And extreme sportsmen don't?" Sawyer banters.

I shake my head. "I need to go check on Reece." Before I smack them up the sides of their heads.

But I'm not an inch out of my seat before Sawyer is dragging me back down, a gentle hand around my wrist. "No. You *need* to eat."

"While you guys sit around and joke about a maniac like Faline?"

"Should've heard my one-liners about the punks in the Sulu Province," Ethan quips.

"Don't get him started," Mitch mutters.

"Don't get me started," Ethan adds.

"You really *should* eat," Mitch emphasizes. "A warrior's caretaker needs as much care and sustenance as the warrior."

"They don't mention that in the superhero girlfriend's handbook, do they?" The satire in Sawyer's tone is backed by the glints in his gaze.

I oblige with a small laugh, though it swiftly peters out. "Hell," I mumble. "If only there *was* a handbook."

"Well, you've got a support team right now, so take advantage of it," Mitch states. "Your man's in good hands. My beloved knows what he's doing."

A girl knows she's living an extraordinary existence when the least surprising thing she's learned all day centers on a purple-haired ninja and Rambo's heir apparent being each other's "beloved." Even more stunning is the realization that I believe Mitch. No matter what state in which Reece wakes up—and dear God, I have to believe he *will*—Kane will be more than able to handle it.

For the first time in the last twenty-four hours, I take my first truly relaxed breath.

Which lasts all of ten seconds.

Before I decide to take Mitch up on his advice and make full use of the three good minds joining me at this table. "So." I ping each of the men with a determined gaze before plunging on. "If this *were* the Sulu Province, what would you guys be deciding to do now?"

"Besides bugging the fuck out of here?" Ethan answers at once.

"Correct," Mitch volleys. "In *most* cases."

"Huh?" Ethan blurts.

Sawyer, with his phone now propped on its holder stand, swipes to a screen displaying a live video feed of what nearly became my murder site—the hangar at Teterboro. I know this because there are a bunch of cops swarming the floor, examining the net that Lydia and I scrambled from and at least ten bodies of bad guys. I close my eyes for a second, thanking God again that my own blood and body parts aren't in that mix.

"Well," Ethan huffs, noticing the same thing we all do about the feed. There's one key thing missing from the scene. One sleek private jet. "Looks like the witch beat us to the punch."

"With her tail between her legs," Sawyer adds. There's no pleasure in his voice, and I understand why. If Faline has been summoned back to the Source by the Consortium, she'll be getting the same punishment that Angelique faced when

Reece escaped their showdown back in Los Angeles. The memory of Angelique's mottled skull almost makes me feel sorry for Faline.

Almost.

There's still all the baggage about the bitch trying to kill 'Dia and me like geese tossed into an airplane turbine.

Yeah. There's that.

"Too bad I couldn't break those legs first."

The comeback to Sawyer's claim is issued by a source none of us expect—and has me surging from my seat before he can do anything about it. As if any man, even as ripped as Sawyer, could hold me back from running to my sister right now. Then hauling her into a fierce hug. Then letting the tears flow, full of humbleness and thankfulness and love, just as hers do. Then holding her tighter even though she tries to pull away and slam her mask of don't-worry-be-happy back on. Then feeling the acquiescence of her body as she realizes I see her—I *see* her—and I'm making it okay for her to just *be* her.

Because that's what sisters do, even if they haven't just been through hell and back together. Because that's what sisters are for, *especially* when they've been through hell and back together.

"It's okay." I whisper it as I stroke the back of her head and the top of her spine, giving her safe shelter in which to succumb to her exhaustion. "It's okay, my sweet 'Dia."

In so many ways, it's the same kind of haven for me too. We can both be strong again in a second, but this unique moment is for the necessity of our mutual wallow. And though I'm sure all the guys at the table, in their own unique ways, understand portions of what's slamming us right now, none of them can be her. The same person who helped me with geometry homework. Who consoled me when that homework frustrated me enough to throw my textbook, which wound up ripping my Leo DiCaprio poster when it hit the wall. Who gave Tasha Northam a black eye for calling me "brace face."

Who wants to do a hell of a lot worse to Faline the Bitch.

After we sway and sob and whisper to each other for a few minutes, I finally let her step back and clear the wetness off her cheeks. I do the same, and we snort back snot before submitting to manic giggles. We'd probably keep going, letting the whole thing devolve into off-key renditions of "My Heart Will Go On" in honor of Leo, but are interrupted by Sawyer politely clearing his throat. We lift our heads in time to see Ethan and Mitch wearing the same quietly nonplussed expressions.

"What?" Lydia charges. "You guys never seen a couple of chicks break down and then giggle it out before?"

Mitch gets in the first comeback to that one. "Honey, not even from the craziest drag queens I know."

Ethan, having finished a bite of his folded pizza, declares, "Speaking of crazy... Will filling us in on that harpy's motives be a breach of national security?" He cocks a defined black brow our way. "Or—gasp—girl code?"

Inside ten seconds, four pairs of eyes lock onto me. Five now, including a newly awakened Alex, who's watching from the couch. It takes me half that time to color from neck to scalp, wondering why I can easily lead a small army of fundraiser volunteers but have no idea what to say as the spokesperson for Team Bolt.

I disguise my desperation behind a thoughtful façade, directing my own gaze toward the windows. It's a clear but cold afternoon on the Hudson, the water like liquid slate beneath a sky just slightly brighter, its expanse flowing with coffee creamer clouds. I long to be gazing at the scene from the crook of Reece's arm, watching old movies from the couch instead of trying to figure out how to give these guys the truth without imparting information that could make *them* targets for the Consortium. But it might be too late for that already, right?

Hell.

The word repeats through my mind, doubled down with intensity, the second Kane reenters the room. While his pace isn't frantic, it pounds the floorboards hard enough to jerk everyone to their feet. His Stallone-on-a-mission expression backs up that grit—and turns my stomach into a knot.

"What?" I demand at once, rushing to meet him. "What is it? Is Reece awake?"

Kane doesn't hesitate longer than a second to answer—but in that instant, his face is hit by such a jarring jolt of weirdness, his bearish brawn taken over by uncertainty, that I yearn for the seconds of being conquered by my stupid blush again.

"You'd...just better come," he finally utters. "Right now." I don't think twice about following him out of the room, but instead of guiding me back to the bedroom, he veers into the bathroom. Once we're there, he speaks again—though the next thing from his mouth isn't any more reassuring than his ominous preface. "*Fuck.*"

Especially because it's the same thought in my head.

All concept of reality leaves my logic. Any remaining grasp on reason slips over the ledge of my rationale. While the shifts are scarily easy to identify now—experience gives a girl that advantage—they're no easier to deal with. Again with the damn lack of a manual. Not even a Facebook group.

But if there *was*, how the hell would I phrase this post?

Hey, gang—LOL—you'll never believe this—the old man's

on his knees in the shower, turning every drop of water into a fresh electron. It's kinda pretty and super blue. Any advice on who to call? Doctor? Plumber? Electrician? Exorcist? Respond with a gif if you want...

But nobody would believe a gif like this.

I don't even want to believe, and I'm looking at it from three feet away.

"He said he needed to get in the shower," Kane explains, past lips that have gone as pale as his skin. "Of course, I noticed the obvious..." Reece's erection, huger and harder than I've ever seen it, is a blatant visual aid. "So I asked him if getting you wouldn't be a better idea."

I compress my lips. "And he probably threatened to carve your balls out if you did."

Kane clears his throat. "Something along those lines."

"Because he thought he'd hurt me if I came to him."

"Will he?"

I reach out, steadying my stance by grabbing the towel rack. Reece's eyes don't open, but he flinches. He knows I'm here but is just too weak to debate the point. Hell, he can't even move to turn off the shower—if that's what it can be called anymore. As soon as the drops from the showerhead hit the air that's charged with his electrical field, they turn into brilliant azure sparks, flaring around and on top of him. It's lightning in a really huge bottle—with a significant refugee caught in the middle of the storm.

Significant?

My ass.

Reece Richards isn't "significant."

He's invaluable. Irreplaceable.

My man.

My more.

The conviction blazes through me as bright as the tempest in the shower, only its flares are more permanent. As the heat embeds itself deeper, it lights the way more clearly for what I have to do now—starting with facing Kane with newly set shoulders and a gaze filled with resolve.

"You did the right thing," I assure him. "Thank you."

My clarity brings his back. He nods, looking less like we're harboring an alien lifeform and should be expecting a knock any second from NASA, TSA, INTERPOL, or worse. "You look like you have a plan." He looks relieved to be stating that too.

"I do."

"So what are we doing here?"

"Uh-uh." I shake my head and plant hands on my waist. "What *I'm* going to do here."

As I expect, the big guy isn't so good with that. "Which is... what?"

"What I have to." I don't elaborate, letting him think I have more of a plan beyond that. "Just keep everyone out of here. The bedroom too." Again, no more details—because again, I don't have them. It's not like I can just yank open the shower door, toss Reece a come-hither smirk, and get him to join me in the bedroom. In attempting to cool off the biggest power surge his system's ever known, he's created his own paralysis chamber.

"*Shit, shit, shit.*"

I repeat it in a desperate mutter as soon as Kane exits to the living room and shuts the door. I have no idea what he's going to tell the others about all this, and I don't care. I *can't* care.

The only thing that matters right now is the man before me—locked down by his own lightning.

But that means he can unlock it—if I can help him. Get through to him...somehow...

The first step to accomplishing that? Making sure my own shit stays locked down and shut tight. Every tear, every reaction, every expression, every emotion—it's all dumped onto the conveyor belt leading to the mental lockbox. If Reece gets a whiff, a glance, or a taste of *my* distress, "thunderbolts and lightning" won't be just a cute rock anthem line anymore.

"So get a grip," I order myself, turning it into a full-on mantra to accompany my slow steps toward the shower.

Toward the man who needs me now more than ever.

Dear God, please don't let it be too late...

"Get a grip. Get a grip. Get a grip." The repetitions come faster as I inch closer. I stop just once, forcing back horrified tears as I behold his empty, unblinking stare. Those eyes, normally so vibrant and in pace with the rapid-fire thoughts in his head, are now stunned and tormented... But after another step, I can see details that weren't evident before. Things that make me want to sob again—in gratitude.

Most importantly, he's not paralyzed. Tiny tremors rack every toned muscle of his naked form, making him look like some beautiful space creature from a planet with a cobalt sun. Even if that was the case, I'd cross the cosmos to get through to him—and I wonder if this experience might feel exactly like that in the end.

But even that recognition won't stop me from trying.

One step at a time.

And for God's sake, keep your grip.

I inhale deeply, pushing air into every cell I can. His

shivers are a good sign, indicating that at least his nervous system is functioning right. I'll gratefully take it—and run with it.

As I creep a little closer, Reece flinches harder. I hope that means what I think it does. If he's reacting to me like this, most of his senses are still engaged too—and that includes his hearing. For now, that's all I need.

At last, just outside the shower stall, I lower into a crouch. Tentatively, I press one hand to the glass. It's warm but not hot. Another good sign.

"Reece," I whisper. "It's me."

He shudders harder. I carefully watch his gaze, my heart handspringing as his pupils jerk, attempting to look at me.

"It's okay, baby. Don't try to look at me. I'm here. I'm not going anywhere."

Inside the stall, the sparks increase in violence and brilliance.

Not good.

"Okay, okay." I struggle to coat my voice in control instead of the panic rushing my veins. "Try to breathe, okay? And do *not* try to move."

I issue it all as an order because it is. But with calculated care, I'm the one doing the moving. Trying not to shift my form in his peripheral at all, I start to strip from the waist down. Thank God all I really have to worry about are a pair of socks and my leggings.

"Good," I praise as he works to comply while I complete my own preparation. Minimizing my motions is like trying to hold a tricky yoga pose. Knowing it's possible and making it happen are two different things. Finally, *finally*, I'm finished—and force the inevitable follow-up thoughts out of my head, in direct contrast to what my naked skin is all but screaming. I'm about to climb into that electro-hell with him...

Because there's no other acceptable choice.

If I fry with him, then we'll face forever together.

But if my theory holds water...

Bad pun. But still a valid idea.

I just need one more element for success. *His* help.

"Okay, baby. Now for the hard part." I lift a hand to the stall's handle, fully letting him notice me now. "I'm going to come in." Brighter sparks, violent and white—and hot. I can feel their blazes through the glass, but I'm beyond being afraid now. "And you can knock the Bolt tantrum off because you don't get a say in this. All I need *you* to do is pull it back inside, okay? I know it'll hurt, baby. I know it won't be easy or any kind of pleasant. But I just need three seconds. *Reece.*" I pound on the word as well as the glass as he quakes even harder. "I'm counting on you, dork. Do you hear me? Three seconds, okay?"

I twist my fingers harder around the handle.

Take a brutal breath in.

Let a harsher one back out.

"On the count of three, Mr. Richards." A hard gulp. A ton of rocks in my throat. Fifty gallons of adrenaline in my blood. "One. Two. *Three.*"

CHAPTER FIVE

REECE

Three seconds.

That's all it takes.

Three fucking seconds in which I'm so terrified of killing her, I gladly eviscerate myself with lightning.

Three horrific seconds in which every fiber of my body is deep fried in agony and every brain cell in my skull is consumed by a silent scream.

Three incredible seconds in which I can do nothing but watch as she sweeps over me, fits her body on top of me, and impales her perfect pussy with the hard length of me.

Three seconds before I lose control inside her...

And she brings me back to life.

"*Emma.*" It bursts from me on a parched croak but instantly turns into a rejoicing moan. "Emma...lina... *Fuck.*" Then various versions of that along with a lot of nonsensical utterings, my own version of speaking in tongues as I worship her with my voice but abuse her with my body. But she takes it, digging her hands against my scalp and sinking her teeth into my neck, continuing to ride my cock through my endless, merciless orgasm.

She came to New York to try to figure out our trust issues. But in three seconds, she's shown me the most beautiful version of the stuff there is. Bursting into my nightmare, ready to die in it by my side if she couldn't save me from it with her passion. Her hope. Her love.

Our connection.

The joy of it rises through me, claiming me in a fresh wave of adoration in return. And heat. And desire. And absolute, electric love.

Every muscle in my body springs to life. My arms are full of fiber-optic force as I slide my hands beneath her sweatshirt and grab her waist in the name of controlling her rhythm. I drive her harder onto me, ramming her down, over and over again, until our flesh slaps loudly in concert with the water spattering around us. With my power redirected into a *much* better receptacle, even the shower can be itself again, raining down as we keep kissing and groaning and tasting and fucking.

Dear God. I never want to pull out of her again.

Part of me wonders if I'll ever be able to.

"I can't stop," I tell her, thrusting even higher as my cock swells even tighter.

"Then don't." Her voice is a whispered plea as her body convulses around my dick. "Reece. *Reece.* Please don't!"

I stare at her face, coursing with water and lust, as she throws her head back in the grip of another climax. The sight, along with her exquisite begging, revitalizes my own endless release. With a primal groan, I let the force of it take over. The heat shooting up my cock no longer feels born of just my balls. It's a conduit for everything inside me, rushing and racing to flood into her. My essence. My soul. My power. My heart. Every element that has made me a real hero, not just a mutant freak...belongs to her.

Is her.

Especially now, as she peels off her sweatshirt. As her nudity gleams before me, slick and wet and perfect. As her limbs wrap me and protect me, all I can ever want.

As her love infuses and completes me...all I can ever need.

⚡

Unbelievable.

Though I never thought it would actually happen, my cock finally hit *E*, and my body swiftly followed.

Now, having let the woman talk me into letting her go long enough so we could stumble to the bedroom and crash on an actual mattress, I've woken from the sleep of the dead—not as much of an exaggeration as I wish—with my arms enveloping silken naked curves, my face buried in dawn-bright hair, and my cock seeking a tight, wet entry point.

There.

Oh hell, yes.

Keeping my lips at Emma's nape, I nudge a thigh between hers so her legs open a little wider for me. She rustles a little, but I still her with one hand atop her thigh.

"It's all right, Velvet." I nip into the curve between her neck and shoulder, ordering myself to take it at least a little slow. After the way I took her in the shower, sore is likely just the start of her condition right now.

But no way am I stopping completely.

This time, I'm not fucking her because I have to.

I'm loving her because I want to.

Though damn it all, the woman's sweet, sensual moan might change that outlook pretty fucking fast—especially when she adds little rolls of her hips, caressing my erection with the firm cushions of her ass. And *especially* when she turns the moan into a mewl before murmuring, "It's not all right, because you're not inside me yet."

Sassy, bossy girl. Sexy-as-hell woman. Her impudence awakens answering instincts in me, compelling me to push on her hip until she's rolled over, flat on her stomach against the mattress. I follow her over, forcing her legs wider with my knees as I slide my hand up, ending only when I push two fingers against her parted mouth.

"Suck."

I grate the directive into her ear, my tone clarifying her options for refusal. There are none. Luckily, and with a willing whimper, the woman complies. As she licks at the digits I sluice in and out of her mouth, I take the chance to fill her in on a few more details of how this is going to go down right now.

"You were in charge in the shower. But we're not in the shower anymore. It's my way now, and you'll fucking enjoy it. Understood?"

With a darker moan, she nods her head—and increases the suction on my fingers. I'm unable to control my approving growl as I watch her plump, perfect lips take my fingers deep inside her wet cavity.

"Holy Christ, Velvet. I'm half tempted to screw my original plans and slide my cock right into that naughty mouth of yours." Because I can't help myself, I insert a third finger past her mesmerizing lips. Then a fourth. "But you already know that, don't you? And you'd love nothing better...to feel my come coursing through your body before it flows down to your cunt and makes you climax from the inside out?"

The new urgency of her sighs is worth the cost of the fantasy on the length of my dick. My skin is stretched so taut it's painful, with every vein shoving at the flesh like snakes under satin. Bittersweet torment. Unreal anticipation.

And at last, the impetus for my next guttural instruction to her.

"Raise your hands over your head. Wrists together." As I raise my dry hand to capture her there, locking her down against the pillows, I pull the other from her mouth, redeploying those soaked fingers to breach the tunnel of her sex. When that carnal passage responds in all the best ways, I stab in a little more. Retreat until I'm nearly out but then slide back in, growling as she gushes all over my digits. I pause only to reach for the nightstand, where Kane parked my toiletries bag after I first woke up and he assumed all I needed was an ibuprofen. Still don't need the ibuprofen, but a fresh growl vibrates off my lips when I'm able to add some lube to this little party.

"Damn!" Emma cries as I work the liquid in by twisting my hand, intruding deeper, shocking her intimate walls. "Ohhhh, dear God. *Damn.*"

"Relax." I trail the word along the curve of her nape, reveling in the honey and spice ambrosia of her. "You'll take what I give you, woman—when I give it to you. And you'll thank me for all of it."

"Yesssss," she hisses. "Yes, Mr. Richards. Thank you, Mr. Richards...*oh!*"

I let her have the exclamation. She's earned it, after what her sweet gratitude has just driven me to do...by how far I've taken my sensual invasion. But now that my whole fist is inside her, I take advantage of the moment. Crank my hand so my knuckles awaken as many of her sensitive nerves as possible. Make her gush with more heady juices and vibrate with deep, primal tremors.

"Damn," I grate against her neck. "*Damn*. Emma. How you're taking me in, baby. How your cunt is opening for me. *Emma...*"

But I let it trail off because I'm unable to form any more words. This is too perfect. *She's* too perfect. I revel in the sounds the next few minutes *do* bring, the air consumed by my rough pants, her high mewls, and the erotic slides of my carnal incursion into her tight, hot body.

But after I dare shove in deeper, she finally cries out.

"Holy...*shit*."

I respond with a savoring snarl. "Holy is right, gorgeous girl." I kiss the valley between her shoulder blades while dipping my head to steal one glance at the place where I'm penetrating her. "I worship you, Emmalina. Holy fuck."

"Mmmm," she replies in a dazed, faraway tone. "Mmmm... hmmm..."

"Is it tight, baby?"

She nods, again with misty languor. "Yes."

"But is it good?"

"Oh, *yes*."

"Then let me make it better."

"Yes. Yes. *Yessss*."

Her scream fills the room as soon as I pull out far enough to free my thumb and pinky—though I leave my other three digits in her pussy and use them to keep her open as I plunge my dick in with one thorough thrust. As my cockhead throbs against her cervix, I flick my thumb around, stroking her clit—and setting her off into an orgasm I've never seen her experience before.

Holy. God.

The tremors radiate from some hidden part of her, ageless and boundless, like a seed of comprehension passed through the ages from Eve herself. By the time the shivers take over her pussy, I'm well on my way to the white-hot eruption seeking to satisfy even that part of her. I don't just want Emma's orgasm. I want to hear the ones she inherited from Eve too. The cries of her very truth. The celebration of her deepest womanhood.

And I get them.

"Reece! *Fuck!* Reece!"

The last note of my name becomes multisyllabic, gasped in chopping sections as I slam harder and harder, chasing my own lightning...

Then capturing it.

And I'm gone.

Lost.

Done.

Bursting. Blazing.

Fucking.

Coming.

I rear back, repositioning my hands at her hips to keep her body locked around mine as long as possible. Like a hose without a shutoff valve, I keep drenching her with my come as ecstasy consumes my blood and amazement takes over my senses.

Yeah. Amazement.

That I'm here. That *she's* here. That we made it, defying the odds again, to hit back at the Consortium harder than they ever imagined—and though they're probably hardly dented for it, at least we're not either.

A thought even crazier than that slams in.

Not only have we emerged unscathed—aside from

enduring a joyride from hell that should be in a Vin Diesel flick and the most memorable shower of my whole life—but the two of us might actually be...*yeah*...better for all of it.

I'm so deep into that consideration that I don't even think to mask its effect across my face when I finally slide out from her and roll onto my back. Naturally, despite the fact that she's entitled to drop into a full sex coma right now, Emma catches every nuance of the expression. "Okay, mister," she prompts, quickly snuggling against my side and parking her chin atop my left pec. "Spill."

I curl my hand in to scrape stray strands of hair from her face. "I thought I just did."

She bats my chest. "You know what I mean. Don't try to hide when your eyes are like that. You've got that Mach-speed thinking thing going on. And don't get me wrong"—with a flare of her own gaze, she runs her fingertips through my stubble—"it's the best damn thing I've seen all day. Now I just want in on whatever brilliance is going on in that gray matter of yours now. Or whatever color it is."

The way her face pinches in, as if she's really trying to figure out what color my brain is, incites my new laugh. Still, she keeps up the persistence, which I return without a blink. From here on, everything about me is an open book for this woman.

"Hate to disappoint, but I think mine's just gray, baby." I pull an extra pillow under my head to raise the angle of my gaze. "All the same, it's filled with wondering about *you*."

"Me?" Her face crunches in new and adorable ways. "Why?"

Gruff snort. "Why, she asks," I mutter. "After she dresses up like the hottest Cinderella on the planet for her ball, only to end the night being held at gunpoint and nearly thrown into a jet turbine. And what does her date do for a grand finish? Oh, that's right. Makes her get into a lightning shower with him. You know, for giggles."

"And, if I remember correctly, a couple of orgasms that the folks at Guinness would never believe."

The impish arcs of her brows tempt me to kiss her forehead. "And then there's what happened after that."

I'm not sure if I'm troubled or relieved by her ensuing chuckle. "You mean the part where you fisted me?"

I clear my throat. "Well, if you have to get technical about it..."

"Oh, my God." Her eyebrows jump higher. "Reece Richards, are you turning Puritan on me?"

"I'm turning concerned partner on you," I snap, though the new stiffness in her form confirms the mistake of letting my nerves do my talking. "You know what I mean," I qualify. "I love you, Velvet."

"You love me as a 'partner.'" Her tone implies the air quotes as she pushes back and leans on an elbow.

"And as a lover." I don't let her get far, turning so we're facing each other. "As *your* lover only. As the man who attends the church of you every time I take a breath." With my leg now thrown over hers and my hand skimming her back, I sweep my lips down her nose. "But also as the jerk who's recognized I might have let my lust—and my experience—carry me too far."

She tilts her head up to the point our mouths quickly meet, though her side of the kiss is a reprimand. "Mr. Richards," she charges. "We've already been here, remember? After the electric Ben Wa balls?" She pauses, looking even more mischievous. "Hmmm. Where *did* you put those? That was kind of fun..."

My rumble cuts her off. "Christ," I utter, with her giggle as my underline. "Fun, hmmm? So is that where you're filing all this? Under *fun*?"

"No." Her fingers, tracing my jaw again, match her softening tone. "You defy every file invented, Reece Richards. You color outside every single one of my lines, and I adore you for it." Her gaze turns a gorgeous shade of turquoise. "And I know you didn't start out just now with that as the plan, if that's what you mean." She laughs once more. "We just got carried away. Imagine *that*."

I take half a breath of relief and repeat with a wry grunt, "Carried away. *Hmmpf*. Was more like your pussy hired a mob of savages, tied me up, and hauled me off to a pyre of lust. But we'll go with carried away if you're happy with it."

She burrows against me, making the world okay again in an instant. "I *am* happy," she rasps into the center of my chest. "And fulfilled. And free." She adds a tender kiss to her whisper. "Free enough to let go for you like that. To trust you and to open up my pleasure to you like that."

Deep gulp, ending between the ribs she's warming with more of her warm breaths. And her precious words. *Happy. Pleasure. Trust. Fulfillment.* So many of the things I want her to have with me and because of me. "I want to fulfill you *every* time, Emma."

"And you do."

"Yeah?" I finish it with a serrated hiss as the warmth of her lips works its way through my whole body. What this woman can do to me with just one brush of her magical mouth...*fuck*...

"Oh, yeah."

And even what her mouth does with simple words...

Compelling me to sweep down, taking over every delectable curve of it with my own. Then to plunge in, penetrating her with my tongue, stealing her air with my command, sucking in her heat until *I* can't breathe...

Consumed by her.

Connected to her.

Many minutes later, when we finally drag apart, I cup her cheek while stroking the sleek line of her eyebrow with my thumb. "You're so beautiful, Emmalina. So perfect."

Her gaze swirls, a teal and turquoise lagoon, as she leans her cheek into my hold. After a long sigh, she whispers, "I wouldn't be anything but dead right now if it weren't for you." She presses her fingers, tapered and graceful, atop mine. "And because of what you did, *you* almost died..."

"Which wasn't your fault," I rumble, filling in her tearful silence. I curl my fingertips in her hair, tugging just hard enough that she understands my vehemence. "You understand, Velvet? It *wasn't* your fault."

She closes her eyes now. Compresses her lips. "If I'd only been thinking faster..."

"In the second and a half Faline gave you to make that call?" I scoff. "And yeah, I *know* it was only that long. There was footage from a delivery camera mounted over the kitchen entrance. I know exactly how things went down with you and Faline—probably better than you do." I hate that my explanation surges fresh tears to her eyes. I rejoice that I'm able to ease them with a firm grip on her nape. "Every decision you made was the right one, Emma. Those fuckers would've raped or even maimed your sister to keep you in line as the good little bait for me." I get a fun whirl with the rigid grimace now. "God knows, I've seen the Consortium do worse."

In the space of two blinks, she's stuffed the tears away. She lifts her hand, forming it over the fresh timpani of my heart as memories—nightmares—claim me again. "But known a lot of that 'worse' for yourself too."

There's nothing close to vacillation in her murmur. The woman has woken me from too many of the flashbacks that keep stalking my sleep to question its truth. But her forehead furrows, causing me to watch her closer. To see the unanswered query in her eyes now...

"What?" I finally prompt. "Spill." I hope that brings at least a smile but fail. She's tense, licking her lips...searching for the right words.

"Back...in the hangar," she finally mutters. "During your high noon with Faline..." She sits up but maintains her clasp on the center of my chest. "She called you Alpha Two."

Ah.

There it is.

I rise up—so she can see all the admiration in my regard. "I'm surprised you remember that."

She blushes, but only a little. So damn stunning. "Hard to forget," she explains. "That's not a typical endearment."

For a second, my jaw tightens. "Faline was never dear to me."

"Then what was she?" Before her fingers turn to cold sticks on my chest, I know the question isn't easy for her. Hell, it's not easy for *me*, but *easy* was Reece Richards version one point oh. The update on my app includes lots of not-so-fun moments filled with not-so-fantastic memories...

"The queen bee of the mad scientist hive." I wish I could write off the comparison as a creative twist, but it leans more toward reality than I want to admit—and now have to. As my mind's eye fills with images of the Source's hexagon-shaped rooms, as well as what was done to me in them, heartless insects and their honey-sucking proclivities are an eerily perfect analogy.

Fuck. Fuck. Fuck.

"I never knew her name until tonight, though—or even had more than fuzzy impressions of her face. But her voice..." I keep Emma's hand locked atop my chest with a brutal squeeze around her fingers. "When you wake me up from my nightmares, that's the voice that keeps echoing in my head."

In an instant, Emma is next to me again. No. *More.* With a sweep of creamy skin and white sheets, she wraps herself around me, legs around my waist and arms wrapping my neck. "She can batter your head, but she can't have your heart and your spirit."

"Damn right." My whisper is full of love and gratitude. "Those belong to you now." I savor the kisses she trails from my nape to my face, letting her conclude the journey with a long, lush meld of our lips and teeth and tongues.

When we part slightly, I fill my lungs with determined air and stare back at her with the same intent. "You asked a question," I finally state. "And...I haven't answered it yet."

She shakes her head, her face crunching with agony. "It's okay, Reece. I— I don't need to—"

"You *do* need to." I grip the back of her neck to keep her gaze locked on the mandate in mine. "You need to because *I need you to.*" I kiss her softly. "Because if we're going to keep trusting each other, that means telling each other even the shitty stuff."

Her features purse again, though I sense it's for a different reason now. The watery wobble beneath her reply attests to that truth. "Okay," she rasps. "*Okay.*" She bobs a fast nod. "Even the shitty stuff."

She's right—yet even though she is and this is going to be agonizing as hell, the moment isn't as disgusting as I'd expected it would be. Well, hell. Maybe the memes are right. Even the tough parts of the road are better when walked with someone you love.

Still, I have to haul in another long breath, giving me time to shut down a bunch of circuits in my psyche. Only the strongest connections can stay online for this disclosure.

One more breath.

Here I go.

"We...were rarely called by our real names there." Knowing she realizes the "there" to which I refer, I just keep going. "Not in our bedrooms, and not in the labs. Makes sense, I guess. If you want to keep a prisoner in line, dehumanize them. It also helps if you don't want anyone to know who their true neighbor is. Not that talking was ever a thing, since Faline was fond of those rubber mouth bits..." Weirdly—but maybe not—I break into a sharp laugh. "Above all else, the policy probably helped keep the paperwork more organized. *There's* a plus for *someone*, I guess."

Emma is quiet—on the outside. In the darkest eddies of her gaze, I can see the ink of rage and revulsion. I'm nauseated, having to be the bearer of her horror like this, but there's no easy way to put all this. It's my baggage, and it's not fucking Louis Vuitton.

"So yeah, I was Alpha Two." That part comes out softer, almost like a fond reminiscence. In a sick way, it is. *Alpha Two.* He was me, for all those months that completely altered my life. If I don't accept the memory of him, then I'm rejecting everything about him...everything about his experience that changed me in so many ways.

He was me.

He still *is* me.

Just not all of me.

I can't get a better summons back from those reflections than the gentle combs of my woman's fingers, taming the hair back from my face.

"So you never spoke to Alpha One?" she ventures. "Or Three?"

I shrug, trying to throw off some of my tension, but the memories have taken over me like hawks on a field mouse. "Neither of them," I mutter. "Though I know there weren't just alphas at the complex. I heard the docs referring to prisoners from an omega unit too."

"Omega." Her features crunch, giving away her deeper thoughts. "What do you think that means?"

"Probably the same thing you do."

"Males and females?"

"It makes the most sense, especially with Angelique confirming they strung *her* along with promises of getting her into the program someday."

Her whole face lights up with a triumphant smile. While I could spend hours reveling in that magnificence alone, she sweetens the moment by sitting up and pumping a victory fist—while the sheet stays exactly where it is.

Ding, ding, ding.

Me for the win.

I don't waste time reaching for my championship rings, either. Yes, both of them—in the form of the taut, puckered circles of glory at the centers of her firm, gorgeous breasts.

Fuck me, she's so perfect.

"*Reece.*"

She punctuates that with a sharp gasp as soon as I twist and tug at her erect tips.

"Hmmm?" I drawl, easing my touch into languid strokes.

"Are...are you even listening to m—" A new breath, hotter and heavier, as I gently scrape my thumbnails across her stiff nipples. "Mmmmm," she moans instead. "Oh. *Mmmmm.*"

"I'm listening to every word, Velvet." I pull harder, savoring the louder shriek that bursts from her. "Men. And women. Got it."

A shiver courses through her. "And now...you've got me..."

"No, baby. *You've* got *me.*" I pull her closer so I can coast my tongue over her bottom lip and then bite in at the small curve at the corner. I love these little parentheses of her mouth, as well as all the unique things I discover about her each and every day. The tiny mole beneath her left breast. The way she likes being bitten at the crest of her hip bones. Even how she has to rewet her toothbrush in the middle of her morning scrub.

I love every damn thing about this incredible woman. And I want to spend the rest of my life proving it to her. Learning every idiosyncrasy about her...

Before the RRO gala went to hell in a massive basket, I was prepared to tell her that too—and not just with words. But right now, I can't fathom leaving this bed to go hunting for what's left of my tux, including the velvet box I'd stashed into one of its pockets. If the ring is gone, it's gone. It's just material shit that can easily be replaced.

I can't replace Emmalina.

I don't ever want to think about trying.

Just as I can't deal with thoughts of being anywhere but

right here, right now. Not past the few inches I allow in order to whisk the sheet off the rest of her body or the few seconds it takes me to gather her even tighter...lowering her molten, wet core over my erect, ready cock.

At once, my world is right again.

Complete again.

Connected again.

"*God*. Reece!" Emma sets a pace of rolling, rutting intent, scoring my shoulders with her nails and filling my face with her she-beast breaths. "Need...this. Need...*you*."

I lift my head, blazing the heat of my desire up at her. "This? Right here? This cock blazing into you? Fucking deep into your pretty cunt?"

Because I've never needed anything worse than this. Than her body. Her trust. Her passion. Our unity.

Those fascinating lips of hers quirk into a joyous smile of her own. "You're a bad, bad man, Mr. Richards."

"So I've been told, Miss Crist." I seize her by the waist and flip her onto her back in one caveman move. My dick never leaves the torrid sleeve of her pussy. "But maybe I'd better show you, just to be sure."

As I plant my knees, I let my hands glide down until I'm shoving at her inner thighs, spreading her wide for my deep, demanding thrust. As she bursts with an ecstatic cry, I croon, "That's it, Velvet. Scream for me. *Louder.*"

She moans as if conflicted but scratches down my torso with such passion, I get an idea of which side of her will win. Still, she utters between breaths, "All the guys are awake. They'll hear..."

"That's the idea." After giving her two seconds to gape at my wolfish grin, I lean forward to bury my face against her neck. With her knees over my shoulders and *my* knees positioned wide, I'm able to stab my cock deeper into her than ever before.

And she screams.

"Yes, Emma."

Another thrust. A louder shriek.

"*Yes*, Emma."

Yeah. Definitely loud enough for all the guys to hear now—though the final *gotcha* is actually on me. I don't care if they hear anymore. For that matter, I don't care if the whole West Side hears. All that matters is my body, buried inside this woman. My heart, held tight by this woman. My soul, kept safe with this woman.

With those weapons in my arsenal, even going after the Consortium doesn't daunt me anymore.

CHAPTER SIX

EMMA

I look out the plane window to see the landscape below bathed in the dark-amber sunlight of a Southern California autumn afternoon, and it's better than beholding any gilded castle in Europe.

We're almost home.

I squeeze Reece's hand to communicate my silent pleasure—almost shocked when all he does is smile, kiss my forehead, and return the pressure. Half of me expects the man's command for me to scream about it, since that's a lot of what I've been doing for him during the last seventy-two hours. But with every one of those occasions accompanied by an equally blinding orgasm, I'm the last girl on earth complaining about a purse full of throat drops and a face stuck in perpetual blush mode.

He did allow at least a *few* breaks from the lovemaking marathon. The first was our obligatory "faceoff with the firing squad" on that first night in the apartment, enduring the catcalls and mock applause from Sawyer, Lydia, and the rest of the gang when we'd finally stumbled out of bed for some sustenance and a fast debriefing about how things had gone down with Faline. The group consensus was that the woman hijacked the jet that almost became a murder weapon, taking the crew and the few henchmen who could limp aboard with her.

After that point, our team was divided about opinions. Sawyer, Kane, Mitch, and Lydia solidly voted that the bitch's flight plan was anywhere *except* back to Spain and the Source and that she had a contingency plan in place for an alternative destination from which to scramble a new team to pursue Reece. But I'm siding with Reece—along with Ethan and Dan—in thinking the woman is a more important player in the Consortium's universe, and she likely authorized her own mission in the name of "course correction" after Angelique's fuckup at the battle of El Segundo three and a half months ago. And no, my mind wasn't made up by mindless worship to my man. It was given in validated trust after everything Reece relayed from his experience inside the Source.

But while the group is split about where exactly Faline finally ended up, every one of us is thumbs-up about that landing pad being somewhere outside the States. For the time being, the woman has slipped away to lick her wounds in anonymity—giving us all a second to catch our breaths and formulate our own strategy in the war against the Consortium.

Because now it really is war.

As soon as our powwow at the apartment concluded, Dan Colton and Ethan Archer gave their polite farewells, both having wives and businesses to get back to. Alex Trestle, Mitch Mori, and Kane Alighieri stayed a little longer, enjoying the new meal that Reece insisted on ordering in for us—directly from the Obelisk's kitchen. After dinner, Reece had done a shitty job of feigning a yawn and declared to everyone that he and I were bound for bed.

That night, I gave him lots of screams.

The next morning, everyone else was gone.

A quick check on my phone had supplied the text from 'Dia, reassuring me that Sawyer was personally supervising her trip back home. She had no idea where Alex, Mitch, and Kane had disappeared to, but I wasn't worried about any of those men not being able to take care of themselves. Alex, with his love of disguises, seems theatrical, so he likely disappeared into the crowds of Broadway for a few days of bingeing shows on the Great White Way. Mitch and Kane, the other pair of lovebirds in our bunch, have probably slipped off to a warm-weather destination for some well-deserved downtime as a couple.

I'm relieved and grateful that Sawyer saw to my sister's safety, for more reasons than one, but didn't press 'Dia for more details beyond that. Once we're home in LA, that won't be the case. Priority one within the next week? Getting that girl to lunch for some serious girl-to-girl "debriefing" time, especially about Mr. Foley.

Okay, maybe not priority *one*.

One gaze up into Reece's face brings me that reality fast enough.

His gaze, intense as quicksilver, glistens even brighter as he looms into my personal space and drops a soft, sensuous kiss on my slightly parted lips. When done, he pulls back an inch before growling one question for my ears only.

"You ready to give me some more screams, Velvet?"

I feel the fresh flare to my eyes. "H-Here? N-Now?"

And why? Cracking the mile-high club isn't new for the two of us, thanks to several flights together on the Richards Resorts private jet. The only reason we didn't take that aircraft for this trip was due to the required departure airport:

Teterboro. So we flew commercial first class, meaning if he really needed my "scream" that badly, he had five hours in which to drag me into the first-class restroom and have his wonderfully wicked way with me.

He *had* five hours. Past tense.

We're now fifteen minutes from our final descent, which is why I'm gawking at him like half his brain really *has been* sucked into a jet turbine.

"Hmmm," he finally intones, the masculine angles of his face tightening into the mode between worshiping me with his gaze and ravishing me with his body. "So tempting, little bunny, but I have a better idea."

"Which is?"

"A surprise."

I perk a little, indicating I'm all ears, but he pours on the aura of enigmatic even thicker, remaining mysterious but attentive during the rest of the flight, the entire landing, through the VIP suite arrival process, and then out to the private parking lot, where Zalkon is already loading our bags into a sleek silver Range Rover.

"Okay, *this* is new," I quip as Reece leads me toward the luxury SUV by one hand. "And that too." I don't hide my double-take as Zalkon passes off the keys to him. To Zalkon, I tease, "You double-shifting it out here, mister? Meeting and greeting someone else? Though I have it on good authority that awards season isn't for three more months, so don't you dare try to fleece me with any of the Hemsworths."

Z chuckles, his white teeth contrasting with his burnished Armenian skin. "Nothing of the sort." He exchanges a rapid glance with Reece. *More* secrets. *Gah.* "Have fun on your special field trip," he drawls, adding a wink as his special version of torture.

"Oh, for the love of—"

Reece cuts me short by pulling me close and landing a firm kiss on my fuming lips. Then deepening it with his tongue, rolling mine with knowing hunger until I'm moaning and gripping his neck with horny fervor. When we drag apart, he doesn't let up with the sexy razz, letting a smile start in his eyes before taking over his lips from the middle out. I don't think my heart's fluttered as hard since watching Enrique Iglesias turn Jennifer Love Hewitt into a puddle of sunset-colored goo in the "Hero" video.

"Get in the car, you little minx," he whispers in a voice dipped in the same sensuality. "We're burning daylight."

I refrain from pointing out that it's only three o'clock, because I suspect the point will fall on deaf ears. The man does love staging surprises—at least for me. Speculation flies across my mind about whether he's pulled stuff like this on his other girlfriends, those legions who came before me, but the anxiety leaves my head as fast as it came. The time has come to stop worrying about whether I measure up. The guy climbing behind the wheel, still with that boyish smirk across his lips, has earned my effort to get over that shit once and for all. Some days, like today, it'll be easy. Others, it won't. But from now on, he at least gets my best attempt to forget I'm a very mortal girl on the arm of an electric-blooded god.

"Reece?" I'm yanked out of my private pep talk when he turns right at Imperial instead of left to get on the freeway toward the Brocade. I'd assumed we'd head there and spend the night in his penthouse suite, since he'll likely want to be debriefed about what's happened while he was in New York making sure I didn't get run over by ambulances and turned into a human smoothie. "Where are we..."

"Throw on some music, baby," he deflects. "And enjoy the day. It's a good one."

He's right. It's a perfect afternoon, and it becomes even more perfect when he takes a right at PCH, heading along the ocean until we hit Playa Del Rey. At the Santa Monica Pier, where tourists turning into lobsters mingle with local kids on their way to the roller coaster and Ferris wheel, we rejoin the coast and sing along to the alt rock station as the Pacific waves glitter in the sun like a billion diamonds atop rolling blue satin.

After passing the cliffs of Tuna Canyon and sharing a few stoplights with Lamborghinis and Ferraris through Malibu, Reece turns the car up a road I would've missed under normal circumstances. All right, maybe not a *road* road. The strip of pavement can barely be called a two-way thoroughfare, with no sign to identify it or painted stripes to delineate lanes.

As we climb higher into the canyon, the road definition gets even looser—though holy Mother Nature does the scenery take up the slack. While I've known these canyons are out here, I had no idea they were this open and wild, with rolling hills as far as I can see, dotted with yellow and red wildflowers blazing between sage and berry bushes. When we take our first true curve, giving me a view of the route we've just taken, the sea spreads out far below, an azure panorama that sucks the air from my lungs.

"Holy...ssshhh..."

Reece's grin just grows more arrogant. Damn him, he knows I won't do anything about it in my current stunned and babbling state.

We climb even higher.

The road twists a little tighter.

The vistas earn even more of my colorful commentary, leading to the exponential jump of Reece's smirking swagger. Yeah, even guiding this big car on this dinky road, the man is the chiseled, magnificent definition of *swagger*.

At last, he turns right again. A dirt road this time—the whole "road" assignation *really* up for grabs now—with the car's tires digging in for traction as we scale a steep hill to a flatter but equally rugged summit. At the top, the road levels out, so Reece cranks the wheel so the Rover is parallel on the road.

And optimal for transporting me into another world.

When he turns off the ignition, I really do wonder if he's somehow just bolted us off the planet and to another realm. As I feel my jaw slowly plummet, I struggle to open my brain wide enough to allow all this beauty in. The breeze across the ridge smells of sage and lavender and sea mist. The hills all around us, flowing to meet canyons of rugged crags in so many shades of brown and amber, look painted against the sky.

And *this sky*...

Wow.

It's vast and huge, already twinkling with a few bold stars directly above, but shaded in the lemon, tangerine, and strawberry meringue of the sunset down along the water.

The sough of my bewildered breath keeps me company while Reece jumps out and runs around to open my door. I let him help me out, but when he tugs me toward the rear of the Rover, I tug free, needing to savor my mesmerized reverie for a few seconds more.

But after those few seconds, I realize mesmerized isn't going to cut it. I'm standing here, rejoicing in being alive, less than a week after the night I almost died. Would I be reveling so fully like this...without that?

Thankfully, my heart sends back an instant answer.

Yes.

Because anywhere I am with this man, and anything I do with him, is worth the celebration...

A thought he seems to have culled right out of my head—*what's freaking new?*—as demonstrated the moment I join him at the back end of the car and take in the luxurious white tablecloth he's laid out across the tailgate, topped with a plate of my favorite macarons from Bottega Louie and a bottle of Dom chilling in a steel bucket. Next to that, the best part of the spread—a pair of crystal glasses etched with sleek lightning bolts.

I'm no sooner done with my overwhelmed sigh than Reece reaches for me, drawing me between his long legs braced against the side of the car. The twilight turns his gaze into a captivating cerulean, but the purpose in his embrace and intensity across his face are what arrest my attention the most now.

"Hey. What is it?" I underline the quiet question by framing his strong face with my hands.

He smiles again. The brashness is gone. This time, his expression is full of wonder that matches my own...and yet there's a focused kind of curiosity that makes my heart do some extra somersaults and my belly tingle with anticipation.

I fight the urge to press him too hard for his mysterious thoughts, but it's not easy. This moment isn't my script to write. He's got his own words for it, and I wait, dealing with all my expectant tingles, for him to be okay with sharing what's on his mind.

Shit. What *is* on his mind?

Is he returning to the world of crime fighting? Leaving it completely and asking me to run away with him into some government protection program? Breaking up with me?

Oh, God.

Buh-bye, script writing.

"So," he finally says, gazing at me and then sweeping his regard out across the bluffs. The wind starts its sunset surge off the ocean, blowing his hair off his face and making him look like some historical lord about to traipse across the moors. "Do you like it?"

For a second, all I can give him is a perplexed stare. "Do I like what?"

He breaks out in a laugh. I stab him with a tighter glower. "*This.*" He sweeps a hand out, now *really* looking all lord-of-the-moors about it. "All of...this."

The breath hitches in my throat. "Errrr..."

"Answer me, Emmalina. *Do you like it?*"

Now I'm laughing. My mirth is *not* appreciated by the poor man, so I sober up and reply, "It's the most beautiful place I think I've been on this earth. As a matter of fact, I keep wondering if it *is* still earth."

"Well." He shifts a little, reaching back into the Rover for a thick sheaf of papers held together with a big binder clip. "We can make it whatever we want to."

I accept the stack as soon as he slides it in front of me, quickly scanning the top page—before the air doesn't just stop in my throat, but my entire body. I sway, literally dizzy from the words, but Reece steadies me by grabbing both my hips.

"This...this is a land deed," I finally stammer.

"Certainly is." Reece's rumble matches the hills around us. Calm covering strength.

"To...*this* land?"

His gaze is gentle as he fingers strands of hair off my cheeks. "Just about everything you can see right now."

"With my name next to yours...as co-owner."

"Definitely correct again, Velvet Bunny."

I gyrate my jaw a thousand directions, but nothing works to aid words that have fled my whole damn mind. "Are...are you..." *No.* He can't be serious. "When...how...why...?"

"Why?" he finally cuts in, emphasizing with a snort. "That's begun to be pretty obvious, don't you think? Even before everything that went down in New York, I sensed we were headed for this, Velvet. Look at the facts. No way in hell will I ever let you return to that apartment of yours without at least three guards, and though my place on the West Side is secure, it might not be that way forever."

I raise a stare over the sheaf at him. "And fighting the Consortium with everything we've got is going to take extra security and extra space."

He splits a huge grin and lowers a kiss to my forehead. "Which we'll have plenty of out here. A place to live and thrive, to train and fight, with everything custom-built from the ground up, exactly as we need and want it." As he pulls back, his smile grows along with the excited gleam in his eyes. "It's going to be state-of-the-art, Velvet. A huge technical and tracking center there. The main house and pool there." He glances back to ensure I'm following as he points. "And of course, offices and a business center...maybe a huge rec room with all the normal shit that goes in such a thing." He quirks a questioning glance. "You have any idea what goes in a rec room?"

I'm thankful for the chance to laugh, using it as an excuse to step away from him. Truth be known, I need the space. He's talking big dreams about a big life. A *really* big life. The kind of big that comes after the *L* word. The scope of a life we've never discussed with each other...

"Reece." I concentrate on infusing it with encouragement and not chastisement. "It all sounds...incredible..."

"But?" He fills in where I'm going just as he wheels around and fills up the air in front of me. His posture is taut, his lips a tight line, and the chest I raise both hands to draws only shallow breaths.

Nevertheless, I don't back away from my own wary move. "But you can do all of that without *my* help."

His answering growl is instant and vehement. "The hell I can."

"Reece—"

"The *hell* I can," he repeats, bringing along an even bigger tiger to his voice. All the same, he's the one to stomp away now, pacing so hard across the road that small clouds of dust burst beneath his feet. "You seriously think I can do this—any of this—without you, Emma? Do you think I can be even half the man, let alone the *super* man, that I now *need* to be, without you?" He stops. Turns. More dust rising around his feet. More lightning-bright emotion in his eyes. "Without the honor you've taught me to believe in. The strength you've shown me that I have, beyond just these fuckers." He lifts his hands, fingers splayed, before swiping them down to his sides again—and continuing his steady steps back toward me. "Without the heart you've awakened inside me—and the connection you've given it by giving yours in return."

Now I'm the one butted up against the Rover—well, at least the edge of the tailgate—which gives me stability as tears cloud my eyes...and pure love floods my being. "Reece."

I'd run to him if I could, but he really does make me weak in the knees with his determined stride, wind-billowed hair, and entrancing, electric stare. I focus on simply continuing to breathe as he gets closer.

And closer...

And then close enough to allow stuff like kissing me senseless again...

But he doesn't.

At two feet out, he stops again.

And lowers himself to one knee.

"*Reece?*"

He leans over just enough to lift the tips of my fingers beneath his own. Then to raise his face so I can see every gorgeous angle, every loving nuance, every perfect effort that goes into his next words. "I'm not a hero without a heart, Emma—and you're my heart."

From an inner pocket of his sports jacket, he pulls out a blue velvet box. He pops the lid—and spikes my blood pressure. Holy *God*. The ring inside is...outrageous. No, really. That's the only word I can conjure as I gawk at the stone the size of my own eyeball, its dark-blue facets surrounded by tiny diamonds, nestled against indigo velvet.

"Holy...Reece..."

"It's tanzanite," he tells me. "It's supposed to have properties of connection and communication. Most importantly, it opens hearts to the possibilities of the universe—which is exactly what you've done for me, Velvet." When I don't say anything for a lot of long seconds—when I *can't* say anything—he utters, "Don't freak out, okay? If this is too fast, then just accept it as a symbol of everything you are to me, and everything I *want* you to be, of all the *more* you are to me." His lips twist a little. His jaw clenches. "But for God's sake, Emma, *accept it.*" He jerks for a second, as if the strangest thought in the world has just jolted him. "Unless...you don't want to accept it?"

Through my tears, I laugh and jerk his hand hard. "Would you just shut up and put that damn bowling ball on my finger?"

Once he's returned a laugh and fulfilled my order, I'm able to see that the rock isn't going to really put someone's eye out if my hand slips. I *do* notice that the sight of it on my finger has turned my man—my *fiancé*—into an even more devastating sight of masculine pride and burgeoning love. And how I do love him. With everything I am and everything I will be, connected to him by a power beyond even the flimsy four-letter word I use to identify it with...bound to him by a magical electricity that intensifies and grows as he finally tugs me in close and kisses me like the human transformer he is.

Marrying a power cell won't come without its challenges. There'll be craziness, heartaches, and yes, probably more danger. Hell, the last week has proved that one clearer than anything. But unplugging isn't an option. *Not* loving Reece Richards will never be an option again. And I wouldn't want it any other way.

As the sun dips completely into the ocean and the stars transform from tiny sparks to full blazes of light, Reece folds me close, nuzzling his lips into my hair.

"Hey...woman of mine?"

"Yes, man of mine?"

"What do you say we go home?"

I burrow tighter against him, sighing as my ear fits over the center of his chest. The heart to which I am forever connected.

"Baby, we're already there."

Continue the Bolt Saga with Part 7

Pulse

Available August 28, 2018
Keep reading for an excerpt!

EXCERPT FROM *PULSE*
PART 7 IN THE BOLT SAGA

CHAPTER ONE

EMMA

Riddle me this...

Is it possible to drown in agony and soar in ecstasy at the same time?

And could I get any cornier about swooning over my secret fiancé?

"Don't answer that," I mumble to my libido—because the struggle gets even more real, surpassing all clichés and hashtags—as I watch my man, standing on a ridge close to the driveway of our freshly built canyon home, helping a construction crew drill a tunnel into the side of a mountain. The other guys are clad in jeans, T-shirts, and hardhats. Reece Andrew Richards is wearing nothing but his shit-kicker boots, tight leather pants, and a whole lot of sweat. The crew members are using a couple of jackhammers and lots of other loud equipment. My shit-hot fiancé is using only the bright-blue lightning erupting from his fingertips. And every jolt reveals new definition in the tantalizing muscles of his tall, rippled body...

Blatantly reminding me of the excess energy he'll need to burn off after the excavation...

Ecstasy.

But then agony. I tear my gaze away from Reece as I remember the two extra members in his audience today.

So I plaster on an awkward smile for my future mother-in-law. And his.

Kill. Me. Now.

⚡

A giggle bursts off my lips. As in, a real laugh. Wait. Is this me, enjoying lunch between the only two women on the planet capable of making me capitalize the word Stress?

That's not true either. One more name belongs on that list.

Faline.

But today isn't for dwelling on the bitch who still haunts my nightmares. It's for building on the dream of forever with the man who helped me survive her. Who literally swooped in and saved me from her.

Who strides in like a modern-day Errol Flynn now, rocking those incredible leather pants, a billowy black shirt he's just thrown on, and even a black scarf of some sort tied around his head to keep his gorgeous but sweaty hair off his face.

And stealing my breath all over again.

Damn.

Reece is delicious even without his rugged boots. He likely kicked off the filthy things at the front door when he came in. His bare feet hit the tiles with undeniable strength as he approaches, and the air practically shudders from the impact of his presence. I'm not the only one who feels it. I can see how his energy impacts both Trixie and Mother—though clearly, their intimate parts aren't as swept away as mine...

Or Anya's.

It's impossible to ignore how the woman is affected by my pirate stud, with the pulse in her throat quickening and the roses in her cheeks growing, but it's not like poor Anya—or nearly any other woman who comes in this close contact with him—can help herself. It is what it is, and I deal with it in new forms every day. Short of ordering Reece to turn the new tunnel into a prison cell instead of Team Bolt's high-tech command center—and chaining him inside for the rest of his life—there's nothing I can do but deal with the discomfort and trust our connection. That inexplicable, incomparable bond that seems to strengthen between us every day.

That ignites anew in his silver-gray eyes as he walks straight toward me...

And kisses me...

And floors me all over again.

***This story continues in* Pulse Bolt Saga: Volume Three!**

ALSO BY ANGEL PAYNE

The Bolt Saga:
Bolt
Ignite
Pulse (August 28, 2018)
Fuse (Coming Soon)
Surge (Coming Soon)
Light (Coming Soon)

Honor Bound:
Saved
Cuffed
Seduced
Wild
Wet
Hot
Masked
Mastered
Conquered (Coming Soon)
Ruled (Coming Soon)

Secrets of Stone Series:
No Prince Charming
No More Masquerade
No Perfect Princess
No Magic Moment
No Lucky Number
No Simple Sacrifice
No Broken Bond
No White Knight

Cimarron Series:
Into His Dark
Into His Command
Into Her Fantasies

Temptation Court:
Naughty Little Gift
Pretty Perfect Toy
Bold Beautiful Love

**For a full list of Angel's other titles,
visit her at AngelPayne.com**

ACKNOWLEDGMENTS

A story like this doesn't happen without the passion and dedication of an incredible team. All the members of my own Team Bolt: you are such superheroes, each and every day, and I'm so grateful to all of you for believing in this world and these characters!

The Waterhouse Press team: you never saw the "weird one" in the Misadventures bunch. You saw the untapped potential of an electric mutant and his ladylove and taught me that different really can be spectacular. I cannot express how moved I am by your love, light, guidance, patience, passion, and belief in this project. Meredith, Jon, David, Robyn, Haley, Jennifer, Yvonne, Amber, Kurt, Jesse...you are a publishing family beyond compare.

And in that family...there are the two big siblings who have been so much more than an editing team for Reece and Emma. Scott Saunders and Jeanne De Vita, you are the ones who have turned my humble little stories into the shiniest superhero magic. You are my inspirations, my champions, my teachers, my cheerleaders—but more than anything, the two mentors who have made me a better writer. I cannot thank the heavens enough for your presence in my life, and on my writing journey.

Every single incredible member of the Payne Passion crew: Thank you for all the love and encouragement you lend me on a daily basis. You are my lights!

Martha Frantz: You keep all the gears turning, and sometimes I have no idea how. You're amazing, and such a blessing to me. Thank you!

Victoria Blue: Some days, you just keep me going, period! I am so thankful for your love and support in my world.

Gratitude and incredible thanks to Regina Wamba, the goddess who has labored so hard on the Bolt covers, as well as Anthony Kemper and Hannah Lundquist, for bringing Reece and Emma to life so beautifully.

To all the geeks and freaks and "different ones": Thank you for living your truth, sharing your scars, declaring your bruises, and celebrating your strength. You are the electricity in my blood! Glow forth!

ABOUT ANGEL PAYNE

USA Today bestselling romance author Angel Payne loves to focus on high-heat romance starring memorable alpha men and the women who love them. She has numerous book series to her credit, including the Suited for Sin series, the Cimarron Saga, the Temptation Court series, the Secrets of Stone series, the Lords of Sin historicals, and the popular Honor Bound series, as well as several standalone titles.

Angel is a native Southern Californian, leading to her love of being in the outdoors, where she often reads and writes. She still lives in Southern California with her soul-mate husband and beautiful daughter, to whom she is a proud cosplay/culture con mom. Her passions also include whisky tasting, shoe shopping, and travel.

Visit her at AngelPayne.com